FIGHTING FOR ANNA (MICHELE LOPEZ HANSON #2)

A WHAT DOESN'T KILL YOU TEXAS
ROMANTIC MYSTERY

PAMELA FAGAN HUTCHINS

SKIPJACK PUBLISHING

CONTENTS

FREE PFH EBOOKS

Before you begin reading, you can snag a free Pamela Fagan Hutchins *What Doesn't Kill You* ebook starter library by joining her mailing list at https://www.subscribepage.com/PFHSuperstars.

ONE

AN AIRBORNE STRING mop charged at us, a white curtain of deranged fringe. But of course it wasn't a mop—it was a dog, and its squatty legs pumped hard, propelling its low, elongated body, with its tummy barely clearing the ground. I smelled it, too—a coppery, foul scent—and I tensed from years of experience with animals in my father's Seguin veterinary practice. Yet, the dog looked familiar, and I was more respectful than scared.

"Get back." I put my arms out to either side of me, as if that would protect my teenagers from whatever the terrified little dog brought our way. "A scared animal is a dangerous one."

I heard the eye-roll in my seventeen-year-old son's voice. "We're not babies anymore, Mom."

I glanced at Sam. He had the Lopez coloring but his father's height. Over six feet and muscular in a zero-body-fat kind of way. He had on khaki shorts and an Astros T-shirt, and his dark brown hair flopped across his forehead.

The dog panted and darted in front of me, and I caught a glimpse of one eye open wide, its white rounded. "Hey, I know you, don't I?" I said, as if she would understand me.

I *did* remember her, from the neighbor's. Gidget. That was the name of the neighbor. An oddly seventies-sounding name for an oddly endearing woman. The dog's name also started with G. I ran through possibilities quickly. Gretel. No. Gretchen. No. Gertrude. Yes, that was it. Which was another oddity, like the names for the woman and the dog were reversed. I'd fallen in love with Gertrude last spring, when Gidget invited me over to her little white farmhouse. She'd asked me to help her write her memoirs, since I was an editor and a published author. I'd agreed—charmed by the woman and intrigued by her years as the force behind a hip Houston art gallery—then forgotten about it in the wake of my mother's death.

Until now. A flush rose toward my face. Ugh, memory problems, on top of hot flashes, fatigue, and allover body pain. But no, my gynecologist insisted it couldn't be early onset of menopause at forty-one. He'd offered me birth control pills and antidepressants, but no empathy.

Annabelle spoke in the high pitch of a teenage girl, although at eighteen she was rapidly approaching womanhood. "Is it hurt?"

Okay . . . add trouble focusing, like on the crazed dog and my kids, to my list of symptoms.

Sam snorted. "It's so ugly it hurts. What is it? Some kind of mash-up between a wiener dog and a sheep dog?"

I raised a brow at Sam, but secretly added pug to his list. "She might be hurt, Belle."

The dog stopped in front of me, yapping frantically, like it was talking directly to me. Something was wrong with her eye, really wrong, but the little canine was whirling in circles by then. Between that and all her hair, I couldn't get a good look at it. Was the reddish brown in her dreadlocks blood?

"What is it, Gertrude?" I crouched and held my hand toward her, palm up.

She reversed course with her back end turning separately from her front, like an articulated bus.

"Oh my God, did you see her turn?" Sam leaned over, laughing.

"She's so cuuuute," Annabelle squeaked, clapping her hands.

Gertrude sprinted into the woods, away from the three of us and the dilapidated summer camp travel trailer dubbed the "Quacker" by Sam because of the brand name Mallard emblazoned on its side. Stopping once, Gertrude looked back at us—one eye wonky—as if to say, "Hurry up, already."

She tugged at my heart. "I'd better go after her."

"I'm coming, too," Sam said.

"You dropped your phone, Michele," Annabelle said from behind me. "Some guy named Rashidi is texting you. Who's Rashidi?" she called.

I pretended not to hear her, because I sure wasn't going to tell her that a gorgeous Virgin Islander I'd met at my friend Emily's wedding in Amarillo wouldn't quit texting me. I hadn't answered him, so I'd hoped he'd stopped. I wasn't ready. I might never be ready again.

"Aren't you coming?" Sam yelled back to Annabelle.

I heard her feet start up after us. Breakfast and too much coffee sloshed in my belly. I had a head start on them both, but even though I'd done an Ironman triathlon less than a year before, my conditioning was no match for their youthful athleticism. Sam played elite high school baseball, and Annabelle was headed to the University of Texas on a swim scholarship. And both were about to leave me alone for the summer, as of today—Sam working a summer baseball camp that moved around the country, and Annabelle getting a head start on the fall in Austin. I couldn't think about it without my eyes leaking, so I forced it away.

The little dog had wheels, and the distance between her and us grew. We thrashed through the bushes and brush like a herd of stampeding cattle, my snake-proof pink-camouflage cowboy boots adding to our thunder. I tried not to think about snakes. Snakes in the grass, snakes hanging from trees, snakes under bushes. Copperheads, rattlesnakes, water moccasins, and coral snakes, all native to south central Texas, something I'd have to get past if I was going to make it through my summer in the country. *Mongoose, mongoose.*

Gertrude dashed under the bottom of the barbed-wire strands at the three-way juncture of poles and fences that marked the edge of our property and the two parcels adjoining it. A new metal sign had been affixed to the outside of Gidget's fence, but facing the next property over from ours. It read FUTURE SITE OF HOU-TO-AUS LONESTAR PIPELINE.

We skidded to a stop, and I put my knee-high boot on the bottom wire and pulled up on the middle one. "Here."

Annabelle ducked through, using one hand to hold her mass of long, curly blonde hair off her pink tank top and out of her face. Sam followed. They started running again.

"A little help, please?"

Annabelle understood me first. "Yeah, thanks a lot, Sam," she teased. She mimicked my actions with the barbed wire.

I'd never been past our fence, and only up to it once or twice. When I'd visited Gidget, I'd driven on a dirt road that wound an extra two miles before cutting back to her place. I crouched, my butterfly pendant falling out of the top of my shirt and swinging forward to smack me in the teeth. I lunged under the higher strand into new territory, catching the back of my shirt on a barb. I heard a tiny rip, but I pulled through anyway. A piece of trash on the ground caught my eye, and reflexively I grabbed it and stuck it in my jeans pocket to throw away later.

"You've got a hole," Annabelle informed me.

It was an old Hotter'N Hell Hundred T-shirt from a bicycle race I'd done with Adrian, Annabelle's father. The ruined shirt was just another piece of him slipping away, a tiny sliver of my heart excised and gone.

Gertrude had stopped, and she was barking at us, her voice a cattle prod.

"Hold on, Lassie, we're coming," I said.

Neither kid laughed, my humor a few decades removed from theirs. We ran on through gray-trunked yaupon holly trees that scratched us up as much as the barbed wire, and I wished I had a coat of fur like Gertrude's to protect me from it. The thick vegetation was pretty from a distance, but up close it gave me the willies. Poison ivy, spiders, and the aforementioned snakes and yaupon. It was dark back there, too, the cedar, mesquite, and oak creating a canopy made denser by thorny vines and bee-attracting honeysuckle.

Sam turned around and ran backwards. "So, where are we—" His words were interrupted when he hit the ground with an "oomph," butt first, palms next.

"Are you okay?" I extended a hand to him.

He lifted one of his up, and it was covered in something brown and mushy. He waved it back and forth in front of his face, sniffing. "Gross."

I withdrew my hand.

"What is it?" Annabelle leaned toward him, then backed away quickly. "Ew, poop."

"Help me," Sam said, shaking his hands to fling it off.

Gertrude started barking at us again.

"Sorry, son. I've got to see about the dog."

"Yeah, me, too." Annabelle giggled.

I zigged and Annabelle zagged around him.

"No fair!"

"Wipe it off on the ground and the leaves." I laughed, and Annabelle skipped. Literally, she skipped, and it warmed me inside.

Sam caught up with us. The scent of something rotten flooded my nose. At first I thought it was Sam, but it was dead animal stink, not manure stink. A few running paces later it started to recede. I didn't want to know what it was. There were lots of critters out there, and all lives had an expiration date. We just didn't have to face it personally in modern society very often.

Or at all, most of us. Another thing I'd have to get over to survive my summer.

My breaths were coming in short pants now, and I couldn't hear anything except the yips and barks of Gertrude. She broke from the tree line, and I saw Gidget's clapboard house in the clearing. Gertrude scrambled toward it, running full-out. I wanted to stop and put my hands on my knees, but I kept going. Sweat trickled down my temple and onto my cheek. Annabelle was in front of me and Sam a good ten yards in front of her. A gate was ajar in a picket fence that could have used the attention of Tom Sawyer. Gertrude entered with Sam hot on her heels. The dog bounded onto the porch and disappeared.

My stress meter inched up. What had the dog so frantic?

Sam stomped up the wooden steps and came to an abrupt halt. He leaned forward, then stood. "You guys, there's a broken window with blood on it, and the dog jumped through it and ran inside."

Annabelle joined Sam, and I caught up with them. The porch sagged under our weight.

My heart was booming, but I didn't want to jump to conclusions that would upset Sam and Annabelle. I knocked but there was no sound from the house, and no one came to the door. "Gidget?" I called.

Nothing.

I took a step to the left and pressed my nose against the intact upper half of the window, my feet crunching the broken pieces on the porch. I shielded my eyes with my hand, trying to see past the glare of high morning sunlight against glass.

"What is it?" Annabelle asked.

I scanned the room. Gertrude suddenly appeared and rushed the window pell-mell, her bark piercing. I jumped back, falling into my step-daughter. She stumbled a little, and I righted myself.

"I'm not sure," I said. I braced myself, hands on the window frame, paint coming off in dry flecks on my palms. I brushed them off on my jeans and tried again. This time I was able to follow Gertrude with my eyes, and they led to the right, in front of a coffee table and faded tweed couch. A bundle of worn clothing lay piled on the wood floors, twitching. Hands and feet and a gray-haired head protruded from the bundle, and blood trickled from Gidget's forehead into a pool beside her.

The sight of Gidget was like a jolt of electricity, short-circuiting my brain. "Adrian." I exhaled, frozen. My forehead slumped against the glass. "Mom."

"What?" Annabelle asked, her face right beside mine. "Michele, are you all right?"

I sucked in a deep, careful breath. For a moment, my mind had filled with macabre pictures from my nightmares, a flash of my husband, Adrian, crumpled lifeless beside his bicycle on the side of the road, murdered a year ago by a crazy stalker in her car. Then one of my own mother, puddled, dead, alone. She'd had a massive stroke only six weeks ago, and Papa had found her.

I winced. "Sorry. Hit too close to home for a second."

Annabelle nodded, her eyes huge.

I squeezed her shoulder. "Gertrude's owner, Gidget. She's in there, on the floor."

"Oh my God." Annabelle pressed her face to the glass.

Sam did the same above her head.

"We've got to help her." I rattled the locked doorknob and shouted, "Gidget, can you hear me?"

Still nothing.

I pushed, but the door wouldn't budge. I knew I should call 911, but first I had to check on Gidget. "Sam, we've got to bust through the door. On three?"

He crouched in front of the door, and I did the same beside him.

I said, "One, two, three."

We threw our combined weight against the flimsy old door, and the jamb gave with a splintering of wood. Sam and I half fell through as it swung open. Annabelle followed us in.

The house reeked of burnt coffee. I put the back of my hand to my nose and stumbled forward. I crouched at Gidget's side, careful not to slip in her blood. I dropped my hand from my nose and reached for her wrist, pressing my fingers against the inside of it as it jerked spasmodically, and I searched for a pulse. It was very faint, but it was there. My eyes darted around the room. Were we the only ones in the house? I knew Gidget had a troubled medical history, but that didn't necessarily mean she'd landed on the floor without help. There was nothing to suggest a struggle, though, no over-turned lamps or tables, and I didn't hear any noises to indicate an intruder. I'd have to search the house in a moment. Meanwhile, Gidget was the priority.

"She's alive. Call 911," I said.

"Um, I don't have my phone."

Not a surprise. Sam never had his phone.

"I've got yours," Annabelle said, already pressing the numbers on the keypad.

I was afraid to move Gidget, but we needed to stop her bleeding. "Find me a rag, please, Sam. Wash your hands first." I thought again about the possibility that Gidget had been attacked. "And be careful."

He disappeared.

Some cruel puppeteer kept pulling Gidget's strings, her body jerking spasmodically, and I wished I could cut them. Instead, I smoothed steely curls away from her temple on the dry side of her forehead and they sprang back into place. Her pale skin seemed gray, the lopsided red lipstick garish against it. I put my ear next to her mouth and my hand on her sternum. She was breathing, just barely, with long lapses between each breath. I opened her mouth. Her tongue wasn't obstructing her airway, which was good. I heard water running from down the hall.

"Gidget, are you okay?"

No response.

Gertrude crawled on her belly, her gnarled locks pooling on the floor and soaking up blood and some kind of brownish liquid. She inched as close as she could get to Gidget's head, knocking into a broken coffee cup that skittered out of her way. For the first time, I got a good look at the dog's face. Beneath the dreadlocks crowning her forehead, one of her eyes had popped partway out of its socket, hanging just over the bottom lid. She looked like something from a B horror flick.

"Poor Gertrude," I said, using my most soothing voice. "I'll fix you up as soon as I can, I promise." Summers and weekends with Papa had taught me most of what I needed to know to help animals—including genus homo sapiens—in minor emergencies, thank goodness. I'd put many an eye back into its socket, especially with the dog breeds whose eyes were on the outside of their skulls. Like Gertrude's were, bless her heart. She licked Gidget's face, seeming not to notice her own injury. I brushed locks back from Gertrude's face like I had Gidget's, with the same result.

Sam returned with a yellow hand towel.

"Put it here, and press." I pointed at Gidget's cut.

He positioned it tentatively.

I put my hands over his, applying more pressure. "Like this."

He complied. "Why is she jerking around like that?"

"Seizure."

I stepped back, taking in the scene. Gidget was birdlike in a voluminous snap-front housedress. Her high cheekbones slashed across her face, over a pursed mouth now barely sucking in enough air to keep her alive. Concern had tightened Sam's brow at the same time compassion softened his eyes. He put his free hand on Gidget's shoulder, as if to stop her spastic movements.

I heard the 911 operator on speakerphone. The voice and static crashed through the living room like a wrecking ball. "Nine-one-one, what's your emergency?"

Annabelle's eyebrows rose. She shrugged at me, a clueless gesture. *Teenage girls. Teenagers in general.*

I shouted so the phone would pick me up from across the room, and I motioned for Annabelle to move closer, which she did. "My name is Michele Lopez Hanson. We found my neighbor collapsed and in a seizure. She's unconscious, bleeding from a head wound, and barely breathing. I don't know what happened to her, but we need an ambulance."

The connection crackled behind the loud voice. "Where are you calling from?"

"I'm not sure of her address. Out near Serbin, between Giddings and La Grange." I gave her my address. "It's near there."

Before I could explain further, the operator shouted, "What county is that? Lee? Fayette? Washington? They all come together out there."

"Lee County. Gidget—my neighbor—isn't on the same road as me. She lives about two miles away by car, but maybe a quarter mile as the crow flies."

The voiced boomed. I still couldn't tell if it was a man or woman. "Gidget? Gidget Becker?"

Of course, with a name like Gidget in a small town, the dispatcher knew who she was. "That's her. We're at her place."

"I'll dispatch the ambulance and the sheriff's department." Then, more softly, "Poor thing. Another seizure."

"Thank you." I looked into the eyes of my kids. They looked scared. I tried to sound confident. "What should we do for her in the meantime?"

The voice softened, solemn and more feminine. "Pray."

TWO

ANNABELLE NUDGED Sam away and took over at Gidget's head wound. She was a herder, that one. She stayed on the line with the dispatcher, who engaged her in a hypnotic back-and-forth. I knew Gidget was in good hands, as good or better than my own. I wasn't what you'd call the Mary Poppins type. I was better at getting my hands dirty and trying to fix things than I was at *caring* for people, even if I knew my way around a trauma.

I stepped away from Gidget and whispered to Sam, "Can you give me a hand with Gertrude?"

He nodded and followed me into the hallway. "What do you mean?"

"I'm going to get some supplies, then I'm going to need you to hold her while I fix her eye."

"Her eye?" He leaned down to get a look at her face. "Oh. Wow. That's sick."

"Yeah. Sick." I patted his arm. "I'll be right back."

I trotted down the hall toward the bathroom. Stunning original art in vivid colors—a Picasso-like sunflower in oil, a crumbling brick façade in watercolor that read "Dr Pepper"—crowded both sides of the hallway and most of the walls in the house. Gidget had given me a tour before, and half of them were her work, the other half a who's who of contemporary art from around the world, some of them created for her as thank-you gifts. There were three doors at the end of the hall. Two were closed. One opened to the bathroom, where a lone abstract of the farmhouse in watercolor hung askew above the toilet, signed by Gidget.

It was a long, narrow room. From the age of the house (early nineteen hundreds, maybe?), it had to be half of a repurposed bedroom or something. The countertops were four-by-four cracked yellow tiles and dirty grout, with a white porcelain undermount sink. A chrome-rimmed medicine-cabinet-type mirror hung above the sink, but yielded nothing except pill bottles when I peeked inside. The bath mat, also yellow, was shag, and from the water damage to the wood floors, the mat didn't appear to do much good. The shower curtain was white, as was the rust-stained tub. I still had an eye peeled and my ears attuned for signs of foul play, but saw nor heard anything suspicious. Maybe since Adrian's murder I assumed the worst. Not everything was a murder mystery.

Behind the bathroom door were floor-to-ceiling cabinets in cheap wood, painted a color that was almost white. *Jackpot*. The door to the largest cabinet was stuck shut, and I had to throw my weight into it to pull it open. I found a first aid kit inside, plus other useful supplies for committing veterinary malpractice on the fly. I grabbed gauze pads, saline solution, Vaseline, Q-tips, and another hand towel. I scrubbed my hands with soap and hot water, then soaked two of the gauze pads with cold water.

"Everything okay, Belle?" I whispered to her as I crouched on the other side of Gidget, by Sam and Gertrude.

She nodded, her eyes less wide. "Is she going to die?"

"She might."

"She's really old, isn't she?"

I stared at Gidget, unsure. She looked ancient. Not just her skin and hair, but her style. Her curly bobbed haircut was the most current thing about her, really, and even it had gone out of style long ago. But she'd told me not to let her appearance deceive me, that severe medical problems and living too hard had taken a toll. "Younger than you'd think."

The dispatcher broke in to talk to Annabelle again.

As quietly as I could, I said to Sam, "Hold her completely still. I have to put her eye back in the socket."

Sam's jaw dropped. "You can do that?"

"Papa taught me." So well that I'd flirted with following in his footsteps, but had ended up at law school because of the smells in a vet practice.

Sam stroked Gertrude's back. He looked a little pale. "Uh . . ."

"Watch out for the broken glass."

He didn't move.

I put my hand on his knee. "You can do this, Sam."

Swallowing, he lowered himself into a cross-legged seated position and pulled Gertrude into his lap.

She yelped and wriggled.

"I'm not gonna hurt you, girl. Mom might, but not me."

I put the sopping wet gauze pad over her eye, as softly as I could. She flinched. "Shhhh." I dipped two fingers into the Vaseline and removed the gauze pad. "You should look away."

"Why—"

I smoothed the Vaseline all over Gertrude's eye.

"Oh my God, Mom, gross." His voice was panicked.

"It's okay, Sam. Don't scare the dog."

Gertrude had hunched down into the hollow between Sam's legs. She was shivering, but otherwise hanging in there.

"Good girl." I gently dripped the saline solution around the eye and into the socket, then I picked up a Q-tip in my greasy fingers and used it to unroll Gertrude's lower lid fully. I held the lid in place with the thumb of my other hand. I unrolled the upper lid, securing it in place with my index finger. The tissues holding Gertrude's eye to her socket looked intact as far as I could tell. She wasn't bleeding, and the area didn't even look swollen. These were great signs, and a miracle. How the yaupon and running hadn't damaged it, I couldn't fathom. I cleaned some debris away with the gauze, then drew a slow, deep breath. Sam echoed mine. I closed my own eyes for a moment, imagining the tissue I was about to handle as fragile as a raw egg yolk. Gently yet firmly, I pressed against it. Thanks to the Vaseline, it slid right back into place with a tiny plop. Gertrude whimpered, then shook her head. The breath I'd been holding came out in a rush.

"Holy crap, Mom, you're a rock star." Sam's grin was enormous, and he ruffled the hair hanging behind Gertrude's ears. "Good girl, you're going to be just fine."

I flipped the gauze pad and put the fresh side over Gertrude's eye. She shied away from my hand, and I grinned like Sam. The dog could see. "Hold this here."

Sam put his hand over the pad. "How long?"

I stood. "As long as she'll let you."

I worked my hands through Gertrude's fur, stopping to clean a cut on her shoulder. When I'd doctored her as best I could, I stood, interlaced my fingers behind my back, stretched them down and away from my shoulders, and rolled my head. My neck cracked three times in quick succession. As I released the tension, I got a better look around me. Peeling wallpaper with tiny flowers on it hung from the top of the walls, a surreal contrast to the expensive gallery of art over it. Cobwebs draped from the corners and dust covered picture frames and glass fronts. The faded wood floors were buckled and scarred. The place was old, small, run-down, forgotten. Like its owner.

I squatted beside Annabelle.

The dispatcher said in her rough voice, "The EMTs are almost there, sweetie. You're doing real good. We're all praying for you and Gidget."

Annabelle shook her head at me. "She's breathing really slow."

"You need me to take over?" I said under my breath.

"I've got it."

Pride in her shot warmth across my chest. "I'll be back in a second, then."

I gathered the pieces of broken coffee cup before one of us ended up needing stitches. I followed the smell of burnt coffee through the adjacent dining room and into the kitchen. The room was tidy, not a dish or crumb on the white-tiled countertop. No, that wasn't quite true. Gidget had left a coffee stirring stick on the counter, the wooden kind with a knob on the end. I tilted it sideways. It was the kind with sweetener that melted into the coffee, and all the sweet treat was gone. It smelled odd, though. I picked it up and sniffed it. Soured creamer? I set the pieces of cup beside it. I moved them around a little. A Ferris wheel. Texas State Fair 1965. They had coffee on them, but it was dark, and it didn't smell of cream. Then I turned my attention to the burnt coffee.

A vintage yellow percolator-style coffee pot with orange butterflies was plugged in on the counter. The stink was coming from it. The darn thing would probably burn the house down soon. I jerked the plug out of the wall, my Vaselined fingers slipping on the cord. I used my less greasy hand to turn on the water faucet and squirt dish soap, then I lathered both hands up and stuck them into the stream until the water ran clear of suds. I shook my hands as my eyes roamed the tiny kitchen for a towel, taking in the old white refrigerator and white oven with a stovetop. No paper towels. No rags. No dishwasher, either. I semicircled toward the dining area and saw a roll of paper towels on the table. I used a few on my hands, then threw them in the trash. It was full to overflowing, with a milk carton, egg shells, bacon packaging, some pink happy birthday wrapping paper, a white bow, and a UPS envelope on top. I turned back toward the table and saw a stack of mail and papers beside the paper towel roll.

I hesitated with my hand on them. I'd promised to help write Gidget's memoirs, even if I'd forgotten about it. It didn't make the papers my business, per se, but it probably made it okay for me to glance through them, and it certainly made me feel curious and a little proprietary. I looked back at Gidget. I couldn't ask her permission, yet I had a strong feeling she'd give it.

Holding my breath, I rifled through. Correspondence, both opened and unopened. A Bluebonnet Electric bill. A Lee County property-tax statement. A letter from the IRS. Texans for Wendy Davis mail. Something with a return address from Lee County Seismic and another item from Eldon "Greyhound" Smith, a bigwig attorney from Houston who I'd heard had slowed down to a country practice in Round Top. A manila envelope with Montrose Fine Arts Gallery in the return address. Another letter, from the office of Julie Herrington Sloane, the campaign manager for Boyd Herrington, U.S. Senator, Texas. I started to dismiss it as political junk mail, but realized the address and postage were handwritten and authentic, rather than machine created. At the bottom, old letters tied with a pink satin bow, no postage or return address on them.

My heart beat harder in my chest. I picked the letters up for a closer look and smelled something roselike waft through the air. MY DARLING DAUGHTER was written on all of them. From Gidget's mother to her? The thought was like a physical blow, a shove catapulting me back to my mother's service. Standing at her casket with me, Papa had broken into sobs, and with my arms around him, he'd confessed that I had a brother.

"We were so young. Cindy couldn't . . . I didn't . . . *Dios perdóname*. We gave him up for adoption. And every year we regretted it more."

I'd pushed back from him and stared with my mouth open, blindsided to learn I was not her only darling, or his, either.

His shoulders heaving, his face in his hands, he'd said, "She tried to find him. We both did. He should be here. He should be here."

Annabelle shouted, jerking me back into the present. "Michele, I don't think she's breathing."

I shoved the mail aside and ran to Gidget.

The 911 operator asked, "Do you know CPR, hon?"

Two cops burst through the front door, guns drawn.

"Sheriff's department!" The first man through the door yelled. "Everyone put your hands where I can see them."

I put my hands in the air and shot a significant look at the kids. Both of them had turned immediately toward me for a clue as to their next move and their hands went up a nanosecond later. We'd had many conversations about complying first and explaining later with law enforcement. And from the flared nostrils of these two deputies to their dilated pupils and dramatic entrance, it was clear this was the most excitement they'd had in their careers. Which had to have been short, because neither of them was much older than Annabelle or Sam. We had to be careful not to spook them further.

"Gidget has stopped breathing. Are the EMTs here?" I said. When they didn't answer immediately, I slung my head in the direction of Gidget. "Shall we start CPR or will one of you do it?"

Behind me I heard the 911 operator. "Hey, guys, these are the people that found Gidget having another seizure. They've been a real blessing to her."

The man in front, a Hispanic man about three or four inches taller than my own diminutive five foot two, kept his gun up, but the white deputy behind him lowered his without holstering it.

The Hispanic guy spoke again. "Who are you?" His voice was shaky.

I used my firm maternal voice. "We're the neighbors. But what's really important is that Gidget's not breathing. One of us needs to start resuscitation, *now*."

The Hispanic deputy's gun drifted down, so I lowered my hands. In my peripheral vision, I saw Annabelle's and Sam's hands drop, too. Behind the deputies, a paramedic appeared. She was tall, thick, and muscular, and I felt better immediately at the sight of her.

"Where's Gidget?" she asked.

I pointed. "Right there, ma'am. She just stopped breathing."

The woman pushed through the deputies, her mouth pursed down so far she looked like a bulldog. "Hell's bells, don't you two have the good sense God gave a turnip?" She knelt and began resuscitation efforts.

As I watched her, for the first time I noticed the faint flashing blue and red lights against the far wall of Gidget's living room. I swallowed, and something lodged in my dry throat. What had started as a somber day, with Annabelle and Sam bidding me goodbye as they were leaving me for weeks, if not the whole summer, had turned crazy. This was not how I wanted our last memory together to go. I wiped away the sweat trickling down the side of my face against my hairline.

The Hispanic deputy puffed up. "There are signs of a break-in."

Another paramedic came through the door, this one a man pushing a stretcher.

"We understand, sir." Not really, but it seemed the right thing to say.

"Is Jimmy here? A handyman sort of guy?"

"There's no one here but us. Maybe we could answer your questions outside?"

His face pulled tight across his cheeks and jaw, and I knew he was still only a hairsbreadth away from doing something I'd regret later.

The second deputy finally spoke. He was tall, thin like a razor, with sparse blond hair and faintly green eyes. "Sounds like a good idea to me, Tank."

Tank, if that was his name, nodded. He put his gun back in his side holster as did his partner. "This way."

Gidget had a decent-sized front porch for the age and size of her home. Once upon a time it had even been a cheery, welcoming white. The paint was coming off in large patches now, and what was left was streaked with mold. A wooden-plank bench covered the left span of the porch. Without warning, in my mind I saw a bonneted woman shelling peas from this bench, smiling at the laughter of children nearby. I shook my head to clear it.

Watching the deputies carefully for clues on how to act, I sat in the middle of the bench. The kids took a seat on either side of me. Both of them had been grilled mercilessly by the cops after Adrian's death. It had left a bad taste in all of our mouths, even though in the end I earned their grudging trust, if not respect, when I was the one to find Adrian's killer. One thing we had definitely learned was that all deaths are suspicious until proven otherwise. Another was that the best suspect is the one right in front of you. And lastly, the better part of valor is keeping your mouth shut. So, rather than start babbling our explanation, we sat silently and waited for the deputies to make the next move.

Tank took a cloth from his back pocket and mopped his brow. It might have only been early June, but here in the Roundtopolis—as locals called the cluster of towns where my property was located, with the area famous for the national phenomenon of Antique Week as the hub—we'd hit triple-digit temperatures and nearly that in humidity. At least in Gidget's living room, there'd been some air conditioning. Not much, probably because of the broken door and window. But come to think of it, I'd noticed it being warm when I was there before, too. Gidget had apologized and told me she didn't have two wooden nickels to rub together. She had served me watery coffee, black, and I was glad I'd channeled my mother at the last second and stopped at H-E-B for a coffee cake. Tiny Gidget ate about two-thirds in one sitting.

Tank spoke. "I'm Deputy Vallejo." The name Tank fit him. He was weight-lifter thick through the chest and shoulders. His short-sleeved brown uniform shirt strained around his bulging upper arms, and veins popped from his forearms. Maybe he juiced? That could cause aggressive behavior, like his overreacting when he came in. "Let's start with names and where you're from." He nodded at me.

I drew my first easy breath since his arrival. Without fully realizing it, my internal tension meter had shot up near to redline. Not that it hadn't been stressful finding Gidget, and helping her and Gertrude. But scary cops were a personal threat, and that was a different breed of cattle. "I'm Michele Lopez Hanson. I have a weekend and summer camp next door, and I usually live in Houston."

I squeezed Sam's hand. I could feel its dampness. He'd been suspect number one for quite some time in his stepfather's death, and cops would probably always scare him.

He cleared his throat and spoke, then Annabelle took her turn. I followed up by explaining how we ended up here and everything that followed, until the deputies had shown up.

When I'd finished, Tank aka Deputy Vallejo said, "Where were you this morning?"

"Breakfast in Round Top at Espressions."

Junior broke in. "Is that the place where you sit at the same table as strangers?"

Annabelle smiled at him. "Yeah. We sat with a bunch of old guys. Then we came home to get our stuff and say goodbye, or whatever. Sam has to get to the airport, and I'm moving to Austin with my cat, Precious."

I suppressed a grin. Annabelle and that cat.

The two deputies looked at each other long and hard.

I put on my sweetest smile, remembering that people told me I looked like Eva Longoria when I flashed one. I might be past forty, but it still seemed to work. The two young deputies smiled back. "So why don't we give you our contact information? In case you have follow-up." I smiled even bigger.

"All right," Tank said. "Me and Junior will give you a call if we need a statement. Or something."

In the background, I heard the female EMT. "I think she's gone."

Gertrude sat like a sphinx on the Quacker floor, waiting for the door to open so she could return to Gidget's side. She refused food and water, but tolerated the cold packs for her eye, which I applied every hour. I didn't eat, either, and the dog and I spent the evening alone, together. I had some work to do, but I decided to go install my new wildlife camera before it got too dark out.

I slid off the bed and grabbed the camera. Gertrude started jumping when I opened the door, about half an inch vertical clearance per hop.

"No. Sit."

She continued her crazed lunging and leaping. I opened the door, holding my foot across it to keep her in. She tried to wriggle under it, her toenails scrabbling against linoleum, and I shut it quickly behind me. I went around back and tied the webbed straps of the camera around a tree, with the camera pointing across the cleared area toward the tree line. I heard frenzied scratching and more yips from inside the Quacker.

"No," I shouted.

I made sure the camera was on with batteries aligned properly, then shut and latched the cover. I jogged back to the door. The dog was still freaking out, so I positioned myself to block her escape and pushed my way in past her.

"Gertrude, honey, shhhhh."

Her barking subsided into whines. She threw herself on the floor, her face between her paws, her eyes sad and betrayed. If a dog could cry tears, she would have.

I kneeled beside her and rubbed her ears under her cords of hair. "I understand, Gertrude. I truly do. Gidget is gone, and you don't realize yet that it's forever. But I can't let you run off. You're snack-size for a coyote."

I'd been referring to losing Adrian, but as I spoke the words aloud, I realized that Gertrude had lost not just her closest companion, but more of a mother figure. I felt a sob well up in my chest, but I forced it down. *Yes, Gertrude, I understand. Times two.* I slid out of my flip-flops and rummaged in my supplies for something to use as a leash, since it was clear I wasn't going to be able to let her out unrestrained. I found a stretchy clothesline that would do and set it on the table by the door. Then I positioned my laptop beside it and turned it on. I changed clothes while it booted up, and as I slid my jeans off, I felt an object in one of the front pockets. I pulled it out. It was a dirty business card. I remembered finding it at our fence line. I brushed the dirt off, and my heart shot into my throat. Adrian Hanson. I covered my mouth with my hand. It felt like a message from him, an encouragement. Or at least a reminder that he had been here, that this was *our* place. I propped the card in the window at the head of my bed, then stepped back.

The laptop was ready for me, so I sat in front of it, massaging Gertrude with my toes. My composure came back to me slowly. I opened my browser and typed *Gidget Becker* into my Google search box. It pulled up the Montrose Fine Arts Gallery and a slew of historical pieces about the art scene. I scanned a few. Her name was always linked with her partner, Lester Tillman. I wondered if anyone had told him yet that she was gone. I added the word *family* to my search. The results didn't change much, and the only appearances of the word were in relation to the "family-like" relationship the gallery had with its artists. I tried adding *parents*. This time when I hit enter, the site locked up, so I hit refresh. It seemed to be trying, but nothing happened, and finally the failure message appeared on the tab.

After two minutes of beating my head against the screen, I decided to check my data. Now that I was in the boonies, I didn't have the luxury of an "all you can eat" plan anymore. I'd run out of data after only a week before I realized just how much I was using. I'd bought more, for a large upcharge, and I'd drilled it into the kids' heads: don't stream data, don't pass Go, don't collect two hundred dollars.

So I shouldn't be out yet. I accessed Exede's site. It came right up, and the meter was redlined.

I was alone in the dark in the woods in the middle of nowhere, without my kids and having lost my husband and mother, and now I didn't even have *data*. My tension meter shot up to 10 and the needle kept moving. I wanted to scream and curse, but my mother had impressed upon me since a young age that cursing wasn't ladylike. She'd turned a deaf ear to my doing it in Spanish, though. In an emotional implosion, I opened my mouth, ready to unleash in the tongue of my ancestors, but instead of *caca*, the word that came out was in English.

"Shit."

Lightning didn't strike.

"Shit, shit, SHIT!" I yelled.

Gertrude cocked her head at me, but nothing else happened. The Archangel Michael didn't appear. I wasn't swallowed up by a giant hole in the earth. My mother didn't rise up from her grave.

Something started bubbling up inside me. Anger. Red hot anger. My secretive mother had died. My secretive, restrictive, judgmental mother wasn't here anymore to tell me what to do. I could do whatever the hell I wanted.

And what I wanted to do was scream every word she'd forbidden me to use. "Mother-effing SHIT!" I repeated it a few times, trying out different conjugations and combinations of the F word until my voice broke and trailed off.

I could feel Papa's sad eyes on me as real as if he were standing an arm's length away. He wouldn't yell. He'd just say, "Oh, Itzpa, my little butterfly," his voice somber. But he wasn't here, and I wasn't his little Itzpapalotl anymore. The Aztec goddess with the knife-tipped wings was strong. She was beautiful. She was a warrior. That wasn't me anymore. I was a middle-aged woman who used to have a life. Who used to have a love that lit her up like a sparkler. Whose kids didn't need her anymore. I felt closer to death—not just Mom's and Adrian's, but my own, and, today, Gidget's—than to life. Old, speeding toward the time when my body ceased to function like a woman. Black and sinful inside, defiling my mother's wishes with my words. More like the Tlazolteotl of my *abuela* Isabel's whispered stories. Tlazolteotl, the Moon Goddess. The eater of filth, the giver of life, the bringer of the moon, and the absolver of lust and sins of the flesh.

"Tlazol," I whispered aloud. Tuh-LAH-zull. My tongue tangled on the –tay-OH-tull, but that was as it should be. Teotl was the designation for a god. Without it, Tlazol was just . . . the moon, waxing, and in my case, waning, darkness everlasting.

I don't know how long I sat there, my thoughts black and my heart heavy. But after quite some time, I realized I could barely breathe. I shoved my laptop back and put my forehead on the Formica surface of the table. It wobbled on its collapsible leg, but its coolness was soothing. I was a little in shock. A warm, scratchy sensation surprised me. Gertrude had somehow wrapped her body in a C curve of fur locks around one of my ankles and was working the other over with her sandpaper tongue. The emotions I'd been holding back burst out of me. Tears rolled down my cheeks, my back heaved, sobs ripped up and out. And all the while, the little lost animal kept up her ministrations.

I leaned around the tabletop and patted the floor. "Come, Gertrude."

She stared at me and kept licking.

I was beginning to think she was completely untrained. I scooped her in my arms and pulled her into me. She switched her attention to my collar bone.

I buried my face in her funny coat, and hidden there, I said, "I'm sorry, Mommy. I'm so sorry. I didn't mean it." Tears still fell, but my breathing slowed. I focused on my breathing. Adrian would have told me to visualize myself in my happy place, if he were here. I tried, but I didn't know where that was anymore, so I just kept breathing.

When I was washed out, I finally scooched Gertrude to the seat beside me. We made significant eye contact, each telling the other we would be fine.

"Can you love a Tlazol?" I asked her.

In reply she made a sound somewhere between a snort and choking.

I laughed and wiped my eyes. "I guess that's awesome? Now, let's see what's going on with that data."

She nodded. Or at least I thought she did.

I texted Sam and Annabelle. *"Out of data. Please tell me neither of you streamed."*

Annabelle's answer came almost instantaneously. *"Not on my laptop."*

"But somewhere else?"

"On my phone so I wouldn't use your data."

"Was it set to wifi?"

"Um, yeah, so I won't run over my data plan."

I groaned and clicked on BUY MORE DATA. Cha-ching. I'd have to do a better job with my instructions next time.

THREE

My brand new canine alarm clock woke me with toe licks before sunrise. I opened my eyes to a blurry view of her googly ones.

"Bed hog," I muttered. "Nine-thousand-degree bed hog." One I was glad I'd bathed before bedtime the night before.

She wagged her tail.

I rolled onto my side. My sheets were soaked in sweat, but I really couldn't blame Gertrude. This was not an unusual occurrence these days.

"What time is it?" I asked her.

I got no answer, so I checked my phone. Five a.m. The exact time Annabelle's cat, Precious, had always woken me each morning. Gertrude barked.

"I'm up." I swung my feet out of bed and onto the twenty-year-old carpet around its base. I cringed. It felt like steel wool, and I didn't want to think about how it had gotten that way.

Gertrude sailed off and landed hard on her squatty legs, then put her paws on my shins.

"You sure are demanding." I jammed my feet into boots and tied the clothesline to Gertrude's collar. I threw the door open and gestured toward outside. Gertrude stared at me, her eyes shocked.

"Yes, you're doing this by yourself." I pointed into the darkness. "I'll be right here on the other end of this." I jiggled the clothesline.

The dog whined.

"Go," I said.

Gertrude lowered her head and moped her way to the door. She gave me one last plaintive look before slinking outside. I played out slack in the line, looped the other end around my wrist, and shut the door. I went into the tiny Quacker bathroom, but before I'd even finished, Gertrude was letting me know in no uncertain terms that she was not an outside-alone-in-the-woods sort of dog. I reconsidered my stance on cats. Precious didn't bark and hadn't needed to be let in and out on demand. I opened the door and Gertrude flung herself back in, panting.

"What's the matter?" I leaned down and ruffled her ears. "Scary out there?"

Her breathing slowly returned to normal. Adrian had wanted to get a dog. I smiled at Gertrude. Not one like her, though. He'd wanted a long-legged, brave-hearted companion for trail runs and mountain biking.

I turned to my training schedule taped to the mini-fridge. It was comforting to me like a favorite blankie or pacifier is to a child. I never went without a training calendar, not since Adrian lured me into my first triathlon. The Excel spreadsheet document was color-coded by type of workout. Today was green—a rest day—and that meant sleeping in. I looked at Gertrude, who was snuffling and sniffing around the Quacker floor. Loudly. Okay, so the extra shuteye wasn't happening.

"You know, Gertrude. This five a.m. thing works great most days of the week, but Mondays are sacred. We sleep in on Mondays. Got it?"

I enunciated each word and held eye contact. She nodded, or something like it. She was a sweet dog, and I had no right to keep her if Gidget had family that wanted her. I'd have to look into it. At a minimum, I needed to call around and see if I needed permission from someone to keep the little beastie until decisions were made.

Even with Gertrude here, the Quacker felt empty today without Sam and Annabelle. Yesterday it had seemed overcrowded. We'd fit in our Houston house perfectly, and I wasn't sure whether I'd ever be able to part with it. All those memories. All those beautiful, beautiful memories. However, if I was successful at country living this summer, I had a decision to make. Sam had only one more year of high school. I could move out here full-time after he graduated. I'd only be able to afford to build a house here if I sold the Houston house. Or I could keep the Houston house and just visit this place and the Quacker occasionally. Or even sell it and move on from Adrian's dream, somehow. But for now, I only had to figure out how to live three months in a twenty-eight-foot trailer, alone, except for Gertrude, maybe, while I gave the country a test-run.

I piddled around for the next half hour, serving oatmeal in paper bowls for both of us since there was no dishwasher in the trailer. I'd pick up dog supplies later. After tidying up and showering, I still had half an hour to kill before my seven a.m. Skype call with my boss. Before I even consciously decided, nerves prickled my skin. I wanted to look for my brother.

Ever since Papa told me about him, I'd been curious. I'd been hurt about the secret my parents kept from me. I'd been scared of this brother's reaction, and scared of mine. Papa had filled me in on a few more details, and I'd done some research. Enough to know that I could put my search out there on the Texas Adoption Registry. I just hadn't done it yet. I stalled, loading one more pod in the mini-Keurig. Madalyn's Backyard Pecan, which was bigger on aroma than flavor. My kind of coffee. Then I opened my browser, prayed for courage, sent up a quick "I love you" to my mother, and dove in. I'd prepared what I wanted to say in advance, over and over. I filled in blanks on autopilot, hurrying so I didn't have to think.

I'm looking for my brother, as was my mother before she died. Click, type, enter. I added details about my parents, our heritage, his birthdate, what we all looked like, and where he was born. *Please contact me.* Click, type, enter. I was done with five minutes to spare before my call. Now it was out of my hands, and all I could do was wait. I let my head fall back against the seat cushion and felt the first flicker of excitement. I had a brother out there somewhere. Someone who shared my DNA and might look like me.

The Skype tones sounded on my laptop, and a posed picture of my boss, Brian, filled the screen. I picked up on the first ring and the screen pixelated then settled upon a video image of his smiling, ruddy face and thinning red hair.

"Good morning," I said to him.

"There's nothing like an early tee time," he said. He unzipped his puffy blue Texans Starter jacket two inches. Never mind that it was summer. Brian was a year-round fan. That and a user of sports analogies and expressions whether they made sense or not. I'd learned to interpret him with a straight face.

"Tell me about it. I had an eventful last twenty-four hours, and getting up early was tough."

We'd scheduled my calls deliberately on my rest days. Brian knew all about my triathlon training. In fact, Juniper Media was the company that Adrian had written for, and the publisher of our best-selling triathlon training/relationship book—whether or not those two subjects usually went together, it seemed to work—*My Pace or Yours: Triathlon Training for Couples.* Juniper's *Multisport Magazine* prospered based almost entirely on advertising and subscription income in the two months leading up to the triathlon world championships in Kona, Hawaii, each October. When Adrian died, there was never a question in Brian's mind whether I would continue in my husband's honor and compete in the race (and document it every step of the way). The race had been big for the magazine, for the book, and for me, mostly because it helped me along in the stages of my grief and recovery.

"I admit I'd expected you to postpone our call."

I laughed. "Well, you've got me with wet hair and barely awake instead."

"Care to share your tumultuous experiences with your coach and mentor?"

"My neighbor died yesterday, and the kids and I were the ones to find her."

"I'd expect you to be down for the count today," Brian said. He frowned and pulled at his chin.

"Yeah. Brought back a lot of unpleasant memories, for sure. It also brought the neighbor's dog."

I turned to Gertrude. "Here, girl." I patted the seat next to me. She backed away a few steps. "Come on, Gertrude." I patted again. When she didn't respond, I hefted her up beside me, then lifted the front half of her body so she was in the frame. I heard a release of air from her back end as I waved a paw at Brian.

"Meet Gertrude, an early riser." A rotten egg scent made me add, "And a little stinker." I waved a hand in front of my nose as I squeezed her with the other arm. She made a little "oomph" sound.

Brian snorted. "That's one ugly dog. Looks like she took one to the kisser."

I hugged Gertrude to me. "You're going to hurt her feelings."

The dog squirmed, and I set her down.

"Are you going the distance with her?" Brian's eyebrows went up, as did the pitch of his voice.

"Don't know yet. We'll see. In the meantime, I've got to shoehorn taking care of her into my overloaded social calendar." I kept a straight face.

"Ha! If there's one thing I know for sure, it's that you aren't a heavy hitter on the social scene."

I raised my hands in front of my chest. "Guilty as charged, your honor. The weird thing is I felt a real connection to the woman. My neighbor. I'd planned to help her write her memoirs."

Brian shook his head. "I'm hoping you'll write your Kona memoirs instead."

I ignored his jab. "She was all alone, Brian. Kind of like me now." I grimaced. "And she was a Houstonite with a really great story."

"Who is she?"

"Gidget Becker. She owned an art gallery in Montrose."

"Gidget Becker? I know exactly who she is."

Gertrude chuffed at me from in front of the door, and I shook my head at her. "How?"

"Oh, twenty-five or thirty years ago, early days at Juniper, we used to do an annual *Who's Who in Houston Sports*. One year we showed up at an honoree's house for pictures. A player for the Oilers. He was with his girlfriend, a hottie named Gidget Becker, both of them stoned out of their heads."

My mind flashed big eighties hair and shoulder pads, a wide waist belt and bright-colored leggings, and lines of cocaine on a mirrored table. "Wow. Well, she was something else. Her death has hit me harder than I would've imagined, and it would have been an interesting book to write."

When I was still a wife and was also a recently published coauthor, I had dreamed of writing books on my own. In fact, my mind had been whirling with ideas for a time-traveling romantic fantasy cozy mystery. If such a thing even existed. Writing took me by surprise, because Adrian had brought out words in me. Words that I'd never known were there. Words that when combined with my overactive imagination—as my mother called it—could maybe do great things. That was heady stuff for an editor. We were usually just the grammar nazis or punctuation police. But when Adrian died, so did my words. I'd hoped to overcome my internal word block with Gidget and her story.

"It's been a tough season for you." Brian nodded. "And I'm serious about those memoirs."

There would be no triathlon memoir, but I kept it to myself. That topic was too personal, too painful. "So what do you have for me this week, boss?" I leaned toward him and steepled my fingers, resting my chin on them.

He clicked with his mouse. "I just sent you an email. In addition to your regular work on the subscription website and the blog posts, I've sent you an article on 'sports in the wake of the same-sex marriage ruling.'"

I sat up straight again. "How edgy of you. But the Supreme Court hasn't ruled on it yet."

"We need to be ready to lead with the chin if they pass it."

"When, you mean," I said, nodding. "Not if."

I thought about my triathlon buddy, Wallace, and his partner, Ethan. They wanted to marry. When the Supreme Court passed same-sex marriage, I'd be standing by their side if they'd have me.

"You know," I added. "The HERO ordinance and the coalition opposing it are bound to come to some kind of resolution in the next few months as well. Last I heard it, the Texas Supreme Court had ordered the city council to put it on the November ballot." I was referring to the city council's hotly contested amendment to add gender identity to the categories protected under the Houston Equal Rights Ordinance.

Brian cleared his throat. "That has everyone in town up in arms. The religious Right has taken their gloves off."

"I've seen." A commercial was running on Houston stations warning parents of young girls about the dangers of men-identifying-as-women using women's restrooms as an excuse to harm kids. My suspicion was that people had probably been using the restroom of their choice regardless of what junk they had in their trunks, and that the law would make little practical difference. But it could make a big difference in people feeling less different and more respected.

"Its impact is limited to Houston, though, and we're international."

"Sort of," I said, and pushed some hair off my forehead and behind my ear. I should've gotten it cut before I left the city. "But it's happening elsewhere, too. I think we should be ready."

Brian nodded. "Okay. I'll find someone interested in taking a swing at it. But I worry we'll lose subscribers on the Right if we don't oppose it."

I shook my head at him. "Journalistic integrity. We've got to stay in the middle."

"Oh, she hits below the belt." He sighed. "But I agree with you about journalistic integrity, as you'll see in the article I emailed."

"Great." I put my hands on the table, then slid my forearms down and rested my weight. Dang dog and her early rising.

"Keep me updated out there in Godforsaken Nowhere."

I rolled my eyes. "How about we call it Nowheresville? That other might offend your religious Right readers." Nowheresville. I liked it.

He laughed, and we chatted a little before signing off. By then, Gertrude was snoring beside me, her warm furry body pressed against my bare thigh. I felt a tug at my heartstrings. Time to get her squared away.

Work could wait.

Gertrude and I walked out to my Jetta. I had nearly sold it last year after Adrian passed away, but instead had gotten it fixed and spiffed up. It reminded me of him. Everything reminded me of him, really. I sighed and set Gertrude up in the back seat. Then I hopped into the front to find her sitting primly beside me in the passenger seat.

"Gertrude . . ."

She kept her eyes averted from me. Poor thing had lost Gidget and suffered an eye trauma and was stuck with a stranger. I decided to overlook it. I put the car in Drive and swung it around onto the dirt driveway from my trailer, past our idyllic pond with its reeds, lily pads, and sunning turtles. On either side was heavy forest of oak, cedar, and yaupon, like the rest of the countryside, except for the parts that had been cleared for fields and pastures. My property—my Nowheresville—was especially dense because it was a parcel of land that had never been worked before. Or at least not in the last fifty years, given the size and density of the trees. Black-eyed Susans brightened the tree line, and a few other springtime stragglers butted up to the road with pops of pink, purple, red, and white.

I liked the forest and the privacy it provided me, but I did want to thin the yaupon and brush around the Quacker for more breeze and visibility. The skinny-trunked yaupon with its little green leaves and red seasonal berries tended to choke off all other plant life, too, and was harder to chop down than a sequoia—plus it had roots with a death grip on the center of the earth. Figuring out a way to eradicate them would go on my long list of summer projects.

From the driveway, I turned onto a gravel lane, then a few minutes and a handful of cattle guards later, I headed north toward Giddings on pavement. That's where we passed a run-down farm that always caught my eye. I'd never met the owners, but the place was a real eyesore, and worse, it was a nose-sore. The long, narrow barn structure reeked of *caca del pollo*. The chickens weren't exactly quiet, either. Gertrude jumped up onto her hind legs and put her front paws on the door so as to get a better look and whiff of them. I tugged her collar gently.

"Down, girl."

She ignored me.

"Down." I pulled harder.

She still ignored me.

"Down!" I said in a tougher voice, and forcibly pulled her back onto her bottom. She shot me a dirty look. "Good girl."

My cell phone rang. Nobody called me except my kids or my boss, so I picked up on speaker without looking at the caller ID. "Hello," I said.

"Michele?" A man's island accent enveloped the interior of the car. It was so thick I could almost hear steel pans playing in accompaniment. Gertrude eyed me quizzically.

"Yes," I answered, and my heart started pounding like runaway hoofbeats. I only knew one man with an island accent, and that was Rashidi John. It was his voice lilting in my ear now. Apparently ignoring his texts didn't work.

"Ah, Michele. It Rashidi. How you doing?"

Small talk. I didn't know how to make small talk. I'd never been any good at it, and since Adrian died, any ability I once had was gone altogether. "Ummm, I'm fine?"

It wasn't that I didn't like Rashidi, or that he was hard on the eyes. He wasn't. Very, very easy on them, as a matter of fact. He had dreadlocks just past his shoulders that Gertrude would die for, and skin the color of buttery, melted chocolate. He had twinkling eyes a shade darker than his skin and . . . I stopped myself. *What the hell am I doing?* I was sitting here all but drooling, when I wanted him to leave me alone.

"I so glad to hear it," he said, his accent wafting over me like silk. "I text you, but I not hear back, so I calling to tell you I coming to Texas. For an interview."

"Oh," I stammered. "Congratulations."

He went on, his accent growing thicker. "Yah, mon, it a big deal."

I couldn't even remember what it was that Rashidi did. I bit a fingernail and tried to think of a graceful way to get off the call as my heart thundered on traitorously.

"Well, I hope your interview goes great," I said in a bright voice.

Rashidi didn't take the hint, but he did start to talk without his accent. When we met in Amarillo, he'd called it "Yanking"—to talk like a Yankee. "Texas A&M. Is that close to Houston?"

"Oh no," I said. "It's a good hour and forty-five minutes away from Houston."

I crossed my fingers, not wanting to admit to him that I was only an hour away at my summer place.

"Wait, Katie told me you were living elsewhere this summer?"

He was referring to my Baylor Law School roommate, a mutual friend of ours. One I was going to kill. "Um, yes, I am."

"How far's that from A&M?"

"About an hour," I admitted.

"Great! I'll come see you. Maybe you can give me a tour."

"Goodness. Wow." My hands started sweating on the steering wheel. I bit another fingernail.

He slipped back into his island accent. "I comin' Friday night. I drive out Saturday morning to your place, a'ight?"

Think fast! Think fast! If he came to Nowheresville, I'd have a harder time getting rid of him. In College Station, I could leave on my schedule.

"How about I come to you instead, and we can have dinner?"

"Or meet halfway," Rashidi said. "I'll text you Friday. We'll plan then."

"Okay," I said, my voice weak.

At a stop sign, a truck pulled up next to us with a big yellow Lab in the back. It looked at Gertrude and away again, dismissing her. Gertrude barked hysterically and threw herself against the window. I accelerated and Gertrude pawed the window and howled.

"What's that?" Rashidi asked.

"That's a Gertrude," I said. "Long story."

"You can tell me Saturday."

"Okaaaay," I said.

And we ended the call.

My brain immediately started spinning. What had I done? Had I really just committed to an evening with a man who was interested in me? What would Adrian think? Not that I really believed my dead husband was watching me, literally. But right after he died, he'd visited me. Or I thought he had. It was hard to be sure, but it had felt completely real. I could hear his voice and see his face and even feel his touch. Then it had just stopped, and it was like he died all over again. I didn't want to fill the empty place he'd left behind with anyone but him, and, yeah, a part of me hoped he would fill it again someday. Maybe this qualified me for a 5150 pickup, but what else would you expect from a woman who'd been convinced she was a knife-winged butterfly and saw things she knew were nothing but a figment of her imagination?

But I wasn't going down that mental rabbit hole. I had to come up with an excuse before Saturday that Rashidi couldn't talk me out of. I could do that. I would do it. It would be okay.

The Giddings Country Vet Hospital appeared on my left. It was a yellow house converted to a clinic. As I pulled around to the side, I discovered that what looked like a small house from the front had been expanded with the same yellow siding. Metal kennels honeycombed along the side and back of the extension. Dogs of every shape and size barked at us as I pulled to a stop and parked the car. Gertrude was giving lip back to them with everything she had.

"Hush, Gertrude," I said to her. It was like spitting in the wind.

I gathered up my handbag, a worn-out zebra print that I'd been vowing to replace for months, and picked up Gertrude's clothesline leash. She clambered out of the car with swagger, still barking ferociously. Her white dreadlocks stood up a little on the rough of her neck. The mutt pulled off small and ugly with a lot of attitude, and I admired her for it.

We walked around to the front of the clinic, Gertrude straining against the leash to get back to the kennel area. There was a sign in the window by the front door: SEEKING PART-TIME VET. It was 7:59 a.m. and the clinic opened at eight, so I tried the door. It was unlocked.

I dragged Gertrude through the empty waiting area, her toenails surely leaving scratch marks as she dug in, and up to a long, broad counter. No one was manning it yet. The reception area was in what had probably been the parlor and dining area before the remodel. There were upholstered chairs and leather benches scattered around the exterior of the room and a book-shelf displaying dog food, leashes, toys, chews to clean dogs' teeth, pill pockets to help them swallow medicine, and other standard veterinary clinic fare. But the shelves also held cross-stitch samplers of Bible quota-tions and a needlework rendition of Noah's Ark. The space smelled antisep-tically clean, which was amazing considering the animals and their bodily fluids. Bodily solids, for that matter. My father's large animal clinic had smelled nearly this good, and I knew it took a Herculean effort from him and his staff to keep it that way.

A man's voice interrupted my perusal, in a deep southern accent. "May I help you?"

I turned and found a large white man of maybe thirty years of age dressed in green scrubs. A scar marred his features from the top of one cheek to down under his nose and across to the far corner of his lip.

I smiled at him. "Yes, I wanted to see if you could take a walk-in."

"What's your pet's name, ma'am?" He poised his fingers over a keyboard.

"Her name is Gertrude."

"And your name?"

"Well, my name is Michele Lopez Hanson, but Gertrude's owner is Gidget Becker."

The man looked up at me quickly. His voice deepened. "Ms. Becker? I heard she's—" He stopped, leaving that awkward gap in conversation that happens when people are uncomfortable mentioning the dead.

"Yes, she's deceased. I'm her neighbor and the one who found her."

"I'm so sorry, ma'am. So you live out near that big new pipeline they just announced?"

"Um, maybe." I remembered the sign on the outside of Gidget's fence the day before. It bore looking into. "And thank you. Anyway, Gertrude had a big fright yesterday, and she managed to break through a window to go for help. I think when she did, she knocked out one of her eyeballs."

I slung Gertrude up and onto the counter.

The man immediately made friendly noises and reached toward her with his palm up. "Good to see you, Gertrude. Had a tough time?" He scratched her belly. She lifted one leg in the air and kicked it spasmodically.

"I was able to get her eye back in. She seems none the worse for wear, but I wanted to get her a checkup and some supplies."

I paused, and in my silence he said, "You know how to pop an eye back in a dog's head? That's pretty intense for most people."

I smiled. "My father's a vet, and I helped him out a lot when I was growing up. And with her eyes outside her sockets, it wasn't that hard. I'm guessing she must have some kind of pug or other googly-eyed dog in her lineage"—I gestured at her—"even with this long coarse fur and dachshund body."

He nodded. "I'd have to agree with you."

"Do you think you can work her in your schedule?"

He nodded. "Why don't you come around the end of the counter and through that door." He pointed. "Gertrude and I will meet you on the other side."

He picked up Gertrude and they disappeared behind a wall then reappeared in the doorway. I followed them into the interior. Narrow hallways led to closed exam rooms and scales on one side of the hallway. The man put Gertrude down.

"Nice leash." He grinned. Gertrude followed him far better than she had me. He gestured toward a closed door and pushed it open. "Let's take her in here. Oh, and I'm Dr. Miller."

"Nice to meet you, Dr. Miller. I'm Michele."

Once we were inside, Dr. Miller poked and prodded on Gertrude and her eye socket. "It looks like it must have popped out cleanly and gone back in the same way. She appears to be seeing fine," he said as he held up a treat and moved it in all directions on the right side of her head, watching her eye track it. "Good job."

"Thanks."

"I'll send you with an antibiotic in case of infection. Now, let me pull

Gertrude's records." He typed rapidly on a laptop, his large fingers striking each key precisely. I knew because I was watching his letters appear on the screen, and he made no mistakes. "So, she has a prescription for heartworm medication and one for fleas, ticks, and all of that. Honestly, we gave Gidget the meds free. She sure loved this dog, and she took very good care of her." He stroked Gertrude's long, matted hair off her forehead.

"That is so kind of you. And I'll pay for today, of course."

"I appreciate that."

Eying his computer and the records about Gertrude, I gestured at it. "Dr. Miller, I was wondering if you know who Gertrude should go to, like from your records. I mean, I'm happy to take care of her. I'd even keep her permanently, but I don't want to overstep."

He shook his head. "Oh, I know the answer to that without looking. Gidget was on her own. She didn't even drive. A gentleman of about her age would bring her and Gertrude in for their visits."

"Do you remember his name?"

"Ummm—"

"Jimmy?" I asked, giving him the name the deputies had asked me about.

"No, not Jimmy. Ummm—"

I interrupted his thoughts again with the only other name I knew. "Ralph?" The mutual acquaintance through whom I'd met Gidget.

Dr. Miller did a fist pump. "Yes, Ralph. I'll see if we have his—"

"I know how to get in touch with Ralph. And thank you."

"Is there anything else you need, then?"

I pointed at the filthy little animal. "I don't suppose you guys do grooming?"

He laughed. "Absolutely. Can you pick her up at ten?"

"Works for me."

"Let's go back to the spa, Miss Gertrude." He scooped her under his arm and the two disappeared.

I wanted to head to the library—that's where Gidget's friend and (apparently) chauffeur, Ralph, usually hung out to work on the Giddings Historical Society Newsletter, for which he was the editor—but it didn't open until ten. I made a quick trip to the grocery store, the pharmacy, and 290 Grind for coffee. When I returned to the lobby of the vet clinic, a Hispanic woman was behind the counter. She reminded me of my Mexican *abuela* in that she was almost as wide as she was tall, and not very tall. I'd always thought of my *abuela* as a Latina Weeble, and those were my genes —and my future if I didn't stay fit.

The woman greeted me jovially, and I settled in to wait. I'd barely had time to take my phone out of my zebra bag when the door from the treatment area flew open and Gertrude steamrolled through, pulling a teenage girl behind her. The girl had long, skinny legs, a bad case of acne, and a beautiful laugh. She handed the leash to me.

"Good luck, ma'am," she said.

"Thank you." I shook my head. *What have I gotten myself into?*

Gertrude beamed up at me. She wiggled and danced, shaking her bright white dreadlocks around her. She was far too small to be related to Puli sheepdogs, but her coat bore a startling resemblance. I settled up for the damages, including dog food and a leash. Then Gertrude and I were on our way.

Like at the vet, we were practically the first ones to the library. Giddings wasn't a tiny town by Texas standards, but neither was it what you'd call metropolitan. It fell somewhere in that range where citizens expected big-town services on a small-town budget. Their library, though, was big-town quality. It resided in a tan-brick building with a stucco façade and a giant swatch of blacktop in front for parking. I suspected a conversion from a strip retail center.

I debated whether to take Gertrude in. I felt sure only service dogs were allowed inside. "You don't look like a service animal to me," I said to her.

Gertrude wiggled.

"All right, here's what we're gonna do," I told her. "I'm going to leave the car running and the air conditioner on and you're going to stay inside and be a very good girl. Deal?"

She wiggled at me some more, making her fringe ripple.

As I walked down the walkway from the side parking lot, I looked back at the Jetta and saw Gertrude in the driver's seat, standing on her hind legs, with her front paws at ten and two on the steering wheel. I shook my head. I approached the double glass doors at the front of the building. A colorful poster faced out from inside the door. Giddings Public Library Annual Fundraising Drive. Spaghetti dinner! Raffle! Silent Auction! Proceeds to benefit YOUR LIBRARY!

I pushed through, making a mental note to put the event on my calendar. I walked through the vestibule into a familiar musty odor. Old books and high humidity. A large bulletin board held another copy of the fundraising flyer and other small-town staples: a roommate-needed announcement, a stock trailer for sale, a lost-cat poster with tear-off strips for the phone number to call if "Kity" appeared. I took one, thinking I might be able to offer them my editing services for their next poster.

I passed the circulation desk on my right and headed for the tables behind the computer stations where Ralph usually worked. While I'd only been in his presence a few times, we'd exchanged emails, too, so I knew him better than I knew anyone else in town. When we met here last spring, he'd been excited that I was an editor and author. He'd hit me up for articles for the newsletter, and he'd introduced me to Gidget. The rest was history. But there was no Ralph in sight today, nor did I hear him. Even though the library was a quiet zone, Ralph held court without regard to the rules, and no one seemed to mind.

I circled back to the front counter. It had been empty moments before, but now a petite woman with a crown of chin-length grayish-brown waves was stacking returns in a book cart. Her pink sweater set buttoned at the neck, where it met up with a strand of pearls. She looked familiar.

"Excuse me," I said.

She stopped and studied me with eyes that were a watery blue. "May I help you?" Her voice had the barest of tremors to it. Almost like vibrato.

"I'm looking for a fellow named Ralph that I've met in here a couple of times. He—"

She interrupted me. "Yes, Ralph's quite a regular." She smiled and the skin on her face crenulated.

I took a step closer to her. "Exactly. Have you seen him?"

"No, not today, but he usually comes in around noon on weekdays."

"Okay, thanks."

"Are you a friend of his?"

"Sort of." I waffled my hand. "I wrote a few articles for the historical newsletter and helped him bring it into the digital age."

The smile reappeared on the woman's face, this time lifting the corners of her eyes up in graceful swoops toward her hairline. "You're the author. The one who's writing Gidget's memoirs."

I felt my face crease in surprise. "I am, but how did you know?"

"Oh, Ralph and Gidget were over the moon about it. After Gidget met with you, he brought her in a couple of times so the two of them could put her thoughts together for you." She leaned toward me. "Personally, I can't wait to read it, even if there's folks in town who think you shouldn't put someone like her on a pedestal. I'm Tabitha Rope, by the way." She touched her sternum for a moment. "Beautiful pendant."

I shook her hand. "Thank you." Adrian had given me the enameled monarch locket. It was soldered shut with a picture of us and a smattering of his ashes inside. "Michele Lopez Hanson. And I'm sorry to tell you this, but I'm not so sure it's going to happen now, seeing as how the source of my information is no longer with us."

"Oh dear. I'd heard Gidget passed. It's just so sad. I didn't know her all that well myself, although we both grew up here just a few years apart in age. Maybe Ralph could be your source."

Tabitha looked twenty years younger than Gidget. I adjusted my mental tabulation of Gidget's age downward. "Did you go to school together?" I asked.

"We would have, except Anna—that's what she was called back then—went to the Wendish school."

"What's Wendish?" I asked.

"It's a religion, or more accurately, a Lutheran denomination of Christianity. The Wends came from Germany to Texas in the 1850s and set up a big community here that thrived through the middle of the last century. And they're the ones who don't like the idea of this book." She came around the desk and led me toward a display across the room.

"Wendish," I said again, following her. I liked the word, but it was new to me.

"We have a really nice Wendish display this summer." She gestured to a glass-fronted case in front of her. Bonnets, like the one I'd envisioned yesterday when I pictured an eighteen-hundreds woman on Gidget's porch. Colorful carved wooden eggs. Old letters addressed in a Scandinavian-looking script. My father's best customer was an old Norseman who ran cattle on a ranch a few miles outside of Seguin. I remembered his singsong accent, and how I'd marveled when he spoke in his native tongue. I'd even seen him write in it once when he made notes about a course of treatment my dad had prescribed for one of his young bulls.

"This is great." Continuing our line of conversation about Gidget's schooling, I said, "So, the Wends didn't let their kids go to public school?"

"They didn't used to. They left Germany to escape religious persecution and discrimination." She reminded me of my high school history teacher, her eyes twinkling as she shared this slice of the past with me. "They wanted to practice their own religion, their own way, with their own culture and their own language. That included educating their children. I remember some of the old-timers around town speaking Wendish when I was a kid, but by then, it had mostly died out in favor of German and English. Turns out that over here they had more in common with the Germans than they'd thought. Assimilating was a necessity for survival."

"I grew up with a Baptist mother, a Catholic father, and an Aztec-leaning grandmother, so I can understand the Wends' situation. It's kind of like being caught in the Holy Bermuda Triangle." It also reminded me of the rumblings I was hearing from Christians in America more and more frequently of late, over things like the HERO dispute I'd talked to Brian about that morning. So many of our ancestors in the United States arrived here for freedom of religion. I made a mental note to keep that in mind as I edited the gay marriage and HERO pieces for Juniper.

She laughed. We walked back to the circulation desk. "We carry your book, you know," she said, winking at me.

"I like hearing that."

She went around behind the high counter. "I think Gidget's story will be interesting. After she ran away—"

"Ran away?" I said.

"Um, yes. She decamped to Houston without a word to her parents not long after she graduated high school."

"She hadn't told me that," I said, and pursed my lips. An artistic young woman escapes her strict religious upbringing and small-town life. She goes on to become a fancy art gallery owner who hobnobs with celebrities just a few years later. It *was* a good story.

"Her life was pretty glamorous by Giddings' standards."

That part—the glamorous stuff—Gidget had begun sharing with me. The doors whooshed open behind me, and we turned as one toward the newcomer. It was a young mother with two little boys, possibly twins. They were gap-toothed and freckle-faced and scuffling their cowboy boots along the floor. Sweat trickled down their young faces. The mother had a steely determination to the set of her mouth and her narrowed eyes as she gripped the neck of each boy. The two youngsters were trying hard to look innocent.

I turned back to Tabitha. She was smiling that beatific smile again.

She whispered, "Those boys are a handful." Her voice returned to normal. "So where were we? Oh yes. When she came back, it was as if she'd given up the life a lot of us would've liked to have had in her place." Again she lowered her voice. "Ralph told me someone dumped her at her family's old homestead, lock, stock, barrel, and dirty dishes from the sink."

"That's just so awful!"

Tears created a hazy film over her eyes. "I didn't see Gidget much, but Ralph talked about her a lot, and I'm gonna miss her."

I pictured Gidget, alone, scared, and destitute in her house. But not alone. She had Gertrude. That thought jerked me upright to all of my five foot two inches in height. "Gertrude," I exclaimed. "Ack! She's out in the car. I enjoyed our chat. Thank you so much." I turned and fled back to where I hoped my unlocked and running Jetta was still parked as Tabitha called out a farewell.

Gertrude was none the worse for her time alone in the Jetta. In fact, she looked downright *entitled* in my seat, curled up with her nose tucked under her long, funny hair and her sides rising and falling rhythmically with her sleeping breaths. I almost felt guilty about waking her and shooing her into the passenger seat. Almost.

I turned the radio on to KTEX. The DJs were cracking jokes about same-sex marriage and the HERO ordinance. I decreased the volume until the music came back on. I'd forgotten to leave a message with Tabitha for Ralph, but I had his email. I shot one off to him via my phone from the parking lot, asking him to get together as soon as he could. I checked for messages from the kids—none—and stalked them on Instagram and Facebook. Nothing new, and it brought that sad, lonely feeling from the night before back to me.

I zoomed home, Gertrude riding shotgun, and parked the car in the shade of a line of oak trees next to the Quacker. I turned off the car and ferried the bags from the trunk into the trailer. The heat was so intense I nearly melted, which surprised me. I was raised in Seguin, so I knew heat. We weren't that far away in miles, but we were light years apart in humidity. Here, it was damper. The hots were hotter, and the colds were colder. And we still had four months of summer temperatures to go before things cooled off in the latter half of October.

As a result, the air conditioner in the Quacker was running at full throttle. Condensation dripped from it onto the warped linoleum floor. Replacing that floor was near the top of my "projects" list for the summer. Gertrude buried her head under the pillow on my bed where she'd leapt, uninvited, as soon as I'd opened the door and let her in. I guess the previous night's sleeping accommodations constituted an open-ended invitation.

I quickly put my groceries away. Coconut water, almond butter, bananas, brown rice, a sweet potato, formerly frozen chicken breasts, prewashed and-now-wilted salad leaves, Paul Newman's balsamic vinaigrette dressing, and a bag of mangoes. I lifted a mango and inhaled its sweetness. *My life for a pint of Blue Bell*, I thought, but the company had temporarily shut down production because of listeria. I couldn't wait for them to reopen, even though I didn't eat much ice cream. Only when I wasn't feeling so great, which lately was most of the time.

When I'd finished with the groceries, my thoughts turned to Gidget, even though I should have gotten to work on Juniper edits. My conversation with Tabitha had fueled my interest. When I visited Gidget's house in the spring, she'd given me a box of pictures and documents. I'd tucked it away in the storage compartment underneath the couch seat without even opening it. I figured I'd have plenty of time in the summer.

I burned with a sudden, urgent need to see what was inside. So I pried up the couch seat compartment lid and saw the gray plastic tub. I lifted it out and onto the table. A hot flash ripped through me, so I wetted a paper towel and held it to my forehead and the back of my neck before returning to the mystery box. I pried the snap-on lid off, watching for scorpions and brown recluse spiders. Gertrude hopped off the bed and trotted over. She put her feet up on the seat and sniffed the box. Her body went rigid and she whined.

"Ah, Gertrude, you smell your mommy? I'm sorry." I ruffled her fur behind her ears.

I set the box aside and lifted the first document from inside, holding it up to the light. It appeared to be a legal document in the language I'd just seen at the library: Wendish. The only thing I could read on it was what I thought looked like "Anna Becker" typed in a blank. I set it aside and dug deeper into the box, pulling out all the contents. I realized I was holding my breath, so I released it. Even though Gidget had given the box to me, I felt like I was snooping, like I needed to tiptoe and not make a sound.

Gertrude hopped up onto the bench seat to the folding table. Her sad eyes followed me as I made stacks on the aged blue upholstery of the couch, sending up puffs of dust that made her sneeze. Then I started sorting the piles, trying to put them in rough chronological order. The oldest documents in the first pile. The newest ones to the far right. And a large group that I couldn't identify in a stack in the middle. There was a photo album in the middle stack. I leafed through a few pages. A picture of a little blonde girl in a pinafore, standing beside her parents and grandparents, possibly, in front of Gidget's house a long time ago. It was the same album Gidget had flipped through with me.

I turned further and found several more portraits in front of the same house. I followed a reverse timeline as the old couple in the first picture regressed in age, surrounded by various family members and vehicles—a vintage sports car, a horse and buggy, a mule and plow—and, finally, was only half the couple and then none of it: the man as a young boy and then pictures without him, with older people in foreign-looking farming clothes and late eighteenth-century hairstyles. The women wore those bonnets like the one at the library, too. The white house was brand new, and the barn was half the size it was now.

I thought for a moment, counting back generations and estimating the age of the house. I had guessed that Gidget's house was old. But it was possibly as much as 150 years old. The history in a building that age, the lives it had seen, the tragedies it had endured, and the joys it had celebrated sent a thrill through me. I trailed two fingers over the oldest black-and-white photo. Oh, how I wanted to tell Gidget's story, if I possibly could.

She'd been so excited when I agreed to do it. I certainly hadn't planned to say yes.

"But don't things happen for a reason in life, dear?" Gidget had said in her little girl voice.

How do you say no to something like that? So I didn't.

"I can't afford to pay you, my darling, but I'll leave you something in my will," she had added, as she patted my hand.

But I wasn't doing it for the money. I was doing it because it was the first thing I'd wanted to write about since Adrian died, which is what I said when I told her not to be silly, to leave her things to her family. She'd smiled with her lips, and her eyes had gone somewhere far away.

Just then, the air conditioner in the Quacker sputtered and died, bringing my thoughts rudely back to the present.

An English expletive hovered on the tip of my tongue, but I got hold of myself. *Honor thy mother by not being a sullen brat, especially at your age.* I switched to *español.* "*Caca del toro.*"

I turned the air conditioner off and then back on again. Nothing happened. I opened the door and looked back at Gertrude, but she snored, pretending to be asleep, even though one of her eyes was open and watching me. Smart dog. I stepped out into the heat and went around to the breaker panel, as my body kick-started its sweat response from zero to full throttle. None of the breakers were marked, so I flipped them all off and on. Back inside, I tried turning on the unit again, but all I got was a deathly quiet.

"*Chingate,*" I said to it, and kicked the base of the bench seat. What was I going to do without an air conditioner?

The unit had only been off for about three minutes, but already the temperature seemed to have risen ten degrees. Gertrude stretched with a disapproving look on her face.

"How about you do something useful and fix my air conditioner," I said, and she yawned with a little squeak at the end.

I had to figure out what to do about my temperature crisis, but it was too hot to think. I took my laptop and phone and set up camp in the back seat of the Jetta, AC on high, with Gertrude by my side. Too close by my side, in fact. I pushed her nine-thousand-degree body six inches away.

I pulled up a browser and started searching for RV repair and air conditioning repair. A knock on the front driver's side window made me yelp. Gertrude jumped to her feet and emitted a low, menacing rumble from her throat. The two of us looked out the window together as I hit the lock on my door. Unfortunately, it locked only my door, leaving the other three open.

An old white guy with bulging eyes to match his bulging belly peered in the window. He wore a straw hat and voluminous denim overalls at least as old as he was. Gertrude's rumble morphed into enraged barks and lunges at the window. There was a canister of pepper spray on my key ring, plus I had a guard dog, so I opened the door.

"Hush, girl," I said, and the man stepped back to let me out. "Hello. May I help you?"

Gertrude rocketed out of the car and rushed him, growling. He held her at bay with one large dirty boot. Still he didn't speak, just stared at me with those disturbing eyes. It was awkward, uncomfortable.

"Stop it, Gertrude." She didn't. "Sir?"

His lips barely moved. "I'm your neighbor. Down the road a ways."

"I'm Michele. Nice to meet you." I stuck out my hand, and he took it, which sent Gertrude into a new bout of hysteria. His palm was dry and callused. We shook.

He was silent again. Or maybe he didn't want to talk over Gertrude.

I raised my voice. "What's your name?"

"Jimmy Urban." He licked his lips one time.

Gertrude took it up a notch and started snapping, mostly at the air, but I wasn't going to risk getting sued if she accidentally connected with flesh. I hauled her back to me by her collar. She yowled in protest, sounding like an alley cat in heat.

Half leaning as I held her, I shook my head. "I'm sorry about the dog. Are you the Jimmy who works for Gidget?"

He narrowed his eyes to slits, and his mouth pursed into a bitter-lemon frown. "I ain't her boy."

I suddenly wanted far away from him. I covered up my tension the best I could by picking up Gertrude and hugging her to my chest. "I was told that a handyman named Jimmy comes by to help her out."

"Don't mean I work for her." He stuck his hands in his pockets.

All I could manage was a stutter under his withering stare. "Well, I'm sure you've heard about . . . well . . . that Gidget is dead."

He nodded once.

I noticed a bulge in his left cheek. Chewing tobacco. I prayed he didn't spit. I focused on the tops of the trees. "I was the one who found her."

"I know."

What a rude old booger! "Well, there doesn't seem to be much I can tell you, does there?" I smiled instead of telling him to piss off.

Gertrude squirmed away from me and landed on her feet. Her locks were still raised at her neck, but she quit barking. Instead, she sniffed around so vigorously I was afraid she was going to hyperventilate.

I took a deep breath for patience and regretted it. Jimmy smelled like a bad mix of old spittoon, manure, and BO. Not that there was necessarily a good mix. "I'm trying to figure out who I should talk to about Gidget. Like family or whoever might be in charge of her estate."

"Why for?" he said, and he spat. A brown, foamy pool of tobacco juice, right at my feet.

I took one large step to the side and willed myself not to gag. "Because I want to see if I can be of any help to them."

He stared at me. So long that I thought he wasn't going to say anything —until he muttered, "Ain't nobody but Anna."

His use of her childhood name struck me. "So, you don't know who I should talk to."

"Don't see why there's a need to."

I gestured at the dog. "Gertrude, for one."

"I'll take her," he said.

My arm hair bristled, and I looked back at the dog. She was still giving Jimmy the stink eye. "I don't think so," I said. "Nice to meet you. Have a nice day." I nodded at him, opened the door to my car, and started to get in.

"Why you in your car?" he asked.

I stopped, pulling my hair back and fanning my face with the tail. "The air conditioner inside my trailer just quit."

Without another word, he walked over to the Quacker and let himself in. I'd decided I wasn't scared of the old guy, but that didn't mean I was going in there alone with him. I moved two feet away from the Jetta, dropped my hair, and crossed my arms over my chest.

Five minutes later, if that, I heard the unit kick on and roar into service.

"Well, what do you know?" I muttered. "Old *bastardo*."

He came out, wiping his hands on his overalls.

"How'd you do that?"

He grunted. "Closed the vent and reset the breaker."

"But I reset the breaker outside."

"Not that one. The one inside."

It was like pulling a hen's teeth. "Inside?"

"Under the seat."

Good enough. I'd find it from that last bit. "Thank you. So there's not really a problem with it? Other than operator error?"

"Didn't say that."

All righty, then.

He got in his maroon Silverado without another word and drove off.

FOUR

GERTRUDE and I went back into the Quacker. I couldn't believe I'd left the vent open. That wouldn't be happening again. Once the Quacker got a snoot of heat inside it, it sure didn't cool off fast. It was still warm and steamy, even though the cold air was pumping out at Mach 5.

It was too hot to work, but not to talk. I hit speed dial on my phone for Katie—time to grill her about Rashidi—but I got her voice mail. I didn't feel like leaving a message. On a whim, I dialed Emily, whom I'd become friends with through Katie. I wasn't much of a girlfriend type of woman, and it wasn't lost on me that my few friends were referrals from someone assigned as my roommate a decade ago.

Emily answered on the first ring. "Michele!" Her voice had that "Ama-RILLuh" twang to it.

"How are things with the newlyweds?"

She tittered. "I'm not getting enough sleep!"

"That's not something to complain about."

"Who says I'm complaining?"

Now I laughed.

"But how about you? Did you get moved out to the boonies?"

"Into my trailer out in the middle of Nowheresville, which is even less glamorous than it sounds. The air conditioner quit today."

"Noooooo," she gasped. "What are you going to do?"

"It's fixed, for the moment. But if it keeps cutting out, I'd just as soon hotfoot it back to Houston. Literally." With my new pet. I scratched behind

Gertrude's ears, and she sighed. I leaned closer to check on her eye. It was looking good. Still, it had been hours since it had attention. I got up and made a cold rag for it. I wanted to keep it clean and counteract the effect of the heat.

"Don't give up so soon. Get a repairman in."

I laid the rag across Gertrude's eye. She sneezed and tried to shake it, but I was firm. "Maybe this whole summer in the country wasn't meant to be without Adrian."

"You'll never know if you only half try."

Sweat trickled down my neck. "Even if I get it fixed and stay, how long can I stand being in this little trailer?"

At first, going through my things and bringing just enough to tide me over for three months had felt liberating. I learned I had lots of stuff I didn't need. But sitting here in the hot Quacker, all of a sudden I felt a lot more attached to those things than I had a week ago.

"*Aha.*" Emily's voice sounded smug and amused.

"Aha what?"

"You called me for a pep talk."

"Commiseration. Sympathy. A pity party."

"Nope. You want cheering up. And to be talked out of going back, because you don't want to go."

"I don't *know* that." But didn't I? What was left for me in Houston, anyway? Sam had only one more year of high school, and Adrian was gone. Annabelle was at UT, and my job could be done anywhere. I wasn't social. The few friends that really mattered to me lived hours away to the north and to the south. "But let's say you're right, for argument's sake."

"I'm totally right."

"If you are, maybe I need a little more space to live in. A house. Maybe I'm not a trailer kind of person."

"You could rent something bigger."

"But then I'm not *here*, the place Adrian got for us." At least here there were memories of him, or rather, I could imagine him here. We'd never actually been to this place together. He'd picked it out and bought it for me as an anniversary surprise. My sight unseen. But when I did see it, it took my breath away. The rolling hills, the trees and flowers, the clearing in the middle of our own enchanted forest. It was beautiful. And harsh for a woman alone, at times. Then I thought of Gidget's place. "The next door neighbor's house might be available. That would almost be *here*. The closest I could get."

"See? You did call me to cheer you up. Your positive side just came up with a plan."

We ended the call, and I slumped back in my seat, my brain buzzing over Gidget's place.

At four thirty, I pulled into the parking lot of Maria's, a stucco-fronted restaurant with inset squares of colorful Spanish tile in the façade. I'd thought I'd find it empty, but it was packed. I entered, looking for Ralph—who had emailed me to meet him there—and inhaled the comforting scent of meat frying in lard. When my eyes adjusted to the change in the light, I found the darkish interior filled to the gills with the fifty-five-and-up crowd. Actually, I didn't see anyone younger than seventy except me.

A hostess glanced across a few tables at me, looking harried, and mouthed, "Be right with you."

I waved her off and searched from face to face until I found Ralph. He stood to greet me. His hair was white and thick, his blue eyes solemn but alert in a tan face with a lighter forehead. He towered over me, strong and tall with broad shoulders. I stuck one of my small hands out to shake, grasping thick fingers that provided him no end of grief in trying to publish a newsletter digitally.

"Good evening," he said.

"Good evening." I sat, and after a moment, he did as well.

"Thank you for meeting me," I said to him. "It's good to see you again."

"And you as well, although I wish it was under different circumstances."

I reached for the menu tucked into the ring in front of the napkin dispenser.

"Oh, you won't need that." He pointed across the room. "Everybody comes for the buffet. Sorry to tell you, but they don't extend my discount to guests under the age of fifty-five."

I dropped the menu. "That's okay."

"So," he said. "How are you settling in?"

I shook my head. "Going broke on data."

"Ah, the joys of country living."

"I've been here in my trailer for a week. So far what I've learned is it's too hot for my air conditioner, and not having well water or a septic system means I'm toting equal amounts of liquid in both directions."

He laughed. "When my wife was still alive, we toured the country for a few years in an RV. She didn't like getting her hands dirty, so I did all of that kind of stuff." He spread a napkin in his lap and took long seconds smoothing it out before he reestablished eye contact with me. "I heard you were the one who found Gidget."

"Yes, my children and me. Well, not really children—my young adults."

He looked toward the center of the busy restaurant and cleared his throat. "You know, the sheriff's department isn't so sure she died of natural causes."

I felt a familiar, unwelcome tightening in my stomach. "Why is that?"

"Said she may have been poisoned."

"Poisoned?" I said. "Why would they think that?"

"They assumed she died from a seizure, at least at first. She was sure prone to 'em. Then they noticed some things that didn't fit, so they're sending her off to Austin for a full autopsy."

Gidget, murdered? A chill came over me. Why would someone poison a sweet, harmless elderly lady? And if it was poison, it couldn't have been on a whim. Poison took premeditation, and that meant a strong motive. I worried it around in my brain for a second, until I noticed the long silence.

"Sorry," I said. "I'm just gobsmacked. Do they have any suspects?"

The waitress interrupted us. "Whatcha drinkin', hon?" she said, smacking a piece of bubble gum. She had peroxide-blonde hair and wore it in a high ponytail that lifted the sagging skin around the edges of her face, pulling it ten years tighter.

"Iced tea, please."

"Sweet or unsweet?"

"Un."

"You doing the buffet?"

"Yes, thank you."

She blew a bubble that quickly popped, then nodded, tapped her order blank with a pencil, and said, "Be my guest."

I eyed Ralph's Corona Light. "Oh, and a rocks margarita."

"You got it."

The buffet was enormous. One island for hot dishes: red, green, and white enchiladas, crispy beef tacos, fajitas, tamales, beans, rice, and *queso*. Another for salad and an entire three-cart string of desserts. I made it back to the table a full five minutes before Ralph. He had a plate in each hand and nothing green on either, except *verde* sauce and a small square of Jell-O nearly obscured by the mountain of whipped cream three times its size and dripping down its edges. He didn't show any ill effects from the way he ate, though. His waist and hips were trim with no paunch. Possibly due to the well-worn New Balance running shoes on his feet.

"Word is you put Gertrude's eyeball back in her head as good as Dr. Miller could have."

I laughed. "Sounds like word gets around."

He bit into a crispy beef taco, the shell breaking and crumbling, and juice dripping down his fingers. He nodded, finished chewing, and said, "It does, especially when we have a famous author—heck, a celebrity—move right into our midst. But me, well, I'm just an old landman, retired. I don't know much except what other people tell me."

I sipped my margarita through a straw. It was yummy. Having lived in Texas all my life, I was very familiar with landmen. They are the people who do the acquisition of subsurface mineral rights from landowners for oil and gas exploration, so that whatever company they represent will own any minerals they find in the ground. "Did you work around here?"

He chased another bite with some milk. "For near to fifty years."

"That's impressive. And you're a runner."

He dipped his head. "Yep. How'd you guess?"

I chewed some of my salad before I answered. "The tan line on your forehead, the shoes, and the fact that despite how much you eat you can squeeze between the booth seat and table."

He laughed. "Thank you."

We ate in silence for a few minutes. I finished my salad and moved on to tamales with meat gravy. They were moist and delicious.

I paused between bites. "I'm still in shock that Gidget may have been murdered. She's the reason I asked you to get together, of course."

Ralph shoveled in a forkful of enchiladas smothered in sour cream and cheese, then swallowed the bite whole. "That's what your email said. What can I do for you?"

"I'm hoping to get in touch with whoever is in charge of her estate. Family, if she's got it, or—" I shrugged. "Anyone."

He pointed a thumb at his chest and took a bite of a sopapilla.

"You're family? I didn't know you were related to Gidget."

He put the back of his hand against his mouth, talking as he chewed. "Nah, I'm the independent executor for her estate. Or her will, I mean."

"*Is* there any family?"

"Not that I'm aware of."

"So you're the one I need to ask about Gertrude."

"What about her?"

"I have her. I need to know what you'd like me to do with her."

He set his fork down, and the rice he'd just dipped in *chile con queso* fell off onto his plate. "I was gonna call you anyway. Not about Gertrude, but about writing Gidget's story. That really meant a lot to her—the thought of somebody helping her get it all down on paper."

"Yes, I could tell."

"After she met with you, I helped her gather her thoughts a little. She didn't tell me her whole life story—we weren't that close—but from what I know of it, she's had a tough time."

A possible source of information. "Did you make notes?"

"I wish we had." He worked his rice back onto his fork. "We didn't know we were going to run out of time."

The bald statement made my eyes sting. And to learn that there was no documentation was a blow. "I heard that she was dumped here penniless after spending most of her adult life in Houston."

"Yep. Of course, I only got to know her because Jimmy came to me. I guess you could say she hit me up first about her story, but I wasn't what she had in mind. Then you came along."

A man stopped at our table, his thick, short body and dark aura familiar.

"Deputy Vallejo, good evening," Ralph said.

The street clothes—jeans, roper boots, and a snap-front western shirt—had camouflaged Tank.

"Ralph, good to see you." Tank squinted at me. "Ms. Lopez, isn't it?"

"Michele Lopez *Hanson*, yes."

One side of his mouth puckered. "I hear talk that you're poking around into Gidget Becker's affairs."

"I'm not—"

"If you were from around here, you'd know we don't take kindly to folks compromising our investigations. Since you're not, consider this your warning."

"You've got the—"

"Have a nice night." He nodded at Ralph and slipped through the tightly clustered tables away from us, without listening to my reply.

"—wrong idea."

Ralph shook his head. "That boy has always been a hothead. Don't let him get to you."

"He's unsettling, that's for sure."

Tank was leaning over a table, handing something to a man across from him. The man was several decades older, with darker skin but lighter hair by virtue of age. I drained my margarita with a few hard pulls on the straw.

Ralph followed my gaze. "That's his grandfather. He raised Tank. He's about Gidget's age, I'd guess."

"I wonder if he knew her."

"Hard to say. She left so long ago, she wasn't much more than a tall tale to most folks."

"I guess she must have been in pretty rough shape when she got back."

"That's true. Jimmy—he was friends with her back in the day, helps her out some—"

"Oh, I've met him," I muttered.

"—says she'd improved a lot. It was her neighbor Lumpy that discovered her, though."

"What do you mean, 'discovered her'?"

"He saw signs of life at her old family place and dropped in. Said she was confused, couldn't even figure out how to use her phone. Was talking nonsense. That the place was filthy and she didn't have any food."

"She could have died."

"And probably would have. Gidget calls her former business partner "the crook." Seems to be some real bad blood between them, and I got the impression getting dumped out here had something to do with him." He tossed a few bites into his mouth and swallowed. Kind of like an overage frat boy with a beer bong.

"But she never mentioned anyone besides this partner? No family? No friends?"

He grunted an "uh-uh," not bothering to stop eating this time. He scooped up the last of the refried beans on his plate then scraped up a little bit of the sauces and juices that had run together and added them to his mouth. He had four times as much food as me, and I was only half done. He turned to his dessert selections: *pan dulce*, *arroz con leche* with cinnamon, and lemon pie with an enormous meringue.

"You need another 'rita, Miss?" The gum-popping waitress stopped, hip jutted out, small drink tray overhead.

"Um, no, thank you."

Ralph held up a finger. "I'll take another beer."

"Coming right up."

Then Ralph shocked me by pausing with his fork poised above the plate. "That little dog saved her, you know."

It was my turn to talk with a full mouth, and I put my hand over it. "What do you mean?"

"Jimmy gave her the pup a few years after she came home. After that, he said every time he went over there, a little bit more of the old Gidget was back."

So Jimmy had a greater claim to the dog than I did, although she clearly hated him, so I wasn't going to feel guilty that I was exercising squatter's rights. And Ralph's explanation about Gidget and Gertrude made sense. Many studies showed that people who lived alone fared much better, both mentally and physically, if they had an animal companion.

"How long had she had her?"

"Well, I can't say for sure, but as long as I've known her, which is over a year."

"What do you think will happen to Gertrude now?"

He twirled his fork in his rice pudding. "Either someone will offer to take her, or she'll end up at the pound."

I shook my head so hard, I flung my hair in my face. "I want her." The dog had already made my life less lonely. Like she'd done for Gertrude.

Ralph beamed and gathered up a nice big bite of lemon meringue pie. "That would be just great." He chased his pie with some rice pudding.

I beamed back. "Thank you. Oh, and Gidget gave me a big box of her old photographs and stuff when we met. I still have it. I was supposed to use it to help me in writing her book."

He nodded. "Good, she has loads more where that came from." There was a dab of meringue from his lemon pie beside his smile.

"So, you still want me to go forward with the book?"

"Oh yes," he said. "It was her last wish, after all."

The project made no rational sense, yet I'd so desperately wanted to hear those words. Tank's dark face flashed in my mind. To hell with Tank. This wasn't any of his business, and I wasn't interfering in their investigation. I was fulfilling Gidget's last wish.

Ralph pushed his plate back with two bites of pie still on it and patted his stomach. "What brain cells she didn't fry doing drugs in the seventies and eighties weren't helped by whatever was wrong with her health. There may be nothing at all to her story. Then again, she's generated some pretty interesting rumors over the years. You never know."

"You never know," I repeated, although it didn't matter to me. I wanted her story for me and for her. If anybody else read it, that would be the cherry on top. "Can you give me access to her place so I can make copies of things?"

"No problem. One thing, though, her attorney called me today. He's giving me a copy of the will tomorrow. I don't know who's going to inherit, but he helped her with it. He's a good guy. I sent her to him. If anything changes, I'll let you know."

"Sounds good." I took out my wallet and a credit card. "Now, you came because I asked you for help, and I'm picking up dinner."

He grinned. "Well, why didn't you tell me that on the phone? I would've picked somewhere a little fancier."

I laughed.

When I opened the door to the Quacker, Gertrude shot out like a musket ball from a rifle. Apparently she was rather excited to see me. That, and she had to water the plants. I stood with the door open, waiting for her. I remembered what the heat would do to the air conditioner, but only after it shut itself down.

"Oh no." My voice sounded whiney, and I couldn't afford the emotional dip. I was about to get on Skype with the kids and Papa. Luckily, I'd stopped at Tractor Supply to get some small fans on my way home, so I could keep air moving, at least. *Think positive.*

Gertrude scrambled inside. I plugged one fan in on each side of the trailer and turned both on high. Sweat ran down my torso within minutes. I lifted my hair off my neck, catching a whiff of myself as I did. I needed a shower, but first I had to set up the group Skype, and if I was going to be on time, I'd have to hope the laptop gods would intervene to accelerate the start-up sequence. Five minutes later, I answered the call, which I was supposed to have initiated; one of my eager-beaver, tech-savvy kids beat me to it.

I heard voices and laughter before I saw faces. It was so good to hear them that my heart hurt, both with the good kind of pain that comes from loving, and the bad kind from missing, like with my mother and Adrian.

"Mom, where were you?" Sam asked, and Annabelle said, "I thought I was the one who was always late."

Papa said, "Hello, Itzpa." He had become so frail, so quickly, after my mother died. His almond-colored skin sallowed and his clothes hung from him, but tonight his eyes were less glassy. More clear and attentive. Beside him on the screen, Sam was a two-generations-diluted version of his grandfather. With skin a bare shade lighter, Sam's dark hair had the sun streaks that Papa's used to get when he worked outside.

"How's baseball camp?" I asked.

"It's super awesome being a counselor. All the kids think I'm awesome. Terrence is a counselor, too, and he treats me so awesome," he said, referring to an older kid he'd lifeguarded with at the pool near our Houston home, "like I'm his age or something. It's like, I don't know, super awesome."

We all laughed.

"You are super awesome," I said. "And Belle, what about you? Are you settled in?"

A face appeared behind her blonde poufy halo of hair. Jay, her boyfriend. He was a good-looking young man with a buzz cut orangish from constant chlorine exposure. He waved at me.

"Hi, Mrs. Hanson."

"Hi, Jay."

Annabelle wrinkled her pert nose with its light dusting of freckles, and her green eyes shone. "I moved in and we started summer school classes today, or whatever, and I had my first practice with the team. No coaches because it's summer, but everybody's getting together for workouts and stuff." She giggled. "It's super awesome!"

"Ha ha," Sam said.

We continued chatting. The kids were high-spirited and mostly oblivious to Papa and me. When they had finished telling us about everything that was super awesome, I asked, "Okay, you three, so who's coming to visit me first? I could use a support team for my bicycle race this weekend."

Annabelle said, "Jay's taking me to see Luke Bryan, or I would totally come."

"So, Belle will be shaking it for the catfish way down deep in the creek. She's out. Papa?"

Papa frowned. "You know how it is in the summer." His practice partner still had kids at home, so Papa covered most of summer weekends. Suddenly, I remembered I'd posted a message looking for my brother that morning. I wanted to tell Papa about it, but now wasn't the time.

"And you already know I can't come because of camp," Sam added.

"Convenient excuses, all of you," I said. "But that's okay. I have friends who will be there."

Annabelle piped in, "That guy Rashidi who's been texting you?"

You could have heard a pin drop until Sam and Papa exclaimed, "What?" at the same time.

"Whoa, whoa, whoa." I held one hand up in the stop gesture.

Annabelle said, "So, is he coming or not?"

"He lives in St. Marcos. You know, the island? Across the ocean."

"That's not an answer," Annabelle pointed out.

"Did I tell you I'm writing a book? It's about the woman who died Sunday."

"Don't try to distract us, Mom." Sam scowled at me.

Papa nodded. "They're smart kids, Itzpa. Answer the question, or we're going to think you're hiding something from us."

Sam crossed his arms. Annabelle crossed hers, and then Papa wiggled his eyebrows and crossed his arms, too.

"He's going to be in College Station," I said. "But that doesn't mean anything. He's a friend of Katie's."

"It's okay with us." Annabelle smiled to match her halo, small and sweet. "You should be happy."

I couldn't be happy without Adrian, just less unhappy, and none of them understood that. I didn't expect them to, so it was okay.

Papa nodded, his face thoughtful. "It's time, Itzpa. It's time to live again."

The kids started bobbing their heads, too, but I shook mine. "I'm not discussing this."

Papa smiled and held up his hands. "Okay, okay."

We rung off with an agreement to Skype again the following Monday and stay in touch in the meantime. My software made the signing off noise three times—one for each of them—leaving me alone again. Gertrude hopped up beside me and put her head on my leg. Well, not completely alone. I stroked underneath the soft hair hanging over her eyes, and she wagged her ragged tail.

"What are we going to do, girl?" I asked Gertrude. "It's only eight o'clock."

She kept wagging her tail and watching me, expectantly, as if I was going to answer the question for her.

"Fine. I have an idea." I jumped up and made a cold compress and held it on her eye, ignoring her chuff, while I let my mind float freely. It settled on an appreciative thought toward my new roomie. "Thank you for not pushing me about Rashidi."

Gertrude wiggled out from under the compress to lick me.

I tossed the wet gauze toward the sink. It almost made it. The fans had done a good job, but it was getting pretty hot. I shooed Gertrude down and lifted our seat. There was another breaker panel, just like Jimmy had said. And one switch in the off position. I snapped it into place. I left the seat up and tried the AC switch. It roared to life, and I shut the seat.

"Hallelujah."

Gertrude jumped back onto the cushion. I joined her, and without consciously making a decision, my fingers found the keys of my laptop and took me to the dashboard of my blog. Although I tried to forget it most of the time, I did have one, forced on me by Juniper's former publicist, an evil witch named Scarlett. I'd barely done anything with it, but her firm had posted as me to promote *My Pace*. I poked around the admin area a little. The PR firm had built up quite a following. Thirteen thousand people, strangers with an interest in triathlon. Or Adrian, more likely.

But they no longer controlled what I did. I went into the settings and changed the name of the blog to *Her Last Wish*.

I began to type.

I met an old woman and an ugly dog a few weeks before my mother died. And then the words flowed like water.

FIVE

Tuesdays started with a swim, but on this Tuesday morning, I had to make an emergency stop in town first. Half an hour earlier, I'd opened the spigot to transfer the contents from the tank to the pootainer, and the stench had blown me backwards. In my mind, I saw a giant green cloud with a face, arms outstretched, flowing toward me, like a stink ghost. Unfortunately, the contents didn't flow for long. The hose was as old as the Quacker itself, and with the pressure of hot *caca*, literally, the hose burst open and several gallons ended up on the ground instead of in the 'tainer.

The green cloud went nuclear. I lifted my shirt over my face and ran, gagging. I shut the trailer door and leaned against it from the inside, pondering my options: go out and clean the mess up myself, now, or go out and clean it up myself, later. Tears leaked out of my eyes. I touched the butterfly locket on my clavicle and said, "Oh, Adrian, this would have been funny if you were here." Then I realized I'd desecrated my necklace with dirty fingers and cried harder.

I wiped my tears on the back of my arm and went outside to take care of the mess. I looked at my hands mid-process: covered in filth. *Tlazol*, I thought. Confirmation of who I had become. I cleaned up then checked the 'tainer. The good news was it was about half full. I backed the Jetta up to a small black trailer I'd bought for just this purpose. Then I positioned the Jetta and trailer so that I could roll the 'tainer up the trailer ramp, secure it in place, and take it to a dump station, all without ever having it anywhere near my vehicle.

Yes, it had been awful, and it still wasn't fun. But finally I spied the RV park with the pay-to-dump station. I dropped in their office first and bought a new hose, which made the second stage of the transfer process much less exciting than it had been in stage one back at the Quacker. Afterwards, I trudged to the restroom, feeling filthy and dejected. They had a bar of Lava soap by the sink, and I nearly wept with relief. Papa had sworn by it and kept a bar at every wash station in his clinic. I scrubbed and scrubbed and scrubbed and scrubbed until my skin was raw and my locket was sparkly clean.

Five minutes later, I parked at the Giddings Public Swimming Pool. I walked to the pool, tore off my cover-up, and dove in without breaking stride. The water was a shock to my system, in a good way, cool without being cold, warm without being hot. I didn't love to endurance swim, really, but I loved the water. I took a few minutes to glide weightless and sleek. Clean and fresh. Beautiful. I knew these were underwater illusions, but I didn't care. Kids had started filling the pool, splashing and screaming. I didn't care about them, either. When the water had done its magic on me, I put on my goggles, ear plugs, and MP3 player. I selected seventies music in honor of Gidget, and "Stayin' Alive" pumped through my ears. I pushed off the wall in one of the lap lanes and began.

I planned to swim for forty-five minutes. Because of my body pain, it was critical that I substitute even more swimming in place of running and bicycling. Compared to Adrian and Annabelle, I was a manatee in a school of marlins. Like Annabelle, Adrian had swum on the UT swim team. So I manateed my way along in the Giddings pool. After a couple of laps, I noticed someone jump into the lane next to me. Right before I flipped at the wall on my next turn, I lifted my head up out of the water. It was a woman roughly my age tucking long dark hair into a cap, putting on her goggles, and getting used to the water. I resumed my all-kick, barely-pull crawl.

I ended another lap and the woman pushed off, putting us side by side. I expected to pull away from her within a few strokes. Just because I wasn't as fast as Adrian and Annabelle didn't mean I wasn't a solid swimmer, far faster than the general population. But the woman beside me matched me stroke for stroke.

Okay, I thought, *she's obviously overexerting herself because she's just started. I'll pull away from her after a couple of turns.*

But fifteen minutes later we still were in perfect unison. My hypercompetitive self kicked into gear.

Maybe she'll quit before me. I'll swim farther. She's just a short-distance swimmer.

But after another fifteen minutes, she was still swimming, and we were still neck and neck. I pictured myself dolphin-diving under the lane rope to come around behind her. I could hold onto her ankles, weighing her down so she couldn't keep up with me.

Probably not a good idea.

At exactly forty-five minutes I hit the wall and pulled myself up out of the water. My nemesis kept going, so I grabbed my towel and made for the bathrooms. I showered and was dressing when a woman with long dark hair came out of the shower.

Probably my nemesis.

We nodded at each other, and she smiled. "Nice swim."

My competitive feathers were still ruffled. I tried to smile, but it felt like it came off as a grimace. "Thank you. You, too."

On my way out, I dug for my phone in my purse. I had voice mail. I hit play as I walked up on a magenta pickup truck of a vintage year parked on the driver's side of my Jetta. Two perfectly mannered golden retrievers were in the truck bed.

The message was a hang-up from an Unknown number.

"Hi, guys," I said to the dogs. Their tail wags thumped against the pickup bed.

My phone rang. I didn't recognize the number. "Michele Lopez Hanson." I stuck my phone between my ear and shoulder, cradling it as I opened the Jetta and threw my bag into the passenger seat.

"This is Eldon Smith," a man's voice said.

I knew that name. Everybody in Texas knew that name. Eldon "Greyhound" Smith was one of the most rich and famous plaintiff's attorneys in the state. He'd made a killing off asbestos work and breast implant class action litigation.

"I'm the attorney for Ms. Anna Becker," he continued.

"Who?" I asked.

He cleared his throat. "Anna Becker. Some people called her Gidget."

"Oh, right. Sorry."

Really, Michele? You, a former attorney, get on the phone with one of the top lawyers in Texas, and you can't do better than that? I hadn't practiced law in years and didn't think about attorneys much. Tried not to think about them at all. And still I was reduced to a speechless, quivering, baby-lawyer on the phone with this man.

Greyhound—because that's how I thought of him—said, "I was wondering if we could meet."

Again, no flicker of intelligence to help me out. "Why?" I asked.

"Ms. Becker made a bequest to you in her will."

I dropped myself into the driver's seat, a sack of potatoes. Air escaped my mouth in a soft "pffft." She'd done it. She'd told me she would, but I thought I'd talked her out of it.

"Are you there, Mrs. Hanson?"

"Sorry, just stunned."

"I really believe we should meet and discuss it before the terms of the will become public."

The car was sweltering. I finally recognized this fact and turned it on so the AC could run. "What did you have in mind?" I asked.

"Lunch at Royers, tomorrow."

"That would work." I turned the AC to high. We set a time and traded contact information, phone numbers, emails, and such. "Could you say what it is she left me?"

I heard a voice in the background. "Greyhound? George Bush for you on line two." A female voice, cheerful but firm.

He muffled his phone, but I could still understand him. "Dubya or elder?"

I couldn't hear her answer.

To me, he said, "I'll tell you all about it at lunch."

After we hung up, I sat in the car, feeling weightless and out of place and time. A woman I had met only once wanted me to write the story of her life, and because of that, one of the top lawyers in Texas had just called me and hung up to speak with a former president of the United States of America. But the weirdest thing of all was that Gidget left me something in her will. She'd been thinking about me after our meeting. Meanwhile, I had put her crate of treasures in the Quacker's bench-seat compartment and never thought of it or her since, until her death forced it back into my mind.

It was a weird feeling, and not in the good *X-Files* kind of way. In the "I need to do better" kind of way.

SIX

La Mariposa the Second was possibly the most beautiful bicycle on the planet. She certainly didn't deserve to be ridden by a shriveled-up, has-been athlete like myself, but that was her fate. I coasted the last ten yards as I braked to make the turn home onto my jarring dirt driveway. I'd risen at dawn to ride before the worst of the heat—after coyotes kept a shivering Gertrude up half the night (and thus me)—but still, it was over ninety degrees, and in the humidity, that felt like a hundred and eighty. My jersey was soaked with sweat and clung to my body like a wetsuit.

I made the turn and pedaled slowly through trees and then past the pond for the last third of a mile. The Quacker was positioned near the back of our rectangular acreage. *Our.* I couldn't help but still call it "ours," because Adrian had bought it for us to enjoy together. The truth of the matter was that now it was just mine. Me. Solo, except for one ugly little dog.

I stopped at the trailer and was greeted by Gertrude's urgent barks. Her black nose and white locks of hair were pressed against the window over the queen-sized bed.

"Hi, Gertrude. I'm coming." I had clipped out of the pedals back at the gate in case I needed to put my feet down to catch myself on the rocky dirt road. I swung off and leaned my bicycle against the trailer. I opened the door, and Gertrude met me with enthusiastic kisses to my shins, which became even more enthusiastic when she tasted the salty sweat. Her rolls of hair stuck to my leg, soaking sweat off me like a sponge.

"Stop it," I said, and gently pushed her away. I rubbed her ears but she leaned back into my legs.

I hid La Mariposa the Second behind the Quacker, locking her to a post. It broke my heart not to ride her more, but my poor aching body wasn't up for it. I loved the feeling of flying with the wind in my face, when riding didn't hurt. But it hurt all the time now, and it didn't seem there was anything I could do about it.

It took me half an hour after my bicycle ride to cool off, shower, and serve Gertrude and myself our breakfast. Dog food for her, a Quest bar for me. Technically, it was ten o'clock and past respectable time for breakfast, but I wasn't going to tell anybody if she didn't. I had about an hour left to fit in a little honest work before I had to leave to meet Greyhound Smith for lunch.

First, though, I texted Wallace in Amarillo. *"Are you guys still coming down for the rescheduled race this weekend?"* It had been rained out, a rare occurrence in Fayetteville, Texas, and even rarer that the weather hadn't touched us thirty miles away.

Last I'd heard, he and Ethan planned to stay in a bed-and-breakfast Saturday. I was looking forward to seeing them, but part of me prayed he would back out of the race. Then I wouldn't have to ride in it and either pretend it wasn't hurting as bad as it was or give in to the pain and ride like the old hag I'd become.

I booted up my laptop. Other than the article I was helping edit, the one on the general impact of gay marriage on sports, everything else in my inbox was specific to a particular sport, and all of it usually written, edited, and posted on the same day. That fit my lifestyle. I was able to work in short bursts, just-in-time, at all hours, instead of making face time eight hours a day. I needed to get the gay marriage piece moving, so I started with it. It was clean and well constructed but preachy and logically flawed. An hour flew by with my virtual red pen flying, slashing, cutting, incising.

My alarm went off on my phone, which I'd set when I started working. Experience had taught me I could get lost in the *Chicago Manual of Style*. I got so lost this time that I hadn't noticed Wallace had texted me back. Yes, they were coming. They'd see me an hour before the race. *Ugh.*

I threw on one of the least-casual summer outfits I had brought with me: knit khaki skirt and shell with a little white jacket. When I was packing for a summer of work-from-home in the country, I never dreamed I would be meeting Greyhound Smith.

Just about the time I got dressed, the air conditioner kicked off again.

"Dios mío," I said.

I hadn't left any doors or windows open. I checked the outside temperature on a thermometer perched at the window. It was 101 degrees. Unseasonably warm for June, it portended hellish heat for the rest of the summer. And it was clear the Quacker's AC couldn't handle it. Great. There was no time to do anything about it now, and it was too hot to leave Gertrude there. No reason why I couldn't bring her with me, now that Gertrude and I were "official."

I picked up her brand new zebra-print collar and leash—which, yes, matched my handbag and made us look like a Hispanic episode of *Keeping Up with the Kardashians*, or it would have, if only Gertrude had been a Chihuahua—and slipped them on her.

"Don't you look pretty now?" I said.

She sat up on her bottom and lifted her front legs. She rose slightly and hopped in a circle.

"Look at you. That's fancy. Come along now." I gave her leash a gentle tug, and for once she followed me like a lamb.

Once inside the Jetta, she jumped into the passenger seat like she'd been doing it all her life. I sighed. At least she hadn't claimed my seat. I fired up the engine, and we got underway. The air conditioner blew hot air for the first couple of minutes. When the temperature grew colder, Gertrude and I tilted our faces toward the vents.

We were headed to Round Top, which would have been a ten-minute drive if direct. But alas, it was not. I drove north to 290 and then east until Carmine, where I could then turn southeast, and finally south, and eventually get there in half an hour. And that's only if we were lucky enough to be driving there when Antique Week was not in session. Antique Week fever grew hotter every year. There were now two weeks in the fall, two weeks in the spring, and one week in the winter. Heck, there were probably other Antique Weeks during the year that I just didn't know about. What I did know was that you didn't drive to Round Top from the south or the north during any Antique Week, or at all, if you could help it. The whole Round-topolis became gridlocked with junkers, antiquers, food vendors, and shoppers. Round Top had grown so hip you could now find the likes of a former senator, Boyd Herrington, a famous attorney, Greyhound Smith, the top-selling country artist in Texas, Gary Fuller, and the Junk Gypsies of TV fame all within a population of less than one hundred.

Kvetching about the circuitous route aside, the drive was gorgeous. A wet winter had brought the wildflowers out in force. Even though bluebonnet season was long over, the bright reds and yellows of the hardier flowers remained most of the summer. I secretly thought they were prettier anyway. And the rolling hills of green grass and trees were spectacular as well, reminding me of my girlhood-bedroom sheets, right out of the drier as my mother shook them out, billowing, to put them back on the mattress.

I let off the gas as I rolled into Round Top proper. As I cruised past the Mercantile, an old magenta Ford pickup like the one from the pool was waiting to pull out. Not that I would expect there to be more than one of a truck like that. A woman with long dark hair and pale skin was driving. I stared to be sure, and I was. My swim rival. She entered traffic (little that there was) behind me. I turned at the square toward Royers, but she continued south.

I parked nose-in right in front of the restaurant just as someone pulled out. The exterior looked like it had been attacked by a street artist with schizophrenia. I hadn't been yet, but they were famous for their pies. So famous they'd spun off a separate establishment—Royers Pie Haven. I'd tried to cajole Adrian into a side visit there once during a bicycle ride. He was a man of iron will when it came to processed sugar, so I lost that battle.

I decided to leave the car running with the AC on like I had at the library, and trust in the goodness of my fellow man to let me retain possession. Gertrude put her paws on the arm rest and barked, but I steeled myself against her emotional blackmail and shut the door behind me. When I reached the entrance, the hostess peeked out and saw the dog in my car.

"Is that Gertrude?" she asked.

I took a closer look at the woman. Ear disks, tattoos, and a hair color best described as electric violet. "Why, yes, it is," I said. "How do you know her?"

"Ralph brought Gidget and the unforgettable Gertrude in for lunch once. Gertrude is a friend of the restaurant. Why don't you bring her around back and she can play with our other dogs?"

"That would be wonderful."

We walked together to the car to collect my keys and dog. An ecstatic Gertrude led the way as we circumnavigated the restaurant.

"My name's Stacy Gifford," she said.

"I'm Michele Lopez Hanson."

"Are you the writer?" she asked.

I was beginning to think everyone in a three-county area knew me, or at least *of* me. I had some catching up to do. "I am."

"We'll all be lined up to read Gidget's story when you're done."

"That's good to hear."

She turned around. The back of her shirt read PEACE, PIE, LOVE. When we got to the back of the building, she opened a U-latch gate.

Gertrude walked sideways like a crab through it, ahead of me like she owned the place. Two dogs rushed her—a Pekingese and a Pug. They ripped at the grass with their feet and strutted a little while Gertrude celebrated with joie de vivre.

"Bud's real good to us about bringing in our animals," she said.

Bud and his family were the owners. I hadn't met them, but I'd bet they knew who I was, since everybody else did.

"Shortcut." Stacy opened the back door and held the three little dogs out with her foot, gesturing for me to go in. We passed the bathrooms on one side and a copier/fax machine the size of an eighteen-hundreds printing press on the other. Then we entered the tiny dining area. The scent of beef flooded my olfactory system and sent it into a virtual orgasm. The tables were small, and the space between them even smaller. Stacy had to turn sideways, and even then it was a tight fit between chairs. My shoulder knocked against a piñata hanging from the wall. The decorations inside made the outside look mentally stable. Every speck of the ceiling and the walls was plastered with T-shirts, letters from customers, posters, drawings, and other lighthearted Texas paraphernalia.

Stacy made her way to the divider between dining room and kitchen. Colorful T-shirts hung along it from the ceiling like nautical flags. "You need a table, right, hon?" she asked me over her shoulder.

"Actually, I'm meeting someone here. Um . . . Greyhound . . . I mean Mr.—"

She pointed to a table for six where five people were sitting, across the restaurant. "I've got you guys down there on the end. See Greyhound?"

Seating at Royers was family style. Greyhound had to be the sixtyish guy, sipping a Shiner Bock and reading the menu. Everyone else at the table was involved in an animated discussion.

"Yes, thank you so much. And nice to meet you."

"You, too. I'll be watching for that book to come out."

Greyhound hadn't seen me yet, so I detoured back to wash my hands. When I reached our table, I put a hand on the back of my chair to hide its slight shake. I was nervous to meet legal royalty and about finding out what Gidget had left me.

"Mr. Smith, I presume." I smiled.

Greyhound stood, pushing his chair back as he did so. It bumped into the wall, and he knocked into the woman seated next to him. She flapped her hand as if to say she'd pay it no nevermind. The table in front of the lawyer shook. Ice cubes surfed in glasses of tea. All this from a man who couldn't have been more than five six or so and probably didn't weigh a lot more than me.

Once he looked at me, I recognized his face from thousands of TV interviews and state bar association promotional fliers for seminars that bore his name. He looked exactly like his photos, just older.

"And you must be Michele Hanson."

We shook, then he proceeded to knock about the table and chairs as he sat back down. A one-man wrecking crew.

"I took the liberty of ordering you a sweet tea," he said.

I would rather die than drink sweet tea, but I didn't tell him that. My mother's Southern manners instead brought out the words "How kind of you." I took a diminutive swallow. I was a Dr Pepper girl. Diet Dr Pepper as I got older and Dr. Zevia when Adrian had entered my life and convinced me of the dangers of chemical sweeteners. I was a far cry from the unhealthy woman of six years ago, pre-Adrian. And in some ways more extreme than when he was alive. Carrying on his legacy, I guessed.

I picked up the menu. "What's good here?"

"Everything. You won't find a better restaurant, even in Houston." He took a long swig of his beer. Moisture rolled down the bottle. His eyes had a satisfied gleam when he put it down.

Since Houston was the restaurant capital of the state and, to some, the world, I took that as a ringing endorsement. I set the menu down. I'd spied the beef tenderloin sandwich, and that was all she wrote.

Stacy swooped down to our table, her hands splayed on its top. "What're y'all having?"

I pointed to the beef tenderloin sandwich and potato chips. "Medium rare, please. With a water, and, oh, a Shiner Bock, too."

Greyhound ordered a salad with beef and another Shiner.

"So, of course, I've heard of you, and it's an honor to meet you, Mr. Smith."

"Please, not Mr. Smith."

"Should I call you Greyhound or Eldon?"

"Either one'll work." He gave me a tight, small grin and fiddled with his silverware.

"So, you said you wanted to see me about Gidget, that she left me something. I don't know which is stranger to me. That she left me something, or that you're her attorney. She had to be a pro bono client. And I've always thought of you as a litigator of huge cases, not as an estate lawyer."

Stacy plunked a glass of water and two uncapped amber bottles on our table. Foam bubbled up to the lip of mine. I reached for it. A midday beer was decadent—not how I usually rolled. I tipped it back. Delicious. And within seconds, my nerves were less of a problem. Greyhound put his elbows on the table and leaned in. I mirrored his motions.

His voice was barely a whisper in our tight quarters, although the raucous conversation next to us continued unabated. "When I moved out here, I gave up my city practice. It's mostly about community now."

"That's great."

"Gidget came to see me after she met you. She had me change her will to leave her house, land, and most of her personal property to you. As payment for writing her story."

My mouth dropped, and I sat up straight again. The sounds in the restaurant magnified—the clatter of silverware, the *whop* of bodies against the swinging door into the kitchen, voices, voices, so many voices all around me, with words jumbled together in nonsense. Nonsense like Gidget leaving me her house and her land.

"You're kidding me!" I laughed, a brittle sound.

My teeth found my thumbnail and chewed it ferociously. He shook his head but didn't say anything. I watched the motion of his head, back and forth, back and forth, like the swinging door to the kitchen. The frenzied movements inside the restaurant seemed to make the floors and walls tremble. Around me chunks of ceiling fell to the floor and onto our table. A waiter fell, screaming, and a table toppled over, sending plates, silverware, and drinks crashing, splashing over.

I closed my eyes to clear my vision. *Not helpful.* Tension meter reading: 7 out of 10. I felt a stab of pain and realized I'd bitten my nail down to the quick. In my mind I heard my mother's voice: "Get your hands out of your mouth, Michele."

I dropped them to my lap. "So, she left me everything?"

Greyhound's voice was calm. "Almost. She left an old Jaguar and its contents to a daughter."

I grabbed my beer and swallowed. When I set it down, my hand jerked and sent it on a crash course for the floor. The twenty-something guy next to me caught it before a drop spilled, returning it to the table without a break in his group's conversation.

"A daughter? Gidget had a daughter?" It was hard to name my emotions. Excitement about the story. Sadness for Gidget, who had lived alone, with no mention of a daughter to her friends. Pain, as another parallel to my mother stared me in the face. And much more. I grabbed my beer like it would anchor me.

"She claims she did."

"So, who is she? Where is she?"

"I have no idea. Neither did Gidget. I'm not even sure the daughter exists, but that will be up to the independent executor to determine."

I listened with every bone in my body because Greyhound was whispering so softly now, I had basically been reading his lips. "Ralph," I said, and he nodded.

"Did she give you any clues that could get Ralph started?"

"She claims to have left plenty of evidence behind for Ralph to find her. So, if she's real, I trust that he will."

"For Gidget's story, the one I'm writing? The daughter's a big part of it."

He shrugged. "Could be." But he didn't offer any more information.

My heart hammered in my ears, drowning out the laughter of our table mates and other restaurant sounds. Those letters I'd seen. Unopened, "My Darling,"—they might have been to her daughter. Why would she write letters to a daughter unless she was real? As real as the brother my mother had given away. A burbling sob rose in my throat, but I fought it down. A daughter. It was she who should inherit, not me. I wasn't entirely sure how much property Gidget had, maybe twenty acres, plus a house and farm buildings and equipment. Sure, it was old, but I did a rough number in my head based on the $200,000 Adrian had spent on our place. Gidget was giving me a gift worth possibly twice as much as Nowheresville.

Greyhound interrupted my thoughts. "I want you to understand something, Michele." He drummed his fingers then motioned me so close his lips were at my ear. "Gidget was of sound mind, sound enough to write a will, but that doesn't mean the daughter is real. Gidget was messed up for a lot of years. It's common knowledge and she didn't deny it. In and out of rehab. Gallivanting around the city on the arms of artists, athletes, and celebrities, not a one of them tethered to reality."

It was like I was in a trance, still close to him, but looking out over the other diners. "But, if she had this information, how come she never found her herself?"

"Exactly," Greyhound said, sitting back. He knocked over my barely touched sweet tea glass. The liquid flowed across the table and waterfalled into my lap. I squeaked and jumped up. So did Greyhound.

"Oh my goodness. I'm so sorry."

I grabbed my napkin and started blotting my cream-colored dry-clean-only skirt. After I did the best I could on my clothes, I sat back down, right into a lake of tea. I decided not to make a big deal of it. I lifted my tush and tucked napkins under it. Greyhound mopped tea up from the table where it had run toward our table mates. They laughed all the harder for it.

Stacy arrived with our food. "Can I get ya anything else?"

A dry outfit. The name and number of Gidget's daughter. And a psych evaluation for myself. "I'm good."

Greyhound added, "Me, too."

She gave us the okay sign with her finger and thumb.

"What is the rest of Gidget's estate?" I waved my hand in the air toward all the other stuff that might be out there.

Greyhound didn't answer. He lowered his head, closed his eyes, and prayed softly, although I couldn't understand him with the background noise. Then he took a bite of his salad. My tenderloin sandwich languished unattended, growing cold. Just when I thought he'd forgotten my question, he answered.

"Who knows what she's got stockpiled in there? She lived off Social Security and a meager savings account that will be exhausted by her final trip in the ambulance." He took a sip of beer as I wondered if he knew about her art collection, then he directed his attention to his salad while he continued talking. "You know, you don't have to write her story. It's not a requirement of accepting the bequest. Nobody's going to care what an old druggie has to say about ancient history."

Old druggie? His words made me wary, and angry. Very angry. My tension meter shot up to a 9. Not care what she had to say? Everyone I ran into was dying to hear Gidget's story.

So I decided to deflate the giant, blow up the elephant in the room. "If I say I won't write the book and can't take the bequest, and nobody can find the daughter, then who gets it?"

He shrugged. "Nobody. Or, rather, the state does."

I had a thought. "What if she has another will—an older will?"

He shook his head. "Completely superseded by a new, valid will."

"And, if the will you did for Gidget *isn't* valid?"

He picked up his napkin and wiped his mouth. "Well, anyone contesting it would have to overcome my testimony to do that. And they won't."

"Yes, I understand. But what if they did?"

"Then, I guess, if there's an old will, it might be valid."

I nodded. "So, was there one?"

He looked away from me. "I honestly have no idea."

I pushed my food away, suddenly not hungry. "You've given me a lot to think about," I said. Not the least of which was Greyhound's reason for meeting with me to tell me things that Ralph could've told me himself. "If there's nothing else you have for me, I need to leave. Unfortunately, I have another . . . thing I have to get to." I signaled Stacy. "Can I get a to-go box, please?"

"Sure thing, hon." She whirled with a tray over her head and started distributing dishes at a table next to us.

"I'm sorry. I've upset you. I think that last bit came out differently than I meant it. Please accept my apologies."

He was smooth, but it did help. "Thank you."

"It was all I had for you. And I've got lunch." Greyhound called after Stacy, "Check, too, please," and she shot him a thumbs-up. Greyhound pulled out his wallet. "Decisions like these are a lot like Band-Aids, Michele. Best just to rip them off quickly."

SEVEN

I sat in the car with Gertrude, trying to process everything I'd just heard and failing miserably. Operating on autopilot, I thumbed through the messages on my phone. I came to a text that made me freeze up: Rashidi.

"Google Map show Brenham halfway. I want to see the land round there."

I had blocked Rashidi's dinner invitation out of my mind. I slumped over the steering wheel. How was I going to wiggle out of this? Instead of answering him, I hit speed dial for Katie. She answered on the first ring, out of breath. I reversed out of the parking space and pointed the Jetta toward home.

"Hello," Katie said. Pant, pant.

"What's got you hot and bothered?"

"I'm chasing"—pant, pant—"Thomas." Pant, pant. "He's run off with"—pant, pant—"a pair of scissors."

I heard a long, drawn-out scream and "No, mama, they're mine!" in a young voice.

Katie's voice was firm. "You're going to time-out."

Loud crying. Very loud. Meanwhile, Gertrude, worn-out from her impromptu playdate, snored in harmony with the crying. Forte.

"Do you need me to call you back?"

"No." Pant. "I'm"—pant—"putting him in his room."

I heard a plop and then a scream of "I don't want to," followed by Katie saying, "I'll be back when your time-out is over." A door shut with a click.

"Okay," she said. Pant. "Where were we?"

Gertrude bicycled her legs, dreaming.

"You were reliving my past."

She laughed.

I turned left toward Carmine. "And I was calling one of my oldest and dearest and hopefully much wiser friends."

"Well, I'm sorry, you dialed the wrong number," she said. "But you've got me now, so what can I do to help?"

"You can tell me why you gave Rashidi my phone number, and if you're aware that he's trying to get me to meet him this weekend."

"Oh, that," she said. "I, well, I was sure you wouldn't mind."

"You mean you were sure I would, and that's why you didn't ask me."

"Possibly something like that."

An enormous John Deere tractor was chugging along half on, half off the road in front of me. I eased out to pass. The road was clear, so I went around. Inside the cab, a teenage boy was singing at the top of his lungs and banging the steering wheel. He waved at me with a grin, and I pulled past him, waving back.

I sighed. "Katie, it's too soon for me. I may never be ready to date again. I'm good. I have my memories with Adrian and—"

"Michele, I thought you wouldn't mind because Rashidi is a nice man, who doesn't know anybody in your area of the world and would like you to be his friend."

I winced. When she put it that way, I should get over it and be nice to Rashidi. Sweet voices babbled in the background.

"Are they walking yet?" I asked. Katie had twin daughters who were about a year old.

"Nearly. I'm thinking about tying them up and putting that off for a couple of months."

"You could go to jail for saying things like that." I entered Carmine, didn't blink, and made a turn onto 290.

She snorted. "Not if the officer who answers the call is a mother."

"True," I said. "And I'll be nice to Rashidi. But please be sure he's not coming here with ideas that will lead to awkwardness and disappointment."

"Rashidi is a big boy, Michele, and you're a big girl. The two of you will figure it out."

"I don't know why I continue to let you believe that you're my friend," I said.

"Shhh," she said. "Your voice is hurting my head."

I gave up. "How is Nick doing?"

"Nick," she said, and lowered her voice. "Is wanting to have more kids. That man is barking up the wrong tree."

"Whoa," I said. "I think three is a really nice number to end on."

I heard thuds, thumps, and clanks. I pictured her unloading the dishwasher.

"Well, he is pretty cute. So I'm not going to say an accident couldn't happen, but I'm trying to get him in to see a really nice doctor who could end all my worries."

About that time, I heard a shattering of glass.

"Oh, shit!" she said. "I gotta go before the girls crawl into broken glass. Love you. Be good to Rashidi."

"If I even end up seeing him. Love you, too."

We hung up.

I looked at Gertrude, who was stretching herself awake. "That wasn't a lot of help."

She wagged her tail. Ten minutes later, we pulled up to the Quacker, which I had completely forgotten had no air conditioning for the last few hours. It was like stepping into an oven, which made it hard to breathe. Gertrude whined, and her tail drooped. I threw the breaker under the bench seat and turned the AC on, but I knew it was going to be a long time —nightfall, maybe—before it cooled off.

I turned to the dog. "Gertrude, let's give this rust bucket time to cool and go get the My Darling letters from your old house."

We fled the Quacker, and Gertrude's tail flew back up to its normal height. From the air-conditioned comfort of the Jetta, I texted Ralph for permission, and within seconds he agreed to meet me there. Soon we were passing the smelly chicken farm and making a right turn toward Gidget's. The trees were less thick on this road than on the one to Nowheresville, because it was more recently farmed and "improved." As we rounded the last corner before reaching Gidget's place, a large white passenger van passed us in the other direction. It had a door magnet on it that read KOUNTRY KLEANERS. All they needed was KLUB at the end and the message would be crystal clear. The driver was a woman about my mother's age, with shoulder-length dark hair, but she didn't look at me or wave. Not local or just rude?

We sailed through Gidget's cedar-post-and-barbed-wire entrance, bumping over the cattle guard. A large stock tank (which I called a pond on my place since I didn't have livestock) with high earthen mounds at its edges was only a few yards back from the right fence line. A few elderly Herefords and two Boer goats grazed in the pasture on the left. The cows and goats were color coordinated in their white-and-reddish-tan coats. They looked up from their grazing as we passed, but only for a moment. The house was tucked into trees straight back from the entrance, although the driveway wound back and forth a little on the way there. The trees extended in a big box around the pasture. The far right edge of the trees led back through the woods to the Quacker.

The picturesque white house with its picket fence, big red barn, and grain silo made me envision the olden days. A farmer in overalls with a pitchfork, some chickens in the yard, a couple of kids chasing a dog, and a woman in a bonnet and long-sashed cotton dress hanging laundry. I smiled, then blinked them away.

A thunderous boom shook the ground, but there were no clouds or lightning to account for it. I stomped on the brakes and hollered. It felt like a bomb. A part of me entertained the idea of a terrorist attack for a split second. Then my mind flashed images of magma from the center of the earth hurtling upward and ripping a gash in the surface. Or it could just be an earthquake. Before I could gather my wits, a white Ram pickup the size of a Sherman tank pulled up behind me and honked. Not a hands-on-the-horn, solidly blaring city honk, but a tap-tap, neighborly country honk. Still, I jumped. I eased off the brake, coasting into the area between the fenced yard and the barn that looked most like parking space and was nearest to the side gate. This house was built long before people demanded attached garages with their three bedrooms and two baths.

Gertrude jumped out, excited, her stubby legs scrambling over grass up to her belly. I stood beside the gate while a man backed the truck in. I didn't like him being there, but I didn't have any proof that I had a right to be, myself, so I wouldn't be mentioning my objections. A bumper sticker on the back of the truck read NOBAMA. There was a black diamond-plate toolbox in the truck bed and a gun rack with a rifle in it across the back window. He got out, and when he stood, he towered over the cab. From the tips of his boots up to the crown of his cowboy hat, he was over six five. His long legs looked skinny below a middle hanging over his blue jeans waistband and stretching the buttons on his checkered shirt. All he needed was a big tin star on his chest and he'd be a cartoon sheriff.

He tipped his hat as he walked toward me. "Howdy. My name's Lumpy. I live"—he pointed to his right—"over there. Who are you?"

His name threw me for a second. He was too big to be one of the Seven Dwarfs.

"Michele Lopez Hanson." I held out my hand to shake his, and he took it like a gentleman takes a lady's and gave it a squeeze. I wondered if a curtsy was in order. "I'm—"

"That Mexican girl that writes books, ain't ya?"

"Yes," I said. "And I'm—"

"The one who found Gidget and's keeping the little yapper."

I smiled but it was the kind that feels like it's stretching your cheekbones with the effort not to show the expression is fake. I opened Gidget's gate and said, "Do you have any idea what that explosion was a minute ago?"

He nodded and—I swear to God—hooked his thumbs through his front belt loops and rocked back up on his heels and then forward onto his toes. "Seismic testing. Exploration company's got a big project going on."

"Aha. Thanks."

"It true that Gidget left you this place in her will?"

Mierda. Something new for people to talk about. I kept my smile pasted in place but didn't answer.

When I almost couldn't stand the silence any longer, he said, "Well, if she did, we'll be neighbors. I'd be more than obliged if you'd let me give you a hand every now and then."

The way his eyes roved up and down my body gave me the impression that the hand he'd like to give me would be planted on my culo. The same one that was stained with half a glass of Royers sweet tea.

"Well, aren't you nice?" I said in my best imitation of my mother's voice. "Thank you so much. You'll be the first one I call if I"—I stalled out trying to think of something less rude than need my septic tank cleaned out —"need something."

"This has got both my home and cell numbers on it." He reached into his left front shirt pocket and pulled out his wallet. He held a business card out to me, and I stepped forward to accept it. "When you're settled in, we can talk about the contract I had with Gidget to sell me this place."

My radar quivered. "Excuse me?"

"Gidget was selling out to me. My parents bought from hers originally anyway. Her family used to own hundreds of acres out here."

"Do you have a written contract?" Because he wouldn't be buying real estate from a dead woman without one. Or anyone, in the state of Texas.

"Well, no, but we'd agreed on all the particulars."

Which meant bupkus, but I'd have to tell Ralph about this. "Huh." I stepped back again. "Well, thanks again, Loopy, and you have a good one, now."

"Lumpy."

I stared at the card in my hand. It really did say Lumpy Baker. Loopy, Lumpy, Grumpy, or Sleepy, I wasn't going to be calling him. "Sorry. Lumpy."

I shut the gate and walked to the front of the house. I chirped for Gertrude, and to my surprise, she trotted along behind me as if she were an obedient creature. As I stepped onto the porch, another of the earth-rending booms split the silence and shook the house. This time I didn't make a sound, but I grabbed a column. I turned back toward my neighbor.

"Those seismic guys are pretty close." He tipped his hat. "Have a nice day."

I stood there acting cool, but I didn't have the keys. I pretended to watch him drive away. Luckily, he drove past Ralph, in a Nissan Murano, coming in. I turned and saw cardboard taped to the broken window where Gertrude had broken out to go for help, and the new doorknob and repaired door and frame that looked like it had all been wood-glued back together. I sat down in a porch swing on the opposite side of the front door. Its paint was chipped and peeling, but I didn't think it could do any further damage to my skirt. I patted the seat beside me, and Gertrude leapt up and moved in close. The porch was shaded so the direct sun wasn't hitting us, but she was a hot tamale anyway. I scooted her a couple of inches away. She moved back, and I scooted her again. She won.

"Michele," my new friend called out in his super-cool-old-guy voice.

"Hi!" I swung and waved and snuggled my dog.

"What was Lumpy doing here?"

Looking for Snow White? "Claiming Gidget had agreed on terms for him to buy this place."

Ralph came up the steps. "Opportunistic SOB."

"Yeah. But he admitted he didn't have anything in writing."

"Because there was no agreement. He's always trying to make a deal." Ralph threw the keys in the air and caught them. "How about I open the house and crank up that AC?"

Crank up, as in it wasn't on. Oh no. "We'll be right here, hanging out."

A second later he joined us. I used my toes to still the swing. Gertrude ducked her head and wagged the back end of her bus at the same time as her tail, but they weren't always going the same direction. Ralph handed me the keys, then he gave her a few scratches before he leaned back on the porch railing.

"For me?" I held the keys up.

"Yep. Spare set. You're about to get it anyway, so let yourself in and out as you need." He snapped his fingers. "I almost forgot. I have a friend who knows your mother. She wants to meet you."

It was like a punch to the gut. "Knew. She passed away recently."

"I'm so sorry."

"You didn't know." I gave him a weak smile. "I'd love to meet her." I used my toes to push off and start the swing rocking again. Ralph watched me, saying nothing. "Mom and I were so different. We didn't always get along. I've found out recently there's a lot I didn't know about her."

I rocked and Ralph shoved his hands in the pockets of his khaki shorts. The silence lengthened.

Ralph cleared his throat. "I heard you had lunch with Greyhound today. Did he tell you the news?"

I nodded. "I can't believe it. Did you have any idea she was going to leave this place to me?"

"Not an inkling. I knew she wanted you to get paid, but not how. And her mentioning a daughter in the will, that's a total surprise. She never said anything about a daughter to me. No one has."

"What about a Jaguar? Is there one around here?"

"Not that I've seen."

"The day I found her, there was a stack of letters on her kitchen table. All sealed, all addressed to My Darling. Did she have a sweetheart? If not, those could be to a daughter."

"No sweetheart," Ralph said. "Maybe she does have a daughter."

"Greyhound doesn't seem to think so."

"I got that impression, too. Any clues in those letters as to where we'll find her?"

I noticed he used the word "we" and smiled. I really did want desperately to be included. "I didn't open them. I will."

"All right, well, I have to get back to town. Doctor's appointment." He walked toward the gate but kept talking. "Greyhound's at the court filing the will for probate right now. Then we've got two weeks to see if anybody comes forward to contest its validity. After that, I think my work's pretty easy, except for that finding the daughter no one knew about part."

"Yeah, that one will be tricky." We waved goodbye as he fired up his engine.

But, I thought, I have a sneaking suspicion finding her daughter was at the heart of her last wish.

EIGHT

I GOT up from the swing after Ralph was gone and went inside. It was hotter than the Quacker. Much hotter. While Gertrude happily ran around, sniffing and snuffling, I checked the thermostat. Ninety-six degrees. Good Lord. My life had turned into Dante's Inferno. I needed to make this quick and get out of here. I went to the kitchen table, expecting to see the My Darling letters, but I went through the stack of mail one piece at a time, twice, and the letters weren't there. I considered searching, but I had the keys. We could come back anytime now without bothering Ralph to meet us.

"Gertrude, where are you, girl?"

I heard her toenails and followed the sound. The heat was blinding, or maybe it was just the sweat in my eyes. I swiped at them, smearing moisturizer with sunscreen into my eyes. It burned like a son of a gun. I found Gertrude in Gidget's room. She was running around it, looking stressed and confused.

"Come on, girl," I said gently. "We're going to melt in here."

She perked up at my voice. I locked the door and, with Gertrude in my wake, walked back to the car. She got in without argument, but put her head between the paws of her short legs. I was sad for her, but relieved. I'd been afraid she'd insist we stay. We drove back to Nowheresville, both of us quiet and in our own thoughts.

The air conditioner had cooled the inside of the Quacker down to a just-bearable eighty degrees. Compared to Gidget's house, it was an igloo.

Closing up a house for days in the Texas summer heat with no air conditioner was no laughing matter. I stripped my tea-stained clothes off, down to my bra and bikini panties. Gertrude and I flopped down on the bed, side by side in front of the fan.

"We don't have to get in a hurry." Might as well give the house time to cool down and knock a few things out here. I turned to the dog. "I don't know about you, but that tenderloin sandwich is calling my name."

Eating in my skivvies felt too nudist camp to me. I wanted clothes on, but the smallest scraps of fabric possible. I put on my white wicking running togs, the kind with vents. I dumped the beef tenderloin sandwich onto a napkin and sniffed. Yum. I tried a bite. It was magnificent, even cold, with grilled onions, a creamy horseradish sauce, and Swiss cheese. I'd pulled the lettuce and tomato out before I boxed it up earlier so it wouldn't get soggy. The toasted bread was still crunchy.

Gertrude came and sat at my feet and whined.

I got my laptop going while I continued enjoying my sandwich, and Gertrude continued to act mistreated. I offered her one of the onions, and she pulled her nose down, back and away from it. I laughed out loud.

"You already ate," I reminded her.

She shook her head as if to disagree, so I gave her the benefit of the doubt and a bite of tenderloin. It was gone in an instant. She begged for more. I offered her the last potato chip, and she smacked and chomped happily for two seconds before begging again.

"That's all there is."

I let her lick the Styrofoam clean while I pulled up my work email. There were no crises. I navigated to the *Her Last Wish* blog. I reread the post I'd written the previous night and noticed that it had seventy-five likes. Surprising to say the least.

I clicked "Add New" under "Posts" and started typing.

For the title, I wrote "Surprised Doesn't Cover It," then moved down to the body.

When I decided yesterday that I would honor the last wishes of Anna "Gidget" Becker by writing her story, no matter the cost to me, I meant it. She was a woman who rose from humble and challenging religious and cultural origins, who went on to rule the art world in Houston for decades, and who partied with some of the most famous names of the seventies and eighties. A woman who returned to her roots and who and what she was in the beginning. A woman who, I learned today, hid a painful secret and lost everything, but wanted her story told so badly that she left me her family farm in her will to incentivize me to go through with my commitment to her. I don't know how I feel about that yet. I guess her family's home has to go to someone, and, on paper, she has no heirs. But she made another bequest in her will. She claims to have a daughter. An unnamed, unknown daughter she gave away many years ago, and she wants to give her old family Jaguar to her. Without going into too much detail, it's hard to know whether this daughter is real anywhere except in Gidget's imagination, but I know in my heart that this is the reason she wanted me to tell her story, and if her daughter is real, to find her. I'm not going to lie. It's pretty personal to me. My own mother died less than two months ago. We didn't have a super relationship, but at least we had one. Daughters deserve to know their mothers love them. For that matter, so do sons. And my mother, like Gidget, maybe, mourned a son she gave away many years ago and never found again. I'm going to find the truth about Gidget's daughter and give that to Gidget. I'm going to give this daughter Gidget's story, and I'm going to try to do the same thing for my own mother and brother.

Tears fell on my fingers as I typed. I stopped. Was I getting too personal? I looked at everything I'd written. Gidget's information was all public since Greyhound had filed the will with the court. But what about my mother? She hadn't shared her secret with her friends. I had Papa's blessing, but she wasn't being given the choice. She hadn't even told *me*. But something about it still felt right. Like she was looking down, and I finally had her approval. *Oh, Mom, what I wouldn't give for another chance to really know you.* My tears fell harder. I lowered my head, touched my butterfly necklace. It was warm.

"What should I do, Adrian?" I whispered.

Of course, there was no reply.

Help me know, God, please help me know what to do, what's right.

I decided to give God and Adrian a little more time to answer me and clicked Save on the blog post. I pulled up Weather Underground to check the temperature. It was down to ninety-six from a high of ninety-eight and maybe would get down to ninety-two before sundown. Was it cool enough to run in? It didn't seem like a good idea, running in this heat, especially when I'd already bicycled in it today, but I felt the tension building inside me. Uncertainty. Grief. Responsibility. Loneliness. A fear I couldn't place. And the only way I knew to quiet those demons once unleashed was to pound the pavement with my feet. To run it out. To run away from whatever was out to get me. To keep running, because, if I was still, even for a second, it would catch me.

I poured coconut water into flasks for my fuel belt and put water in the reservoir for my swamp-fan hat. I put on some sandal-type running shoes with mesh toes, which were excellent for the heat. It was all I could do to prepare myself for what was out there, except for one last, most important thing. I grabbed my Shuffle and clipped it to my waistband and shoved the earbuds in. I took off at a run down the trailer steps, catching a glance of Gertrude's reproving gaze before I slammed the door.

I turned the volume up as high as I could stand. My legs and arms moved in rhythm with Beyoncé's "Crazy in Love." The dirt roads were easiest on my legs, so I took a right at the end of my driveway. In a quarter mile the paved road gave way to gravel. The yaupon, cedar, and oaks were thickly clustered out that direction, and the land was perfectly flat. All the leaves were still green, as was the grass peeking out on the edges of forest. Wildflowers bunched together between the edge of the road and the base of the trees. The green and the flowers wouldn't last much longer. The cycle of life for flora was achingly short and bittersweet, and the gift of a longer season totally dependent on the vagaries of the weather. A teeny sob burst out of me as I realized it wasn't only flowers with short, bittersweet lives controlled by forces other than themselves.

I sucked air in greedily as my body adjusted to the sudden exertion of running and crying. It tasted dusty, like a truck had passed by too quickly and not long ago. I breathed through my mouth. The dryness of the dust made me feel parched immediately. Mind over matter, I told myself. I was well hydrated. I could wait fifteen minutes before I drank. If I didn't, I wouldn't have enough fluids for the whole run.

The music changed to "Crazy Little Thing Called Love," the Dwight Yoakam version. My pulse slowed as my body adjusted to the punishment I was inflicting upon it. Fully warmed up, I lengthened my stride and concentrated on a mid-foot strike with as little contact with the ground as possible. I wanted to float. I wanted to fly. I wanted to *ascend*.

Freed from the consuming demands of the beginning of a painful run, my mind started going places it shouldn't. I hated when Adrian's absence was sudden and razor sharp. I slipped my fingers down to my necklace. It was hot and damp.

"Adrian," I whispered, just as I'd been doing these last ten months, as I'd struggled to find him. No answer.

Stop it, I told myself. He's not there. Just stop it. Focus on what's real. You're stronger than this. You're not going down into this pit again. Remember, people count on you.

Fine then, an evil part of my brain said. What would you rather obsess about? How about being alone, and not just this summer, but after next year, completely alone all the time?

I ran on.

"Wide Open Spaces" began to play, and I slowed my pace in time to its rhythm.

My thoughts continued, bullying me, but I fought back, forcing a change in mental direction. There were people in the community that had helped Gidget for years. If I waltzed into their town, accepted this gift, and moved to her place on a promise I hadn't kept yet, there were bound to be hard feelings. *I* didn't even think it was fair. But it wasn't like I could say, "No, I think it should go to Jimmy or to Ralph or whomever." I either took it or I didn't. And if I refused it, and we didn't find a daughter, the state would get everything. That didn't honor Gidget's wishes. I didn't know what to do.

Luckily, I didn't have to make a decision yet. Probate was just starting. What I would do was start working on Gidget's story and just let things play out. It was all I could do, really.

The passage of time worked, as it always did when I was running, and my mind let go of my troubles. Blessedly, I lost track of everything until, sooner than I'd expected, I was back at the entrance to Nowheresville. I began running the final stretch to the Quacker, picking up speed, pushing myself into the best sprint I had left in me. The music was still pounding in my ears, so when a car pulled up beside me, I felt its vibrations before I heard it. I jumped to the side and ripped my earbuds out.

It was a sheriff's department vehicle, a Tahoe. Tank.

He rolled his window down. I stopped, hands on my knees, lungs heaving. I mopped sweat off of my forehead and cheeks with the back of my hand. My mood, which had finally leveled, went south again as soon as he spoke.

"I hear you've had a windfall."

I couldn't read his eyes behind his mirrored shades, and the rest of his face was expressionless. The sun seared my shoulders, and I itched. I reached around to scratch and found a tiny gnat flailing in my sweat. I flung it away with dripping fingers and tried to slow my breathing. "It's hot," I said. "I need a drink. If you have a question, please ask it."

"We can go in your place if you want."

"No, thank you."

I detected a slight grin around the corners of his mouth. I'd learned too much about dealing with law enforcement in the wake of Adrian's death. I didn't trust them anymore, not until they'd earned it. Even if Tank *wasn't* a deputy, I wouldn't be confined in that small space with him, or any strange man, especially not wearing the tiny garments I had on. My hands slid down the sides of my thighs where the shorts tapered, covering myself.

He patted the seat beside him. "I can turn the air conditioner up in here."

Another non-question. I didn't respond.

"Suit yourself." He turned the air on high anyway. It blew like a norther at him.

Pendejo.

"Ms. Becker's will looks an awful lot like motive. Don't you think?"

I crossed my arms over my chest. "Not when I didn't know about it before today."

"Who's to say you didn't? Know about it before today, I mean."

Tank didn't know Ralph had told me the sheriff's department suspected poisoning and was waiting on the autopsy. "Hold up. Didn't Gidget die from a seizure?"

"Haven't ruled out anything yet. You have any theories or information you want to share with the sheriff's department? Now'd be the best time to tell us if you do."

"I wish I could help, but I thought she had a seizure and died." I dipped my head at him and picked my earbuds back up.

"But if that changes, you'll let us know." He shook his head. "With the research you're doing for your"—he made air quotes on either side of his head—"book."

"Of course."

He put the Tahoe in gear. "Just remember what I told you at Maria's. There's a fine line between research and obstruction, and out here, we don't care who you are back in the big city." He U-turned in the grass in a circle around me, like he was herding me. I jammed my earbuds back in my ears, my hands shaking. It was Taylor Swift, and her perkiness was jarring. I ripped them back out.

I was a little worried and a lot angry. Gidget's bequest was the perfect excuse for the cops to bark up my tree. I stomped back to the door of the Quacker. Gertrude nearly had an attack of apoplexy she was so excited to see me. She'd been cooped up, and I'd been out running and playing. Tank's visit surely hadn't helped.

"Come on, girl," I said, and started trotting back toward the road.

She ran in circles in the clearing beside me, her long, low body giving her the appearance of slow motion as she darted back and forth, chasing yellow butterflies. I touched my own butterfly, the one hanging from my neck. The sun was sinking, and its rays were already less direct than a few minutes earlier. My body cooled, and as I breathed deeply, I got a whiff of earth and pond water and cedar. It was a clean smell, and I held it in a few seconds on every inhale. On our way back to the Quacker, I popped around back and retrieved the chip from the wildlife cam. A small wave of excitement coursed through me, chasing away a little more of my tension. It would be my first time to get a look at what was out here when I wasn't around.

I let Gertrude up the steps before me, then shut the door quickly behind us. The air conditioner was still running. Gertrude went straight to her water bowl. I showered, luxuriating for the full two minutes of hot my tank held. I threw on shorts and a T-shirt. While sucking almond butter from a spoon, I popped the camera chip into my laptop and scrolled through. Frame after frame showed blowing grass. There was one of a butterfly, and a few others of birds.

Then the computer cycled through to the nighttime pictures. A rabbit. An opossum. A raccoon. And then—my jaw dropped open—a bobcat. Comparing it to the rabbit a few frames earlier, it was roughly three times Gertrude's size. I squinted at it in alarm, enlarging it to full screen.

Just then, the air conditioner cut off again.

"Dammit!" I yelled. It wasn't on my list of no-no words from my mother.

The heat took over like a fast-growing fungus. I wondered if Gidget's house had cooled off. I thought about the little fence around Gidget's yard where Gertrude had lived, safer from bobcats. I picked up my phone, hitting a number in my recent calls.

"Hello," Ralph said.

"This is Michele." I used my serious lawyer voice. "Any chance that the independent executor of Gidget Becker's estate would like to rent her place to her beneficiary pending resolution of probate?"

"Wow, that was something," he said. "Are you okay?"

I reverted to my normal voice. "My air conditioner keeps cutting out, on top of everything else. I'm ready to commit hari-kari."

He chuckled. "Rental income for the estate. Someone to keep an eye on things. Since you're the beneficiary, there's no problem with eviction. Sounds like a great idea."

I bounced up and down on my toes. "Hallelujah."

"One condition, though."

"Anything."

"You help me find Gidget's daughter."

I snorted. "Like you could stop me from it."

"Good. How's five hundred a month sound?"

"Far too little for a place like that, but it fits my budget. How soon can I move in?"

"You've got the keys. It's all yours."

When we ended the call, I whooped aloud and danced in circles with Gertrude in the tiny space. I threw Gidget's box of treasures into the trunk of the Jetta, then went back into the Quacker. I packed two suitcases of essentials as quickly as I could and gently removed Adrian's business card from the window and put it in my wallet.

Gertrude whined to go out. I thought about the bobcat again, and the coyotes I'd heard yipping the night before. "No, ma'am," I said to her. "Not without me."

After I reset the air conditioner and prayed it would cool things off before Christmas, I grabbed the chip, my handbag, and the suitcases, opened the door, and we went out together. After I'd reloaded the camera, we made tracks to G

NINE

THE FIRST NIGHT IN A NEW-TO-ME, 150-year-old house with all its creaks and groans and strange noises was like my first night in the Quacker. I barely slept, even after I'd found clean sheets for the bed, taken a bonus ten-minute shower just because (and appreciated every second of it), and had a glass of warm almond milk to chase down my melatonin. When I finally nodded off, it was nearly daylight. That didn't last long, because somewhere close—like right outside the window, from the sound of it—was a rooster. A flock of roosters, maybe, getting their cock-a-doodle-doos on before dawn. I put the pillow over my head, but I couldn't block it out. Gertrude was making the transition much more easily than I was. After all, this had been her home. She had ignored her dog bed at the foot Gidget's bed and claimed her place on the pillow beside me as her entitlement.

The rooster didn't let up, so I trudged to the kitchen, Gertrude trotting along with me, too perky by half. I needed coffee, *rápidamente*. I contemplated the percolator. My Mississippi grandmother had one almost just like it. I took the lid off, and the smell backed me up a few steps. I filled the sink with hot soapy water. After a scrub and a rinse, I put fresh water in it and assembled the chamber and tube. I found some filters in a drawer and a half gallon of Hy-Top coffee in the tiny pantry. I ladled coffee into the filter and plugged the percolator in.

Gertrude was watching me closely, I suspected for signs that I was going to do the right thing and feed her.

"Me first."

I stared at the coffee pot, but nothing happened. I knew better than to watch a pot.

"Fine. You first."

I searched for her bowls and didn't find them inside. I decided to check the backyard, and when I turned the doorknob, it was unlocked. *So much for not having the key yesterday.* Gertrude tumbled into the yard for her constitutional, and I went inside with the bowls. She was back by the time I'd filled her water, dancing around me in a frenzy like she hadn't eaten in years, her locks hiding the taut, round belly I knew was there. There was a half-full twenty-pound bag of Ol' Roy dog food on the pantry floor. I dumped some in her bowl, added water, shook it to wet the kibble, and set it beside the water, inside the back door.

Gertrude gobbled it down without saying thank you. I stepped out onto the concrete patio in the backyard. There was no back porch to speak of, but there was a wooden picnic table—bench style—and enormous fig and persimmon trees. To me they were exotic, and I couldn't wait for them to ripen. A rust-and-black-feathered rooster strutted by outside the back fence.

"You look like dinner."

He cocked his head without breaking stride.

There was a trail into the woods behind him. I padded toward the fence in my bare feet. It was too early in the season for burrs, but still I placed my feet down as if I were walking through landmines. My feet sank into the soft grass, ankle-high. Honeysuckle grew up the back fence, and beyond it I saw yellow-blooming cactus by the pump house. Just then, I heard a rustling sound and froze. Something black was moving in an S-curve pattern. Snake. I screamed bloody murder. I tried to get a look at it as I backpedaled full speed toward the house. Those two things were not compatible, especially since the snake was moving away from me faster than I was from it. Thus I had no idea if it was venomous. It was probably just a harmless rodent-eater, but I went back in the house and closed the door anyway. *Boots,* I told myself. *Boots.*

When I reentered the kitchen, the coffee pot was percolating loud and fast. The smell was pure heaven. While it finished up, I studied my surroundings. A business card was stuck to the refrigerator with a magnet that said TODAY IS THE DAY THE LORD HATH MADE. I smiled and opened an upper cabinet to the right of the sink and found cups. The coffee mugs were old and chipped, with little bluebonnets on them that looked hand-painted. They were very different from the broken State Fair cup Gidget had used last Sunday. I peeked around the kitchen. The broken pieces and stir stick were gone. I snagged a bluebonnet cup and set it by the coffee pot, which was still making noise that told me it wasn't ready yet.

It made sense that the broken mug and stir stick were gone. The sheriff's department should have processed the scene if they suspected a poisoning, and they would have collected evidence. I chewed the side of my bottom lip, lost in thought. I'd touched the pieces and the stick that day. Not ideal.

The percolator quieted. I poured a cup to the rim and stepped past Gertrude, who had stretched out on the mat by the back door, a sated glaze to her eyes. I stood over her and took long sips of too-hot coffee. It burned a little, but it was worth it. My wakefulness increased another notch. Evidence. The missing letters. Now it made sense. But I decided to be thorough. I grabbed one of the Quest bars I'd brought with me and unwrapped it, walking around with it and my coffee, looking for the papers in drawers and cabinets with no success. I went to the garbage can to throw away my wrapper, but the bag and contents had been removed. I got a fresh liner from under the sink.

It seemed like the cops had done a thorough job, and I was grudgingly impressed. I rifled through the mail remaining on the table. I would let Ralph know about it. The letter from Lee County Appraisal District was marked PAST DUE.

I wandered back to Gidget's room. I put my second cup of coffee down and collapsed on the bed, just to rest my eyes for a second, and didn't wake up until it was afternoon.

Even though I'd slept past noon, Thursday had been productive for me. I'd set up an appointment for Internet contract transfer and hookups (for Monday, no matter how I begged it be sooner), squeezed in a swim, and worked into the evening on Juniper business, tethering to my phone and using the connection to publish the blog post I had written and saved the previous afternoon.

Friday was off to a good start as well, despite waking again as the cock crowed. I poured myself a second cup of coffee and took it with me to the bathroom, along with my phone. It was too early for me to call Ralph, so I texted him, remembering I'd forgotten to tell him about the mail the day before. *"How about I inventory G's things? Useful for search for daughter and probate. Also, there's a stack of mail. Bills, one maybe past due property taxes?"*

I wasn't going to feel guilty about my day job, because my focused six hours yesterday were like two eight-hour days of productivity in the office. In fact, I wasn't going to feel guilty about anything. I was meeting Rashidi in Brenham tomorrow, mostly to be a nice person. So I got virtue points. It was also partly because he texted me again the night before, and Southern women aren't raised to say "no" except to sex before marriage, and not always even to that. Neither my mother nor Gidget had, that was for sure.

I planned to stay ragged today, so I only washed my face, brushed my teeth, and applied deodorant. I stepped out of the bathroom and walked down the hall—all three steps of it—to Gidget's bedroom. I threw on an old pair of Adrian's boxer shorts and a tank top sans bra and gathered my hair into a ponytail without a mirror. Ready.

I stood with my hands on my hips and surveyed the bedroom from one corner, making a circuit with my eyes. It wasn't large. And Gidget had a full-sized bed in it. Well used. I had to roll to the middle to find a slightly level spot. The walls around the bed were shiplap paneled. Most recently, they had been painted an off-white, but an old eggshell-blue color showed through where there was water damage on one of the walls. More exquisite art hung throughout the room. Sun-faded curtains of blue checkered fabric covered the windows, but there were no blinds. A pine chest of drawers, pushed against the longest wall, with photos in a variety of sizes in cheap metal frames on its dusty surface. I picked up one of a young Gidget with a dandy-ish man and brown-haired woman then put it back in place, careful to align it so it re-covered its dustless spot. There was a clothes hamper in the corner just to the left of the doorway, with a sour smell and a pink flowered housedress hanging out one side of the closed lid. A pair of black ballerina-style house slippers was on the floor beside the hamper.

Closet first, I decided. I opened it to the powerful scent of mothballs. It wasn't very large—just one shelf with dresses hanging from a full-length rod. The kind a single woman of sixty-five years of age who never left home would wear. On the floor were a pair of rubber boots, some orthopedic-looking walking shoes, and more slippers. The shelf at the top of the closet held folded sweat pants, sweat shirts, and a quilt.

I dictated into my voice app, "Women's personal apparel, assorted, used," and on the next line, "quilt."

I forced myself to look under her bed (only dust bunnies), then moved to the dresser drawers (which resulted in "more women's personal clothing, used, assorted"). I certainly wasn't going to list out every used pair of underwear and stretched-out bra. Before I left the room, I lifted the mattress off the box springs and found a two-inch scorpion. I yelped and dropped the mattress, then realized it was dead. I lifted it again, glad I hadn't missed an eleven-by-seven-inch sealed manila envelope and an old 20-gauge shotgun. I checked to make sure the safety was on and leaned the gun against the wall. I rummaged through the bedside table. I added heating pad, family Bible, and shotgun shells to the inventory, along with the gun. I flipped through the Bible to see if the birth of Gidget's daughter was recorded, but no dice. I left the manila envelope on the bed, unopened for now.

I decided to inventory art next. Room by room, I lifted the paintings from the wall hangers and catalogued each title, artist, and date with a brief description. Many of them were dedicated to Gidget on the back, with lots of love and thanks. They were all originals. I recognized names, like Robert Rauschenberg, and the list of artists themselves was a starting point for research into her life. Some of the pieces were so stunning they belonged in a museum or at least a gallery.

I had a sudden realization. Ralph obviously had no idea about the value of the art. Greyhound didn't appear to know it existed. Gidget had been living hand-to-mouth, art rich and cash poor. Had she sold just her Rauschenberg, she would have been in high cotton the rest of her life. We'd have to get an art appraiser out here, and hold an auction. The inheritance taxes on these would be so high that most of them would probably have to be sold off to keep them from bankrupting the beneficiary—me.

I decided I preferred Gidget's work over the others. So much so that I spent an hour rearranging all the paintings to create a gallery of her abstract watercolors in her bedroom. Seen together, they told the story of her heritage: the homestead, a church, a mule and plow, a family picking cotton, and—my favorite—a nighttime landscape with fireflies and a blood moon. I made Gidget's bed and unpacked my suitcase into her drawers, then moved the bag into the closet. It helped bring the rest of the room up to the standards of the majesty on the walls.

Gertrude was a trooper, napping in whatever room I worked in. I rewarded her with a bite of my Quest bar when I stopped for a late lunch. I was sick of them, and I really needed to make a run back to the Quacker to get the rest of my food.

I tackled the spare bedroom next. Gidget had taken me into it last spring. It didn't have a bed in it, but it did hold a standing clothes rack and box after box after box of her personal belongings. She'd set up an easel in the corner to the right of the window, and clean brushes and bowls sat on the drop cloth at its base. There was a cheap set of shelves beside the easel.

Three exquisite hand-painted birdhouses perched there, two of them finished and one partly done.

I spent the next two hours meticulously cataloguing her personal items. Notwithstanding the financial value of the art, these were Gidget's treasures. The seventies bell bottoms that she'd shown me and the padded shoulders of her eighties power jackets, the stacks of albums holding photographs of her with artists and at openings. In some of them she was wearing the clothes on this very rack, receiving from the artists the paintings I'd found in this house.

Again, a light bulb went off. The provenance—if that was the right word—of the paintings was proven in these photographs. They'd be important evidence to the appraiser. I leaned closer toward a picture. It was Andy Warhol and an ethereal Gidget in a flowing white linen gown and macramé belt. He was holding a square package wrapped in brown butcher paper and twine, beaming, and she looked giddy, her head on his shoulder and arms around his waist.

I hadn't seen an Andy Warhol in the house. I would have flipped out if I had. But this picture suggested I should keep my eye out for one. I pulled the plastic album sheet away from the picture, very slowly, and it made a ripping sound as the adhesive released. I tried to pry the photo up, but the adhesive wouldn't let go. I went to the kitchen for a knife, then carefully sliced between the picture and the page when I returned to the spare bedroom. The album gave up the photo. I flipped it over. ANDY AND ME, 1982, HOUSTON. I studied the background in the photo. It appeared to be the front of a townhome with pink bougainvillea. I'd seen it in other photos. Gidget's place? Maybe I could get an address from some of her old records, whenever I found them. Talk to neighbors. Learn about the Gidget outside the gallery scene. I was getting more and more excited about the possibilities.

I flipped another page in the album. Folded sheets of paper with handwriting and signatures on them and honest-to-God envelopes with stamps and post markings. Letters addressed to My beautiful Gidget. The plastic sheeting gave way with a ripping noise and I fished the letter out. Could these be love letters from the father of Gidget's baby? Had I found him? My heart slammed in my chest. I unfolded the first one. The handwriting looked familiar for some reason, and I flipped over the paper monogrammed with the name ANDY WARHOL and on the back signed Andy. I held the paper, rubbing it between my thumb and forefinger, then scanned the letter quickly. He was talking about a painting that he had almost completed.

Could he be the father? I had an impression he was gay, but maybe not.

I pulled out another letter from the album. It looked like there were about ten altogether. I compared the date on the envelope to the one I had just read. It was several months later. I examined the remaining letters and compared them all. They were all the same size and shape, with the same handwriting, and were in date order covering roughly a one-year period.

I unfolded the second letter and read it quickly. It was reporting progress on the painting and professing undying love and friendship. He asked Gidget if she wanted to accompany him to an opening in Paris.

I kept reading the letters. From the flow it appeared that Gidget didn't join Andy in Paris, and the content remained largely the same. He loved her madly. He missed her. He was working on the painting, his gift and homage to her. And he couldn't wait to see her again. Each letter also included tidbits about his social life and the other things he was working on. The last letter said, *I loved seeing you* and *The painting is exactly as I dreamed it would be, only better.* The date of the last letter was November 3, 1986.

My hands levitated with the notes, like they were holding air. These letters from Andy to Gidget about this supposed painting, these were artifacts of tremendous value, historically, even if the painting didn't exist. And they were hidden away in Gidget's Wendish family home. A never-before-seen Warhol painting hinted at, and a friendship not previously documented. I felt a thrill of discovery at the same time as an irrational jealousy. She'd kept this information private for a reason, and I didn't want to violate her wishes. But if it turned out to be relevant to my search for her daughter, how could I keep it quiet? He was a larger-than-life pop-culture icon.

I replaced the last letter in its envelope and carefully put them back in the order I'd found them inside the album, then smoothed a page with one last loving touch. Gidget and Andy, 1986. My adrenaline surged. I tethered my laptop to my phone's signal. I Googled Warhol. A fact jumped out immediately. He'd died only three months after his last letter to Gidget. My chest tightened. I narrowed my search to his sexuality. The signal hung up for a moment. "Come on, come on," I urged it. When the results showed up on the screen, I read greedily. Multiple sources claimed he was celibate, possibly a virgin. They cited his devout Catholicism, and speculation was rampant that if not for his faith he would've been out as a gay man.

I sighed.

No mention of a pregnancy or baby or daughter or of being a father. But the letters did talk about secrets and things only the two of them knew. Maybe they were referring to secrets he was keeping for her, not secrets about Andy and Gidget. It was impossible to know, but tremendously exciting. I took a picture of the photo of Andy and Gidget, and emailed it to the blog. "Oh, the Possibilities . . ." I titled the post.

I shut the album and stood, my knees cracking, my hips aching. Gertrude snuffled in her sleep. I arched my back, stretching. All I had left in this room was the stack in the corner, but it was enormous. When I got to it, though, I saw that it was one large piece of furniture covered by a sheet. Armloads of clothing had been draped on top of the sheet. Once I'd catalogued the outfits and moved them to the hanging rod, I removed the sheet to reveal a black safe.

"Yay!"

Gertrude wagged her tail but didn't open her eyes.

It looked like my Papa's gun safe. Tall. Bolted to the floor. Hinges on the left against the wall. A combination lock. I jiggled the handle. It didn't budge. I stepped back from it. Now that the long dresses and sheet were gone, I saw two round-toothed disks on the floor and a pile of metal filings. I took a closer look at the hinges and realized someone had tried to cut them open. Maybe Gidget had forgotten her combination?

I heard a ding from the direction of the bathroom. My phone. Still puzzling over the safe and the obvious attempt to break into it, I grabbed my phone from the bathroom counter. Or tried to, anyway. It fell to the tile floor.

"Oh no," I groaned.

Gertrude galloped in to see what the problem was, skidding the last few inches and overshooting my phone. I picked it up and turned it over. The screen was shattered but intact.

I shook my head. "This is why you always spring for the OtterBox, Gertrude."

She leaned her head back trying to get a look and toppled sideways.

I was able to read the message even though the screen was toast, but just barely. It was a thank you from Ralph that I'd let him know about the mail. I sent him back a quick message. Well, I sent it back quickly after typing it slowly. The shattered screen really gummed things up.

"Ralph, this house is holding MILLIONS in original art. And a treasure trove of letters between Gidget and Warhol, who claims he painted her portrait!!! We need to talk. Later. For now, what's the safe combination? Also, someone tried to cut it open. Do you know anything about that?"

Then I remembered the envelope unopened on the bed. I didn't know how I'd forgotten it—except for the fact that in the last year my brain was an absolute sieve. I hustled back to it. Maybe the combination was in there. I pried the flap open and dumped the contents out on her bed.

There were a number of papers—legal documents. I looked at the first one. A Power of Attorney granted to Lester Tillman. A Last Will and Testament. A Bill of Sale for her part in the ownership of the Montrose Fine Art Gallery to Lester Tillman for $50,000. The will and bill of sale were executed on the same date, six years ago. The power of attorney was dated "as of" a year prior to that. I cringed. I sincerely doubted that $50,000 was the true value of her ownership unless the place was going out of business or close to it. I'd have to check. I paged through the will. In it, she'd left everything in a charitable trust to be used on behalf of causes benefiting the arts in Houston with Lester Tillman as the trustee. I smelled something stinky, and there wasn't a dead rodent around. I moved Lester Tillman up on the list of people I wanted to talk to about Gidget.

My phone dinged, interrupting me before I had finished going through the envelope. Ralph, again: *"WOW, my hands are shaking as I type this. About the combination: I don't know, and No. Be careful!!!"*

As I walked down the hallway, I thought about the unlocked back door and had to agree with him. Sometimes people read about a death in the paper and took advantage of empty houses—ransacking them when they knew the owners would be gone. Gidget's death had been a big wave in a small pond.

A man's voice called, "Anybody here?" from inside the house, and a door shut. Heavy footsteps approached in the hall. My heart leapt in my throat. I remembered the shotgun in the bedroom, but it was too late. The rack of clothes blocked the closet, and a tower of boxes did the same to the window. There was nowhere to run and nowhere to hide. I flexed my knees and rocked up on my toes.

A large, doughy face appeared in the top of the doorway, one I recognized.

"Loopy?" I said.

"Lumpy," he corrected.

My heart rate slowed, but it converted to anger. I gritted my teeth, fighting to control it. "I didn't hear you knock."

"Well, I—I just stuck my head in and called."

"Next time, knock." I crossed my arms over my chest. "If you could be so kind, I need to get decent."

"Oh, sorry." He backed up fast, his boots loud. As loud as the silence that followed.

I stalked into the bedroom and found a housedress in the closet. I threw it on like a robe, snapping it from sternum to waist. I met him back in the living room.

"If you don't mind me saying so, Ms.—"

"Mrs. Hanson."

Confusion flickered across his face. "Mrs. Hanson, where's Mr.?"

I didn't soften my words to make it any easier for him. "Dead."

"Oh, golly, I'm so sorry." He didn't look it. In fact, he looked . . . optimistic.

"I was just going to say you sure are a pretty woman. You look like that Mexican actress that used to live in San Antonio."

I didn't smile. "Thank you. Now, are you here for something?"

"Well, I saw your car out front and, um, I wanted to see if I could help you out any."

I thought about it for a second. My first inclination was to say no and send him packing, but he *was* the nearest neighbor. One who kept a very close eye on things. "Have you seen anyone other than me coming in and out of the house since Ms. Becker died?"

He pulled at his bottom lip, and I smelled the smoke as he tried to come up with an answer that I would like. "Well, there's Jimmy, he comes by regular."

I held up a hand. "You mean Jimmy Urban?"

"Yes."

"Anybody else?"

"Not that I've seen. Ms. Becker didn't get a lot of visitors."

"Did you visit Ms. Becker?"

His face turned pink at the edges. "I can't say I did all that often, but I was around if she needed me. I was the one who found her all those years ago when she first came back."

In my mind I pictured a possible Mrs. Lumpy at home and tried to decide whether or not she would be happy with Mr. Lumpy's visits to me. I decided she wouldn't care one way or the other. He wasn't wearing a wedding ring, but that wasn't unusual for people who worked with their hands, I'd found. Assuming he worked at all, and didn't just spy on me.

"Did you see who dropped her off, or when? Back then, I mean."

"I saw a big van one day. Coming and going. That's why I dropped in that next day. But I reckon that was about five years ago or more."

"And you haven't been here, except when you've come by to see me, since Ms. Becker died, have you?"

He shook his head.

"I have somewhere I need to be, but I do thank you for stopping by." I held the front door open.

He tipped an imaginary hat and walked to it.

I said, "If you need to visit again for any reason, please call first. Or at least knock."

"Sure thing." He made one last attempt to look down my housedress.

As I closed the door, a hot flash exploded through my body. I wondered how much longer men like Lumpy would keep coming around, comparing me to Eva Longoria and trying to sneak a peek down my top.

Not very long, I thought.

TEN

Saturday morning came early again, and my stomach exploded in butterflies. I was meeting Rashidi today. I thrashed the covers off of me, and Gertrude moaned in protest. Well, if I was going to have to drive to Brenham for dinner, I needed to get started around here. I got the coffee going and put my cheek down on the cool tile countertop. I woke from a lock-kneed, drooling doze when the percolator started burbling. I was sore from yesterday, and I hadn't even moved to the barn on my inventory yet. I poured my coffee and took it to the living room. I'd spread the envelope's contents there one last time before bed. After Lumpy left, I'd had a chance to look at the last few things in it. I held up the first one, an old picture of Gidget, probably known as Anna back then, and another little girl in the rumble seat of an exquisite antique sports car. The man standing beside it had a proud look on his face. *Did Gidget have a sister?* I tilted the second one into the natural light streaming in from the windows. The same man, a woman about his age, Anna, and the other little girl, in a small wooded clearing with a straw picnic hamper. They were sitting on a checkered cloth with a picnic spread out in front of them, big smiles on their faces. The last picture was more recent, but still old. Gidget—in her twenties?—at the gallery, with what looked like Lester, and another woman with short dark hair. The back said LESTER, JULIE, AND ME.

Gertrude strolled into the living room and executed a mobile upward dog pose.

"Nice form."

She looked from me to her food bowl.

"Nice try."

She huffed.

"All right, because you said please. And because we're going out to the barn this morning, and you'll need your strength."

Gertrude pranced behind me to the barn half an hour later. I'd poked my head in there once the day before. It was dark and smelled like manure. But this morning, I threw open the double doors facing the house and flooded it with light. Hay bales were stacked along one side with a few bags of livestock feed thrown in a pile beside them. Tools with rust-tarnished surfaces and weathered wooden handles hung from the wall. The barn's second story was a U-shaped loft. A ladder perched against it near the tool area. Three stalls made of open slats of wood lined the facing wall, but there were no animals inside them. At least, no farm animals. From Gertrude's immediate interest in the area, rats and other critters I wasn't so sure about.

What I didn't see was a Jaguar.

I climbed the ladder to check the loft, just to be sure. No Jaguar had levitated to the second story. I sat on the edge with my feet dangling, taking it in. I closed my eyes and breathed deeply. The manure odor had dissipated with the doors open. Mostly now I smelled hay and dirt, a little bit of mold, and goats. Good smells. Smells that reminded me of house calls with my Papa long ago, when I had perched in many a loft, watching him.

My brain switched slides on me to this barn, sixty years ago. Gidget's father in overalls with a straw hat and a pitchfork, throwing hay into the stalls for a mother cow and her calf. A milking stool and pail sat outside the stall.

"Daddy," a little girl's voice shrieked from outside my vantage point.

A happy noise. Not a scared one.

The man smiled. "In here, Anna."

"Take me for a ride in your car, Daddy."

Her father had levered up another forkful of hay and tossed it to the cow.

"When you finish your chores."

I opened my eyes. Hay particles and dust were floating through the air into one of the stalls, but the man and his daughter weren't there.

So far I hadn't seen a single thing that hinted at the location of the Jaguar, or Gidget's daughter's whereabouts. I was praying there'd be something in the safe. A receipt for a storage unit. A safety deposit box number and key. A deed to another piece of property that I hadn't learned about yet. A note from a friend inviting her to store her vintage automobile at their place. A plat to this farm would be nice, too, come to think of it. An address and name for Gidget's daughter would be best of all.

"Where's the dang car?" I muttered.

Gertrude put her paws on a post, peering up at me and wagging her tail.

The thought of doing the barn inventory this morning, or anytime, was daunting. But I had a productive idea: I could visit the oh-so-pleasant Jimmy. About the safe, the car, the daughter, and the price of tea in China.

Back in the house, I found Jimmy's address. I grabbed my handbag and Gertrude's leash, calling to her as I walked through the back door and out the side gate to my car. She bounded over the tummy-high grass, her funny body long and thick, her locks and ears flapping. She was always making me smile.

It turned out that Jimmy didn't live far from Gidget. That was the good news. The bad news was that he lived at the stinky chicken farm.

The ammonia stench overpowered me from inside my closed car. "Stay here, girl."

Gertrude snorted.

I held my hand over my mouth and nose and marched to the front door. I rapped it sharply with my knuckles. After a few moments, when I didn't hear any noise inside, I smacked it with my open palm.

"Come on, come on," I said under my cupped hand.

Gertrude started barking in a pissed-off-dog way. I followed her line of sight. Jimmy was heading toward me. He looked a heck of a lot like my vision of Gidget's father, except in blue jeans and red chamois and with buggier eyes. His big work boots were covered all the way to the base of the uppers in chicken poop. He lifted a hand in greeting. I lifted my free hand to wave back but kept the other one over my face.

"You all right?" he shouted.

I nodded and held up a thumb. When he was standing five feet from me, I said through my hand, "I was hoping I could seek your advice on a few things."

He stopped. "What fer?"

"For my book. About Gidget."

He motioned to two metal gliders on his front porch. His house was not a lot different from Gidget's, although it had been more recently painted. A rich, buttery yellow with sparkling white trim. I took a seat. He didn't. I was glad to be in the shade, but felt a little power-played.

"Do you know the combination to Gidget's safe?"

He raised his bushy white eyebrows. "Uh-uh." He put his thumbs in his pockets.

I took that as a no. "Rats. A lot of the things Ralph and I need might be in there."

"Huh," he remarked.

He was beginning to irritate me, so I smiled. "Also, I was wondering if you've been by her house any this week."

"Uh-huh."

"Oh, good. What for, exactly?"

He shrugged. "Cover the window. Replace the doorknob. Fix the jamb and door. Check on the goats and cows. Look after the chickens. That kind of thing."

"I've only seen a few animals. I remembered a lot more. From once when I visited Gidget."

"I brought most of 'em over to my place. Easier to care for 'em."

"Oh my," I said. "Okay."

"I'll bring 'em back. I figured whoever"—he emphasized the word—"inherited would appreciate it."

"I expect so." I clasped my hands in my lap. "Where are the chickens?"

He gestured out toward his hen house.

"How many? Animals and chickens, I mean."

"Five cows, eleven goats, twenty-three hens. Plus some pregnant Herefords and Boers I didn't want to mess with."

"You missed one rooster. He serenades me in the mornings."

He smirked. "Wondered where he got off to."

"While you were there, did you check on things inside?"

He shook his head. "Not 'cept the window and doorknob. Didn't reckon there was any need, since you took the dog."

"Yes, right. So you didn't take any letters from the kitchen?"

"Uh-uh. Saw 'em. Didn't take 'em."

Something about his answer niggled my brain, but it didn't yield specifics. I decided to let it background process. "Did you check the doors?"

His forehead wrinkled. "I opened the front door by prying out the nails holding it shut. Went out the front after I'd fixed it. Locked it. Didn't check the others. Why should I?"

"No reason. The back door was unlocked when I got there yesterday. I'm trying to get a fix on when that happened."

"Could be it was never locked."

"True." But why would the police leave the scene unsecured? "Did you see anyone else there?"

"I woulda told you if I did."

"Okay." He was an ornery old cuss. "The art in that house is worth millions. Do you have any idea why Gidget was living like a pauper?"

He nodded. "Said they were her treasures, and she'd rather starve than give 'em up."

I wasn't surprised.

"How's your air conditioner?"

He was surprisingly kind, deep down. "Not so good." I frowned. "I've given up on it. I'm staying in Gidget's place for now."

"Why's that?"

I'd assumed he'd heard. "Um, Gidget's will?"

He shook his head and hitched up his overalls.

"She left the place to me."

His eyes batted once, twice, but his expression didn't change. "Why fer?"

"She wanted me to write her story."

He still didn't change expression, but his eyes grew darker and the skin around his mouth, tighter. "Huh." Then, "Wait here."

He shucked his boots off at a jack by the front door and disappeared into his house. When he returned, he handed me the keys to Gidget's house and a page torn from a spiral-bound notebook, its crinkly edges still attached. On it, he'd written a phone number.

"They'll fix your air conditioner for ya. Tell 'em I sent you."

"Thank you." I stood up. I needed to get out of there. My nose was growing used to the smell. "Just one or two more things."

He jammed his feet into his boots.

"Did Gidget have a Jaguar? An old one?"

"That fancy car of her father's?" he asked.

"I don't know. Tell me about that car."

He shifted on his feet, looked around like someone might overhear him telling tales. "Old man Becker saved some British heir during World War II. The family was so grateful they gave him an old SS 1. He was right proud of it."

"Wow, yes, that sounds like the one I'm looking for."

"Hasn't been around the house since her folks passed. I reckon that's fifteen or twenty years ago."

"Did she have friends or another piece of land or a storage unit? Anywhere else she might keep it?"

He looked at me like I might be slow. "I never saw anyone else out there with her, except for Ralph."

His sorta answers caused my fists to clench. I flexed them. "Well, thank you." I stuck out my hand.

He wiped his on the sides of his dirty jeans, and I cringed. We shook and I headed back to the Jetta. I opened the door, to Gertrude's delight, and he called after me, to her consternation.

"She used to have a friend. Lucy. Works over at the Lutheran church."

"Which one?" I shouted over the dog's hysterical barking.

"The Wends."

I nodded. "Thank you."

He looked at his feet, kicked at something on the ground, spit. "I'm purty sure I saw Lucy driving away from Gidget's place in her brother's van. Friday, maybe. A few days before Gidget passed."

I didn't want to make too much of it, but it seemed like we'd had a breakthrough, and I accidentally peeled out in my excitement. When I looked back, he was watching me go, his hands on his hips. The last I saw as I drove off toward Serbin, he was walking over to his old pickup truck, cell phone to his ear.

ELEVEN

"BE GOOD," I told Gertrude. Once again, I left my car running and dog guarding it.

She may have batted her eyes innocently at me. It was hard to tell since they were covered in locks.

St. Paul Lutheran Church and its plain white facade didn't look like much from the outside, but I knew better. Adrian and I had toured it along with the other Painted Churches of Texas a few years before. I stepped through the doors and was hit by a memory so vivid I could almost feel Adrian's lips on my forehead. We'd stood inside this sanctuary, gazing in awe at the unexpected abundance of color. Murals crowded the walls. The columns, floor, and baseboards shone like marble.

Adrian had put his arms around me and kissed me below the hairline on my forehead. "I feel God here."

How was it I kept finding myself caught in a space between then and now, and why did the past feel so much more real to me? I wanted to go back there, with him, but I couldn't. I was here, now, with nothing but the memory of him. I touched my butterfly and let the doors swing shut behind me. "I do, too. And I feel you, my love."

A woman's voice broke me out of limbo. "May I help you?"

I put a hand over my eyes to help them adjust to the change in light inside the nave. I searched for her, my eyes roaming wooden pews facing an elaborate altar. An elevated organ—almost suspended in midair—was even with the pulpit, above the ground-level seating for the congregation. It gave me the feeling of looking up in reverence at the same time as down in gratitude and admiration. As hard as these people's lives were, they took the time to honor God and show their faith through worship, even when they probably didn't always find Him very benevolent. The Sunday school I'd attended as a child was training pants next to this. And my gradual distancing from religion since then made me squirm, like God could see me more clearly in here, and was disappointed.

"Yoo-hoo," the woman's voice called from above. An angel?

I lifted my gaze. A narrow upper balcony ringed the sanctuary, it too filled with pews. She was standing with one hand on the railing, leaning out toward me, smiling and waving. Golden light haloed around her hair, but she was just a woman.

"Yoo-hoo," I answered.

"I'll be down in just a sec."

"Thank you."

I ran my hand along the top edge of a pew. It was varnished smooth and sealed tight.

"There you are." Her voice was beside me now.

I turned to her. "Here I am. I'm Michele Lopez Hanson."

"And I'm Lucy Thompson. I've heard about you."

The only surprise would have been if she hadn't. "All good, I hope."

"Yes, indeed. Must be quite a change from the big city."

"Well, it's definitely less anonymous." That wasn't exactly true. My privacy in Houston last year was zip. Painfully zip, like running naked through Reliant Stadium when it was filled to capacity. But that was then. I was mostly over it.

She smiled, controlled, from her lips to her pleated navy gabardine pants and white blouse. "What can I do for you today, Ms. Hanson?"

"Please—Michele. I've come about"—I started to say *Gidget* but changed it at the last second—"Anna Becker."

Her brown eyes cast down, and her lips trembled. "I was afraid you were going to say that. Why don't we have a seat."

Lucy lowered herself into the pew. Her soft brown hair, chin length, swung forward, hiding her face for a moment. Then she lifted her head. While her face bore wrinkles, the skin was pale and mostly smooth. She looked so much younger than Gidget it was hard to believe they were friends and contemporaries.

I sat beside her and turned to face her, as best I could. "You were friends with Anna."

"Oh yes, we were friends. But that was a long time ago."

"Tell me about it. About her."

She looked up at me, her head tilted to one side. "Is this for that book you're writing?"

"Mostly. But not completely."

She nodded. "I heard Ralph is supposed to find a daughter nobody knew she had and give her some lost car. And you're helping Ralph."

"And he's helping me. If we find her daughter, she's part of the story."

She drew in a sharp breath. "I'm not sure that's a story that would need to be told."

"I'm sure Gidget had good reason for wanting her story"—I waved my hand in front of me—"out there."

"I have faith the Lord knows best in all things."

Ouch. "So, about Anna?"

Her voice sounded resigned and a little sad. "You can call her Gidget. Seems like everybody does now." She took a hymnal out of the pew in front of her. It looked nearly as old as the church itself.

I waited her out.

"First thing you need to know is that Anna Becker was a sweet girl and the best friend I ever had." She put the book in her lap and started fanning the pages. "And the next thing I ought to tell you is that Gidget Becker was trouble and lived a life that shamed her parents and her community." Her lips grew tight, and I could see she was struggling not to cry. "She left poor Jimmy at the altar, you know, when we weren't even twenty years old."

I put a hand up. "No, I didn't know. Altar? Jimmy?"

She laughed, a bitter sound. "Well, I guess that's where it all starts. And Jimmy sent you to me." *So he'd given her a call, warned her.* "Can't believe he didn't tell you himself. The old fool, out there spending his good time and money on her after what she did to him." She smoothed her lips, which had puckered as she spoke. "Shows you the kind of godly man he is."

"So, Anna was engaged to marry Jimmy?"

"She was, and we were all at the church waiting for her to show up, when word came she'd run off."

"Wow."

She dipped her head.

"So, you were her friend then. Did you see it coming?"

"I hate talking about this—mind, I've kept it to myself for more years than you've been alive—and I resent that it's at her instigation, for something I don't find . . . savory." She put the hymnal up and clasped her hands in her lap, her knees together.

Again, I sat in silence, waiting. I could feel the story burning its way out of her.

"Oh, all right. We were working together. Waitresses. At a diner in Brenham. Taking classes at Blinn. A red convertible Cadillac pulled up one day when we were working. One with longhorns on the front end, very tacky. An older man in snakeskin boots was driving, but older's all in the perspective." She shook her head. "Younger than I am now. A young man and woman were with him, in their twenties. Anna got their table. She used to do this thing. She'd draw on the paper placemats or people's bills. Caricatures, or whatever caught her fancy, and sign them."

I raised my eyebrows.

"She was good, I'll give her that. Wanted to be an artist since we were little. Won every contest and award you could imagine. But her father wanted her to do something practical, plus there wasn't money to send her off to some ritzy art school."

I thought of Gidget's work. She was more than good.

"Well, after they left, Anna was beside herself. The man had written his phone number on his bill and left it with her. She said he'd offered her a job, working for him, and a sort of 'scholarship' to art school at the University of Houston."

"Oh my." I crossed my legs and gripped my knee, trying to contain my excitement. I wished I'd brought a notepad with me. Some kind of biographer I was. Taking out my phone and starting to record now wouldn't go over well, I was certain of it.

"Yes, oh my. Her parents said no. As well they should have. It seemed highly inappropriate, not to mention unlikely. I thought she'd given up the idea until the day she didn't show up for her own wedding." She closed her eyes, and when she opened them, she sniffed. "At the time, some people suspected she ran off with a former minister of the church."

"Really?"

"She'd made eyes at him a time or two, and he moved away around the same time. But who knows? She just disappeared. Folks these days wouldn't believe that could happen, what with Facebook and such. But back then, well, that's more than forty years ago, and if you wanted to be gone, you were. Seventy miles away could be like another continent. She didn't write home. Didn't come back to see her folks. Nobody knew what she was up to. Her parents gave her up for dead, and her their only child. Not even any nieces or nephews, since both of her parents were only children as well." She made a tsk noise. "Jimmy went on with his life and married a nice woman, now deceased." She licked her lips. "And then a few years after she'd left, *Gidget* showed up in an expensive car. She'd gotten herself an art gallery and was living high, with a new name."

"That's good?" I asked.

She looked at me from under her eyelids like *Are you kidding me?* and said, "How'd a young girl like her get money for an art gallery, much less that car she was driving? There was no wedding ring on her finger, either."

"Did you see her?"

She snorted. "*Gidget* didn't darken my door."

Her pain about Anna was so palpable it hurt *me*.

"So she became Ms. Big Shot in Houston. We'd see her in magazines, at parties with the wealthy and degenerate. She always looked two sheets to the wind, if you ask me. And I know for a fact she had to take the treatment for drugs and alcohol."

"Did you ever talk to her again?"

"Oh yes indeedy, I did. She came back for her parents' funeral—let's see, that was seven years ago—and tried to speak to me. Here." She waved a hand around us at the church. Her lips pressed together, grew tight, and then shook ever so slightly. She lowered her voice. "I said hello and tried to act as the Lord would have wanted me to, to set an example of forgiveness, but it was hard, I'll tell you. It was hard. Her mother had died of breast cancer, and her father shot himself when she took her last breath. And she shows up here, as if she'd been a good daughter."

I gasped. Tears sprang into my eyes. I could relate to that kind of loss.

"I'm going to tell you something. I never married." She raised her chin, as if I was judging her. "My brother Bubba went off and started his seismic business. Lee County Seismic. He's been real successful. But our parents are older. They needed me. Do need me."

"I understand."

"Later that night she came driving up to my house. Her visit was very strange. Not to mention she looked awful. Like a drug addict. She made me repeat what she said to me, as if it mattered."

"What was that?"

She recited it to me like an English assignment. "If anyone were to ask me where I was the happiest, it was in the rumble seat, giggling with you on our magic picnics in the woods. It's like I left my heart there and never found it again."

"What did she mean?"

"I haven't the foggiest."

"Could it have anything to do with a baby? A daughter?" I'd held back on asking, fearing it would be too "unsavory" for her to address.

Her eyes flashed. "I'm sure I don't know. There were rumors. I never put any stock in them. I can't imagine why her will—"

My phone alarm went off. I'd set it so I wouldn't be late heading back to Gidget's to get ready to meet Rashidi. We both startled, and I jumped to my feet. "My apologies. I'd almost forgotten. I have an engagement and have to dash. This has been amazingly helpful. Thank you so much."

"You're welcome."

"Just one more question." I smiled to soften it, because it was an abrupt shift. "Were you at Gidget's place last week?"

Her eyes widened. After a long pause, she said, "I haven't been to see Gidget since I was nineteen years old."

Not according to jilted, widowed Jimmy. I sensed she had more to say, whether she was willing to or not, but I was out of time. "Thank you, Lucy. If you think of anything else, you can find me at Gidget's. And if I have more questions, how do I get hold of you?"

She nodded, holding her shoulders high and her back straight. "Here. Or call information for George Thompson. That's my father."

For the sake of propriety, I walked to the door, but once outside I ran to the car and raced down the back roads toward Gidget's. I'd compartmentalized so well today that my anxiety about dinner with Rashidi had stayed at bay until now. Once unleashed, it couldn't be contained. I wanted to go back over my conversation with Lucy, to record the important points on my voice recorder. Because she'd said some hugely important things. But my hands were shaking too hard to hold my phone, so I just hung on to the steering wheel with both hands and concentrated on remembering to breathe in after each exhale.

TWELVE

I STRODE into Home Sweet Farm trying to show more confidence than I felt. Why did meeting Rashidi have me so bunged up? My nails ached to be bitten, my mind threatened its fanciful tricks, and a body-punishing run sounded *bueno*. Edward Lopez had laughed at me when I'd get like this. He was the epitome of calm, cool, and collected. But it had driven Cindy Lopez crazy. She'd see it coming before I did. Papa would soothe me. Mom would seethe. "Really, Michele, people are staring at you. Hands out of your mouth. Come back from wherever you just escaped to in your head, and sit still." And other mantras on the same theme. I stopped mid-stride on the creaky old floors, smack in the middle of organic produce. Did she see it in me because she knew it in herself? Lord knows she could be uptight and controlling, and I had inherited that (and fought against it) from her. But had her mind taken her on flights of fancy, too? Was I more like Mom than Papa?

I reached for my butterfly necklace and gripped it tightly. It felt cold. Just as I was about to bolt, I heard Rashidi's voice. His sexy, lilting island voice.

"Michele, over here." He was out in the biergarten.

My stomach felt funny. "I'm sorry, Adrian," I whispered. "I shouldn't have come."

Rashidi walked into the store toward me, acting like he didn't notice I was impersonating a marble statue. Heads turned as his smile and brilliant white teeth lit up the place. Objectively speaking, he was a very attractive man. Maybe a hair under six feet. Dark skin that refracted the light. Dreadlocks tied back at the nape of his neck. Lean, very lean, although still muscular. But his onyx eyes were his best feature. They were like bottomless pools. Smart, kind, with a sense of fun shining in them.

I didn't want to notice. I couldn't help but notice. The first time I laid eyes on him outside a courtroom in Amarillo, I'd noticed. Everyone was being introduced to everyone else outside the surprise wedding of our friends Emily and Jack. When he had taken my hand, he looked into my eyes with such probing intensity that I'd felt naked.

He'd held onto my hand and pulled me a little closer. "So nice to meet you, Michele."

It had scared me then, like I was scared now. He was a threat. A threat to the life I didn't want to let go. So if I didn't *want* it, then why was I reacting to him like this?

I knew the answer. It came from that part of Tlazolteotl I had suppressed. She wasn't just the goddess of filth, but of vice and sexual misdeeds. She was the patroness of adulterers. The forgiver of sexual sins. She was the reason my traitorous mind and body were acting this way, when my heart said no, and with Adrian gone no more than a year. I stiffened. She was another way I was like my mom.

He'd reached me now, and instead of taking the hand I held out to him, he wrapped me up in a hug. He smelled so delicious it made me dizzy.

Stop being ridiculous, I told myself. He's not a chocolate lava cake. He's a person.

I swallowed hard and patted him on the back, pulling away from the warmth and hard contours of his chest. He let me go, but held onto my shoulder.

"You a sight," he said, grinning. "Come. I have a table and a pitcher of Holy Crow beer."

This brought my first feeble smile. "Welcome to Brenham."

He let go of my shoulder, but somehow caught my hand and pulled me along behind him as if leading me through a crowd, even though there was barely a handful of people around. My hand started to sweat. *Go away, Tlazol. I reject you. I am not you.*

Rashidi had claimed the end of one of the biergarten's long picnic tables, closest to the stage. In front of the instruments and microphones was a sign: the Anthony Moreno Band. Apparently they were on a break, and while the biergarten was nearly full, there was no one else within six feet of us. It was as if we were completely alone.

"Did you order any food?" I asked him as we sat. There was a pitcher of beer and two cups.

His island accent disappeared. "No. I'm not hungry yet. You?"

I wasn't, but I needed something in my stomach besides craft beer. On the other hand, I didn't want to drag this out any longer than I had to. I was starting to get control of myself, to win the battle over the moon goddess. "No, I'm fine," I said.

He poured me a beer and took a sip of his own, then stuck a toothpick between his teeth. The band members started taking the stage, rejoining their instruments. They launched into a song, and they were so loud that talking was impossible. "Amy's Back in Austin." They were good.

For the next half hour, they played country, pop, and rock. We drank the dark beer, which I liked. It was a stout, which I liked, too, since it smoothed my edges out faster. Between songs, Rashidi told me about his job as a professor of botany at the University of the Virgin Islands and his specialty, aquaponic farming. It was actually very interesting, and hearing about it helped settle my nerves even more—and keep the Tlazol thoughts at bay. Without realizing it, I emptied my glass, which Rashidi had topped off several times. I felt loose, or looser, which was saying a lot for a woman whose first husband said she was wound so tight, she sprang when he touched her.

I smiled.

"What're you smiling 'bout?" Rashidi asked.

"I don't drink very often. My lips feel funny."

He squinted at me, the toothpick back in his teeth. "They don't look funny."

Suddenly, I felt dizzy. The way he looked at me didn't seem like the way a friend would. "Listen, Rashidi, I need to tell you something."

"What's that?"

A tall man with gray hair, white at the temples, and the most recognizable face in Texas walked by. He caught me staring and nodded at me. A burly guy followed in his wake. They sat at the table closest to the door.

"Do you know who that is?" I clasped the top of Rashidi's hand.

He flipped it over and we were palm to palm. "Who?"

"That's Boyd Herrington."

"I know the name. Why do I know it?"

"He's a U.S. senator, from Texas. Big-time Tea Party conservative."

"He lives here?"

"Not in Brenham, but close to here."

"Ah."

I pulled my hand away.

Rashidi looked at my hand for a long second, then back up at me. "So you're an editor." The toothpick waggled in his teeth.

I explained my job in Houston.

"But you're living in the country, right?"

"I am."

And this is where the stout took over. I started rattling on about moving into a new house and researching a book I was writing about the former occupant, who'd left it to me in her will and who maybe had a daughter that no one had ever heard of and I had to find along with an antique car. When I'd finished, I gasped in huge lungfuls of air.

Rashidi busted out laughing, and his accent returned. "We need food in you belly." Then, "We take you car?"

I gave him a thumbs-up.

"But I drive."

I gave him two thumbs-up.

In the car, I directed him to the town square. We grabbed a table outside at 96 West, an eclectic tapas/fusion restaurant with truly arresting local art. The server lit the candle at our table. As Rashidi ordered a bottle of Machete red, I studied him. He was the polar opposite of Adrian. Adrian had been blond with beautiful green eyes and a permanent tan to his very fit body. He didn't like going anywhere he couldn't wear cargo shorts, a race T-shirt, and flip-flops. Rashidi had on dark jeans and a collared shirt despite the heat. Adrian loved words, like me. Rashidi loved plants and the little fish that nurtured them in his aquaponic world. I wasn't even sure whether aquaponic was one word or two. Or hyphenated. I giggled. I was a little drunk.

We studied the menu in silence until a waitress reappeared with our water and wine. I should have said, "No, thank you," but instead I said, "Yes, please." Rashidi was a vegetarian, so we ordered a tableful of tapas, everything from hummus to yucca fries and black bean, pumpkin, and quinoa sliders.

I held up my glass. "Last one. I've got a bicycle race tomorrow." Which was going to be bad enough without a hangover.

Rashidi raised his eyebrows. "You'd best eat pasta and a lot of bread, then." He'd found another toothpick and stuck it in his teeth.

I took a sip of my wine and nodded, my head wobbly.

My phone alarm went off at six a.m. As I rolled over to grab it, nausea almost sent me sprinting to the bathroom, but I held very still. It went away, and I hit snooze. My little canine heating pad wriggled closer to my bum. As I rolled back over, I bumped into another body, this one not a canine.

I screamed and shot upright.

Rashidi yelled "yah" and was on his feet before I could blink.

Gertrude yawned loudly and extended her body full length into the spot I'd vacated.

"What the matter?" He grabbed me by both my upper arms.

"You," I said. "What are you doing here?"

Rashidi grinned.

"You not remember?"

"I remember having dinner at 96 West in Brenham and red wine and—"

He nodded.

I stopped.

"And—?" he prompted.

"And that . . . well . . . that's where I go blank. I hardly ever drink—and then just a glass." I was so mortified I could barely look him in the eye, but was relieved that he was completely dressed in the clothes he'd been wearing the night before. I looked down at myself. So was I.

"Oh, Michele," he said, then started to Yank. "You don't hold your liquor."

"Apparently," I muttered.

"I drove you home. The couch is too short for me, too lumpy for you. We fell asleep in here." He bumped me with his shoulder. "And nothing happened."

I whispered, "Oh, thank God."

"Hey, I'm not that bad." He pulled an exaggerated sad face.

I wasn't ready to laugh yet. "It's not that."

"Yah, you gave me an earful a'that last night. You're not ready. You're married even though he's gone. I understand."

I drop-sat on the bed.

He wagged a finger at me. "But you agreed we'll be friends. And you said you're racing this morning."

"Oh no." I leapt up again.

I scrambled around the house, grabbing water bottles and coconut water along with Gu and yet more Quest bars. I heard the sound of the coffee percolating in the kitchen. The scent wafted toward the back of the house, promising I'd feel better soon.

I swigged water to down three Excedrin. Another wave of hangover roiled through my gut. I leaned over to brush my teeth, and my whole body protested. Sleep matted my eyes, so I splashed water on my face. I crammed my hair into a scrunchie—once I had on a helmet it wouldn't matter anyway. I threw on my bicycling shorts and a tank jersey, all in bright orange, yellow, and black, to match La Mariposa.

Rashidi hollered, "You got any travel mugs?"

"No," I shouted over my shoulder. "Use whatever you can find."

I took the bicycle and my bike bag and loaded them in and on the car. I had downsized to a rooftop bike rack a few months ago from the larger rear-hatch model Adrian and I had used. This one still felt wrong.

Rashidi came out the door, bearing two bluebonnet mugs. I was confused for a moment and spoke before I thought. "You're not coming with me, are you?"

"It that or I stranded," he said, island style.

All right by me, I thought. I didn't want to have to explain him to Wallace and Ethan. But that wouldn't be nice. It wouldn't be what friends would do. "Up to you."

He set the mugs on the roof of the Jetta and opened the passenger-side door. *All righty, then.* Gertrude put her paws as high on the gate as she could. She barked, a pouty yip.

"You've got water, food, and shade, girl. You're going to survive."

I slipped into the driver's seat and drove as fast as I dared toward Fayetteville. I saw the magenta pickup outside a cute little shop I'd never noticed before, on the outskirts of town. Flown the Coop. I made a note to check it out, when things slowed down.

Rashidi was so quiet the first twenty minutes I thought he'd gone to sleep, until he let out a low whistle. "It's really pretty here. A deer!" He gestured with his right hand, sloshing coffee.

"It is." I took my cup and sipped. My stomach didn't like it. "Can you grab me one of those bars out of my bike bag?" I pointed to the back seat with my nose.

Rashidi held his coffee aloft and half pivoted toward the back seat. His cup rose higher as he leaned for the bag, almost to the ceiling as he grabbed a chocolate chip bar.

"One for yourself, too, if you like."

He scoffed. "I'm not eating mystery food."

I vaguely remembered him explaining his dietary principles the evening before.

"Do you want me to stop for something? This area is mostly country gentleman farms, so there's a few gourmet grocery stores. Lots of organic whatnot." We were driving through Round Top.

"Nah, I'm fine. They have food where we're going?" He bit the end of the wrapper off a toothpick he fished from the depths of his front pocket after handing me my bar, spat out the plastic, and pulled the toothpick out with his teeth. I itched to pick the wrapper up, but I didn't want to run off the road, so I resisted.

"Well, it's a town. A small one, but I'm sure there'll be something. At least a gas station with a banana."

"That'll work," he said.

Blessedly, he left me mostly to my thoughts. I was mortified that I was about to ride a bicycle in front of my friends and him. They were under the misimpression I was a triathlete. I was also mortified that I hadn't quit *noticing* Rashidi. He radiated vitality. I wished that my body—no, more than that . . . my whole person—wasn't reacting to him. It felt like cheating on Adrian's memory as this interloper intruded on an activity that had always been ours alone.

We coasted into the parking lot of the quaint town square in Fayetteville. It was a little after seven and already filling up. Bicycles and spandex were everywhere.

I parked the Jetta. "If you want, you can take the car and go find a place to eat."

"Nah." He pushed his door open. "I'm good."

I was used to going places with Adrian. He was not only well known on the triathlon scene, especially in Texas, but he was gorgeous. A blond Adonis. A Brad Pitt in his prime. But it turned out that was nothing compared to showing up with Rashidi. As I started unloading my bicycle, people stopped. Jaws dropped. Conversations ceased. Here in the continental United States, Rashidi's island looks were exotic. He was dark and mysterious, new and sexy. And he was with me.

I wanted to crawl back into the car and hide. Almost everyone here knew who I was. Adrian's wife. The reluctant and really crappy Ironwoman. His coauthor, the media darling of Texas sports last year. Houston's favorite daughter of the moment, looking like a harridan after a night of partying.

Something drew my eyes down to my chest. There was a giant scarlet A painted across it. My mother's voice in my head said, *"No, Michele."* The A morphed into a T for Tlazol before my eyes. I closed them as Mom grew sterner. "*I said no.*"

"Is that you, Mrs. Hanson?" A young man's voice, and it sounded confused.

I turned. Annabelle's Jay. "Well, hello. What are you doing here?"

He pointed toward the bathrooms. The tiny frame of Annabelle Hanson with her dandelion bloom of hair approached.

I forgot about Rashidi and my scarlet letter. I ran to my stepdaughter. She ran toward me, silly and exaggerated. I picked her up and swung her around me, both of us laughing.

When I'd put her down, I said, "You guys! You surprised me."

Annabelle beamed. "We did?"

"I thought you had a concert."

Jay swung a long, ropey arm down and around Annabelle. He was as tall as she was short and his swimmer shoulders about as wide as she was tall.

"The concert was last night. Belle really wanted to be here."

She poked him in the ribs. "And you said you'd do anything for me."

He blushed. "Just about."

A hand clasped me on the shoulder. I winced, feeling guilty I'd forgotten Rashidi.

But it wasn't him. "There you are, sunshine."

"Wallace!"

My old friend looked like a glossy ad for Pearl Izumi bicycle wear in his ocean-waves-themed bike shorts and jersey. Just the perfect shade to bring out the blue in his eyes. After a bone cruncher of a bear hug, I introduced him to Annabelle and Jay.

"Where's Ethan?" I asked him.

A model-thin ebony figure stepped from behind Wallace, who was roughly twice the second man's size. I'd only met Ethan once—like with Rashidi, it had been at Emily's wedding. Ethan was in street clothes, but his outfit was a shout in the library: neon-green-and-pink plaid shorts with a pink polo shirt and Top-Siders with pink ankle socks. After introductions and warm greetings, he threaded his arm through Wallace's.

"Aren't you riding?" I asked him.

He made a face. "I'd rather be eaten alive by fire ants."

"That's how I feel." Papa's voice surprised me. He put an arm around my waist and squeezed me. "I managed to break away from my four-legged patients."

Tears pricked the corners of my eyes, and I laid my head on his shoulder. "Papa, you came."

"I did."

Annabelle squealed and dove into his other shoulder.

Around me, people were looking at each other with smirks and raised eyebrows, their eyes just past me, to Rashidi.

Before I could turn around and introduce him, he removed his toothpick and spoke in his most Continental voice. "Good morning. I'm Michele's friend, Rashidi John."

Stunned silence met his announcement. I wanted to disappear, and I wiggled my nose, *Bewitched* style, because you just never know when it might start working, and I had nothing else to try.

Annabelle broke the tension. "You're the one who texts Michele."

"Yah, mon. She pities me. I had nothing to do and she said, 'Come on, nothing like a small-town bicycle race at the crack of dawn on a hot Saturday for a good time!'"

Everyone laughed and welcomed him. I felt as awkward as I had at sixteen in my white debutante gown. Me, the short dark one adrift in a sea of willowy blondes.

Wallace pointed at me. "Michele, you and I need to get moving."

I realized we had a cruise ship full of guests in need of direction. "Why don't you guys head to Espressions in Round Top? It's on our route. Wallace and I can drop in and say hi."

Annabelle clapped. "I love that place."

I handed Rashidi my keys, and Wallace and I walked our bicycles toward the starting line.

Wallace spoke through the side of his mouth. "What's going on with you and the dreadlocked Taye Diggs, there, missy?"

It wasn't as uncomfortable to me as Annabelle meeting Rashidi had been, but close. Wallace had been a regular in the triathlon scene in Houston—before he was transferred to Amarillo with Child Protective Services—and Adrian had introduced us.

"Not what you think."

"And why isn't it? He's yummy."

I side-eyed him. "Too soon."

"Hasn't it been a year?" Wallace asked.

"Not even eleven months."

"You're going to have to start living again at some point."

"I am living. See, this is Michele living—racing bicycles."

He shook his head. "This is Michele hungover, toting her hot date from the night before."

"Not a date."

He squinted and slipped on his sunglasses, then smiled wide. "You may not be ready, but Rashidi is."

"Just friends."

"Doesn't make me wrong."

"How's it going with Ethan?"

"Transparent redirection. And he's wonderful."

"When and where are you guys getting married? I need to put it on my calendar."

"I think we're going to wait for the Supreme Court. We don't want to have to run out of state like we're a dirty little secret."

"Good plan," I said.

He lowered his voice and leaned toward me. "We tried to get a cake for our engagement party. It didn't go well."

"What happened?"

"The baker declined on the basis of religious beliefs."

"Oh no!"

"The funny thing is, I understand. Religion is a protected right. I just think there's a lot of things religious people pull from the Bible that eventually get shit-canned. Multiple wives. Killing your children. Owning slaves. Hmm?"

A man pushed his bicycle through the crowd. He lost his balance and knocked his bike over, landing on me.

"Argh!" I fell into Wallace.

"Whoa, there." Wallace caught me before I hit the ground.

The other guy was prone, tangled up in our bikes. He stared up at me. "Michele Lopez Hanson?"

I squinted in the bright sun, trying to get a better look at his face.

"It's me, Blake Cooper." The dark-haired, fit Dr. Blake Cooper owned a sports injury clinic in Houston. He and his staff had helped me through injuries on my way to the Ironman. And he'd hit on me, until I made it clear he should stop.

"B-B-Blake, hello." Heat rushed to my face. I could see Rashidi with the rest of our cheering section, standing on the sidewalk ringing the square. Wallace was covering his mouth, hiding a laugh. Blake was grinning as he climbed to his feet and righted his bicycle. I was dying.

"Great to see you, Michele."

"You, too."

"I'd love to take you to lunch sometime."

"I'm not living in Houston."

"Do you still have the same number?"

"Um . . ."

Wallace cut in. "Yes, she does."

"Great!" Blake said. "I'll call. We can catch up."

The starting gun fired, cutting off conversation. I clipped in and began to pedal.

The pack made its way out of town at a leisurely pace, with a few hotshots sprinting out ahead. Even at this speed, my body struggled to warm up. My heart was sprinting when it should have been jogging. I couldn't catch my breath, and I realized I was anaerobic.

Wallace sat straight up, steering with his fingertips. "The only reason I'm not grilling you about Blake is because you look rough. Are you okay?"

"I'm not sure. It isn't going well."

He nodded. "You must have drunk your body weight in something."

"It's more than that. Long story."

He frowned, and I focused on the ground in front of my front wheel. I wished that it was Adrian beside me. I could confess my fear that at forty-one my body was betraying me as if I was twice that age. If it was getting this bad this young, how much worse would it be later? How much longer would I be able to be active and do whatever I wanted, whenever I wanted?

"You go ahead," I said. I wasn't going to hold him back. He would wave me on if the situation was reversed.

"If you're sure."

I nodded.

Wallace saluted me. "I'll see you in Round Top?"

"Perfect."

His ocean-waves jersey surged ahead of me as he wove in and out of traffic and chased the leaders. I breathed easier with nothing to prove and no one's ride to mess up. However, my car was in Round Top, and I had to get there by pedaling. The next twenty-seven miles were a hellish ordeal. It never got any better. I drank coconut water and sucked down chocolate Gu trying to spark some energy, but nothing worked. I popped three more Excedrin, but I knew they weren't the cure for what was ailing me. I'd tried every over-the-counter painkiller available over the last few months. Orally and topically. I'd tried yoga and meditation. Nothing was working. Nothing. Riding in the back middle of the riders, I barely took notice of the countryside. I quit worrying about wind resistance and gave in to my pain and sat up.

An interminable length of time later, I passed the Junk Gypsy world headquarters. I finally dropped down on my handlebars again as I gasped my way to the top of the hill into Round Top. Wallace was standing on the side of the road in front of Espressions. Sweating, overheated, and demoralized, I clipped out when I reached him.

"I'm toast. You go on without me."

He touched my elbow lightly. "I'm sorry you're feeling so bad."

I smiled with all the perkiness I could muster. "I'll be fine."

"Don't be so hard on yourself. And next time I see you, no excuses about not going on with your life. Adrian wouldn't have wanted you to die with him."

Tears sprang to my eyes.

We hugged, tight and sweaty.

"Ride safe."

"Always."

He rode away, standing up in his pedals. I was glad to see him go, because what he'd said, however kindly meant, stung. He was wrong, and as much as I loved him, I didn't want to hear it. I knew Adrian would want me to be his forever. If the roles were reversed, I would want him to be mine forever, too. I reached for my butterfly necklace. It was shockingly, inexplicably cold, and I dropped it back on my chest.

I leaned La Mariposa against the outside wall of Espressions. Inside, I found Rashidi, Papa, Jay, Ethan, and Annabelle gazing in rapt attention at the most recognizable man in Texas. Boyd Herrington, the U.S. senator Rashidi and I had seen at Home Sweet Farm the night before, was holding court, and looking good doing it. He had just enough gray at the temples to look wise and distinguished.

I waved to John, the proprietor and occasionally the resident musician for Espressions.

John boomed, "Welcome back, Michele."

Annabelle jumped up. "Hi, Michele. We didn't know you guys were here yet."

Ethan stood, too. "Where's Wallace?"

"He went on ahead. He'll pass by again in about fifteen minutes."

Ethan lowered back into his chair. "Sounds good."

"I'm going to call it a day, though. I'm not feeling well."

Rashidi had an open chair right beside him, and he shoved it back so I could get in it. "Will coffee help?"

"Maybe." I gave him a tepid grin.

"They have yummy scones." Annabelle sat back down.

Papa shoved a plate across the table at me, and I eyed the scones, which had some kind of berries in them. I needed to pass. The white poison of processed sugar. My hand snaked out and snatched one anyway. The statesman at the end of the table nodded in approval.

"Best scones this side of the pond. I'm Boyd." He half rose and stuck his hand out.

I shook and mumbled through a bite of the blueberry confection, "Nice to meet you," holding a hand over my mouth to catch the crumbs falling from my lips.

Papa leaned toward me. "Senator Herrington has just been telling us about his presidential campaign."

"Potential presidential campaign." The senator put a hand out, palm down, like he was minimizing his statement.

"How exciting." I licked crumbs from my lips. "When will you announce?"

"In a couple of months, if at all. We've got a lot of fundraising to do first."

Annabelle bounced in her chair. "I'm going to work on his campaign, or whatever, in Austin. Isn't that so cool?"

"What about you, young man?" Senator Herrington turned toward Jay. "Do you have an interest in politics?"

"The coach would never let Jay have time off." Annabelle patted Jay's hand. "He's going to the Olympics."

Jay was a likely contender in distance freestyle, although he still had to qualify.

"Belle!" Jay protested.

"What? It's true."

Jay's face splotched red. "You're gonna jinx me."

The senator changed the subject. Deft. "Michele, your very proud family has been telling me all about you."

"They're awfully sweet." I snagged a strawberry from the garnish on the scone plate.

"You're one of my neighbors, I hear."

"Am I? I live between here and Giddings."

"She calls it Nowheresville." Annabelle giggled. "Because that's totally where it is." I had shared the moniker with the kids in a group text earlier that week. Clearly, Annabelle liked it.

The senator smiled graciously. "And you're writing a book, I understand?"

"It's not her first one. She has a best seller that she wrote with my dad."

Annabelle's enthusiasm was sweet. And a little embarrassing. Jay and I glanced at each other. I smiled at him.

"Yes. A biography about a local woman."

"Who left you her farm."

Even Herrington had heard all about me. "Yes."

Annabelle gasped. I hadn't told the kids or Papa yet. "Really?" She socked Jay. "We've got a farm!"

The senator fished a card from his wallet and handed it to me. "Fantastic. Seeing as we're nearly neighbors, feel free to reach out to me."

I pulled at my sticky top, feeling uncomfortable that the senator was focusing on my family and me, and that our guests were so quiet. "Thank you. Afraid I don't have mine on me."

"Oh, I know the Becker place. Plus, I have a very industrious staff. If I need to find you, they can."

Just as I was about to change the subject to include Ethan and Rashidi, the senator rose to his feet. And as if he were the King of Siam, we all stood with him as he bestowed the honor of his grand goodbye upon us.

Annabelle was dying to show Jay the Quacker, and Papa wanted to see Gidget's place, too. I led a caravan toward Nowheresville, and Rashidi chatted with me easily as we drove. When we arrived, I stood in the clearing and swept my arm in a circle, encompassing the pond, the forest, and the decrepit trailer.

Papa got out of his 1960 Shelby Cobra, a ride he reserved for nonworking time. "You look like your *abuela*, but this trailer is more like your mother's Mississippi side of the family."

Everyone laughed.

Papa continued, "It's so remote, Itzpa. I worry about you."

I recoiled at his use of my nickname. I was no Itzpa anymore. "It's what Adrian and I wanted."

Annabelle interrupted, "It's great for bicycling."

"Exactly," I said. "Roads with very little traffic and broad shoulders."

Rashidi was walking around the Quacker, inspecting it. "You not afraid a'tall. Like Katie," he drawled.

Instead of responding, I thought of all the things I was afraid of: forgetting Adrian, losing Sam or Annabelle or my father, not living up to my mother's expectations, having to live another fifty years feeling this empty.

Annabelle put both arms around Jay's waist. "Dad said she dives head first with both arms swinging."

Papa laughed out loud. "Michele's won every fight she was ever in, and she was always the smallest one."

I opened the door to divert their attention. "Hurry in or the AC will cut off. And you don't want that to happen."

Rashidi entered first. "Living small is all the rage."

Annabelle and Jay followed Rashidi in.

I put a hand on Papa's arm to detain him. "Annabelle, can you show the guys how everything works in there?"

"Sure," she chirped.

I shut the door. "Can I talk to you for a second, Papa?"

His eyes widened. "Of course."

"I put a new message out, looking for my brother."

His face grew serious. "Have you heard anything?"

"Nothing." I watched a cardinal on the little bird feeder I had assembled two weeks before. It was empty. I'd have to move the feeder and fill it over at Gidget's. Another male cardinal lit on a different perch. "I can't believe I have a brother."

"Does that make you happy?" he asked.

"A little. But also, sad. It's like losing something I never had."

Papa sniffed and then reached in his breast pocket for the little pack of Kleenex he always kept there during allergy season. He fussed with it for a moment. "If you hear from him . . ."

"You'll be the first to know." I patted his shoulder. "You better get in there if you want a chance to see this amazing dwelling, because I can't promise I'm going to keep it a minute longer than it takes to get someone out here to haul it away."

He went inside. The discussion about the remote location reminded me of my wildlife camera. I walked behind the trailer and retrieved it. I wanted to hang it at Gidget's. It still bothered me that her back door had been unlocked, and that someone had tried to cut into the safe. The door to the Quacker opened, then closed. The sounds of people conversing easily floated across the air. I heard a squeal, then laughter.

Rashidi's voice said, "No killing. Here."

I came around the Quacker to see him walking with cupped hands in front of him. He crouched, opened his hands, and stood. A striped lizard ran under the trailer.

"Ew." Annabelle shuddered.

Rashidi brushed his hands on his jeans. He must have been hotter than blazes, but he wasn't sweating. He caught me looking at him and winked.

Next I took the gang to the homestead at Gidget's. Jay and Annabelle wandered off with Gertrude. I led Papa and Rashidi around the place, and told them about the will, the book, and the missing daughter.

"She just gave this place to you?" Papa shook his head. He'd been gushing about the house, the property, and the whole area. His enthusiasm was much higher than I'd have expected. "You'll be seeing a lot of me."

"Good. I miss you."

"I miss you, too, Itzpa. Nothing left for me in Seguin with you and your mother gone."

I hugged him with one arm. "Come anytime. I have a spare trailer in addition to a whole farm. There are actually a lot more animals. They're staying with a friend right now, but they need a good vet. And you could help me research this book."

Rashidi was pulling on his chin, looking thoughtful. "What'd you find so far? On the daughter?"

"Come inside. I'll show you."

I spread the pictures from Gidget's envelope out on the kitchen table to my eager audience of Papa and Rashidi.

Papa put an index finger beside the picture with the old sports car. "1932 SS 1, the precursor to what later became the Jaguar. Only five hundred made. Hard to imagine this car finding its way onto a Wendish farm in Texas. They didn't even start importing new Jaguars into the U.S. until the fifties." He was obsessed with vintage cars. "That car is a serious collector's item."

"So I've heard."

Rashidi drew the picnic photograph closer to him. "This 'round here?" He'd found another toothpick. He must have brought a gross of them.

"I'm not sure," I admitted. "It's been a whirlwind couple of days. I haven't even explored past the house and barn yet."

Rashidi turned the picture over. "There's another one stuck to the back." He held it up.

Papa took it from him, gazing at the new photograph, and held it out at arm's length, tilting his head. "That's Fort Moore. The oldest building in Fayette County."

"And you know this how?" I teased and bumped him with my hip.

"My parents took us to La Grange on a weekend trip, a very long time ago."

"You have a good memory." Better than mine, especially lately.

Papa passed the picture—or pictures, in this case—to me. The Fort picture was of four adults, two of whom were recognizably Gidget's parents. The other couple was younger, maybe ten years or more. Only the back center of the two photographs was stuck, so I pulled the edges apart, slowly, gently. The photographs gave way. Part of the backing from the picnic photo stuck to the Fort picture. There was writing on the back of both. The picnic picture said *Anna and Lucy, Tea Party Picnic, Back 40*. There was more, but it had stuck to the back of the other picture. The writing on the back of the La Grange picture said something illegible, then *Killians*. The stuck backing from the picnic photo obscured something, then I could read the word *Grange* below it.

"Very interesting." I put the pictures back in the manila envelope. "Want to see something else interesting? She has a locked safe."

Rashidi grinned. "The plot thickens."

We walked to the gun safe.

"It opens with a combination, but I don't have it."

Papa crouched in front of the handle and lock. "It's an old one."

Rashidi picked up the disks and ran his finger along the metal shavings on the floor. "Did you do this?"

"Nope, and I have no idea who did."

Papa's eyes and voice were sharp. "Since you've been here?"

"I'm not sure."

He rubbed the shavings between his fingers then stared at the cuts. "The cuts look shiny. New. I don't like it."

"I've got a shotgun, a wildlife cam, and a dog with two-inch legs. I'll be fine."

Papa stood, but he turned to Rashidi. "I worry about Itzpa all the time. This doesn't help."

"I'm no Itzpa, Papa."

"Itzpa?" Rashidi asked.

"Itzpapalotl."

"The knife-winged butterfly. She's a warrior goddess."

I wheeled toward him. "You know about her?"

"Yah, mon. I got sucked into teaching an Aztec mythology class at the university one time."

Papa was standing, but still staring at the safe.

I put both hands on my father's chest and gently pushed him backward until he turned and walked to the living room on his own. "I'm a big girl, Papa. You can call me your Tlazol now."

"You'll always be my Itzpa." He frowned. "Let me set up that wildlife cam before we go. I'd feel better if you installed a security system, though, ASAP."

"Aye, aye." I saluted him.

Jay, Annabelle, and Gertrude rejoined us. After Papa had positioned the wildlife camera to his and Rashidi's mutual satisfaction in the side yard, I kissed my family goodbye. Papa was headed southwest. Annabelle and Jay were going west to Austin. Rashidi needed to go east, and that meant I was his ride. I went for my keys.

This time the Jetta followed Papa's low-slung blue car with its fat white lengthwise stripes out the long driveway to the road, while Jay and Annabelle drove behind us. Rashidi remained silent, and I almost held my breath, praying for it to continue. Papa turned left at the next intersection and I turned right. Soon we were on 290 headed toward Brenham, with Jay and Annabelle going the opposite direction.

"Your family's good people," Rashidi announced.

"They're pretty awesome," I said. "In case you hadn't figured it out, they were a surprise today."

"You friends are nice, too. Katie, Wallace and Ethan, Emily."

"You really know a lot of my people. And you're right. I'm lucky."

He looked out the window, then slipped back into his island-speaking voice. "Katie talk about you, but she leave out you so beautiful."

I put my hand up. "Rashidi—"

"Just sayin' what true."

"It makes me uncomfortable. I wish you wouldn't."

He turned to me with his gentle eyes. "I hold my tongue."

"Thank you," I said.

"For now."

THIRTEEN

THE NEXT MORNING the Internet installation guy woke us up, knocking loudly. At least I assumed it was him. I'd had a bad night, tossing and turning at all the scary country noises.

As I shouted, "Just a moment," I glanced at my phone. Eight a.m. How had the dog and the rooster let me sleep so late? Maybe Gertrude remembered from last week that Mondays were sleep-in days. "Give me a moment."

I heard a man's voice. "No problem. I'll just be getting my stuff set up out here, miss."

"Thank you," I shouted back.

Gertrude rolled over and stretched her long body, her stubby legs pointing out as far as they could reach. She finished up with full-jawed yawn, which showed off her white beard locks. She twisted her torso, and it was like she was hinged in front of her hips so that when she twisted the back portion, the front followed in a time-lapse sequence. Tangled in the blue sheets, she looked like a Loch Ness Monster gyrating in the waves. Morning yoga completed, she leapt from the bed. Her belly sagged and grazed the floor.

I was dressing by the closet when she turned and barked at me.

"Wait your turn, missy."

I was majorly sore today, and I'd only done half the race yesterday. I stretched my shoulders, reaching up as high as I could and groaning as I bent slightly at the waist, then fell forward until my hamstrings screamed in protest. I swayed first in one direction and then back to the other, teasing out my lower back. I rolled my neck slowly, working out the crunchies, reversed it and rolled in the other direction. Gertrude followed every move with her eyes. She looked a little dizzy.

After throwing on yoga clothes, I met the Internet guy outside. He was young and gawky, with red hair and freckles. We settled on a site on the roof, and he promised to knock when he was done, in about an hour.

I set my laptop up on the kitchen table and turned my phone's hot spot on. I was all about Juniper, this being a Monday after all, and technically a workday. I browsed email, triaging as I went. I sent Brian an update on the few remaining projects I had left open from last week, and my plans for the upcoming week. As I'd hoped, that prompted him to send me a new packet of work and a cancelation of our Skype call. I breezed through six or seven pieces for the subscription website and the blog.

One hour passed, then another, until I was pretty much caught up. I pulled up a yoga video from my hard drive and rolled my mat out on the living room floor. About half an hour into it, someone knocked. I paused the video and opened the door. It was the installer wiping sweat off his forehead with the back of one arm.

I gestured in the house, but he shook his head. "I was starting to get worried about you," I told him.

"Sorry, ma'am. I had to stop to take a call from the office."

He didn't meet my eyes.

Wife or girlfriend, for sure. "So, how much longer now?"

"An hour, at the most."

His original estimate was one hour, and another would put us past three. That was a long phone call.

"I'll need to be in the house some."

"Okay. No need to knock." I started to shut the door when I noticed pink surveyor flags at the tree line near the road. My near vision was getting worse lately, but my eagle-eyed far vision was still 20/15, and those flags were on Gidget's property.

"Did you see who put those flags up?" I pointed.

He shot a quick glance. "Yeah, some guys with surveying equipment were out here earlier."

"Really?"

Now he pointed. "They went that way." The direction his finger indicated was through the woods toward the Quacker.

"Great. Thank you."

I donned my pink camo boots and was about to go see what the surveying was all about, but I decided to quickly check the *Her Last Wish* blog first. It had about 150 hits the day before. That meant traffic doubled between day one to day two. I knew I was a fairly good writer, but still, it was shocking.

There was a comment waiting for approval from someone who called herself Maggie: *I'm a junker in Giddings. I'd love to bring you some banana nut bread and introduce myself.*

A neighbor was a potential witness about Gidget, her life, and her daughter. She'd entered her email, so I clicked on her address and sent a short note: *I'd be delighted if you came by. Let me know when you're in the neighborhood.* I included my phone number and hit send. I approved the comment and grabbed a mug of the coffee I'd made and forgotten earlier.

I headed outside and through the woods in the direction of the Quacker. Walking slowly, I saw details I'd missed on our mad flight to Gidget's and our dazed return. The dirt underneath my feet was mostly sand, a colorless sand with occasional rocks. The grass was sparse, choked out by the trees hogging the light above and the yaupon hogging the dirt and water at ground level. There was a layer of dead lichen-covered branches suspended every couple of feet in the yaupon as well. Some of the oak trees reached for the sky and others snaked almost along the ground like they were trying to make a run for it.

I heard voices in the distance. Men. Sound carried through the trees, making it hard to tell whether the source was fifty feet or fifty yards away. The first glimpse I caught of them was a man in a camo cap, blue jeans, cowboy boots, and a long-sleeved plaid shirt too warm for the weather, but perfect for protecting skin from the yaupon and thorny vines. He was leaning over and peering through a tripod-mounted monocular.

"Excuse me," I called.

He whirled toward the sound of my voice. He pushed his hat back on his head. "Yes?"

"What are you doing here?"

He tucked a pencil behind one ear. "And you are?"

My blood boiled, that fast. "The person whose permission you need to be on this property."

His look of disbelief wasn't hard to interpret. Short Hispanic woman in ridiculous pink-camouflage knee-high boots, yoga pants and tank top complete with boobs. Because I've got a more generous helping of curves than I would have liked. I crossed my arms over my chest.

He stared. After a long silence, he said, "My company has the owner's permission."

"What company?" I held out my hand.

He narrowed his eyes.

"A card, please."

He probably wasn't used to being ordered around by half-dressed Texican women in the middle of nowhere, but he dug in his back pocket for his wallet, opened it, and gave me a card.

"You're from Houston," I read aloud. "And you're a surveyor."

"Yes."

"Do you have the name of the 'owner' you supposedly have permission from to be here?"

"Back in the truck." He hitched his hat up and back down again.

Another man's voice rang out. "Bill?" The second guy appeared through the trees, even closer to the property line and the Quacker. He had lamb-chop facial hair, trimmed short, and shoulders the size of a lumberjack. "You okay?" Then he blanched, seeing me. "Oh, howdy, ma'am." He tipped his wide-brimmed safari hat.

Bill looked from me to the newcomer. "Hey, Chad. This lady—"

"—owns the property you're on without my permission." It was a stretch, but nearly true.

Chad pushed his hat back and scratched at his scalp. "Well now, ma'am, I sure do apologize. We were told everything was in order."

"Who told you that?"

"The pipeline that contracted us."

I'd been clutching my coffee cup, and it was cramping my style. I set it on the ground, then put my hands on my hips. "I don't know anything about a pipeline."

Chad looked at Bill. Bill shrugged. Chad's forehead folded into an accordion of wrinkles. "Could I get your name, ma'am?"

I enunciated. "Michele Lopez Hanson."

Chad moved closer to Bill. "And you're the property owner?"

"As soon as probate of Ms. Becker's will is complete. Until then, I am the tenant."

"Ah." Chad rubbed at his hairless chin.

"I'm going to need you guys to pack up and leave." I pitched my voice deeper and laced it with steel. "Please have someone call me who can explain this and seek *proper* authorization."

Chad licked his lips, then rolled them inward, rubbing them together. "Okay, ma'am. We'll do that."

Bill said, "But—"

Chad held up a hand. "Load 'em up, Bill. Can I get your number, ma'am?" He pulled a pencil and a mini spiral notepad from his back pocket.

I recited it for him and repeated my name. "One L," I said.

He looked up at me, squinting, then resumed taking it down old-school.

Gertrude's barks penetrated the forest. After a few days of living together, I knew she wasn't a random barker. We had company.

"Thank you. Good day." I headed back toward the farmhouse, my neck tingling as eyes bored into my back.

Gertrude's barks grew increasingly frenzied. As I neared the tree line, I realized I'd left my coffee cup in the woods, but I heard a woman's voice and decided to go back for it later.

"Nice doggy," she said.

She was trying to pet Gertrude, who was still barking at something behind her.

My jaw dropped. It was an early Shania Twain look-alike, tiny gap in her front teeth and all. I drew closer, feeling a flicker of recognition. She had on a leopard-print miniskirt over black leggings and bright red cowboy boots, the ensemble tied together with a big rodeo belt and buckle. Her upper half was encased in a black tank top with a men's white button-down shirt, open and tied at the waist over a belt with a big rodeo buckle, her long sleeves rolled up. Her hair was teased high and clipped back with the little bump at her crown that I associated with country music stars and Texas beauty queens. The Internet guy was standing on the roof, unabashedly drinking her in.

I smoothed my hands on my yoga pants and tried to look dignified to greet my visitor. She saw me and broke into a lopsided smile with large white teeth.

"Hey, I texted you that I was dropping by." Her voice was gravely, smoky.

I didn't know what to say to that. How did this woman have my phone number?

"I'm Maggie?" She held up a loaf of homemade banana bread wrapped in plastic film.

Suddenly I understood and felt very, very foolish. "Oh, geez. I'm Michele. Sorry, I didn't have my phone with me."

I glanced toward the barn and saw the magenta truck parked in its shade. Two golden retrievers were standing in the bed with their front paws up on the edge. The source of Gertrude's ire, I realized. The truck's doors had magnets that read FLOWN THE COOP.

"If now's a bad time, I can head out the way I came in."

I smiled and shook my head. "Now's fine. And I've seen you before. At the pool in Giddings."

She tilted her head, then laughed. "Oh yeah. I nearly killed myself keeping up with you."

"I'm glad it was hard for you, too, at least." I motioned toward the house. "Come on in. Gidget left it a bit of a mess and I've made it worse, but there's coffee and AC. Do you want to bring your dogs in?"

"Sit," she called to them. They ignored her. "Janis, sit." The smaller of the two dogs sat. "Woody, sit." The second dog sat, as well. "If I ever start letting them out, they'll always want to. Consistency is how I get them to stay put. But thank you."

As we entered the house, I saw it for what it was—a dirty, unlikely hiding place of museum-quality art. "Sorry for the mess," I said.

Maggie's mouth gaped. "The art."

"Spectacular, isn't it?"

"Unbelievable. Is it yours?"

"Looking that way. Want a curated tour?"

I walked her through the house, sharing the information I'd gleaned during my art inventory and saving Gidget's bedroom for last. Like me, those were her favorite pieces.

"If you ever want to sell this one, let me know." She pointed to *Front Porch Pickin'*, which depicted a guitarist. It was melancholy and joyful at the same time. "I can't believe I've been living this close to this house and had no idea her work existed. I didn't even know she was an artist. I met her once, you know."

"Out here?"

"No, about fifteen years ago, in Houston. I played an event at her gallery. She was fascinated with my last name, and it turned out she knew my parents. I never saw her again, although I've heard about her from the locals. My shop is a gossip magnet."

"I saw it yesterday. Do you live there, too?"

She followed me back into the kitchen. "Yep. My record label went belly-up, and the owner gave me the place in lieu of payment on my last album."

"You're a musician?" I poured two coffees.

She bobbled her head. "Not professionally anymore. I blew it all on coke—I mean that literally. Everything. My career, my relationships, nearly my life. Came out here broke and alone. Learned I had a knack for junking. I've scraped by without having to sell my dogs, my truck, or my guitar, and I like the area. I grew up in La Grange, and my parents were getting older. It's nice being close, but not too close."

I handed her coffee. "Wow," I said, at a loss for anything else.

She laughed, a deep-throated, rumbly sound. "I get that a lot."

Now I laughed.

She pitched her voice to a high, squeaky tone and mimed holding a phone to her ear. "Have you heard about Maggie Killian, former darling of the Texas music scene and biggest screw-up this side of Lindsay Lohan?" She blew on her coffee then spoke in her normal voice. "Now I just get high off the paint thinner and varnish and the occasional tin cup of whiskey."

I kept my face neutral, but I realized I'd heard of her. Ten years ago, she'd been a rising star. More like a shooting star. I remembered a few songs. "Buckle Bunny." "I Hate Cowboys." Good stuff. She'd gone down fast and faded out. But here she was, and she looked healthy, happy, and beautiful. "Good for you. I love your truck."

"Bess. She's awesome." She sipped her coffee, then stopped, inhaling it deeply, a sensual appreciation. "I get a booth twice a year at the Warrenton/Round Top antique shows. That's where I really make a killing. Have you been to the shows?"

I didn't want to tell her that shopping wasn't my thing and that anything crafty was even less so. "Not yet."

"HGTV-obsessed urban women by the thousands flock to 'em in a buying frenzy so they can make their new city homes look more like old country ones."

I blurted out my first thought. "Sounds like Hades to me."

"It is. I just try to smile a lot, scan the credit cards quickly, and keep my mouth shut." She set her coffee on the kitchen counter. "I get most of my junk these days from estate sales. The nearer they are, the cheaper for me. So, I run a clipping service online, looking for mention of estate or probate in the area." She grinned. "I'm always on the hunt for window frames, doors, mantels, slabs of wood, furniture, old metal, windmill pieces, and car parts, especially trucks. That's how I found you. Trolling for dead people. Sounds pretty smarmy, doesn't it?"

"Sounds smart." I took a sip of my coffee. "So you saw I'm inheriting this place."

"I did, and I'd love to go through your barn, make you an offer if I see anything my buyers would like. There's things in the house I could offer on, too, if you're willing."

For a moment I was taken aback, but then again, she was a junker, and direct. I liked direct. "Be my guest."

"I'd like to be the first one you let through, too."

I thought about the competitive woman in the pool. Of course she wanted to be first in. "No problem. Want to take a peek now?"

"I'd love it."

We walked out, releasing the dogs to come with us. Gertrude strutted in front of the goldens, showing off her place. I rolled one side of the barn doors back, and Maggie drew in an excited breath.

"A treasure trove." She strolled through, trailing her fingers over things, stopping to admire others. "Someone's already been here picking?"

"What?"

"You've already had someone through?"

"No. I'm basically the only one in here since Gidget died. She had a guy who helped her around the place some. Jimmy Urban. But I don't think he took anything."

"Someone has." She showed me dusty outlines and disheveled trails through the hay on the floor.

"That's disturbing."

A man's voice interrupted us. "Hello? Michele Lopez Hanson?"

Maggie and I looked at each other.

My mouth turned downward in annoyance. I glanced toward the voice. It wasn't the Internet guy. "Yes?"

"I'm Gerald Cooper from Cypress Surveying. The guy on the roof said you were out here." He walked toward me, arm out, card in hand.

I took it. "That was quick."

"The guys called me right after they talked to you. They said you claimed to be the person living on Anna Becker's property in Lee County. I was in the area, so I decided to drop by."

"Not claiming." I heard the edge in my voice. "I actually do live here." I gave him the short version of my tenancy and inheritance.

Maggie touched my elbow. "Excuse me, y'all. Michele, do you want me to step out?"

"How about you come back later this week? This may take a while."

She frowned, disappointed, then reversed it and nodded. "I'll be in touch. Great meeting you."

"Sounds good. You, too."

Maggie whistled for her dogs. She walked out, hips slinging, and Gerald tried to hide the fact that he was ogling her. I would have, too, in his place. Ogled *and* tried to hide it.

When she was gone, I resumed. "Help me understand."

He leaned against the gate to a stall. "We were retained by Lonestar Pipeline."

Ding, ding, ding. A bell of recognition went off in my head. Lonestar Pipeline, as in HOU-TO-AUS LONESTAR PIPELINE, the sign on the neighbor's fence, and the one I'd heard about in town. "And how does this affect me?"

"Well, according to my contact, the attorney for Ms. Becker's estate granted permission to run the pipeline across her place."

I'm a little teapot, short and . . . angry. Water started to boil inside me. Greyhound had given permission for Lonestar to run the pipeline here? That's why surveyors had come today? But he knew I was inheriting. If this happened before Gidget died, he should have told me. If it happened after, he should have let Ralph handle it, and Ralph should have asked me. Ralph. Ralph was a landman. Doubt rippled through me. Could he have a hand in this?

The pressure built inside my kettle and steam whistled through the spout. "Greyhound Smith?"

"Not him."

"Ralph Cardinal?"

"No, I think it's a woman."

"Can I get the name, please?"

"Um, I'll have to get back to you with that."

"Please do."

I followed him out, dispensing with pleasantries. I was pissed. When he'd driven away, I hit Ralph's number in recents. Voice mail answered, and I closed my eyes. "Call me. It's an emergency."

A low-rumbling growl at my feet made my eyes pop open. Gertrude was standing beside me, watching Gerald's truck as it turned onto the road.

"Exactly how I feel, girl." And inside my mind, Itzpa stretched her wings, flexed their knife tips. Only she looked exactly like Tlazol. I felt a surge of something elemental, vital. "And when I find out who's behind this, they're not going to like me very much."

FOURTEEN

GREYHOUND'S SECRETARY transferred my call to him as I marched toward the house, my pulse a military cadence.

"Greyhound Smith speaking."

Innocent until proven guilty, innocent until proven guilty. "This is Michele Lopez Hanson. There are pipeline surveyors here on Gidget's property today. They said Gidget agreed to let them route the Houston-to-Austin pipeline across her place, and they have permission to access the property from 'her attorney.'"

"Not from this one. What's going on?"

The whistling slowed to a hiss. I started from the beginning and told Greyhound the whole story. I gave him the contact information for Gerald Cooper.

An intercom buzzed. I couldn't understand the first word she said, but then heard "Herrington here for you, Greyhound."

"I've got a client here, Michele, but after that, I'll get to the bottom of this."

We hung up. I set the phone down on the couch beside me and drummed my fingers. Was this Herrington Boyd or one of his relations? It was mind-blowing that a man of Greyhound's connections represented Gidget. That Ralph knew him in the first place to refer her. He seemed a couple of rungs higher on the food chain than either of them. I sagged back against the couch cushions, putting the back of my hand against my forehead. I felt a little feverish.

Not now, I said to my immune system. Do your job.

I looked around. I'd had more people through this place in the last few days than in the last year in my Houston house. It was in shambles, and it was time for me to quit blaming Gidget. I went into the kitchen and started washing the dishes by hand, making a mental note to go get the coffee cup I'd left outside, later. I was putting up the dishes after drying them when someone knocked on my door. Again.

It was the installer. I'd forgotten he was here. "Ma'am, I'm sorry, but I'm going to have to come back later this week. I don't have a part I need."

Four hours. Four hours and now he doesn't have a part? My smile hurt. "So, no Internet for me?"

He shuffled his feet. "I'm sorry, ma'am. I'll call you when the part's in."

There was nothing to be done. I shut the door behind him, leaning against it. The feverish feeling increased. My phone dinged. I went to the coffee table and picked it up. Ralph. Good. I needed answers from him.

"Family emergency. Driving to El Paso. Granddaughter coming to live with me for school year. Can you cover for me with Gidget's estate for a few days? Very sorry."

Now didn't seem like the time to grill him about whether he'd had anything to do with Lonestar Pipeline sending surveyors out to Gidget's place.

"No problem," I typed.

His personal situation sounded dicey, but my throat constricted anyway. My little internal kettle had boiled up all its water, and it was time to take it off the burner. Meanwhile, Brian had emailed for help with the quarterly *Archery Collector's Edition*. He'd given it to a junior editor, and it had come off the rails, big time.

I needed free Wi-Fi and a change of scenery. The library promised sanctuary, and after I grabbed coffee and a Voodoo Burger from 290 Grind, I fled for the Giddings library. I spent the rest of the afternoon there, trying to hold myself steady and get work done, only leaving when a librarian I didn't recognize needed to lock up. As I drove home eating the other half of my burger, chips, and fruit, I passed by Jimmy Urban's chicken farm. He was sitting on his front porch, drinking something out of a Mason jar. He lifted a hand, so I waved back. I made the left turn on the road leading to Gidget's place, lost in thought about the pipeline and who I could trust. I didn't see the deer jump out in front of the Jetta until it was too late. I slammed on the brakes and braced for an impact, but it didn't come. The deer bounded into the woods on the other side of the road, unscathed.

Gasping for breath, I put my hand over my throat. My heart hammered into my palm. I had to get myself together. Right now that meant focusing on my driving and getting home alive. I eased off the brake and put my quivering hands on the wheel. I looked both ways, half-expecting a herd of deer now, but I was alone.

That was not the case when I got back to Gidget's, however.

There was a Lee County Sheriff's Department Tahoe parked at the house, with no one in it. Gertrude met me at the gate, which I hit at full speed. She looked sad, like she'd failed me somehow. I didn't slow down to console her. I opened the front door so hard that if the window hadn't already been broken, it would have shattered then.

Tank and Junior were in the kitchen. Both had on gloves, and they were bagging and stashing items in a large black satchel. The residue of black fingerprint powder was everywhere and the cabinets were all ajar. The drawers were open and half of their contents set out on the counters. So much for cleaning up earlier today.

Tank's hand went to his holstered gun. Junior took a step back, farther into the kitchen.

"What are you doing here?" I demanded.

Gertrude skidded to a stop beside me, and I slammed the door.

"You first," Tank said, and tapped the badge on his chest.

"I'm renting the place from the estate. Which you'd know if you'd sought permission to enter."

"Aren't you lucky." He ignored the bit about permission.

I scowled at him. "I'm paying rent. And you may recall I've inherited it."

"I recall." He crossed his arms. "I wonder if you're as surprised as you claim to be about that."

"Oh, please. Now it's your turn. What are you doing here?"

"Ms. Becker's death was officially ruled a homicide. We have a crime scene to process."

"Do you have a warrant?"

Tank used a singsong voice. "It was open. Front door was ajar. We had an obligation to make sure everything was okay. We didn't know anyone was living here."

Liar. I fumed. Well, anything they tried to use would be inadmissible.

Their problem, not mine. "You're gonna find my fingerprints all over every-thing and probably about eight or nine other people, too. I've been sleeping in her bedroom and showering in her bathroom. I've touched everything in the house, because I did an inventory for the estate. I've even given the barn a pretty thorough going-over."

Tank and Junior looked at each other. Tank looked disgusted. Junior looked concerned.

"And you guys better not have bagged up any of my things."

"How are we supposed to know what's yours or hers?"

"I think it'll be pretty easy to tell. I'm the forty-year-old who brought a suitcase with brand new things and a laptop. Everything else is hers."

Junior nodded. "If it's yours, ma'am, you'll get it back."

"Wait a second." I grasped the back of one of the kitchen chairs. "Weren't you guys already out here once to collect evidence?"

Tank's eyes narrowed. "We don't process crime scenes when there's no crime."

"Don't take offense," I said. "It just looked like you had when I moved in."

Tank sneered. "Did you *see* crime scene tape anywhere?"

I sighed. "You're making this so difficult."

"And you've been messing with our crime scene."

"I *live* here." I laughed with no mirth. "And you just told me it wasn't a crime scene until now."

"How convenient for you."

"You're missing my point, Deputy. I saw things here on the day Gidget died that weren't here when I moved in. The back door was unlocked, and someone had tried to break into Gidget's safe."

Tank dropped an evidence baggy into their satchel. "It's only your word about any of it."

"I didn't move the things I saw. Ralph didn't. I asked Jimmy Urban about them, and I don't think he did. So, if you guys didn't, then who did?"

Gertrude tiptoed to the other side of the table and put her feet on the chair. Tank didn't seem to notice her. She gave the satchel a good sniff. Junior looked at me, then the dog, then back at me.

FIFTEEN

AFTER THE DEPUTIES LEFT, I locked the doors and jumped in the shower. I felt dirty. Even if it was the cops, having someone in the house without permission gave me the willies. When I had washed the feeling away and was in a clean T-shirt and shorts, I checked my phone. Brian had emailed me around six thirty. It was seven thirty now.

Emergency meeting tomorrow about the Archery Collector's Edition. Can you be here at 8? I know that's early, but I need you to carry the ball.

I had a voice mail, too. I'd turned my ringer to silent while I was in the library, then forgotten to turn it back on again when I left. It was from Greyhound. I pressed play.

"A Houston attorney just filed a protest to Gidget's will. I'm guessing she's the same one that gave the pipeline the go-ahead. Her name is Nancy Little, and she's claiming to be Gidget's attorney and to have a will. I gave her a call. I'm going to send you the rest of this electronically. Also, I tried to get ahold of Ralph, but he hasn't called me back. If you talk to him, let him know."

I stared at the phone. My stress meter ratcheted up, up, up. I didn't want to read this email. I didn't want to deal with this issue. I got up and got a glass of water and took several long swallows. Finally, my brain had enough oxygen to process thoughts. What *bastardo* was contesting Gidget's will and trying to block her last wish? I felt a cleansing rush of adrenaline and anger. What *pendejo* would send pipeline people here? I wanted to bash some heads. I felt ready for Greyhound's email and pulled it up.

I read quickly.

Ms. Little claims she's represented Gidget since before Gidget left Houston, and that she is also the attorney for Lester Tillman, Gidget's former partner in the gallery. Ms. Little has done powers of attorney for them in favor of each other. Interestingly, Gidget had her aneurysm, then later, when she was recovering, she executed a will leaving everything to a trust with Lester as sole trustee, and signed a contract to sell out her interest to Lester.

I felt a tiny bit sorry that I hadn't told Greyhound about the POA, will, and sale documents I'd found under Gidget's bed. But as an attorney, my caca del toro detector was clanking and whining, as Nancy Little's lack of ethics pushed it to the max. Hello, conflict of interest? Even if both Lester and Gidget had waived the conflict, Little should have run from these transactions, especially given the highly suspect timing and Gidget's recovery from a neurological issue.

Gidget never told me about this will, and I specifically asked her if she had one when she came to me. I've attached the one Ms. Little sent me. The trust is called the Houston Arts Trust, which is to benefit the Houston arts community. Little claims she didn't know about the new will until today, which is why she filed this emergency motion. She says there's no way Gidget had the testamentary capacity to execute this will. We had a bit of a row over that since I know for a fact that she did.

If Gidget supposedly lacked the mental capacity to make a will now, how did she have it back then, right after her aneurysm? And how would Ms. Little know what Gidget's mental state had been recently, anyway? I wanted to scream and punch the walls. This made no sense whatsoever.

I'll have to examine it closer tomorrow. It's my fortieth wedding anniversary and my wife won't forgive me if I miss it because of work. Give me a call. I still can't get ahold of Ralph.

That was the end of the message. It had two attachments: LAST WILL AND TESTAMENT OF ANNA BECKER and BILL OF SALE. I snorted. Second to last, maybe. I shot a quick message back to Greyhound.

Ralph has a family emergency and asked me to stand in for him until he gets back from driving his granddaughter back from El Paso.

I paused, thinking about Gidget's last wishes for her book to be written and for someone to get a bequest to her daughter. About Lester's entanglement and his presence in her life. About her life in Houston, forty years' worth of it. That was where her story was. I had to talk to Lester, and soon. Coincidentally, Brian needed me to come in tomorrow for an early meeting.

Serendipity.

I continued my message to Greyhound.

I'm going to be in Houston tomorrow for my day job, and to work on Gidget's book. I plan to visit the gallery and talk to Lester. Thank you for sending this information.

I hit send. My tension ebbed. Taking action was a good thing.

I shot off a quick reply to Brian: *See you tomorrow morning.*

And then I turned my attention to figuring out how to get Skype on my phone. It was almost time for my Monday-night call with Papa and the kids. I had the app downloaded and was logged in and ready in the nick of time. I moved over to Gidget's threadbare tweed couch. It could use a restuffing. I initiated the call to our group. Papa picked up immediately.

"Hi, Papa." I smiled at the sight of him. "How are you doing?"

He gave me his courtly smile and his steady voice. "All is well here, Itzpa. And how are you?"

Papa had been steady my whole life. The only time I'd seem him falter was over Mom's death, and to a lesser extent, at Adrian's, and even then he appeared unruffled to those who weren't close to him. Unlike me. Everyone could tell when I was having a tough time. So there was no use pretending things were peachy now.

I flopped my hand side to side. "Two steps forward and one step back." I watched my screen carefully as we talked, expecting to hear Sam's and Annabelle's voices at any second.

A text came in. Good. One of the kids. I changed screens to read it.

Papa frowned. "In what way?"

I shrugged. "Everything, I guess."

The text appeared on the screen. It wasn't one of the kids. It was Dr. Blake from the bicycle race: *"Great seeing you. I'd love to catch up. I've opened a clinic in La Grange. I'm there 2 days a week. Your friend Wallace said you're in Giddings down the road?"*

Oh, Wallace, no. I remembered now that Blake had told me he grew up in La Grange. *Dios mío.*

"Tell me about everything." Papa's voice was warm, inviting trust.

It took me a second to recalibrate to my conversation with Papa. "This book I'm writing. It looks like there may be some wrinkles to the story that I didn't expect. I'm heading to Houston tomorrow to talk to some people."

Papa waffled his hand at me now. "That doesn't sound—"

"It's not really that, I guess, since wrinkles make for more interesting books. It's that Gidget left me this place, and now the independent executor has family problems and is disappearing from probate at the same time as a lawyer in Houston claims to have the rightful will and meanwhile has authorized work done on her property and, apparently, entered contracts, as well. Plus, I haven't found a single clue as to a daughter's whereabouts and —oh yeah, I almost forgot—Gidget was poisoned, so it's murder, and the police act like I'm a suspect."

Papa's face grew stern. "That's crazy."

"I know, and I'm sure nothing will come of it, but it's a nuisance. It's weird, but I feel like Gidget picked me out to represent her. That I need to stand in for her, write this book, find her daughter and her killer. Am I nuts?"

My dad nodded. "Very. Someone killed her, and now you want to stand in her place. Just write your book."

"The story *is* the daughter and whoever killed Gidget."

"Just don't do anything that could get you hurt. I—" His voice broke.

My heart broke with it. "What is it?"

"I don't know what I'd do without you, Itzpa."

"Oh, Papa." I leaned toward the tiny screen on my phone. "And I don't know what I'd do without you. You have to take care of yourself, too, because—" I sighed. "Speaking of taking care of themselves, where are the kids?"

"I wondered about that."

"Let me text them. Give me a second, okay?"

"All right."

I flipped Blake's text away and sent a group text to Annabelle and Sam. They hated them, but they'd just have to deal. *"Where are you guys? Your grandpa and I are waiting on Skype."*

I heard from Annabelle almost immediately: *"SRRY! SO SRRY! Totes 4got. Catch u next week."* And then a couple of random, overwrought emojis that were too small to see. I checked myself. Maybe I just didn't have a sense of humor anymore.

"Annabelle isn't going to make it on tonight."

"Is she okay?" he asked.

A deep sadness ripped through my chest. She was breaking away, growing up. She was a good kid. Sweet, loving, far better than I deserved. But it was happening. She didn't need me anymore.

"Oh, she's fine, Papa. Just busy being a teenage girl."

"I remember what it's like to have one of those," he said, and I heard the humor in his voice.

I wanted to laugh, too, but I couldn't. "I'm afraid Sam is a no-show, too."

Sam was completely AWOL. My baby boy who still had one year left at home, who was supposed to (because he was a boy) love his mommy forever. But in reality, he didn't need me, either. Who did need me? Papa? Theoretically. It was nice of him to say so, but I hadn't lived with him in more than twenty years. We talked more lately since Mom died. And I'm sure the fact that he had an adult daughter comforted him, but it wasn't the same as having a spouse or a child who needed you. The ripping sensation started up in my chest again. Now it was tearing away flesh and bone.

"Itzpa? Are you still there?" Papa said.

"Oh yes, I was just, um, sending another text to Sam, letting him know that the call has ended."

"But it hasn't," he said.

"Not yet, but it will soon, well before we hear from him." I gave him a wan smile. "They've grown up."

"Yes, they have, and you've done a great job."

How great a job was it if the kids didn't even cancel the call, with both Papa and me sitting here waiting? But I just said, "I love you, Papa." I flipped back over to his video image in the Skype app. He was a handsome devil. "Any of the local women setting their cap for you yet?"

His mouth curled, partly a smile, partly a grimace. "You know how widowed ladies are."

Now I did laugh. "Aggressive."

"Yes. I'll be happy when they pick on some other old guy. They're drowning me in casseroles and fried chicken and peach pies."

"One of them is going to sweep you off your feet."

"Not yet. But I don't want to be alone. Your mother and I—"

"I don't know how you didn't kill her."

"We had a good marriage. It was easier to be married to her than to be her daughter."

"Well, I still think you're a saint," I said. "I love Mom, but yeah, Saint Edward."

"What about you?"

I wished I had already hit End Call so the conversation wouldn't have gone this direction. "I'm good."

"It's been nearly a year. What about that Rashidi fellow?"

Or that Blake fellow. Ugh. I wished I could unsee his text. "Just a friend," I said. "And I wasn't . . . I'm not . . . Adrian and I weren't . . . well, we were different, and I don't know that I ever want anyone else. I think that he was the one for me and I should just leave it there."

He sighed.

I cut him off before he could say anything else. "Love you, Papa. Gotta go."

He blew me a kiss and the screen faded to black.

SIXTEEN

I BUDGETED two hours to get to the Juniper offices in Houston the next morning for the eight a.m. meeting, but I got up at five. I'd had the luxury of an early-to-bed evening since both kids no-showed on the Monday-night Skype call with Papa and me. I wasn't happy with them, but I was well rested for a soul-cleansing run before sunrise, with the temperature a blessed seventy-five degrees. We weren't yet into the long dog-days of summer when the temperature never fell below eighty degrees at night.

After my run, I drove into the Heights, fighting traffic while I planned my strategy for the day. After Juniper, I'd head to the gallery. Part of me wanted to show up at Nancy Little's office and get her to explain herself to me face-to-face, but the lawyer part of me knew better. That was a job for Greyhound. I barely braked to turn into our metal-fenced parking lot, parked with a stomping of my brakes, and hustled toward the door. I pulled the time up on my phone as I pushed inside: 7:59.

"Michele," the receptionist said. She sounded delighted. "Long time, no see."

"Two weeks," I said to Marsha. "But it feels a lot longer."

"It sure does." She took her glasses off her nose and let them dangle from their bejeweled strap. "Are you joining the others for—"

"Yes, ma'am. Just gonna grab coffee first. Which conference room?"

"All the way to the back. They've got coffee set up in there."

"Thanks." I trotted down the hall.

It was never a good idea to come to the Juniper offices with a hangover or stomach bug. The walls were blanketed with sports paraphernalia in a jarring kaleidoscope of colors that could trigger sprints to the bathroom. Mostly the décor was Houston teams, but Brian commemorated significant events and sports figures as well: pennants, jerseys, cleats, sails off sailboats, helmets, ticket stubs, wheels, and racing silks. It was . . . a lot.

I entered the conference room just before the clock hit 8:01.

"At the buzzer, Michele Lopez Hanson for three," Brian announced.

I squeezed into a chair. A chorus of hellos sounded, and I greeted my coworkers. Juniper wasn't a large company. We had graphic artists, editors, sales people who sold ad space, and marketing and promotional types who focused mainly on getting our brand out in the digital world these days. The rest of our work we contracted out. All the heads of state of our various divisions were present this morning. I was the potentate for editing.

Brian pointed at the beverage cart. Coffee.

"Yes, sir. Thank you, sir." I got back up and poured myself a black coffee and held it aloft to keep it from sloshing out on my walk back to the table.

Brian kicked off the meeting while I struggled to adjust. I hadn't been lying when I told Marsha that two weeks felt much longer. It was odd to be in this space with these people. I scanned the room, trying to feel connected. Jerry—an older guy I'd worked with since I'd escaped from the practice of law and been hired as an under-qualified editing assistant—caught me looking at him and smiled at me. One by one, I took them in. Old, young, short, tall, heavy, thin, dark, light, man, woman. Brian had put together a top-notch team. Very diverse. Very talented. Kind and welcoming. So why did I feel out of step to their tune, like my rhythm had changed in the country?

"We've huddled up today," Brian was saying, "to talk about converting to a virtual workplace. This area of town is hot. I've had offers on the building."

There was collective mumbling and gasping. This was groundbreaking for Brian, even though he had been willing to try it with me. And it had nothing to do with the *Archery Collector's Edition*. The sneaky devil had lured me here under false pretenses.

"Michele is squaring off with it this summer, but I'm looking for each of you to audible in this play to your team. Warm up slow, establish some standards and trust, then bring it on home."

I was reeling. I might not have an office to return to in the fall. Yes, it felt strange to be here, but it was like when you graduate and your parents sell the house you grew up in. You don't want to move back there, but you want to know you can hold on to your memories and your safety net, your *choice*. Brian was taking my choice away. Our very way of working had grown old-fashioned, antiquated, and decrepit. The negative words started piling up in my brain. Was I talking about myself or the building?

"So, everyone's okay with this?" Brian said. "It's a new playbook, but this is a team with heart and resilience." He pumped his fist in the air, and a few people said, "Yeah!" and pumped the air, too. I didn't say anything, just let it soak in. Brian encouraged questions, and people discussed the new arrangement with enthusiasm.

Afterward, as everyone gathered their things and filed out, chattering as they went, Brian put his hand on my arm.

"You have a minute?"

"Absolutely."

I followed him to his corner office. It was catty-corner from mine, which was dark inside, like someone had died. Brian took a seat at his desk, leaning back with his hands behind his head and arms akimbo, a sight I'd seen daily for the last ten years. I wondered how many times I would see it again, if ever.

"You're off your game, kiddo. What's up?"

I was embarrassed to be so transparent. "Oh, you know."

"Your mom dying, Adrian gone, the kids away for the first time. You've got a lot of balls in the air. I'm here if you need me."

I sucked in a breath of relief at his understanding, then heaved it out. "Thanks, Brian. You're a good friend."

"Am I missing anything?"

"No. You've about summed it up."

"Anything I can do for you?"

"Just keep the work coming." I stood up. "I don't like to be bored."

He grinned and got to his feet, Oompa Loompa-ish in his puffy blue Starter jacket. I really loved this man. He was one of the best people I'd ever known, and endlessly hilarious, whether he meant to be or not. "So you're working on the book today?"

"Yes, but I worked ahead this weekend and last night so everything's on target, including the *Archery Collector's Edition*." I gave him a thumbs-up.

"I know you're a straight arrow." He waved his hand.

A thought struck me. "Remember you told me about Gidget Becker at the photo shoot of a Houston Oiler, the one in an old *Who's Who* mag?"

"I do."

"Is there a way to figure out who he was?"

"We had at least one Oiler in each issue."

"I imagine. But maybe the photographer remembers?"

"We had different photographers for nearly every shoot."

"Oh."

"Let me ask around and see, though."

I walked to his door and stopped, turning back to him. "That would be awesome."

"Good luck."

"Thanks, boss." I walked away with heavy footsteps and mixed emotions. So many things I'd counted on were coming to an end.

Houston highways and streets were like a different planet at nine thirty than they were at seven thirty. I cruised five miles above the speed limit down 290 to 59 toward downtown, peeling off at the Main Street exit. I drove into the Museum District and started looking for my street. I nearly missed it and swung the Jetta to the left, barely making the corner and running into and over the curb. *There goes my alignment.* By the time I'd put my car back in the street and driven a few hundred feet, I'd passed the gallery. I swung the Jetta into a U-turn and parked across the street from the scene of my curb-hopping.

Montrose Fine Art Gallery was in a "modern" two-story building that looked as if it had once been a home. The gallery was at least forty years old. Modern then was not the same as modern now, and this house seemed 1960s-modern.

I grabbed my handbag and smoothed my linen pant legs, then straightened the matching jacket, together comprising the second-least-casual outfit I'd taken to Nowheresville. The flat sandals with their narrow straps were not as comfortable as my running sandals. Houston summer clothes felt constricting after a few weeks dressed for workouts and country home office. The front door opened, and I startled. No one was exiting, and there was no hand on the door. Automatic, I realized. On a sensor, maybe, or activated by a button inside. I stepped through. The glare of the sun blinded me as I entered the relative dark of the gallery. I took a few sightless steps, feeling like a mole and trying not to bump into anything that would eat me.

"May I help you?" A young woman. I tracked toward the sound of her snotty voice.

"Just a moment while my eyes adjust."

She didn't reply. I got a fix on her silhouette, and slowly her face came into view. She was a thin-to-the-point-of-anorexic twenty-something with flat-ironed black hair hanging past her shoulders. Thick black eyeliner under flat eyes. Bright red lipstick on pursed lips. Translucent skin. She had on a Dior outfit that probably cost as much as I made in a year. She occupied a tall stool. Her clamped knees were tucked under a glass desk. The top was bare, and I could see through to her hands in her lap. No telephone. No register or iPad. No computer. Nothing. Not even any brochures of the art in the gallery.

A woman about my own mother's age was standing in front of her. She had shoulder-length dark hair blending into a dark jacket of the same color.

"Sorry, Ms. Sloane," the receptionist said, her voice chastising me as the other woman avoided looking at me.

I blocked them both out. And that's when I noticed the art. It was otherworldly. Colorful paint splashed across metal in tall abstract shapes, almost alien. A milky white glowed from the walls, and the floors were an industrial-looking stained concrete.

Her voice grew even snottier. "I said, can I help you."

The other woman studied her shoes.

I smiled sweetly at her. "Sorry, just browsing."

"This isn't Walmart."

I was so shocked, I had no reply. I heard a buzzing noise that I realized was inside my own head. A chainsaw that I wanted to smash through her glass desk. My fists balled. Who did this vapid little twit think she was? I breathed through my noise, pictured the tension meter and willed it down from the instant 9. Behind me the front door opened again. I turned to see who was entering as I took smooth, cleansing breaths. I recognized the face with the Mark Twain mustache immediately. Gidget's partner, Lester Tillman.

I put on my most winning smile, trying to forget the supercilious creature behind the desk. "Mr. Tillman, good morning. I'm . . . Marsha Bryan," I adlibbed, "here from Juniper Media." I stuck out my hand and he took it, a confused look on his face. "We have a ten o'clock appointment for your interview, and I'm afraid I'm early."

The man standing before me looked younger than Gidget had at the time of her death, yet he'd founded the gallery and brought her in as a twenty-year-old. He had to be older than her. I pegged him at seventy. He dressed fortyish, in a bow tie and saddle oxfords with designer jeans and a Ralph Lauren shirt.

"Of course." His Georgia accent evoked ripe peaches. "Right this way, Ms. Bryan." He nodded toward the desk. "Julie."

The matronly woman said, "Um hmm."

I shot a look of victory at the receptionist, but she was picking at her fake nails. I followed Lester across the high-ceilinged apex of the gallery. It was empty except for one sculpture twenty feet high.

Lester caught me looking at it. "Do you like it?"

"Um, it's very tall." I wanted to retract the unflattering statement, but it was too late.

He laughed. "The artist, Henry Chavez, is a very short man. Methinks he's trying to compensate for something. His pieces are selling very well, though. He's the next big thing on the Houston art scene."

His work didn't do anything for me. "Impressive."

Lester opened a hidden door built into a section of paneling. It led to a narrow hallway with gleaming blonde hardwoods. Bare walls created a tunnel feel broken only by doors. Lester turned into one on his left. I peeked back to my right and saw an Asian man about my age. His eyebrows were raised high. I nodded at him, then turned into the room Lester had entered.

The space was small and efficient. A little bitty Apple Air sat in the middle of his desk. Wall posters announced gallery exhibitions for different artists over many years. I recognized Andy Warhol, of course. Most were unfamiliar to me.

Lester gestured to a Keurig coffee maker on a credenza. "Something to drink?"

"I can make myself a coffee."

"Great."

"Can I make one for you?" I smiled at him.

He lifted a tall, stainless steel travel mug from the desk. "I'm good."

I popped French Roast into the slot.

"So, Ms. Bryan, tell me what I can do for you and your publication today?"

I shot him a smile over my shoulder. My coffee finished dripping into the cup, and I took it to the metal chair with spindly legs in front of his desk. The hard plastic under my tush reminded me of school cafeterias.

"I'm writing an article about Gidget Becker." I put my phone on his desk. "Would you prefer I take notes or record?"

He scanned his phone, shifting in his seat. "Ms. Bryan, I confess. I don't seem to have noted our appointment on my calendar."

"Oh my goodness. Well, I'll make it as fast as I can, then. And no recorder." I pulled out a yellow legal pad and pen.

He twirled the end of his mustache.

I hurried before he could respond. "So, how did Gidget come to work with you?"

He straightened his posture. "If you've done your homework, then you know from the many articles written about us that she was the most promising art student at the University of Houston. I was lucky to entice her here."

His tone raised hackles on my neck. I'd fallen asleep reading an article on my phone the night before. What little I'd read was scant on detail, and I knew I needed to step up the research. "Always best to hear it from the horse's mouth. Did she come on as an intern?"

"At first, but she quickly proved herself valuable. The gallery was new, and other than her, it was just me. She was a godsend."

"And became an owner."

"Yes."

"And how did that come about?"

He tugged at his bowtie. "Ownership interest as a reward and enticement. Kind of like stock options, but in a privately held company."

"I see. I'd love to see the papers on that. It's historically significant, now that the gallery is a landmark in the art world."

He laughed, a brittle bark. "Oh, heavens. Didn't I just tell you this place was only me back then? We did it on a handshake. The old-fashioned way, and it worked out just marvelously."

"And you were partners for the better part of four decades?"

He nodded. "Longer than any other relationship in my life except my parents. Neither Gidget nor I ever found the right man." He winked.

"Tell me about your partnership. What kind of work did each of you do?"

"Gidget was a born flirt and was pretty enough to carry it off, in the early days. She coupled that with brains and a personal understanding of what it took to be an artist. She became the face of the gallery. The media loved her and the artists adored her. I, on the other hand, had less success with the human side of things"—his mouth formed a moue—"and focused on the business end."

"Gidget handled the public and was primarily the person artists would interact with?"

He pondered a second. "Unless they needed me."

"Are you an artist, Mr. Tillman?"

"Never any good," he said. "But that didn't stop me from trying."

"What's your medium?"

He looked over my shoulder and waved a hand. My eyes followed his and I saw the retreating back of the Asian guy from across the hall. "Mixed media. It'll be the death of me."

"Did Gidget have any particularly special relationships with anyone that I should talk to as I research the article?"

He looked at his fingernails.

A student of his own appearance.

"Not really. Gidget did remarkably well her first few years at the gallery. She was personal friends with some of the most celebrated artists in the world, and she remained an important figure all of her career. But, she engaged in behaviors that alienated her from anyone who tried to get close."

"What kind of behaviors?"

"Well, it was common knowledge she was a hopeless addict. I've lost count of how many times we staged interventions, sent her to rehab, or carted her somewhere to dry out."

"That's too bad."

He popped the cuffs on his shirt. "No one is perfect. Not Gidget and certainly not me."

"So what about you?"

"What about me?"

"Where'd you go to school?"

"I grew up in Savannah, and I've always been a little obsessed with the art world."

"How did that lead to Houston?"

"I went to school at the University of Texas and stuck around. Started the gallery. Never left."

I gazed down at my notes, scribbled the word Pompous. "Do you know whether Gidget had a daughter?" I cut my eyes up quickly to see his reaction.

He froze. No more pulling on cuffs or bow ties or his mustache. Finally he spoke. "Heavens, no. I don't doubt she could have gotten pregnant. Men flocked to her from the day I met her. That former fiancé of hers showed up." He wrinkled his nose. I wrinkled my forehead. Jimmy? But I didn't interrupt. "A randy minister she knew from her teen years, too. It was a wild time, and she was a wild girl. But I would have known if she had a baby."

I circled my scribble and wondered if people ever talked about my mother like this. I'd punch them in the face if they did. "How did your partnership end?"

He exhaled. "She was in rough shape. She was desperate for cash and asked me to buy her out, which I ultimately did. We executed mutual powers of attorney, in case something happened to either of us. Anyway, thank God we did, because right after her parents died, she had an aneurysm, the poor thing. And that was it, really."

"What do you mean, 'that was it'?"

"She wanted to move home, be done with the gallery. I helped her. She wasn't right in her head anymore. Never was again."

"Did you inherit anything in her will?"

His eyes went dark. "I'm the independent executor of her estate and the trustee for the arts foundation she set up as the nonprofit beneficiary. That was her last and dearest wish, you know, to keep giving to the Houston art community."

I looked him straight in the eye, trying to hide my growing disgust. He was so wrong about Gidget's last wish, and her last will, for that matter. "So I guess the revenue for the pipeline being built through her family place will be the first big infusion of cash for the trust?"

"Yes." He blinked. "Um, I mean, I don't . . . what?"

SEVENTEEN

I HAD LESS than I wanted from Lester, but I could make another run at him later if research and other witnesses didn't fill in the gaps he'd left. As he led me out, the Asian guy I'd seen earlier cat-footed to the door of his office. Without a word, he stuck his arm out toward me and shoved a folded piece of paper in my hand. He put a finger to his lips. I nodded once. He slipped back into his office so quickly he was outside of Lester's range of vision by the time the older man had opened the door at the end of the hall and turned back to hold it for me.

I preceded Lester through the cavernous gallery with its bright, eerie metal sculptures. When we reached the front desk, the snooty receptionist didn't glance up from contemplation of her knees.

"Thank you again, Mr. Tillman."

Lester and I shook. Callouses rimmed his thumb and index finger, but otherwise his hand was silky smooth.

His accent deepened. "If you have any other questions, feel free to call."

Was it my imagination, or did he emphasize the last word? "Absolutely."

The door swung open, spilling heat and dampness into the dry, cool oasis. I held my head erect as I walked out, then straightened my shoulders and leaned into the wall of wet. I glanced back from the Jetta. Lester stood at the glass, making sure I would leave, no doubt. I saluted him and he raised one hand laconically, Kevin Spacey in *Midnight in the Garden of Good and Evil*. I shuddered.

I was dying to read the note, but I decided to get out of view first. I made a few turns then parked in front of a dry cleaner's. A beige Land Rover pulled in and parked on my passenger side. I'd clutched the note in my hand, even as I held the steering wheel. Now it was damp and wadded. Oops. I unfolded it in my lap. It was written in smeared ink on gallery stationery. I stared at the ink blotches, willing them into legibility. I made out *Catalina Coffee, half an hour*. The rest was a lost cause. Well, I knew who'd handed it to me, and I had a place and a time. Or I probably had a time, anyway.

I headed north. Catalina Coffee was on the south side of the Heights, which in turn was west of downtown and north of the arts district. It took about fifteen minutes to traverse the lighted streets between the gallery and the coffee shop. Right before I parked, I saw a Land Rover pass on a side street, the same tan color as the one earlier. Well, we were on the edge of River Oaks, an expensive area. Walking in from the dirt parking lot, I was overcome with nostalgia. Adrian—as a professional triathlete and freelance writer—had been able to schedule his days as he pleased. That included spending them where he wanted to when he worked. His most frequent hangout had been Fioza's, a coffee shop near our house. But his second-favorite haunt was Catalina Coffee.

Sometimes I'd meet him at Catalina after one of his working sessions, and we'd go to lunch. I touched the butterfly around my neck. Warm. I wandered to the counter, lost in memories as I read the chalkboard menu.

"Welcome to Catalina Coffee. What can I get you?" I'd seen this barista before. A young guy with ear disks and unruly light-brown hair. He glanced up at me and did a double take.

"Hey, you're um . . ."

I smiled. "Michele."

He grinned back. "You used to come in here with Adrian."

"Yes, I did."

"I'm real sorry. About him, uh . . ."

"Me, too." I remembered they used to keep expensive Kona coffee behind the counter, just for Adrian. "You don't happen to have any of his Kona left, do you?"

He cocked his head, his eyes searching shelves as he pondered. They lit up. "I'll be right back."

The people in line behind me shifted back and forth, their shoes making impatient noises, but I didn't care.

The young man returned with a bag of Kona, which he held aloft.

"About a fourth of a bag left. Sealed up real good, so the beans are probably still fresh."

I cleared my throat. "Well, then, I'll have an Adrian special."

"One large Kona with almond milk and maple syrup, latte style. For here or to go?"

My eyes burned. I wasn't the only one who remembered my husband and his big splurge. He had an aversion to all things plastic and processed that included to-go cups, even if they were made of paper. "For here, please," I said.

The barista had already started grinding beans. "Have a seat. I'll bring it out to you, Michele."

"Thanks. And I'm sorry, what's your name?"

"Hayden." He raised his voice to be heard over the whir of the grinder.

"Thanks, Hayden."

I took a seat at one of the low-slung metal chairs at a table in the back. I pulled the crumpled note out, scrutinizing it closely. I'd obliterated the writing in the middle of the page, below the legible part. The last blot appeared to be someone's name. The guy who'd handed it to me? I didn't know his name, so there was no way to be sure. He could have been handing it off for Jack the Ripper or—less likely—the snotty receptionist.

Hayden set an enormous mug and saucer in front of me.

"Beautiful. Thank you."

He held up the near-empty bag of Kona. "Do you want the rest? We don't use it because it's too expensive and nobody else wants to pay to upgrade their brew, but I won't tell if you don't."

I reached into my handbag and got a ten. He put the tightly rolled coffee bag into my hand, and I slid the ten into his.

"You don't have to do that."

"Neither did you."

We smiled at each other for a moment, then he set his heel and wheeled around like he was on a skateboard, returning to his work area.

I searched the faces in the room, looking for a familiar one here to meet with me. I got nothing. I scrolled through my email, answered a few, felt guilty for not texting Rashidi to see how his interviews went, flagged a few, felt guilty for not answering Blake, and listened to a voice mail from Ralph telling me he would be staying in El Paso for a day or two while his granddaughter packed.

I decided to make a sprint to the bathroom. It was occupied. Mere seconds later, the door opened. A woman with a five-o'clock shadow and enormous Adam's apple stepped out. She had on a turquoise silk shift and sparkly silver heels. Dressy for midmorning in Houston, but gorgeous.

"Your dress is beautiful."

"Thank you," she answered, her voice a deep bass.

Another woman entered the shop by the back door. The sunlight behind her rendered her nothing but a silhouette. But her voice was very clear. "Excuse me, you can't just use the women's restroom."

I put my fingers to my chest in question. Was she talking to me? But no, she blew past me, after the woman in the shift, who'd hustled out the front, lickety-split in her heels.

I slipped into the bathroom, cringing. I'd seen men in women's rooms before—if the woman I'd just seen was even genetically male, and not just genetically unfortunate. I used the men's room any time the women's was full, as long as it met basic sanitation standards. But I'd never seen anyone make a big to-do about it, until today. This HERO thing had people acting like damn fools.

I returned to my table, eyes on my phone, scrolling through Instagram, stalking my kids. As I sat down, a female body suddenly filled the chair across from me. Simultaneously, my phone dinged with a text. Before I could tear my attention away from the phone, I saw it was from Sam. Since he'd stood us up on Skype, I had left him a voice mail, sent him an email, and inbox messaged him on Facebook, then texted him again this morning at a red light.

I read *"Oh gee Mom, I'm so sorry. You're going to be totally mad at me"* before I tore my eyes away. I looked up at a stranger. "Hello."

"You're Marsha?" she asked.

The woman's hair was teased high and held firmly in place. It was a brilliant orange, flame-like, really, and her lipstick only a shade darker. She was well preserved, surgically so, with the suddenly Siamese look to her eyes, thinness of facial skin, and limp plumpness that screamed *I've had expensive work done.* She was Tlazol, the plasticized version. I was so caught up in her skin that it took me a second to find my manners.

"Yes, and you are?"

She leaned in. "Diana. But I'd appreciate it if you'd just call me an anonymous source."

I pressed my lips together to keep from giggling. Drama much? She was dressed for it, though. Cheetah-print stretch pants, a white tunic with three-quarter sleeves and a cleavage keyhole. I resisted the urge to lean over and check out her feet, but I pictured her stumbling tipsily on three-inch stiletto slings with a pouf of marabou at the toes.

"Okay. Then call me Michele."

She winked. "Sure."

"So, Diana, how do you know me?"

"Jacques called me from the gallery." She sniffed. "We share a mutual contempt for that pretender Lester. He's trying to write Gidget out of her place in the history of the Houston art scene."

"Aahh."

"It's just wrong, no matter what her problems were. Anyway, Jacques said he asked you to meet me here." Her accent was pure east Texas, southeast to be exact. Beaumont or Orange, maybe, but probably something considerably smaller.

"And here I am."

"You can ask me anything you want."

"About . . . ?"

"For your article about Gidget. I know everything. We were the best of friends."

"Great. Would you mind if I record you?"

She touched her cheeks gently with her finger pads, like she was making sure her enhancements hadn't slid off her face. "Of course not."

"And, Diana, not that I would ever use your name, but in case I need to get ahold of you again . . . ?"

"Call Jacques."

"Last name, phone number, address?"

"Oh, honey." She laid her hand across her framed décolletage. "I can't take the risk."

I pressed my phone a few times, and like magic it pulled up the recorder. "How did you know Gidget?"

"My first husband, the cheating bastard, introduced me to the gallery. We were decorating our home. His ex-wife had hideous taste." She placed her palms flat on the table. A perfect red manicure tipped each finger. She lowered her chest onto her hands. Through the keyhole, I could see that her breasts kept their perfect shape even under pressure. "I was just a girl. And he was a horny old bastard who couldn't keep it in his pants. I should've realized, but a girl in love will believe anything."

Again, I had to squelch my urge to laugh.

"I mean, all that money. I was so in love with all his money." She laughed, so I joined in. "I've never loved anything more in my life. Until he left me, and I married an even bigger pile of it. By then, I was thick as thieves with Gidget. I was the one who gave her the nickname, you know."

"I didn't."

"When she came to town she was calling herself 'Anna.'" She said the word as if it tasted like cod-liver oil. "But she was clearly a Gidget."

"She was already at the gallery when you first started shopping there?" I wasn't sure you shopped at a hoity-toity place like an art gallery, but I didn't know what else to call it.

"No, but she was there before I married my second husband. She had taken over meeting with clients. She set up interviews with the artists so we could understand their work better. Helped us select pieces. Sourced art for us when we were looking for something special."

"And she was good at it?"

"She was the best, sugar. In no time she knew everybody who was anybody in the art world in Houston. I took it upon myself to introduce her to the right kind of people—you know, the ones who could blow a wad of cash without blinking."

"What a good friend."

She dipped her head, accepting my praise. Diana, if that was really her name, suddenly sat straight up. "The table service here is terrible."

"You have to order at the bar."

"How gauche."

"I'll take a water if you don't mind."

She weaved her way to the counter. She was not only in heels much like what I'd pictured, but with a platform stacked under the forefoot. I was starting to believe she was three sheets to the wind, too.

She was back in a few minutes and wobbled into her chair. "The boy is going to bring our drinks."

"Great." I had turned off the voice app while she was gone. I pressed record.

"Could you remind me of what we were talking about, hon? I can't quite put my finger on it."

"You were telling me about all the . . . clients . . . you brought Gidget. I guess that's why Lester gave her an interest in the gallery?"

Diana raised her perfectly drawn, pencil-thin eyebrows. "Where'd you get an idea like that, sugar? Gidget had an interest in the gallery when she walked in the door."

I kept my own eyebrows from shooting sky-high somehow. I made a mental note to confirm when she started with the gallery. "Really? Tell me about it."

"I shouldn't, but I know how much it must have meant to Gidget for somebody to write an article about her." She tapped one of her acrylics against her lip. "Let's just say somebody important didn't want Gidget flapping her gums about their relationship."

"So she was involved with someone with money?"

"Then and a bunch of other times. But this guy? He had loads of it, and power, too. Going back generations."

"And he was married?" This seemed an obvious conclusion, but I asked anyway.

She looked up, waited a beat, then said, "Still is, I hear. She must be a glutton for punishment. He's a notorious womanizer—the younger the better."

Hayden placed a tiny cup and saucer in front of Diana. "Your espresso, ma'am." He handed me a bottle of water and winked.

"Thank you."

Diana pulled a twenty from her wallet and thrust it at him.

"Um," he said. "Uh . . ."

She continued to hold it out. "Well?"

"Thank you." He took the money, keeping his eyes on his feet.

"So, you were telling me about Gidget's lover."

"Lester was desperately searching for money for this gallery, and he was tight with the man and his family. They bought Gidget off and propped Lester up all in one fell swoop."

"Was any of this public knowledge?" I twisted the cap off my water.

"Oh, heavens no. That was the condition. She had to keep her mouth shut." She sipped her espresso and made a face. "And get rid of it."

"What?"

"Get rid of the baby."

This was the first confirmation I'd had from anyone that Gidget had ever been pregnant. My heart raced in my chest. "Oh, Diana, that must have been terrible for her."

She took another sip with her pinky straight as an arrow, pointing out to the side. She set it down.

"About as terrible as for any other young woman of her time." She inspected her nails.

I picked up on her hint. "I just can't imagine how hard it was for women before my generation."

She sighed long and hard. "You have no idea what it took to get where I am, let me tell you. It wasn't pretty." And then she smiled. "But it was worth it."

I was sure I did have an idea. I smiled back at her even though I was curdling a little bit inside. "So, Gidget told you she'd had an abortion?"

"Well, she told me she got rid of the baby."

My heart sped up. Doublespeak. Adoption was getting rid of a baby, too. "Did she ever mention the baby again?"

"You mean the pregnancy. Only when she was really wasted. When she'd go all Valley of the Dolls, she'd sob about her baby, her baby, her little girl."

"It was a little girl?"

"Oh Lord, I don't know if it was ever even born, or if it was a little girl or not. I don't think Gidget knew, either. I think she was just sad."

A sweet pain filled my chest. My mother. My brother. "Did she tell anyone else?" I took a big slug of water. Then another.

"She talked about it in front of anybody and everybody when she was wasted. And there came a point in time where she was always wasted. I tried very hard, but she simply got too out of control. It was beginning to impact my reputation at an inopportune time." I must have looked blank, because she added, "Between marriages."

I nodded. "Did you lose contact with her?"

"I stayed on as a client of the gallery. It was heartbreaking to watch that little thing waste herself away. Honestly, she was a sweetheart. I love every piece she ever found for me, and I will always treasure her for that."

I took another sip of water, thinking. "So she was good with the artists?"

"Yes, she was an artist herself. I have one of her pieces. But there was talk, you know"—she leaned forward so far she could have kissed me—"that she was dealing to the artists." She sat back, a smug look on her face.

My mouth fell open. "How well sourced is that?"

"Just rumor, but she was their darling, and they were all using. She was even"—she finger-patted her cheekbones again—"BFFs with Andy Warhol." She half-rolled her eyes. "Everybody in town pandered after her as long as he was alive, trying to get closer to him."

"Wow." But I wasn't surprised.

"I've already told you one. Might as well tell you the other rumor." She winked. "That he painted her portrait and gave it to her."

"Okay."

"Obviously you don't understand, or you would have just screamed. People say he gave her an exclusive Andy Warhol that no one else in the world has ever even seen. If it existed, it would be priceless. The rumor alone cemented her place in the art community. Nobody cared that she was a hot mess. They just wanted to be near the woman that was the subject of the secret Warhol painting."

I opened my eyes wide. "Oh my goodness."

I must have done better, because she nodded and took the last sip of her espresso.

"Is there anybody else I should talk to about Gidget? Old lovers, other friends, special clients?"

"Most of them are as dead as she is."

"What about her lover?"

"Oh, honey, no, no, no. I'm taking that name to the grave. I value my life —what's left of it—a little too much for that." She stood and threw back her helmet of orange hair with a flourish.

"Thank you, Diana," I said. "I may be in touch."

She paused long enough to throw me a smile. Somewhere between her lips and my brain she morphed into the grimacing visage of the horror puppet Chucky. She walked jerkily, the pawn of an unskilled puppet master.

EIGHTEEN

My head was spinning as I left Catalina Coffee. Diana had blown up most of what I thought I knew with choice revelations and a few confirmations. I hit my key fob as I walked, replaying bits of Diana's story in my mind and comparing it to what Lester had told me just a few hours before. I wasn't watching where I was going, and I ran smack-dab into another human.

She cried out, "Hey!"

"Oh my gosh, I'm so sorry." My words spilled out before I caught a glimpse of her.

The angry sneer on her face turned into a tentative smile when she recognized me. "Michele." Scarlett, the publicist who had worked on My Pace for Juniper until we learned she'd been feeding speculation and negative items to the press to keep us trending.

I hadn't seen her since, and I didn't respond to her now. I stepped around her and powered by. My anger at her renewed, boiling in a snap.

"Michele." Her voice was soft.

I stopped but didn't face her.

"I'm sorry."

I still didn't turn around, but I answered her. "Sorry doesn't quite cover the damage you did to my kids and to me. To Adrian's memory. Negative gossip is front-page news, and the correction is last section, last page, beneath the fold, buried in the classifieds."

"I know." She put a hand on my arm. I flinched involuntarily, but I didn't pull away. "I thought what I was doing helped sell more books, and that's what I was hired to make happen. But I hurt you. I shouldn't have done some of what I did without your permission."

I lifted my hair from my neck, suddenly hot. I didn't want to understand Scarlett's side of the fiasco she'd wrought upon us last year, but I'd also had a long time to think about it. From a publicity perspective, what she said was true. "Thank you."

"Can we start over?"

I took the whole package of Scarlett in. Today she'd coiled her hair into black ringlets. Her medium roast skin and pink cheeks glowed. She radiated vitality and sensuality in a red flowing blouse and black pleated pants, with scarlet fingernails and matching shoes. The black-as-pitch gleam in her eyes had softened from tigress to house cat. I didn't want to be best friends with her, but hate was a burden.

I nodded, just barely. "I can let it go."

The feline eyes moistened. "That means a lot to me. You made me a better publicist and human being, I promise. I can't thank you enough for that gift, and I know it came at a very high cost to you."

I exhaled, a long sigh. "You made me a stronger person, but I'm not ready to say thank you."

She laughed, her eyes glistening. "Is there anything I can do to make it up to you?"

I took a beat to think about it. Publicity was always critical for an author and a publishing company. And I was about to write a book that was important to me. "I'll take a rain check."

"Good. What are you up to these days?"

"Telecommuting with Juniper for the summer, from a place in the country that Adrian bought for us. And I'm working on a new book. A biography."

"Really?" She changed before my eyes, crouching on all fours, licking her chops, ready to spring, still wearing her snazzy publicist outfit, but with tiger stripes on her face, neck, and long, twitching tail. "About Adrian?"

Down, kitty. "Oh no. About a woman who just passed away, a longtime fixture in the Houston art scene. Gidget Becker."

"Yes, yes, good." Her eyes followed her prey, unblinking. "I just saw our biggest patron of the arts in the last few decades walking to her car." She pointed to the side street. "Coincidence?"

I felt a quickening in my pulse. "Do you know her?"

"Of her. She's a piece of work."

"What's her name?"

Scarlett moved a ringlet carefully away from her face. "You don't know her name? I thought you were together."

"You jump to a lot of conclusions." I held still, unwilling to beg.

"Darlene Hogg, two g's. Hogg is her fourth or fifth married name. Low-rent east Texas origins. One of those little hurricane-magnet towns where toothless trailer-park residents refuse to evacuate."

I had to laugh. Catty, snarky, and poised for the jugular. That was Scarlett. "Thank you."

"Does this mean we're even?" She raised her left eyebrow without wrinkling her forehead.

I snorted.

She held up both hands. "Got it. You know how to reach me."

"I do."

She threw her arms around me and pulled me close, my body stiff. "You are an amazing woman. I'll deny it if you ever repeat this, but you're an inspiration to me." She squeezed, and I could barely breathe. "I can't have anyone thinking I've gone soft. Scarlett, the piranha of publicity."

I patted her back and slipped out of her embrace. "Well, you're living up to it. Except for right now, I guess."

She released, ducking to hide her face, but I saw her wet cheeks. I was almost speechless. No, I was speechless. The piranha/tigress was crying over me. We parted, me to my car, her inside Catalina Coffee.

Really, what I'd done for her was send her career into orbit last year. Her shenanigans lured people to her. I stood next to my car, lost in thought and staring in the general direction of some town homes across yet another dirt lot, this one rutted and uneven. I opened the door of the car, the suffocating heat reaching out for me. Once inside with the air on, I checked my phone. Sam. I'd already read the part about how mad I was going to be at him, so I skipped forward. *"Terrence quit. People here are a-holes. I want to come home."*

My brows furrowed. Teenagers. I texted back: *"What happened to super awesome? Give it a few days. I love you. And you better show up on Skype next week."* I couldn't help but worry about him a little, but I also felt sure it would pass.

Next I texted Rashidi, because that's what friends do. *"Hope your interviews were great."*

I put both hands on the steering wheel, evaluating my options. I could check on the Houston house, but that seemed like a lot of drive for not much payoff. Our neighborhood in Meyerland was about as safe as it gets in an urban area, and I'd paid my neighbors to keep an eye on it for the summer. I could drive back to Juniper, make a little more face time. I could confront Lester over the difference in his story from Diana/Darlene's. Or I could beat the traffic, grab a late lunch on the way home, and dig in to researching the leads and contradictory information I'd been given.

No-brainer. What a country bumpkin I'd already become. And truly, I should have been researching all this already, but there'd been no time since Gidget's death.

I quickly navigated out to I-10 and took the 99 Loop for variety. I kept the station tuned into The Bull for as long as I had signal. It crapped out in Carmine, so I pulled into the fancy gourmet grocery/Valero station. In my peripheral vision, I caught a dark tan Land Rover coasting down the side road through town, back toward me from the west. I'd developed a paranoia about being followed after the woman who murdered Adrian had stalked Sam and me and ultimately tried to kill us both. No one had believed me then, but I hadn't let them talk me out of what I knew to be real.

The hairs rose on the back of my neck. The Rover was driving the wrong direction, but having seen one like it three times now, I got that old familiar feeling. A bad one that got worse quickly, sending me into an emotional flashback. I was being tailed. That driver meant me ill. Maybe my family, too.

The angel on my right shoulder was raised by my mother. "I'm sure it's nothing."

And the little heathen on my left shoulder, the one I trusted implicitly, said, "Get a clue. The effing Rover is following you."

The SUV turned right toward JW's, the steakhouse people flocked to from a four-county area. The vehicle disappeared from my view, but not before I got a vague impression of the driver. White male, darkish hair, pale face, medium-tall based on his head clearance. I couldn't have picked him out in a lineup unless everyone else was his polar opposite, though. I pumped the gas and jammed the nozzle back in the pump when it was done. The heathen urged me to linger and confront him if he showed up, but the practical little angel said, "Don't ask for trouble."

In the end, my stomach and bladder made the decision for me. Pit stop time. I paid for a package of summer sausage and cheddar cheese out of the refrigerated display and shoved it in my handbag. I made a beeline for the ladies' room, which was decorated in country cute: beadboard paneling with a varnished cedar countertop and homey framed quotes. It was empty, and a growing sense of isolation came over me. I stood before the mirror, out of place. The woman staring back at me had big dark circles under her eyes. She looked tired. And old. I tried for the sake of my self-esteem to believe what people told me about my looks. That Eva Longoria had nothing on me. That if my life were a movie, Jennifer Lopez would play me. But the visual evidence was unmistakable to me. The wrong side of forty and not hiding it well. Frizzy hair. Flat, sad eyes. Short and curvy, but not in a wasp-waisted sort of way. More in a generous-tush way. Adrian had told me my curves are what he liked best about my body—he called my earthiness "sensual." But he was wrong.

I saw my *abuela*'s face in the mirror, and before my eyes Eva became Isabel and morphed into Tlazolteotl, bone earrings stretching her earlobes and a grotesque bone piercing hanging between her nostrils. A red snake draped her neck, and she held a broom in one hand, a bloody rope in the other. I backed up, blinking. The image wouldn't go away. I reached for my butterfly, but in the mirror, my hand touched the nose bone. My Tlazol face sneered. My lips moved, and I heard a rough version of my own voice with an unrecognizable accent. "I am the eater of filth, the giver of life. I bring the moon, and my lust consumes me. I grant absolution for the sins of the flesh." I whimpered, but the sound was only in my head.

I clamped my eyes shut, screwing up my face with the effort of banishing my delusions. I was losing it. *I should drive straight to a mental hospital from here and check myself in. They could give me something so I'd never see Tlazol again.* I peeked an eye open. Tlazol grinned, her teeth black and bloody. Then she faded away, leaving in her place my familiar, scared face.

I fled to the Jetta, turned it on, and threw it in gear. My tires squealed as I left the parking lot. All I cared about was escaping that wormhole into hell I'd stumbled into. I'd never, ever stop at that station again. I sped onto the highway, and an eighteen-wheeler honked and swerved. I pressed the accelerator to the floor. My speedometer hit ninety, ninety-five, one hundred. The Jetta started shaking. People coming the other direction down the highway flashed their lights at me, and I jerked my foot away from the pedal. As the speed dropped, I hit my cruise control at seventy-five. I flexed my fingers. They'd clutched the steering wheel in a death grip, and they were numb. I chomped down on a hangnail on one hand, pulled too hard, and it bled. I'd been holding my breath, too, and I was light-headed. I breathed in and out, slowly, careful not to hyperventilate.

My phone rang and I let it go to voice mail. I didn't want to have to talk to anyone when I was in a tizzy. And I was in a tizzy. A full-blown one. It was terrifying how fast I'd gone there. I'd been strong and surging on my new information just a little while before. What was wrong with me? Was I going crazy? Was my emotional apocalypse tied to the heat that suffused my body over and over each day and through the night, depriving me of restful sleep? Was it from the pain that was always there, like discordant background noise, sapping my strength? I hadn't felt this vulnerable since the Ironman last year when I'd totally lost it.

As miles passed and the visions receded in the distance, I calmed down. It was over. I didn't need a psych ward. My eyes kept darting to my rearview mirror, just to be sure. No Tlazol. *See? You're fine.* The last few miles home to Gidget's were a blur, though. I pulled up to the house and stumbled out of the car and through the gate. Gertrude put her paws on my shins, yapping a welcome. I crouched and hugged her. The butterfly locket rested in Gertrude's fur. My tension meter was below 10 now, but I still needed to take control of myself. I needed to hear Adrian's voice saying *"Visualize your happy place. Breathe in. Breathe out."*

I had only me, though, and when I visualized my happy place, I found myself back at our house in Meyerland with Adrian and the kids, before he died and they grew up enough not to need me anymore. It was vivid, bold, chaotic. Adrian was laughing, Annabelle and Sam were arguing, I was shouting for quiet and order. And it was beautiful.

I started to sob. My wails rent the silence, and my tears soaked into Gertrude's coarse fur locks. I released her, and my arms stretched in front of me. My palms grappled for purchase on the earth, finding only short grass and insubstantial weeds. I was so completely alone with my feelings, with what I was going through, with my entire life, dog or no dog. I pressed my forehead into the ground. Gertrude bathed me with sandpaper kisses as I sobbed until I had no more energy or tears left.

The sounds of a vehicle approaching made me raise my head. The Lee County Tahoe. Tank and Junior. Their footsteps crunched gravel. The gate creaked open and clicked shut. I rose to my knees, then sat back on my heels and scrubbed at my eyes.

It was Tank who spoke. "Michele Hanson, you're under arrest for the murder of Anna Becker."

I didn't move or say a word.

NINETEEN

I'D SPENT my fair share of time at the Houston Police Department after Adrian's murder. But never because I was the one under arrest. Cooling my heels in a locked room waiting to be questioned for a crime I didn't commit was a new one on me. The Lee County Sheriff's Department looked much the same as the Houston city-version, just smaller and with fewer people. Same nondescript room with a big table and uncomfortable chairs around it. Barely any room to squeeze into a chair between the table and the walls, which were completely bare save for scuff marks from chairbacks, briefcases, and shoes. The smell was different, though. HPD had smelled like dirty mop water and burned coffee. LCSD smelled like partially eaten Hot Pockets left in the trash too long.

I'd been nearly catatonic since the time Tank and Junior roused me from the ground at Gidget's place. Tank had refused my request to use the bathroom and change my clothes. They'd told me I could go to the ladies' room when we got to the LCSD building. But they started questioning me as soon as we arrived. I'd been silent except to say "lawyer," "bathroom," and "phone call." Junior had squirmed, and Tank had informed me that in his experience, only guilty people needed lawyers. Then Tank had admired the way his short-sleeved uniform cut into his upper arm, and they'd left.

Still no bathroom, and I was getting pissed off about it. That was a good thing. Anger meant adrenaline, and it was bringing me back to my senses. I picked at my cuticles savagely. The door opened, and a woman I'd noticed on our way in brought a phone to the table. She was wearing a sheriff's department uniform like Tank's and Junior's. She had thirty years on them, though.

She said, "Is there anything else you need, ma'am?"

"Phone book," I said. "Bathroom," I added, for like the hundredth time.

She nodded. "I'll be right back."

A minute later she returned and set a phone book beside the phone.

"Thank you," I said. "Bathroom?"

She nodded. "I'll send someone." She shut the door behind her so softly it didn't make a click.

I had an urge to just go where I was sitting, to show them all, but I didn't want to be left in yellowed white linen pants. Instead I grabbed the phone book. It felt weird in my hands. I hadn't used one in years. Because it was a rural directory, it contained both the white and yellow pages for several towns. Luckily, Round Top was one of them. I flipped to the yellow pages and then to A. I scanned until I found *Attorneys*, then the number I needed.

"Eldon Smith," Greyhound said.

Answering his own phone instead of letting a secretary or service get it? "Greyhound, this is Michele Lopez Hanson."

"Michele? The caller ID said Lee County Sheriff's Department."

"Those yay-hoo deputies showed up at Gidget's place and arrested me."

His voice rose. "For what?"

"The murder of Gidget."

"That's ridiculous!" He was almost shrill now.

"Correct." I pushed my bangs off my forehead. My hand continued across the top and down the back of my skull, grabbing my hair loosely until it got to the ends and slid off.

"What do they claim to base it on?"

"My fingerprints being all over everything in the house. And because I supposedly killed her to get my inheritance."

"Well, that's a load of crap. I can vouch that you didn't know a thing about it."

"I appreciate that, if and when the time comes that you need to do it. In the meantime, what I really need is somebody to help me get out of here."

"I'm on my way."

"And to make them let me use the bathroom," I added, but he'd already hung up.

Luckily, they'd left me cuffless. I folded my arms on the table and put my cheek on one forearm like it was a pillow. I must have fallen asleep, because when the door banged opened and a loud male voice said,

"Michele Hanson," I jumped. Drool had pooled on my arm and was dribbling down my chin.

"Here," I yelped, like a school girl. I tried again. "I'm Michele Lopez Hanson." I wiped drool off my face with the back of my hand.

"I'm Sheriff Kenny Boudreaux." A large man walked in, making the room feel immediately smaller. Sideburns and a handlebar moustache but no beard. Tired cowboy boots. A real ten-gallon hat. Not an old guy, but mature. Probably around my age.

He was imposing, but I waited him out.

"I understand you've elected not to speak to us until your attorney arrives?"

"Correct."

"And your attorney is?"

"Greyhound Smith."

He pulled at his chin. "Greyhound? A good man, an expensive lawyer."

"Gidget's lawyer."

He raised his eyebrows.

Tank poked his head around the doorjamb. "Sheriff? Attorney Smith is here for Ms. Hanson."

The sheriff smirked. "Looks like the cavalry has arrived."

He held up one finger, then turned away and shut the door. I scrubbed away crust and spittle from my lips. It was like I was waking up from a three-day bender, like a real-life Tlazol. The door opened again. The first face I saw was the sheriff's, then Greyhound appeared. He regarded me from behind serious horned-rimmed glasses. The weight pressing down on me lightened some.

The sheriff grinned. "We can talk now that your lawyer is here."

Greyhound squeezed himself into a chair beside me. "No, first I'll speak to my client. Alone."

The sheriff raised his eyebrows, lifted his hat, and scratched his head. "Ms. Hanson? That what you want?"

"Yes, after I get to go to the ladies' room."

The sheriff guffawed.

Greyhound stood. "Come on, Michele." He took my arm, and we pushed past the sheriff.

The sheriff hollered out the door. "Mary Lee, I'm leaving the cuffs off her, so you need to supervise her in the ladies' room, pronto."

The phone-book woman followed me into a white-tiled room with gloomy lighting.

"I won't make you leave the stall open if you promise not to do anything foolish." She didn't meet my eyes.

"I promise." I shut the door behind me, feeling warm toward Mary Lee for that little bit of dignity.

When we exited the bathroom, Greyhound was waiting to take my arm again. He escorted me back into the conference room and shut the door behind us. We were alone. I returned to my same seat. Greyhound set a leather portfolio on the table in front of him and opened it to a yellow legal pad. He got out some number-two pencils and knocked them to the floor. He picked them up. The point had broken off one. The other was intact. He blew on it, then poised it for action.

"Thank you, Greyhound."

"Of course. Fill me in."

I spoke fast, updating him on the search the day before and the missing items from Gidget's, the unlocked back door, the grinding wheels at the safe, Lester's deceit, Darlene's revelations, Jimmy's former betrothal to Gidget, the reverend who'd visited her, the mysterious baby daddy and his rich and powerful family, the grudge Lucy held. Plus that Tank and Junior knew full well I was living at Gidget's, renting it pending probate. He already knew about the pipeline and the will contest.

He took his glasses off and cleaned them with a cloth from a case. "You've been busy."

I nodded.

"Lots of people with motives. They can't like that you didn't call them about the open door and safe-grinding when it happened." He dropped his glasses as he tried to put them back on. The second time was a go.

I shrugged.

"All right. Let me bring them back in."

He opened the door to call for the sheriff, but the man was standing right there, with his minions.

"Ready?" the sheriff boomed.

Greyhound took his seat without answering.

We hold this truth to be self-evident.

The sheriff, Tank, and Junior crowded around the table.

Greyhound didn't give them time to get settled. "Kenny, I don't know what kind of game you guys are playing, but everyone in this room knows this arrest is a total load of crap."

The sheriff steepled his fingers in front of his chest, elbows on the table. "None of us know any such thing."

Greyhound let out a horselaugh, his lips vibrating. "You're just trying to appease your voters with an arrest of someone well known that isn't local. It'll run in the papers and they'll lay off you for a while about Gidget's murder, and then you'll cross Michele off your list. Meanwhile, you'll have ruined her reputation in the community."

The sheriff leaned back in his chair and crossed his arms over his chest. "Her fingerprints are all over that kitchen. Someone slipped Ms. Becker poison orally. Ms. Hanson is the beneficiary of Ms. Becker's will. She found her, conveniently. That's motive, means, and opportunity. I don't know how much more evidence you think we need."

Greyhound just shook his head at him. "Even if we set aside for a moment the fact that I am the one who informed Michele about her inheritance, which she didn't know about before I told her, which completely wipes out motive, and if we discard the fact that she was living in the house so of course her fingerprints are everywhere, and we ignore that you didn't properly secure and process the crime scene in the first place—there are far better suspects. What about Jimmy Urban? He had motive, means, and opportunity, too. I'd imagine you'll find the same for about ten people. Lucy Thompson holds a grudge. Gidget's former partner was holding a will that put all her assets under his control. Word is there's a baby daddy who paid Gidget to abort a child that she gave birth to, a rich and powerful man with a pocketbook and reputation to protect. I could go on. All of them are better suspects than Michele."

The sheriff shifted in his chair but didn't answer. Tank and Junior studied their hands.

Greyhound seized the moment. "Are you going to let Michele leave with me so she can forget any of this ever happened, or are you going to make a horse's ass of yourself, Kenny?"

"Wouldn't be the first time, I suppose," said the sheriff.

Junior's lips tightened, and he coughed.

Greyhound snorted. "Nor the last. And you know I'll sue you and the department to kingdom come."

"I'll tell you what." The sheriff leaned on his forearms. The man had a real problem sitting still and I wondered if he had ADHD like Sam. "We'll let your client go and hold off filing any charges as long as she'll agree not to leave Lee County and—"

"Uh-uh. My offices are in Fayette County. You can't deny her the right to come visit legal counsel."

I was shaking my head. "And my job, my employer's offices are in Houston. I was there today. You'll get me fired if I can't go to my workplace. I own a home in Houston."

"Your *rental* is in Lee County." The sheriff licked his lips.

"And I own property in Lee County. What of it?" I shot back, before Greyhound could shush me. He laid a hand over mine.

The sheriff held up a "stop" hand. "We'd be willing to write in a couple of exceptions on the geographic restrictions."

Greyhound looked at me and then back at the sheriff. "I don't like it. When you end up looking like the jackass to the public, that I mentioned you resembled earlier—"

I couldn't help myself. "I believe you said *horse's* ass, Greyhound."

"You're right." He grinned. "The *horse's* ass. For hurting a nice woman who happens to be a public figure, it's going to be really bad for reelection, and if you ever want a job outside of Lee County, even worse."

"Sounds like you're threatening me, old friend." He paused, but Greyhound just held eye contact with him without changing expression. The sheriff stood up. "She should pay me for this. Isn't any publicity good publicity?"

"Maybe if you're running for sheriff in Lee County," I said. "But not if you use your good name as credibility for the nonfiction books that you write."

He grunted. "Here's my final offer. How about you, Ms. Hanson, sit down with my deputies every other day, starting today, and share with them all that you've uncovered in the *research* you're doing for the book about Ms. Becker."

"Is that what this is about?" I frowned. I already had been sharing. I'd told Tank and Junior all about the cup and stir stick and everything else. Well, not *everything* else. Especially not after today. "All you had to do was ask."

"I'm asking now."

"If I say yes, I can leave with Greyhound, and I won't be charged with anything?"

"That's correct."

"And my name isn't going to be in the papers tomorrow because you guys hauled me in here under arrest?"

The sheriff rubbed one cheek, like he was checking his stubble. "I am terribly sorry, but I'm not in control of the press in Lee County."

Greyhound squeezed my arm. "I'll make some calls." He stood, and I did, too. "That's it, right?"

The sheriff walked out without answering him, and Tank filled the bluster vacuum left behind. "Things aren't as formal here as in the big city."

Greyhound put two fingers in the center of my back as we exited. "That is an understatement of epic proportions."

Half an hour later—after I'd finished debriefing Tank and Junior—Greyhound and I loaded ourselves in his black Porsche Cayenne with its GRYHND vanity plates, and he started it up. "How about we go grab a cup of coffee before I take you home?"

My stomach growled loudly. "Make it dinner and you've got a deal." I thought back on the unopened cheese and sausage in my purse. "I haven't eaten anything in"—I counted back—"twelve hours. And I started the day with a six-mile run."

He shuddered. "Why would you go and do something crazy like that?"

When we were seated in the tiny Giddings Buffalo Wings & Burgers, I placed a hasty order at the counter. A dozen wings and blue cheese. Large fries. An iced tea. I felt qualified for the 5150 burger tonight, but passed even though a half ground-beef, half ground-bacon burger sounded pretty darn good. Another time. Greyhound ordered a coffee.

He set his glasses on the table and they went skittering across it and into my lap.

"Where'd you get the nickname Greyhound?" Obviously, it wasn't because he was sleek, fast, or graceful.

"Rode up to my first law school class in a Greyhound bus." He harrumphed. "It made a lasting impression."

I laughed.

"We need to talk."

I handed him his glasses. "Uh-oh."

I was not in great shape for more bad news, and probably past being able to hide it. My mother had conducted herself according to her belief that emotion made others uncomfortable. Making others uncomfortable was bad manners. Thus, emotions were bad manners. I'd resisted her logic all my life, but now, I found myself turning to her guidance. I needed my mommy. I cast my eyes down so Greyhound couldn't see my tears. I pretended to be busy with some Splenda packets.

When he spoke, his voice was gentle. "You've inherited quite a mess."

I nodded, afraid to speak.

"The contest of the will you already know about. The hearing should be soon. I feel confident we'll be successful with my testimony about Gidget's mental capacity, but Attorney Little claims to have a witness on the ground up until Gidget's final days."

I blurted out, "What do you mean, witness on the ground? She had someone here spying for them?" My anger helped me put aside my other, messier emotions for a while.

"That would be the conclusion I'd draw."

"Those bastards."

"I'll have to testify, and I'll call Ralph and Jimmy. It may delay probate some."

"Fine. As long as Gidget's daughter gets what she's entitled to." My voice only cracked a little.

"If there is a daughter." He cleared his throat. "Little claims the pipeline contract is valid regardless of whether their will is upheld or ours is. She said that Lester had authority to enter contracts on Gidget's behalf under the power of attorney she gave him. I filed for a temporary injunction against the pipeline and the Houston Arts Trust, but it's possible Little will succeed on this point."

"The POA is rotten." I couldn't argue with his logic, but I knew in my gut that Lester had taken advantage of Gidget.

"Probably, but hard to prove."

If Greyhound and I put our heads together, I felt sure we could find something to discredit his version of events. Even though I'd given Greyhound the brief version at LCSD, I told him the story from beginning to end now, about Lester, Diana/Darlene, and Scarlett.

"Do you think we can fight it with any of that information?"

"It's promising for casting doubt. Even better if someone would testify Gidget didn't execute the power of attorney until after the aneurysm. Or that she was incapacitated with substance abuse issues when she did it."

"I'll circle back with Darlene Hogg." I took a sip of my water. "She's not going to like hearing from me, but that's tough."

A waitress appeared with my food. She looked like the young mother I'd seen in the library with her twin boys. I dug in without so much as a thank-you.

"She's crazed." Greyhound explained to her. "Hunger."

The woman shook her head as she left. "Been there myself."

Greyhound reached for one of my fries, knocking the ketchup over. I caught it in my left hand. "There's more, unfortunately. Attorney Little told me she has a client who's filing an injunction to keep you from writing the book. She promises that if you do write it, and it ends up mentioning her client, they'll sue."

I stopped chewing and spoke through a mouthful. "What? Isn't all publicity good publicity?"

Greyhound sipped his coffee, swirled it in his cup, and sipped again. I held both hands out, loose and ready, just in case, until he set his cup down. "The funny thing is that potential defamation is not a winning argument. There's been no harm. And there's absolutely no proof that you have, will get, or will use information that's not true. I have to warn you, though, the downside is that without Gidget here to prove her side of the story, you're vulnerable later. I recommend you get corroboration knee-deep for anything you write."

"I would've anyway."

"Excuse me." A very young male voice interrupted us. Adult, but barely.

We turned toward him. He was skinny and pimply with horn-rimmed glasses and a big cowlick in the front of his short dark hair. He had on country professional attire, which meant his Dickies khakis had creases in them, and his shirt had a collar.

"Yes?" Greyhound said, his voice polite but disinterested, like he expected the young man to launch into a Jehovah's Witness pitch.

"I'm wondering if I might have a word with the two of you. I'm with the *Giddings Times and News*. I wanted to follow up on Ms. Hanson's arrest earlier today for the murder of Anna Becker. Any comments?"

My mouth flew open. My tension meter skyrocketed to redline in a tenth of a second. I was ready to lash this pip-squeak with my tongue. Luckily, Greyhound beat me to the punch.

"Young man, your name?"

He puffed his frail chest. "Brett Upton, reporter."

"May I have a card?" Greyhound held his hand out. His voice was velvety smooth.

The pip-squeak blanched. "Uh . . . I didn't bring them with me. Uh . . ."

Greyhound's expression seemed like one a mountain lion would make, right before pouncing on an injured Bambi. "That's all right, son. Ms. Hanson and I won't be making any comments other than she has been released with no charges filed and is pleased that the sheriff's department recognizes that she had absolutely nothing to do with Anna Becker's death."

The young man turned to me. "Would you—"

Greyhound shook his head, putting a hand up. "I said that would be all. Have a nice day."

Thank God for Greyhound. Anything I could have said in my current state would have only made things much worse. I grabbed a wing. I needed to polish them off before they got cold.

The young man shuffled away.

Greyhound called after him. "Oh, Mr. Upton?"

He turned back, bright-eyed. "Yes?"

"I wanted to caution you about what you and the *Giddings Times and News* print about Ms. Hanson. Do you know who I am, son?"

The young man shook his head. "Ms. Hanson's husband?"

I gasped, dropping a wing back on my plate and splattering buffalo sauce on my filthy linen top. My filthy, ruined linen top.

Greyhound grew somber. "Oh no. Ms. Hanson's husband died a year ago. Murdered. Which you would have known if you'd Googled her right quick before you accosted her for an interview. That's the minimum I would have done if I were a professional journalist."

Red crept up the cheeks of Brett Upton. "I'm sorry, ma'am."

I dipped my head to acknowledge his apology.

Greyhound beamed at the terrified reporter. "I'm Greyhound Smith. Are you familiar with that name, Mr. Upton?"

All the red drained from the reporter's face as quickly as it had appeared. He licked his lips, swallowed, and nodded. "Everybody knows who you are, sir."

"I expect they do. So, when I tell you that you should be very cautious about what you print about Ms. Hanson, do you understand what I mean? Do you *fully* understand?"

"Oh, yes, sir." Upton straightened his collar, then his shoulders. "Thank you, sir." He fled out the front door.

Greyhound raised his eyebrows. "Some bastard in here called the paper." His eyes roved the room looking for signs of conspiracy.

That or Greyhound's vanity plates facing the main drag gave us away.

I glanced after Upton. A beige Land Rover was parked near the street, empty, in the lot that serviced only the stand-alone restaurant. My pulse accelerated, and I glanced around us, looking for a light-skinned, dark-haired, medium-height man. I saw three of them. All were eating alone, and they ranged from Annabelle's age to mine to Greyhound's. And a fourth one was walking to the parking lot: Upton.

The hairs on my arms stood at attention. I couldn't believe I'd forgotten the Land Rover. Then again, my afternoon had gone downhill fast and hard. And even though this beige or taupe or tan or whatever it was Rover was parked here, that didn't mean it had to be the one—or one of the ones—I'd seen earlier. Or that it was following me.

Didn't mean it wasn't, either. I grabbed my glass and gulped a large drink.

Greyhound helped himself to another of my fries. "That kid's going to be way too scared to do you damage."

Upton drove away in a red Prius. That left the men in the restaurant. None of them were watching me. Maybe because none of them were following me?

"Michele?"

I shook my head to clear it. I couldn't let myself drop my basket for the second time in one day. "Sorry. What were you saying?"

TWENTY

GREYHOUND DROPPED me off at my Jetta. The sun was setting, and the entire western sky was orange and pink through the trees behind the house. A forest ablaze. Gertrude met me at the gate, her nose and paws covered in dirt. Our yard, behind her, looked like a prairie dog town. Just then, Gertrude stiffened. She ran with her nose to the ground, then stood with her head low, quivering. After a few seconds, she readjusted her position and started digging frantically.

"No!" I cried.

She stopped mid-dig, posed. It took me a second, but I realized she was digging for moles. That she had actually heard the little tunnelers underground. When I didn't repeat myself, Gertrude started digging again.

"No, no!"

She backed away from her site, dirt clumps falling out of her facial hair.

"Good girl!"

She wriggled her long body toward me, gecko-like. I swept her into my arms, dirt and all, but I held my face away from her attempts to slather it in kisses. I squeezed her, and she grunted. I was relieved to see that her water bowl was still in the shade and over half full.

I hefted Gertrude onto my hip and walked to the door. It was slightly ajar, and I jumped back from it like it was a copperhead. I pivoted around to call out to Greyhound, but the Cayenne was three-quarters of the way to the road and kicking up dust. I shouted and waved but it did no good.

"Will this day ever let up on me?" I set Gertrude on the ground. "Not good. Not good at all."

I got my phone out, considering a call for help. But for what? For all I knew, I'd forgotten to lock the door, and it had popped open when the AC cycled on. Gertrude had been here, and she didn't seem concerned. And who would I call? Ralph was out of town. I didn't know anyone else. Well, Lumpy or Jimmy, maybe. Maggie wouldn't add any muscle unless she brought firepower. I was outside the city limits, which meant the sheriff's department would respond if I made it official. No, thank you.

So I decided to check it out first. I wanted a weapon, and the shotgun was leaning against the wall in the bedroom. The trees in the yard had flimsy branches that would be worthless. I settled on the Jetta's tire iron. I tested it in my hand. If someone was in the house and meant me no good, it would do.

I walked back to the house, reassuring myself. If anyone had been in there, the Cayenne pulling up had surely alerted them. They'd've high-tailed it. I threw the door open. It banged against the wall inside. I quickly stepped in, looking around for movement, stopping to listen for the sound of footsteps, a window, or the back door. But it was completely silent. Even Gertrude, at my feet, seemed to be holding her breath.

"Hello?" I called.

Gertrude huffed. No answer. Like anyone would, if they were hiding in the house. *Jeez, Michele.*

"Whoever you are, I've dialed 911 so this is your last chance to take off." I hadn't, but they didn't know that.

Still nothing. The house was quiet as a grave except for the brushing of Gertrude's fluffy tail as it wagged against the floor. I stomped around the house, slamming and bumping into things to make noise. When I got to the bedroom where the safe was, I stopped in my tracks. New cutting wheels and a fresh pile of metal filings lay on the floor. Ants crawled all over my body, and eyes bored through the back of my head. I whirled, slapping at my arms and legs. No one there. No ants. But someone *had* been here. Moving faster, I tugged on the safe door—still locked–checked the closet in there and in Gidget's room, then rushed into the bathroom and flung back the shower curtain.

Nothing. At least, nothing else.

Except that I'd only checked the house. I fished my phone from my purse and typed in 911. Armed with that and the tire iron, I took off for the barn, leaving Gertrude closed in the yard. She informed me it hurt her feelings, but I blocked her out. About the time I yanked the sliding door open, I remembered the shotgun in the house. A flock of bats erupted past me with an explosion of wings and the stench of urine. I screamed for long seconds until my voice cracked, and I ran out of breath. The bats were gone. I poked my head into the barn. I could see no one, and if they were hiding in the loft, then good on them. I'd run out of desire to sleuth about ten thousand bats ago.

I leaned against the outside wall of the barn and stared at the sky. I was an idiot. What was I doing living out here alone, not even smart enough to grab the perfectly good gun sitting beside the bed?

Someone had been here, trying to get into the safe. Probably the same someone as before. Could it be the beige-Land Rover guy? Had he followed me all the way home today? Or followed me *from* home this morning? Maybe we'd seen him at dinner, but he could have been out here earlier. While I was in custody. He could have gone to the wings restaurant for nothing more than food. Or to terrorize me.

It could be him.

Or it could be anyone.

I stood, brushing the dirt off the back of my pants. The outfit was history, kaput. My phone dinged, and I glanced at it, then did a double take. I hadn't checked my messages since—well, since sometime earlier that day. Probably not since the parking lot of Catalina Coffee. God, was that only today? It felt like a week ago. I had eighteen texts, four voice mails, and fifty-seven emails.

The most recent message was a text from Papa: *"Hope you haven't caught anything but animal pictures on your wildlife cam."*

The wildlife cam! Papa had put it in the side yard where it would catch the front and back of the house. I sprinted to the yard, vaulting the fence. I popped the camera cover open and ejected the memory disk, leaving the cover ajar in my rush. Fearful and excited at the same time, I ignored Gertrude dodging in between my ankles and got my laptop out of the Jetta. I opened it on the front hood and pushed the disk into its slot. The photo software started importing the pictures too quickly for me to see the images. When the import had finished, I clicked to save them on the disk, in case anything went wrong, and started scrolling through them.

There were a couple of thousand pictures, and I scrolled as fast as I could. Nighttime photos. An owl. A cat I hadn't known lived here. Pictures of me and my bazillion visitors yesterday. Pictures from today. A coyote with a rooster in his mouth, the reason for my quiet morning. Poor thing. Photo after photo after photo of Gertrude. Chasing butterflies, digging for moles, sunbathing, watering the plants, barking at squirrels. I reached down and rubbed her behind both ears with my thumb and middle finger. Then I held the arrow button down. The frames flew past me, a day in the life of a farmhouse on hyper-speed. The Jetta jumped into an image. I jerked my finger off the key, then arrowed more slowly. Way too many frames of Michele melting down. Then a picture of Tank and Junior. The two of them taking me away. It made me nauseous.

I scrolled carefully now. Birds, waving grass, a rabbit, more Gertrude. I paused. Exhaustion hit me, sudden and hard, like a head butt from the goat Papa used to keep as the clinic's mascot. I wouldn't give in to it. I couldn't.

With two hundred pictures to go, I saw something. Homo-erectus, hunched over and running fast, like a shadow. Gertrude barreled into view, barking, in the next frame. I gasped and arrowed back to the human picture. It was a blur, a figure in full flight, leaving the house. The image wasn't clear enough for gender or race. I scrolled back a few. Nothing. Forward, slowly. About an hour after the picture of the intruder was taken, the camera took photos of the Cayenne, then me. I kept scanning until I came to the end: my own image, reaching for the camera cover.

For the next ten minutes I mutilated my cuticles as I studied the pictures from earlier in the day, trying to get a fix on when the intruder had entered the house, a better shot of him, an accomplice, a car. Anything.

I got nothing.

I tried not to think about him hiding in the house with me there. It was more likely he'd run out when the camera was between shots. Maybe it had been busy shooting one of the many mole-digging photos of Gertrude. Maybe he'd entered away from the camera. Angled from the front. On the opposite side. The camera didn't have eyes everywhere.

I returned to my one-image capture and blew it up to maximum resolution. It pixelated immediately. "Come on, come on."

Gertrude braced her paws on my calves.

"Not you." I reached around and patted the top of her head. I started dialing down on the size. The image came back into focus enough that I could work with it. But I couldn't overcome the blurring effect of the rapid movement. All I could tell was that it was a person, Caucasian or at least not dark skinned, medium height, dark hair, short or up, jeans, light boxy shirt, and boots. Maybe glasses. Probably a guy.

I clicked to share the photo and sent it to Greyhound. *"Caught this on wildlife cam today. Someone tried to get into Gidget's safe again."*

My phone rang, and I squeaked, startled. Gertrude cocked her head. It was Rashidi. Part of me wanted to ignore the call, to pull my aloneness around me like a hair shirt. Another part of me wanted to hear another voice, to banish the aloneness. That part didn't mind that it was him at all. I pressed Accept.

"Hi, Rashidi."

"I starting to worry." His lilting voice sounded serious.

"With good reason."

"Wah?" His accent grew thicker.

"Long story."

"I got time."

I snapped the laptop shut and walked back into the house with it and Gertrude. I locked the door behind me.

His voice was curt this time. "Spit it out, Michele."

I dropped onto the couch and let my head loll back. "I don't even know where to start. I was in Houston today, for work, and to do research for the book. I got great information."

"That good," Rashidi interjected.

"Yes, but I think someone may have followed me home."

"Why somebody do that?"

"I don't know, and it gets worse. When I got home the deputies from the sheriff's department showed up and arrested me. They accused me of murdering Gidget." I left out my mini-breakdown.

Rashidi drew in a breath. A harsh sound. Then I heard clattering. "I packin' up. On my way."

"No," I protested. "No, it's okay."

The sounds in the background stilled for a moment. "But you home?"

"Yes. Greyhound got me out. He accused the sheriff of doing this as a publicity stunt."

"Good." Rashidi snorted. "I like to kick he ass, that sheriff." I could barely understand his Calypso accent now.

"Yes, me, too."

More clattering and slamming sounded from Rashidi's end. "That all?"

"Well, no." I tried to out-silence him and lost. "Somebody tried to break into the safe again, while I was . . . detained."

Keys jangled, footsteps sounded, a door slammed. I listened, not speaking.

"Go on," said Rashidi, acting like an army general.

"That's it, except I got an image of him on my wildlife cam."

The roar of an engine starting was unmistakable.

"Rashidi, I'm okay. You don't need to—"

"You not talk me out of this." His voice was gentle but determined.

"I have my shotgun and a tire iron. Plus, I've got Gertrude. She'll let me know if anybody comes and—"

"I make your place in an hour. Turn on you lights."

I rolled my eyes. "I wasn't born under a potato truck."

"It make me feel better."

"Who knew you were so bossy?" I said, but I realized I was smiling.

"It okay when someone care about you."

I nodded even though he couldn't see me. "Thank you." I would feel better with someone here. With him here. I walked into the bedroom for Gidget's shotgun. "Hey, Rashidi?"

"Yah, mon?"

I walked out the back door and pointed the barrel up at the sky. "Listen to this." I cocked the shotgun, sending a shell into the chamber, flicked off the safety, and fired it into the air. "It's all good."

He laughed. "I forget you a badass."

We hung up. I made a pallet for him in the spare bedroom then sat on the front porch with Gertrude, scrolling through missed messages and watching for his headlights.

TWENTY-ONE

Rashidi unloaded his suitcase and a bag of oranges. He held them up. "Dinner." I couldn't help but notice another toothpick. The man had a serious toothpick habit.

I opened the door for him, feeling awkward about whether to hug him. "Great. Come on in."

He turned off the accent. "What are the flashes of light?"

That was a puzzler. "Where? What do you mean?"

"Out there. I saw them when I parked."

I strained to see in the darkness. A flash went off. *Aha.* "Lightning bugs, aka fireflies."

"Ah yes. I've read about them. It's a bioluminescence. They're actually some kind of beetle." He didn't seem to want to come in.

"I can give you a bottle later if you want to catch some. Kids around here do it all the time. Poke holes in the top so they can breathe."

"Nah. They're wild."

He finally came in. I led him to the spare bedroom. Gertrude was ecstatic to see him. He crouched, arranging his bags beside his pallet, and she catapulted herself into him. He fell back on the makeshift bed, humoring her.

"She's friendly." He was laughing and fending off her tongue.

Tlazol dog. "She likes you."

When he'd extricated himself from Gertrude's love, he adjusted his knit shirt. It hugged his pecs and exposed a smattering of chest hair in a V neckline. A medallion hung in the V. Adrian had always said V necks were metrosexual. I suddenly realized I didn't agree with him. Like dog, like owner.

"What's that?" I pointed at his medallion.

He reached up, touching it. "Just something my mother gave me." He blinked and shuttered to a flatter look.

"Can I see it?"

He lifted it and nodded.

I took it in my hand. Cold engraved metal, warm on the side where it had rested against his skin. It grated against the gold rope chain, which was long enough that the medallion nestled into the V, but not long enough for me to read it without getting really, really close. I leaned farther in. He breathed into my hair. Heat radiated from his skin onto my face. The dual sources of warmth sent fireworks through my brain. I was close enough to see the pores in his skin, the black, wiry hairs springing from his chest, the contour of his collarbone and muscles beneath his shirt. Normally I breathed deeply to center myself. Now I was scared to. I decided to focus on something disgusting to break the spell Rashidi had over me. Frog guts. Pickled pigs' feet. Baby poop. It worked enough that I was able to read the inscriptions on the medallion. The front was etched with a magnificent lion and the words JAH RULE. I flipped it over. IRIE. These weren't words I knew.

I finally took a breath and musky sandalwood overpowered my senses. I dropped the medallion like it had burned me. Rashidi cocked an eyebrow.

"What does it mean?" I touched the locket on my own chest. It was warm. More than warm. It was hot, hot, hot. Too hot. *Adrian?* I backed away from Rashidi until I bumped into the wall.

"Jah means God in Rastafari. So Jah Rule means God Rules."

"And the back?"

"My mommy"—which he pronounced Mah-MEE, his voice lilting again—"always say 'irie' whenever I lettin' things get to me. It mean, 'it all good, mon.'" He flashed white teeth at me around his toothpick.

I'd never heard a grown man say mommy quite like he did. His voice was warm, emotional. Reverent. I fled to the kitchen. I turned on the hot water tap, pumped soap into my hands, and scrubbed them.

Rashidi followed me. "Show me your necklace?"

I wiped my hands on a dish towel. The old rag predated my move-in. I lifted it and sniffed it. Sour. I washed my hands again and then wiped them on my pants.

"I said," Rashidi repeated, "show me yours?"

When I didn't answer, he reached out and lifted the butterfly from my chest. I grabbed it and pulled it from his hand. I took three quick, giant steps past him to separate us.

"I'm sorry." He bowed his head.

My cheeks burned. "Oh no. I'm sorry." I'd made everything uncomfortable. I wanted to fix it. I unclasped the necklace and handed it to him. "Remember how Papa calls me Itzpa?"

Rashidi nodded, turning the monarch to and fro, letting the meager ceiling light reflect from it. "For Itzpapalotl."

"Adrian wasn't great with Spanish or Aztec words. So he called me his butterfly. He gave that to me."

Rashidi looked up and smiled. "Your bicycle."

"Yes." I smiled and felt the tears. I cursed the tears. I scrubbed them away with my palms.

"Hey," Rashidi said. He moved closer again.

"No, don't."

He held up both hands. "Irie."

That made me smile through the wetness, then something in me broke. "Itzpa," I said, my words shaky, "is young and beautiful. A goddess. A butt-kicker." I chuckled, but the tears still flowed, damn them. "Isn't that funny? They both had me believing it for so long." My tears turned to sobs. Rashidi stared at me, stricken. I had forbidden him to comfort me, and here I was, a total mess. "I'm a dried-up old woman, and all I have is this stupid necklace, and memories to pull from. Like digging them from the dirt. There's a name for that, too."

His gaze on me was strong, intense, laser-like.

I whispered, "Tlazolteotl. The eater of filth. The goddess of the cycle." My voice fell. "From girl to woman to used-to-be."

"No."

"What?"

He spoke in his accent again, and goose bumps rose on my arms. "Tlazolteotl more. She purity, purification."

I froze, transfixed.

"She beautiful like the moon, she the goddess of fertility."

I squirmed. His words, his knowledge was seductive. I had to resist it. "How do you know these things?"

"You forget I teach Aztec mythology?"

"Oh . . ." It came out a squeak. I wished he wouldn't talk in that accent. It did funny things to me.

He went on, his eyes like onyx. "She give life energy to the jaguar, and she inspire protecting the flame of the Old Ones. She wise and brave and powerful—"

I had to . . . "I can't talk about this anymore. Excuse me."

I fled and barricaded myself in the bathroom. *Well, that didn't go so well.* I was an absolute freak. I turned on the water. For the second time that day I let the sobs come. I welcomed them. I used them. I channeled out my grief to the universe. I emptied my bruised and battered innards.

Sometime later, when the sobs had stopped, I splashed my face then turned off the water. I peered into the mirror, afraid of seeing Tlazol again, but all I saw was swollen eyes, red-streaked whites, and dilated pupils. I scrubbed my face hard to dry it. It pinked my nose and cheeks.

"No more crying," I told the woman in the mirror. "I mean it. No more."

With the water off, I heard voices from the living room. Rashidi talking to Gertrude? But no, there was a woman's voice, too. Great. More company when I wasn't at my best. I hustled into the living room, trying to make it look like I was peachy.

Maggie was sitting on the couch going through Gidget's mail and the envelope of pictures I'd found under the mattress. My handbag was at her feet. Maybe the letters had spilled out of it? Maggie set the mail down when she saw me and grabbed a cup of coffee that was in front of her. As I watched, she twisted the cap off a whiskey bottle and topped off the cup. Rashidi had propped his lean frame against one of the kitchen chairs, and he was sipping from his own coffee cup. Something green and ugly wiggled in my gut. I tried to ignore it.

"I take it the two of you have met?"

Rashidi smiled. No toothpick. Maybe he'd run out. "We have now."

I turned toward Maggie. "Coffee at"—I looked around for the time but couldn't find anything but the dark of night out the window to judge it by —"this hour?"

Maggie held the bottle up. "And whiskey anytime. Can I pour you some?"

"Sorry. I've—wait, what are you doing here?"

She stood and grabbed me, pulling me into a hug. I breathed deeply. She was eau de 80 proof, Aqua Net, and sawdust. "I heard about your day."

I bristled. "It's been awful." I pulled back so I could face Rashidi. "There's more I haven't told you," I blurted. "You know my mother died?"

"Yah."

"My parents had a baby before they got married. They gave him up for adoption."

Maggie stood beside me, rubbing small circles on my back. I moved a step away. She said, "I read that on your blog."

Rashidi started pacing slowly, his footsteps rhythmic. "I read it, too."

"Okay, well, this whole thing with Gidget's daughter, with my mother and her son, my brother, it's all mixed up inside me. I've got this crazy feeling that if I find one, I'll find the other."

Maggie pulled me to face her. She put her hands on my cheeks. "Of course you feel that way. I'll help."

Normally I wasn't a very touchy person, but I felt myself giving in to her. It had been so long since I'd been touched, that I found I needed the contact.

I laughed. "How can you help me?"

"I used to sleep with someone who was working at the state registry of adoptions." She patted one of my cheeks and let go of me.

"That's . . . useful."

"Let me see what I can find."

"About Gidget's daughter, too?"

"Of course. We can call and find out if I've been forgiven for being a wrecking ball yet."

"What?"

She thrust me the coffee cup she'd doctored earlier. "Never mind. Drink."

"I don't know if that's such a good idea."

"Drink," she repeated.

"Bossy. All right."

She and Rashidi looked at each other and the exchange of glances was telling.

"You guys are ganging up on me."

This time I laughed aloud. Another confession came barreling out, a non sequitur, but I couldn't stop myself. "My kids don't need me anymore. Sam is coaching all over the country and Annabelle's off at UT. They don't return my calls. I'm totally alone." Sam. I needed to get him on the phone. I took a swig of coffee and two beats later spewed most of it—along with something that tasted like paint thinner—across the room, finishing off with a few coughs.

Rashidi Yanked, "She doesn't hold her liquor well."

"You think?" Maggie shed the top layer of her outfit, a vest of strings attached to each other in a netlike pattern. The threads were a metallic purple. She tossed it on the couch and fanned her face. "This house have an air conditioner?"

"Sorry. I was gone all day and had it off. Things went haywire and I forgot."

Rashidi said, "Praise Jah. I thought it was broken."

I looked at him. Sweat beaded across his forehead. How had I not noticed the heat before? I started to move to the hallway to turn the unit back on, but Maggie grabbed my arm.

"Count heads." Her eyebrows furrowed but her forehead barely wrinkled.

How had a woman who spent years abusing drugs and alcohol managed to stay so youthful, so beautiful? Maybe it was Botox or maybe it was good genes.

"What do you mean?"

"How many people are in here?"

"Um, three?"

"Yeah, that's the number I came up with, too. What about you Rashidi?"

He made a show of counting us. "One, two, tree. I get tree, too."

"I would think . . ." Maggie sniffed. "That even in your impaired emotional state you could see that you are anything but alone." She waved her hand at me. "Now go turn on that AC."

I laughed and did. When I came back, Rashidi had brought a third cup of coffee into the living room. He handed it to Maggie. She poured whiskey into it. Glug, glug, glug, then tossed it back. Liquid splashed on her emerald-green tunic. She'd paired it with a blue jean mini—frayed at the hem— torn black fishnets, and a pair of turquoise high-heeled boots. Her hair was teased up on top, framing her face, and the rest of it stuck out in an electrified mess like she'd just crawled out of an orgy. Her chandelier earrings hung to her shoulders and tangled in her hair. Something in them caught the light from the single bulb in the ceiling and sparkled. She returned to perusing the stack of photos and mail. I took a bigger sip of whiskey.

Maggie gasped. "Oh my gosh!"

"What is it?" I joined her.

"This picture." She waved it at me. "My parents are in it. It's in front of some old building that one of our ancestors built a long time ago. It's not even in La Grange anymore. They moved it to Round Top."

I pulled the picture from her to get a look.

"The younger couple." She pointed to them. "That's my mom and dad."

"They look too young to be friends with Gidget's parents."

"The Wendish community is small."

"Are you Wendish?"

"By ancestry. I occasionally go to the annual festival for some cultural history, but I quit going to church when I was a teenager. They were into it, though, when I was younger."

"That's pretty cool."

"Now that I'm older, I think so, too. Anyway, I can't wait to show my mother this picture." She positioned it on her thigh and snapped a photo, then texted the picture.

My phone rang. The whiskey had started to go to my head already and my focus was *caca*. I held a finger up.

It was Annabelle.

"Hi, sweetie," I said.

She quickly said, "Hey," and then went on with "I'm working on Senator Herrington's campaign. For real. I'll get internship credit, or whatever. I'm so excited."

"That's fantastic." I hadn't voted for the man, but this would be great on Annabelle's resume.

Maggie filled my coffee cup with whiskey. No more coffee. I shook my head at her, and she grinned like the Cheshire Cat.

"I know."

"You're going to be busy. How are you going to fit in school and swimming and volunteer work? No, never mind I asked that. If there's one girl in the world who can organize her life to fit it all in, it's you, Belle."

"No problem," she said. "Jay's a little . . . well . . . I think, he's kinda jealous."

"Jay? Jealous? Why?"

"He thinks I have a crush on Senator Herrington, but, like, he's so old."

I laughed. It felt good to laugh with tears still in my eyes. "He is *way* old, Belle."

"He may be old, but he flirts. I don't flirt back, though."

An oogey feeling replaced the warmth. "Are you sure it's a good idea to work with him?"

"I barely see him. But just think, what if he wins the presidency and I know him?"

"Well, that would be cool. Just don't get to know him too well."

"I won't. Gotta go. Jay's here to pick me up. Oh, you should call Sam, too."

"Congratulations, Belle. I love you."

The phone went dead. It was too late to call Sam. I shot him a three-word *"How are you???"* text, then swallowed some of the searing concoction and yelled, "Gack!"

Maggie laughed.

"Are you okay?" Rashidi asked.

I took another sip. It went down easier. The next one after that, easier yet. Three or four later, the stings of today had numbed. I gave my new friends a thumbs-up.

TWENTY-TWO

THE COFFEE and whiskey had rounded my sharp edges. I'd listened more than talked and laughed until my sides ached at Maggie riffing on her past indiscretions and Rashidi describing his interviews with the Texas A&M extension service. They didn't quite know how to handle a dreadlocked Rastafarian from the islands with an accent they'd only heard in movies. He'd agreed to stay to meet more folks the following week since he was on summer break at UVI—keeping him in College Station was cheaper than another round-trip flight. It gave him a chance to look at housing and explore the area. But instead he was at my place, an area he'd already explored.

I woke up next to Maggie. She'd flung an arm across my neck. The snores coming from her dainty nose and bowed lips were chainsaw decibel. I lifted her arm as gently as I could and set it at her side.

Her snoring stopped for a second. "No, Gary." She mumbled unintelligibly for a moment or two. "Okay, just once more." Then her whiskey snoring resumed.

I sat up, the bed creaking underneath me. My head shouted echoing protests. I'd never been much of a drinker. Even less so after marrying Adrian. Hangovers weren't conducive to peak athletic performance. I was out of practice, and I clamped my hand over my mouth as nausea set in.

The sun had risen, just barely, but there was no longer a rooster alarm clock. And no sound of doggie paws. I put my feet on the creaky wood floor. My outfit from yesterday—stained, sour, and now wrinkled—was plastered to me. My sandals were still on, though one foot had come out of its front strap. The shoe hung from my ankle. I put my hand over my mouth and exhaled. My breath was worse than my clothes. I stepped off the bed with my arms out for balance. My bare toe and flopping shoe landed on something both hard and soft.

"Umph."

The room swayed, tilted, then righted itself. "Sorry," I whispered.

Maggie snored on. Rashidi rolled away from my foot. "That okay."

Even his whisper was a sexy singsong that called out to the Tlazol in me, but I told her to bugger off. "What are you doing in here?"

"I move my bed thing."

Obviously. I sidestepped along the bed to the bathroom. When I got to the kitchen a few minutes later, Rashidi was working the coffee maker, wearing only his blue jeans. My eyes gobbled him up before I could cut them away, and heat flushed up my chest, neck, and cheeks.

His skin glowed. His lean body was sculpted with a rippling six-pack and long legs. I tried to replace his image with Adrian's. Paler, thicker. The images flickered and competed.

Rashidi put his hand to his head. "I think we partied too hard last night. I'm not used to that kind of t'ing."

"Me, either."

I studied the floor and blurted, "Would you like me to go get your shirt?"

He laughed. "Sorry. In the Islands it's no big thing. Your house, your culture, your rules. No problem." He disappeared for a moment, then returned pulling a shirt over his head, leaving me with one last glimpse of his pronounced abs and ribcage. When his face appeared through the neck of his shirt, he had a toothpick again. What was it with him and those things?

"I'm afraid I don't have much food."

Rashidi peered in the refrigerator while I stayed rooted in place like a statue. "Eggs. Milk." Then he opened the pantry. "Granola." He nodded at me. "Plenty."

I managed to get myself moving. "So, do you have plans for today?" I melted butter in a skillet and whisked eggs.

Rashidi was pouring powdered creamer in his cup. He heaped spoonful after spoonful of sugar in next. "No eggs for me."

I wondered if he'd have room left for coffee. "I'm not totally clear on the vegetarian thing. Do you ever eat eggs?" I poured eggs into the skillet and stirred.

He dribbled coffee into his mixture, then poured a second cup, black. "Sometimes. Eggs never alive. Not flesh." He handed me a coffee.

"Thank you."

Rashidi poured granola and milk to the rim of a bowl, then set his toothpick beside his bowl. "I was t'inking," he said through a bite of granola and milk. "I'll open that safe today." He pointed at me. "And you'll report the man who broke in your house?"

I didn't like being told what to do overmuch, but the way he said it sounded more like a suggestion than an order. I spooned half the eggs onto a plate. "All right. I've some work to do for my day job. And the Internet people are coming back this morning, supposedly, to get things working here." I ate standing up, like him. "Do you have someplace you have to be that I'm keeping you from?"

Before he could answer, Maggie appeared, crumpled and bleary, but still a jolt of sexual electricity.

"Good morning." I watched for Rashidi's reaction to her from the corner of my eye.

There was none. He just took another bite of his granola and lifted a spoon to her in greeting.

"Want some breakfast?" I asked.

Her voice was gravely and awesome. "Please. Have you checked on the dogs?"

She'd brought Janis and Woody with her, and they'd been treated to a night in the yard. Well, Gertrude had her doggie friends, so maybe she didn't feel completely abandoned.

I didn't tell her that all I'd done so far this morning was try not to make a fool of myself in front of Rashidi. "I was just about to."

"Dog food?" She rubbed her pale cheeks briskly and color seeped into them.

"In the pantry."

She grabbed Gertrude's bowl from inside the door. A moment later she was out the back door with another big bowl and the bag of food.

Rashidi squirted soap in the sink and turned on the water. "You get the trailer's AC fixed?"

"I haven't yet. It's been crazy."

He found a long-handled scrubber under the sink. It looked original to the house. He put the rest of the eggs on a new plate, then attacked the skillet. "I'm pretty handy. I'll take a look. If I fix it, maybe I can stay there?"

Gratitude suffused me, for him understanding his presence here made me uncomfortable. In a love it/hate it kind of way. "That would be great."

I grabbed a dish towel and set up a drying station. *I have friends here,* I thought. *New friends.* It was odd. Even odder that I kind of liked it.

Maggie burst back into the kitchen, dewy beads of sweat at her hairline. "Gonna be a scorcher."

"Rashidi and I were just making our plans for the day. What are you up to?"

She wolfed down the eggs. "I don't open the shop on Wednesday, and I'm lusting after your junk."

"Could you go through the barn like we'd talked about before? But maybe keep an inventory, and let me know if you see any clues to our little mystery?" I put a bowl and plate in the cabinet.

"Perfect. Oh, and I almost forgot. Gidget has a letter that the county is putting this place up for auction. She hasn't paid her property taxes in a couple of years."

Remembering Maggie rifling Gidget's mail last night, I said, "Oh no." I turned to her, dishes forgotten. "You know, someone told me yesterday there were rumors Gidget was dealing drugs in Houston. Like to the artists. That doesn't jive with a little old lady who can barely make ends meet and can't pay her property taxes."

Maggie went into the living room and brought the letter back to me.

"*Dios mío.*" I confirmed what she'd told me then snapped a picture of it. Gidget owed for three years. Nearly $50,000. I emailed it to Greyhound. *Emergency. Tax arrears sale of Gidget's place scheduled for next month!!!!!* When I finished, I said, "Well, that woke me up."

"Sorry for the bad news."

"Better to know than not to know. Greyhound will take care of it, I'm sure." I scrubbed my scalp around my face, getting the blood going. "So many crap things to deal with right now. I have to report my intruder, at the sheriff's department this morning. Rashidi has some errands, too, and the Internet guy is coming. Could you let him in?"

She snorted. "I can let him in, but I can't promise any more than that. The average number of visits and elapsed time for working Internet out in the country is three visits and three weeks."

"Don't tell me that." I grabbed the empty Balcones Distilling Texas Single Malt bottle from the kitchen table and dropped it in the trash.

Rashidi folded a paper towel. I watched as he slid it under a little spider that was on the window sill above the sink. He went to the back door with the paper towel and spider. Out the kitchen window I watched him release it onto one of the fence pickets. He returned and used the paper towel to wipe up water from the counter.

My mouth hung a little. "Did you just rescue a spider?"

"He's God's creature, too." He threw the paper towel away.

Maggie tossed her hair. "If I get bit by God's creature today, I'm blaming you."

Rashidi flashed his ivories at her around the toothpick he'd salvaged after breakfast.

I shook my head. "One more thing, Maggie. Gidget's will leaves her old Jaguar to her daughter, but I can't find it. Be on the lookout."

"Be still my heart."

I grinned. "While you're at it, if you don't mind, find out who killed Gidget."

Maggie shook her head. "I can't believe you're leaving all the fun stuff for me."

As I rolled down the last mile of the paved road back to Gidget's from LCSD, I tried not to be disheartened. Even with the photo I'd shown them, the deputies didn't take my break-in seriously. I guess the idea of me as a victim didn't jive with painting me as the bad guy. I tried to convince them the person was a suspect in Gidget's death, but Tank suggested maybe I'd just had a friend run by the camera. I felt murderous.

Junior promised they'd be by when their schedules cleared.

Like the twelfth of never, I'd thought.

I drove on. The roadside foliage was noticeably less green in the last few days. We needed rain. Lumpy's pickup pulled up in a cloud of dust at the entrance to his drive. He honked and waved at me. I didn't want to, but I pulled to a stop and rolled down my window. He could have seen my intruder, so talking to him was a necessary evil. He got out and came over.

I stumbled over pleasantries. "Yes?" My conscience pricked me. My mother would've never made anyone uncomfortable if she could help it. Except me, of course. In her world, it was bad manners. "I mean, hello, good morning." My conscience eased. I was beginning to think my conscience was my mother.

Lumpy doffed his cowboy hat at me. "Ms. Lopez."

"Ms. Hanson."

"Uh, yeah." He turned and spit a stream of brown juice. "Did that delivery driver yesterday get you your package?"

My face scrunched up like it did when something made no sense. "I didn't find any packages. I was gone most of the day."

"That's a shame. I gave him directions when I saw him pulled over on the side of the road here. It's that new driver."

"What do you mean?" I asked.

"Our normal driver is a guy named Nacho out of Austin. A Mexican like—uh, a nice guy." He paused, shooting me a glance to see if I had caught his slip.

I wanted to roll my eyes, but not while my radar was going off. "So, Nacho is our normal delivery guy . . ."

He wiped his hands on his shirt front, leaving dark smudges on the tiny white plaid. "Yeah, Nacho. This new guy, I've only seen twice." He stopped, appearing lost in thought.

He was a little off his game. "So, new guy. You've only seen him twice."

"Yes, yesterday when he parked here and a week or two ago. Around the time Gidget passed away, maybe a little before."

My radar pinged again. New delivery driver. Here when Gidget died, and when someone broke in. "Was he driving a Land Rover?"

"Nope. A white delivery van."

A wave of vertigo tipped my world akimbo. Had there not been a beige Land Rover following me? I pulled my laptop out and opened it. I'd left it on at LCSD so it came to life immediately. "Let me show you something." I typed in my password and pulled up the picture. "Is this him?"

Lumpy leaned in. He took off his mirrored Poncherello-from-CHiPs sunglasses and squinted. "Can't rightly say."

"Could it be? What was your delivery guy wearing?" I pointed to the guy in the picture. "Jeans? Boxy, short-sleeved shirt. Light colored?"

He scratched the top of his head. "Well, yeah. Maybe."

"And your guy: medium height? Short dark hair? Caucasian?"

"Uh-huh."

I circled the face in the picture with my finger. "Those could be glasses. Did your guy wear glasses?"

"Yeah, nerdy little glasses."

"So this picture could be him."

"Maybe," Lumpy said. "Why is it so out of focus?"

"It's from my wildlife camera." I hesitated, then said, "Someone broke into the place yesterday."

"I don't like the sound of that." Lumpy stood up, wincing. He frowned and stretched, arching up and back a little bit.

"Did you see anybody else headed toward Gidget's yesterday?"

He turned slightly backwards and launched another stream of tobacco juice. Splat. "Nope. Listen." He crouched eye-level with me. "You need any help out there, I'm a former Texas Ranger. Had to leave 'em on account of my back." His sunglasses still off, I caught a sadness as it passed through his eyes. "I could come right now, take a look around."

"I appreciate it, Loopy—"

"Lumpy."

"I appreciate it, Lumpy, but I have a friend over to help. Friends, in fact."

"You got a feller?" he asked.

"My heart is taken," I responded.

"Well, I guess I'm too late to pitch my hat in. Let me know if that changes."

"Thank you for the . . . compliment. And if you see anything else, let me know."

"Sure will. Hey, I don't s'pose you've given any thought to that arrangement I had with Gidget to buy her place?"

"I'm afraid I haven't. I don't even own the place yet. Do you have my cell phone number?"

I gave it to him. He punched it into his phone, his big fingers making slow work of it.

I drove too fast the rest of the way home, feeling off balance. After Adrian died, my kids and I had been stalked by his killer. I could have just imagined the Rover yesterday. I might not have been followed. But I sure didn't imagine the intruder. I pulled onto Gidget's property. There was a parking lot of cars in front of the house. I slammed on the brakes, stopping in the middle of my own dust cloud. I was so excited about the information from the eighth dwarf next door I couldn't wait to tell Rashidi and Maggie, and these cars looked like a spanner in my works. Who were all these people? I looked from vehicle to vehicle. The truck for the Internet provider service guy, Maggie's magenta Bess, and Rashidi's nondescript white rental Ford Fusion, plus Greyhound's Cayenne and Jimmy Urban's truck.

"Good Lord." I slammed the door of the Jetta a little too hard.

Two golden retrievers and one sausage-like, googly-eyed dog of questionable origin barked at me like I was there to loot the place.

"Hello, I live here!" I shouted at them.

They stopped barking, locking hurt eyes on me. I heard wheels on the dirt behind me and turned to find Sheriff Boudreaux himself pulling up in an LCSD Tahoe.

"Great," I muttered.

I let myself in the gate and rubbed Gertrude's tush. She wiggled and did figure eights around my ankles. I petted Janis and Woody behind their ears. I wasn't sure which one was which without checking under their hoods, but they didn't appear to be offended by my familiarity sans personal greeting.

Boudreaux was out of his SUV. He came into the yard, re-latching the gate behind him.

"I thought Tank and Junior didn't take me seriously."

He gave me a politician's bland smile. "Got a call from Greyhound."

"I'll get him for you. Wait here."

The sheriff raised one eyebrow at me. His smile disappeared. Mine came back as I let myself in the house and closed the door firmly behind me.

The house was crowded, hot, overwhelming. The adults clustered in the front rooms disappeared for a beat, replaced by two barefooted, pigtailed little girls in white cotton dresses, running and laughing, dolls in their hands, trailing the scent of dirt, fresh cut grass, and summer. I shifted my eyes and saw a woman in a calico dress and a long-brimmed bonnet. She was coming in the back door, carrying a basket of string beans. An older boy followed her with a pail of milk. A toothless old woman rocked by the front window, her eyes staring at nothing while she smiled and hummed a tune-less song. "Can a fellow get lunch around here?" a voice boomed. A tall bearded man in a sweat-stained white shirt slammed the door behind where I was standing. He moved through me, whipped his hat off, and bent to pull the pigtails on one of the little girls.

As quickly as they had appeared, they were replaced by Jimmy Urban standing off to my left, shifting from one foot to the other. Greyhound sitting at the table in the kitchen bending Rashidi's ear. Maggie in the living room to my right, arms crossed, foot tapping, as the Internet techni-cian was explaining something to her. And Lucy from the church, walking out of the kitchen with a cup of coffee. I didn't bother greeting anyone.

"Greyhound, the sheriff's out front for you."

"Let him in," Greyhound said.

"I don't feel like it," I retorted.

He looked at me closer, then stood and walked over to me, putting his hand on my elbow. "I asked the sheriff to come investigate."

"You have a lot more pull than I do. I made a report to his deputies and got nowhere."

"I'll take care of it. That and the property tax situation."

I gestured around me. "Speaking of taxes, federal in this case, the estate is a lot larger than you knew. There's millions in art in here. It's not extraor-

dinarily liquid, but there are some paintings in here that could pay the property tax debt as well as the future estate tax liability."

Greyhound squeezed my elbow, nodded, and went out the front door.
Rashidi beckoned me with his hand. I only had to take two steps to
reach him.

"I fixed the Quacker air conditioner."

"Really?" I eyed him dubiously. No toothpick, I was relieved to see.
"How?"

He shrugged. "I cleaned the evaporator coil and added coolant. And
when all the people dem leave, I'll crack your safe."

"Thank you. Very much."

He dipped his head. Then he added, softly, "I have something to show
you from your place."

Equally softly I said, "And I have something to tell you about the
picture on the wildlife camera."

He raised his eyebrows.

Maggie piped in, "Mr. Internet and I are having us a good time."

The young man flushed. Something about his gleaming eyes told me
that being harassed by Maggie was better than being ignored by Maggie.

"I'm almost done, ma'am." He continued fiddling with wires and cables.

"Jimmy, Lucy. To what do I owe the pleasure?"

Jimmy hooked a thumb at Lucy, who had come to stand beside him.
"She's got something to say to you."

I gestured at the table. "Can I offer you a seat?"

Lucy and Jimmy settled in chairs while I poured myself the last of the
coffee.

Rashidi said, "I'll make another pot," and shooed me toward the table. I
took Greyhound's vacated seat.

"All done here," the Internet installer announced.

Maggie crossed both arms over her chest, one hip cocked out. "I'll
believe it when I see it."

"I tested it out good, Ms. Maggie. With your phone's Wi-Fi connection,
too."

"Check it with a laptop," she ordered.

"Use mine," I said. I'd set it on the floor by the door when I first came in.
I pointed.

She went to collect it. "Is there a password?"

There was but I didn't want to shout it out. What was the point of a
password if everyone knew it? I waved her over. "Adrian14," I whispered.

She looked into my eyes, and in a weirdly comforting gesture, she leaned her forehead against mine like we'd been sisters or friends forever. As quickly as she'd done it, she pulled away and went back to the living room to bedevil the installer. Rashidi was whistling in the kitchen, stopping to sing, "Little darling, stir it up."

"Where were we?" I gave Lucy what I hoped was a warm smile.

"Go ahead," Jimmy urged her, but he was looking at me.

Lucy placed her cup in front of her carefully, then lined the handle up on the right side at a precise three o'clock. She clasped both her hands together, and her fingers kneaded each other. Whatever she had to say was becoming more interesting to me with each second that passed. Finally she squeezed her hands together so tightly her knuckles went white.

She drew in a deep breath and blew it out hard. "I didn't tell you the truth."

I froze, afraid to spook her. Afraid she would chicken out.

She closed her eyes. "I told you I never talked to Gidget again after her parents died, but I came to see her the day before she died."

I reached across the table and put my hand over her two clasped ones. They were icy cold. "I'm glad you're telling me now. Go on."

"It was Jimmy talked me into it. He made me see her life was harder than I'd known." Jimmy shifted in his chair. "She was right glad to see me." Lucy's eyes filled with tears, but she smiled. "She cried buckets. I did, too. She was more like herself than she'd been since she was a girl. She even called herself Anna. She asked me to pray with her. She was reading the Bible again."

"I'm so glad you were able to have that time with her."

Lucy's voice quaked. "I told her I was sorry. She said that she was, too. She told me about the book you're writing and"—a sob escaped her throat—"she told me about her d-d-daughter. I lied about that, too, I'm ashamed to say. Anna said she was going to tell you herself, and the secret would be out."

My heart thudded a powerful rhythm in my throat. I became hyper-aware of the sound of the coffee maker gurgling, the door closing as Rashidi slipped out back, the clicking of Maggie's fingers on my keyboard, the breathing of the installation tech as he watched over her shoulder, Lucy's cries, the vibrations of Jimmy's emotions as he worried over her without making a sound. He cared for her, I realized.

"What did she tell you about her?"

"Years ago, that time she'd come to town and I was so angry she didn't visit me, she'd been here to have her daughter. She said her parents gave her away, but that they never told her who or where. I just wanted you to know that the daughter is real, and that she was born in 1975, if that helps you any."

"It helps me a lot." An understatement of immense proportions.

Maggie's fingers started typing, click-click-click. "By golly, the Internet works!"

The Internet guy blushed. "I told you, Ms. Maggie."

"Good job, young man," she said to him.

To Lucy, I said, "Did she tell you who the father was?"

"No, she said she wasn't going to tell anyone his name until she'd given him fair warning. She said she wrote to him and was expecting to hear back anytime."

"Dang. Okay."

"I knew Jimmy went to see her in Houston, and I wondered . . ." Her eyes flitted up, causing more tears to spill as they met Jimmy's intense gaze. "I wondered if it was you."

You could've heard a pin drop.

Jimmy's forehead glistened with little drops of sweat. He stood and adjusted his overall straps. "That ain't none of your business," he said, but again he was looking at me.

All his response did was goad me. "But could you be?"

He growled, "I said it ain't none of your business. So get your nosey nose out of it."

Lucy whispered, "I'm so sorry, Jimmy."

I wondered if her question would ruin her chances of becoming the next Mrs. Jimmy Urban. She grabbed for her cup with nervous hands, and again her knuckles whitened. I was afraid the cup would break. Control. This woman exercised an amazing amount of control, but what did her desperate mannerisms say about the powerful emotions inside her? Watching her and Jimmy, I wondered, too, how jealous she might have been, believing that her old best friend had borne the child of the man she now—and maybe had always—pined for.

TWENTY-THREE

RASHIDI PULLED his rental car to the side of the road on Rummel Square around the corner from Espressions, the coffee shop we'd visited less than a week before with Annabelle, Jay, Ethan, and Papa. On the drive over to Round Top, I'd filled Rashidi in on my conversation with Lumpy, and we'd discussed Lucy's dramatic revelations, Jimmy's angry reaction, and Greyhound's report on the sheriff, who he swore promised action on my break-in. Rashidi was headed to meet with someone about cracking Gidget's safe; I was grabbing more coffee and then would be waiting for him at the library, where the Wi-Fi was free and unlimited.

I turned to Rashidi as the car stopped. "Can I get anything for you?"

He trained his bottomless black eyes on mine. I fell right in them, losing myself in a second. I was way too sleep-deprived and vulnerable. I gave myself a shake, which shimmied my shoulders a little.

Rashidi laughed. "What's that?"

I did it again. "Oh, just a chill. So do you want anything?"

He cocked his head, fiddling with his omnipresent toothpick, and studied me so long I grew antsy. "Nah, no caffeine for me. I'm high on life."

I grabbed my pocketbook and slung my laptop bag over my shoulder, then wiped sweaty palms on my bare thighs. "Text me when you're done with the safe-cracker guy."

Maggie had sent Rashidi to this guy because she'd heard he knew all there was to know about getting into things he shouldn't. What a recommendation. I slid backwards out of the car. Gertrude was in the back seat. I opened the rear door and called her out. She jumped, dreadlocks sailing up in the air, then floating down as she landed.

"Yah, mon." Rashidi gave me a two-finger salute from his brow.

I'd gone two steps with Gertrude sniffing the ground at my feet when Rashidi called after me. "Hold up."

I turned, ready to ask what was up, but he motioned me back to him with his fingers then held his phone up to me. "I forget to show you. I saw this at the Quacker today."

I grasped the phone, my fingers brushing his. Electricity shot up my arm. I lifted my sunglasses partway to get a better look at the screen. It was a photograph of a carving in a tree. A heart, with A+M inside it. I dropped the phone and jumped back. A . . . Adrian. M . . . Michele.

"Where . . . what . . . ?"

Gertrude whined, cocking her head.

Rashidi put the car in park and hustled around to me. He picked up the phone, then grasped my shoulder with a strong hand. "I was working behind the trailer, and I saw it. Covered in leaves, on the back of a tree. I thought maybe you hadn't seen it."

I put my hand over my mouth. "I hadn't."

"Then it's a good thing."

"Yes," I croaked. A message from Adrian. It was like he was talking to me again, although why his message had to come through Rashidi, I couldn't fathom. Still, I'd take it. He had to have carved it a year ago. Probably was going to show it to me on our anniversary, when he'd planned to reveal to me he'd bought the place. Only he died before that could happen. *Oh, Adrian.* I wanted to go back to our place and wrap my arms around the tree. I wanted to trace his sweet carving with my fingertip. I wanted to turn around and find him there with me, alive.

Rashidi typed with one thumb. "I'll send it to you." He released me. "You gonna be okay?"

"Yes." It came out weakly, so I repeated myself. "Yes, I'll be fine. Thank you for showing it to me."

"Of course." He got back in the car and accelerated away from the coffee shop.

I saw him turn and look at me one more time. How did I just resume life like everything was normal and okay after that? I nudged my funny dog with my toe. "Wow. Adrian."

She bobbed her head.

I'd take my time. I took in a deep breath through my nose. I smelled coffee and biscuits from Espressions and the fragrant odor of fajitas from

Los Patrones around the corner. I slowed down and really studied my surroundings, and I noticed a building ten yards back that struck a chord. I walked to it, pulled like a paper clip to a magnet. The old log structure had two arched cutouts in its long rectangular shape. I couldn't tell if it had been a cabin or a stable or some other type of building. It was a beautiful restoration with new but old-looking mortar filling the chinks. As I walked through it, I saw a plaque hanging inside one of the arches.

I skimmed the words. Moore's Fort, the oldest building in Fayette County, moved to Round Top in 1976 from La Grange. I put my hands on my hips. Of course. My father had recognized this building in the photo of Gidget's parents with their friends. He'd remembered it from a childhood trip to La Grange.

Gertrude barked, one sharp yap.

A person walked up and stood near me. "They just moved it here from all of two blocks away. Can you believe it?"

I glanced to my right and recognized Senator Boyd Herrington. "Hello, Senator. My name's Michele Lopez Hanson. We met at Espressions last weekend."

His face lost color, and he took a step back. "Good to see you again. Enjoy the beautiful day here in Round Top." He walked quickly across the street and down the block, out of sight.

Gertrude and I headed toward the coffee house. It was a strange encounter, but he was a politician, after all. I entered Espressions. The interior was small and dark yet somehow colorful and cheerful, too. The proprietor—the same guy from the weekend before—was scrubbing counters.

"Hi, John. Is it all right if I bring my dog in?"

He paused, rag in hand. "Absolutely. Let me know if she needs a bowl of water. Where's the rest of your bicycling entourage?"

Back in Houston, so few people remembered each other. Those I saw frequently still recognized Adrian more than me, even at the height of my semi-celebrity. Yet here in the small towns, everyone knew everyone. I set my bags on the community table.

"It's just me today."

My phone rang. Out of long habit as a parent, I pulled it from my purse to glance at the caller ID. It was Papa, which was unusual. Before my mother's death, she did most of the dialing and phone communication. Since she'd died, I'd been the one to schedule calls with Papa. I turned away from John and tried to keep my voice low.

"Hey, Papa."

"Michele," he said. "How are you?"

I loved his musical accent. Both of his parents were from Mexico, so he couldn't help but pick it up somewhat. I had none of it. "I'm good. I'm in a coffee shop. In fact, the one you were in with us in Round Top."

Papa's voice brightened. "Give it my best."

I laughed. Gertrude pulled on the leash. She'd sniff-patrolled all the square footage she could reach. I let the leash play out to its full length. "I will. What's up?"

He hesitated, and the silence filled my entire being with a heavy dread. Was it bad news? Could he be calling about his health? Was something wrong with Mom's estate?

"Papa?" I prompted.

"Oh, I'm just a silly old man," he said. "Feeling lonely and wanting to hear your voice."

I'd been away from home so many years I only missed my parents when I needed them. My mother's absence was a terrible pain and loneliness, but it didn't pervade my day-to-day life. It was different for Papa. He had lost his lifelong companion. His partner. Like I had with Adrian. While their marriage may not have been the greatest love match of the twentieth century, they had been together for many years. That house had to feel silent and empty.

"I'm so sorry, Papa. Would you like to come visit this weekend or—"

He cut me off. "I would, actually. I've been thinking a lot since your mother passed. I don't know what's holding me here anymore."

"Your practice?" Gertrude tugged, ready for more territory. I took a step forward.

"My practice, yes. But any vet can take care of my clients' animals."

"That's not true. They love you."

"Time would make them soon forget. And every day I remember that the only things in the world that matter to me now are you, Sam, and Belle."

"Oh, Papa." I hunched my back toward John to hide my sudden tears. I reached up to my cheeks to brush them off and my fingers came away slick and wet. I'd promised I would stop all this crying. But surely this didn't count, when I was crying for Papa instead of myself.

"Since you are putting down roots there, I want to come look at some places, too."

"That would be—" My voice broke, and I cleared my throat. "That would be fantastic. When do you want to come?"

"How about Sunday?"

"Sounds great." A sign in a window flashed in my memory: SEEKING PART-TIME VET. "All right, Papa. See you then."

"Love you, Itzpa."

"Love you."

I ended the call and put the phone back in my purse. My face was still wet. I leaned down toward my shoulder and used the short sleeve of my T-shirt to blot my cheeks. First on one side and then the other. When I'd done all I could, I walked to the long, high countertop. Gertrude bounced happily along with me. "Sorry about that."

John was washing coffee cups by hand. "What can I get you?"

I stared up at the hand-lettered menu board on the wall in front of me with unseeing eyes. "Can you do an iced coffee?"

"I can do it iced or I can put it in the blender for you like one of those frap-type of drinks."

"That sounds good. The blender version."

"What flavor do you want?"

"Regular coffee. Honey. And almond milk?"

"Got it."

He scribbled something on an order pad and stuck it on a spike. He tucked the pencil behind his ear. I handed him my credit card. He swiped it and typed on an iPad then swiveled it to face me. I touched twenty percent for the tip and signed with my finger.

"No receipt." I swiveled it back to him.

He handed me my credit card. "Give me just a second."

I went back to the table and took a seat. Apparently there was no such thing as a midday rush in Round Top on a Thursday afternoon. While he prepared my coffee, I scrolled my messages on my phone.

I had a text from Annabelle. "Jay dumped me. What am I gonna do?"

My hand flew to my chest. Jay had been the moon and the stars to Annabelle for the last year. He was her first love.

Before I could answer her, John shouted over the sound of the blender, "You're writing a book about Gidget Becker, aren't you? And living in her place?"

I kept my phone in my hand but returned to the counter where he could hear my answer. "I am."

He turned the blender off and poured the creamy tan concoction into a clear plastic cup. "My father knew her when they were young. They went to church together. If you ever want to know anything about Gidget when she was young, I know my dad would have plenty to say."

"I met another of Gidget's friends from her childhood. Another girl that would've gone to church with them."

John held up a canister of Reddi-wip. "You want me to top it off?"

I couldn't believe it when I heard myself say, "Sure."

He squirted a tower of white foamy topping on my drink. "I'll bet it was Lucy."

"Yes," I said.

"She's my aunt." He handed me my drink.

"Oh, is your dad Bubba?"

"Sure is. Oh, wait." He grabbed a straw in a paper wrapper. He tore the top off the straw wrapper and handed it to me, holding the paper-wrapped end of it.

"Thank you." I took the straw and stuck it in the top of the drink.

"Aunt Lucy's an old busybody. Dad doesn't go to the church anymore. She never married, and I suppose she's just bitter. She and my dad don't get along."

I took a deep pull of my coffee drink. Brain freeze. I put a hand to my forehead and he laughed.

"Well, I know it's cold, but otherwise, how is it?"

"It's great." I winced anyway, brain still frozen. "Thank you. It will keep me cool and awake on my walk to the library." I shouldered my bags and raised my drink to him as Gertrude and I headed for the door. "Thanks again, and I may be in touch about your dad."

He smiled after me. "Good luck."

I opened the door and the wall of heat and humidity hit me in the face. I waved a hand in front of me to cut through the thick air. Not that it did any good. The library was about two blocks away. Small-town blocks, not city blocks. There were no sidewalks. I walked on the asphalt on the left-hand side of the street. Gertrude went nuts pulling me every which way. As I walked along, sipping and trying to control the dog, I remembered Annabelle's bad news. I had put my phone back in my handbag when I was gearing up to leave the coffee shop. I used my free hand to retrieve it now. The bright sunlight made it hard to read the screen. I used voice activation to send Annabelle a text back.

"What happened? Are you okay? Dumb question. I'm so sorry!" I hit send.

In five minutes, I'd reached the library grounds. My arm was sore from Gertrude's pulling. Who knew there were so many squirrels in Round Top? I shook it and changed hands with the leash, looking around me. The Round Top Family Library was housed in an immaculately reconstructed historic church. White clapboard, a metal roof, wonderful Gothic windows, and a tall belfry. It stood beside the tiny Rummel Haus, which was restored in place as an activity center for the library. An old guy was sitting in front of the Rummel Haus at a picnic table shaded by a giant live oak, working on his laptop. I smiled. Too hot for me out here, but more power to him.

I walked under the metal entry arch and up to the double front doors. My mother would have loved this library. In fact, my mother loved all libraries. Unfortunately, it was only as I put my hand on the door that I considered the dog at the end of my leash.

I thought back to the old guy in front of Rummel Haus. At least it was shaded there. I tugged on Gertrude, who gave me a dirty look, and we went back around the corner toward the picnic table. The man was packing up his laptop, and by the time we reached him, he had a messenger bag slung over his shoulder and was standing up.

"Good afternoon," I said to him.

He grunted. "Too damn hot."

"You won't get an argument from me."

I set my bags on the table and pulled Gertrude in as she attempted to sneak off with him. She turned back toward me, her front half, at least; her back half still pointed in the direction she'd been headed.

I shook my head. "You're a mess, Gertrude."

She smiled, her tongue hanging out and her dreadlocks bouncing as she trotted the few steps back. I hooked the loop at the end of the leash under one of the picnic table's feet.

"Behave."

She plopped down for a rest. I connected to the free Wi-Fi. It worked and I wasn't paying by the gig.

"Hallelujah," I said to Gertrude.

She cocked her head toward me.

"Never mind."

A flood of messages poured into my inbox, half of them from Brian. I knew I should feel guilty—and I did a little bit, but I knew he would understand. I typed a quick message apologizing for not writing earlier and explaining the day—*days*, really—full of police and legal woes. I promised him an update and an avalanche of finished work soon. Next I pulled up white pages for Houston and poked around until I found Darlene Hogg. I filled her in: My name really was Michele, I lived out at Gidget's old place in Giddings, and I was writing a book about Gidget, not just an article. Gidget had wanted her daughter's father to know about her, and to get his blessing to find and tell the daughter about him. It was imperative I reach him. I left out how I figured out her identity. Sometimes it's better not to give away all your secrets.

I had so many things I wanted to do, like dig for information on the lying Lester Tillman, Gidget herself, Darlene Hogg in her many marital incarnations, the attorney Nancy Little, the Beckers' registration for their antique car, Lonestar Pipeline, who thought they were routing through Gidget's place, the Houston Arts Trust, and every artist who'd personalized work for Gidget. I needed to post on the adoption boards now that I had a birth year for Gidget's daughter, and read through them, too, to see if she'd left a message for Gidget or her father. I wanted to hunt down any deliveries to Gidget's place in the last few weeks. I should write a post for the blog. I should figure out if Ralph had a tie to Lonestar or to this deal they thought they had to route the pipeline through Gidget's place. Just thinking about how much I had to do to fulfill Gidget's last wishes took my breath away. I would do all of them. I had to.

But I had to triage for now. I needed the property records for Gidget's land. I figured I could get the plat from the county, but first I pulled up Google Earth and put in the address to see if I could get enough information that way, without the red tape. While Google Earth did its thing, I glanced at my phone again. Nothing from Annabelle.

A Cayenne caught my eye as it pulled into the library parking lot and joined the handful of other cars. The vanity plates gave the owner away. Greyhound. He parked, but didn't get out.

Google Earth finished pulling up Gidget's place. I admired the leafy green top view surrounding the livestock pastures where crops used to grow. From above you could see cuts through the trees that appeared to be fence lines separating her property from mine on one side, Lumpy's on another, and someone's who I hadn't yet met in the back. I remembered Lumpy told me that the Beckers used to own all the land, and I pictured it fenceless, years ago. There was a small pond among the trees, and near the back of the property there appeared to be something shiny and red under the canopy of tree branches.

My phone dinged and I looked down at it. Annabelle: *"He's jealous about a guy. It's not my fault."*

Another car pulled into the parking lot and backed in beside Greyhound. I voice-recorded a text for Annabelle, staring at my computer screen, the pastures, forest, and farmhouse. *"I'm so sorry."*

I glanced back at the parking lot. Greyhound was still in the Cayenne with it running. The other driver had left his car running as well, and both drivers had rolled down their windows. They were leaning toward each other. Talking. With a sick feeling, I squinted for a better look. It was Greyhound, all right. And the driver of the other vehicle was Lester Tillman.

Rashidi pulled his car to a stop, blocking my view.

TWENTY-FOUR

WHEN WE GOT BACK to Gidget's, Rashidi's work with the grinder was downright violent. The mild-mannered savior of spiders had returned from his safe-cracking meeting feeling borderline homicidal. He'd driven up to the mobile home where the guy lived and found Dixie flags hanging as blackout curtains in the windows. The guy had a shaved head, and—after he called Rashidi "boy" one too many times and only after Rashidi had enough information to DIY—Rashidi had driven away before he was tempted to "knock he ass out," as he so colorfully put it. I was relieved, because dumbass racist bastards—sorry, Mom—usually traveled in packs, and I was scared to think what they might have done to a black Rastafarian with an island accent who'd decked one of their own.

I was mad, too. At Greyhound. But the reason for my upset wasn't as emotional as Rashidi's, and I decided to just tell him about it later.

I flinched as the grinder we'd stopped at the Mercantile to get on the way back whined, went quiet, then hit the floor.

"Dammit," Rashidi shouted.

The deafening noise resumed. The grinder kicked up a thick metal dust cloud that I was sure was ripping the insides of my lungs like shrapnel. I left Rashidi to it and took myself and a large glass of water to check on Maggie's progress in the barn. Gertrude and her buddies were lounging in the shade next to the piles Maggie was creating.

She emerged through the barn door, her face smudged with dirt and her arms full of old wood and rusted metal. She was probably the most beautiful woman I'd ever seen, even covered in grime. The most poised one, too. I wondered if I would ever feel as confident as Maggie looked.

She crowed, "Have I got shit to show you."

Not the most eloquent, though. "I'll trade you a water for the guided tour." I held a glass up at her.

"Deal."

She dumped her armload on the ground in front of her three large piles. She took the glass from me and gulped until she'd drained it, then set it down in the grass.

She picked up a spiral notebook and flipped to the first page. "I'm separating my finds into those I want to make an offer on and those I recommend you keep—which I'd offer on in a heartbeat, too, but I don't want to be greedy. The other pile is just for things I'd pitch out."

The pile of the stuff that she wanted to make an offer on was enormous and the pile of trash was fairly sizeable. The things she thought I should keep was pretty small.

"Awesome," I said, then filled her in on my eventful trip and Rashidi's terrible one before we started her reveal.

Maggie shook her head. "Well, I don't know if I can top a weird Senator Herrington encounter, Greyhound's odd behavior, or a stone-cold racist, but I do have some eighteen-hundreds wagon wheels and an old cast-iron stove, plus an entire kitchen's worth of pre-electricity gadgets and hoo-has."

"All of that in there? I'm shocked."

"Slow down, little Jaguar," Maggie sang. She continued, something about a sky blue Jaguar and a Thunderbird Ford.

At first I was confused why she was singing. Then I didn't care. My jaw dropped. Her voice was probably the most amazing thing my ears had ever heard. Katie had a beautiful voice, but Maggie was on a different plane.

"Well?" she prompted me.

"Oh my God."

"What do you mean, oh my God? Did you get my hint?"

"Hint? I was listening to you sing."

She waved her hand like she was swatting away a fly. "No, it was a hint. I had a huge find."

"What is it?"

She lifted a beat-up, corroded chrome fin with an SS on it from the ground by the "Michele should keep these" stack.

I wasn't really sure what she was holding. "And?"

"It's a hood ornament. From a really old car. I Googled it. Swallow Sidecars shortened their name to SS when they switched from making motorcycle sidecars to automobiles. Their earliest cars were just called SS models. Then SS Jaguars. Then just Jaguars. So this"—she held it out to me —"was the hood ornament to a pre-Jaguar."

Papa had told me as much when he saw the picture of the car. I reached out for the piece of metal, sucking in a breath. It was small. I ran a finger over the flared top edge. "This proves, at least, that there was one."

"Absolutely," she said. "Now, we just have to find the rest of it. But from a pure junk perspective, this is gold. Anything from this car. Pure gold."

"Pure gold that belongs to Gidget's daughter, if we can find her."

"True."

I took out my phone and snapped a picture of the hood ornament up close. I emailed it to my blog, titling it "Things That Are True."

My phone rang. Expecting a frantic Annabelle, I answered. "Hello? Belle?"

"Nope. It's Blake. Hi, Michele!"

Whoops. Not only had I not answered his text, but he'd left me a voice mail the day before, too. "Blake Cooper. Wow. Hello."

Maggie chortled. "Blake Cooper from La Grange?"

I nodded.

In my phone ear, Blake was saying, "I'd love to meet you for lunch in Round Top one day when I'm working in La Grange."

In my non-phone ear, Maggie was screeching, "Oh my God, I lost my virginity to him in high school!"

My eyes widened at her. I covered the mouthpiece. "For real?"

Maggie licked her finger and touched it to an imaginary stove and made the sound of it sizzling. "He was so hot. Is he still?"

Blake said, "Am I interrupting something?"

"My friend Maggie Killian is saying she knows you."

"Maggie Killian? Tell her I said hello!"

I exchanged greetings between them. "Well, we're in the middle of a meeting, Blake. Thank you for calling. I'll have to get back to you."

"Except you won't."

I laughed stiffly. Damn him for being right. "Sure I will."

After I hung up, Maggie gave me the more detailed version. More detailed than I wanted to hear. I explained my connection to him. Finally I was able to get her back on track. The project. Gidget's barn. Maggie showed me the highlights from the rest of her junking. There was a ton of cool stuff, but nothing else led us closer to Gidget's daughter or the car.

"You're doing great. And I've got to get back to work or my boss is going to fire me."

"I'll come with you. I need water and a cool-down."

We entered the house, and she set the SS fin on the kitchen counter. The high-pitched shriek of Rashidi's grinder assaulted our ears.

She refilled her water glass, then spoke in a shout. "I've probably only got another hour in me before I melt."

"Sounds good," I shouted back.

The whirring of Rashidi's grinding operation stopped as soon as she left. I heard some guttural sounds from Rashidi that might have been expletives, but not the continental United States variety.

"Are you okay?" I called to him.

He muttered something else then his voice brightened. "Irie."

He came into the kitchen with a painted birdhouse in each hand. He set them on the table. His dreadlocks and face were gray where his protective mask had ended. My face twitched.

"I need more wheels for the grinder."

I shook my head. "You need the fountain of youth. You've aged four decades in an hour."

He ducked into the bathroom and yelped. I heard water running and the sounds of splashing. "No towels."

"In here."

He stumbled back with water on his face and his eyes half closed. I grabbed some paper towels from the kitchen counter and handed them to him.

"Thank you." He blotted his face. When it was dry, he picked the birdhouses up and turned toward the back door.

Curious, I opened it for him and followed him out. He stopped at the little oak in the backyard where my wildlife cam hung from a branch. He nailed the first house onto the trunk of the tree with a hammer he'd carried in his back pocket. A warmth spread through me and my emotions bubbled toward the surface.

"Where do you want the other?" No toothpick.

"Front yard?"

His long strides ate up the ground, and I scrambled behind him. He hung the birdhouse in another oak.

"Thank you." It was all I trusted myself to say.

He winked at me, and we went back inside.

"Are you close to cracking the safe?"

He waffled his hand. "I'm figuring it out. Making progress. But it's slowgoing."

My handbag was on the table and I reached into it, grabbing my wallet. I pulled out two twenties. "Here you go. For more grinders."

Ignoring my outstretched hand, he opened the front door. "Room and board." He flashed me a killer white smile, then slipped out.

My phone sounded its text tone. I flipped it over in a hurry, eager for distraction from the fluttery feeling in my stomach from Rashidi's smile.

It was Annabelle picking up where I'd left it in our conversation: *"That's not all. I got fired."*

I shot a text back quick as a flash. *"Oh, honey. What for?"*

"Same thing."

That made no sense. *"What do you mean?"*

I waited, but this time I got no reply. I connected to my newly installed Wi-Fi from the laptop. I opened a new tab and clicked my saved place for the adoption site of kids looking for their parents. Before I posted the entry for Gidget's daughter, I scanned the new posts that fit my search parameters. None of them seemed to be the one—my brother. I scanned again looking for someone that could be the grown-up daughter of Gidget. Nothing. I typed up a searching-for-a-female entry with everything I knew about Gidget's daughter and her birth. I closed the site and checked my email. Nothing there, either—nothing except one from Brian about my absence for the day, which made me feel like a heel for working on Gidget's stuff instead of Juniper's. No problem, Michele. I know you're good for it.

But not guilty enough to stop. In the same tab I opened Google and typed in a search for Lester Tillman. My mind fixed on his face in profile as he leaned out the driver's side window of his car for a tête-à-tête with my attorney. I cursed him and his ancestors in Spanish, then Greyhound's for good measure. He'd better have a heck of an explanation. The search results included the gallery's website and numerous links to articles from art publications. I wanted something historical and comprehensive, as well as the most recent information and articles linking him to Gidget.

None of the search results were what I was looking for. Short on detail, long on fluff. Also, they focused more on the artists and their shows than the gallery and its personalities. As a last resort, I turned to Wikipedia. Although it certainly wasn't a source to rely on, I figured it would be a long shot that a gallery owner would have an entry. Scarlett had tried to put one together for me after *My Pace or Yours* had come out last year. I hadn't been sufficiently noteworthy, according to them. The Montrose Fine Arts Gallery pulled right up, though.

Its Wiki page was long and had a section on personal history near the bottom. I quickly scrolled past the various artists who had shown at the gallery and lists of high-dollar sales the gallery had made. Later I could read everything on this page, especially for mentions of Gidget, but first I wanted a fix on Lester Tillman. The personal history section was sparse. It did tell me his birthdate, which confirmed what I already suspected, that Lester was unmarried and seventy years old. It listed his hometown as Riceboro, Georgia. I Googled it. Population 829. Ha. Savannah, my big toe. Briefly married to Julie Herrington before coming out in his early thirties. There was a picture of him with her, a plain woman with brown hair.

I was interrupted by a knock on the door. Red and blue lights flashed through the window, giving the LCSD Tahoe away. I threw the door open. Surprise, surprise, it was Tank and Junior.

"Long time, no see."

Tank shoved past me without an invitation, forcing me back. Junior followed him, turning to the side so he wouldn't bump into me.

"Is there anything I can do for you guys or are you just here to do what you should've done this morning?" I shut the door harder than necessary, rattling the windows. Well, the windows and one piece of cardboard.

Tank grunted.

Junior set a large tote bag on my kitchen table, knocking my laptop a few inches to the side. He mumbled, "Sorry, Ms. Hanson."

I shut my laptop and jerked the cord from the wall. Tank rubbed his chin. The whiskers growing in were dark and thick. They'd been less noticeable when I went in to see him and Junior that morning.

"Anybody been here that we need to rule out?" he asked.

I threw up my one free arm, exasperated. "You have a picture of who you're looking for. However, the list of people who have been here is the same as when you did the crime scene for Ms. Becker's death. Oh, plus my attorney—Greyhound Smith—the sheriff, Jimmy Urban, and Lucy Thompson. And Maggie Killian."

Junior's head popped up at the mention of Maggie.

Tank didn't react to her name, or any of the others. "Your neighbor said a black man's been casing your place. Have you seen him?"

I counted to ten slowly before I spoke. "If you'll take a look at the picture I sent you, it's clearly not a black man. My good friend Rashidi is a black man with dreadlocks. He hasn't cased the place. He's a house guest."

They didn't comment. I went to the bedroom for my handbag and shoved my laptop in its carrier. I stomped down the hall toting them both.

Tank met me coming from the other direction. "Was anything missing?"

"Like I told you this morning, nothing that I can tell."

He looked into the room with the safe and raised his eyebrows. "Looks like somebody tried to take something."

I followed his gaze to the obvious safe-cracking project. "Yes, it appeared they'd tried to get into the safe. But since then, I've been trying to."

He didn't look at me, just kept his gaze on the safe and walked over to it, put his hands on his hips, and moved in a semicircle around it. I snapped my fingers. He didn't turn.

"Are you listening to me? I did that."

"Not yours, though, is it?" he said softly, not bothering to turn around.

I played the attorney card. "In trying to access this safe, Deputy, I am acting on the instructions and with the permission of the independent executor of the estate, pending probate, and while I am renting this property, furnished, inclusive of everything on it, writing the deceased's biography at her request, and assisting in the search for her daughter." *Put that in your pipe and smoke it.*

"Is Ralph here to verify that?"

"Really? Do you *see* him here?"

He locked eyes with me and didn't answer.

"Effing call him. Please."

He laughed. "Effing?" He lifted his fingers and wiggled them. "Woo. Now she means business."

This was going nowhere fast. I stomped toward the door. "*Pendejo,*" I whispered. I slammed the door behind me, even harder that time.

TWENTY-FIVE

MAGGIE WAS SURVEYING HER PILES, her arms crossed, tapping her feet. She turned at the sound of the slamming door. "What's the matter?"

I pointed at the deputies' vehicle and back at Gidget's house. "They aren't doing anything to rehabilitate my low opinion of law enforcement."

She laughed. "I know what we need to do. It'll make you feel better. Can you leave?"

"Absolutely."

Twenty minutes later we pulled into the parking lot of the Giddings pool. Maggie had steadfastly refused to tell me her plan as we drove.

"This is perfect, except I don't have a suit and goggles." I heard the joy gurgling in my own voice.

"I keep spares in my toolbox."

I had texted Rashidi on the drive, warning him about the deputies. He'd promised to steer clear until they were gone. The last thing I wanted was them harassing him or, worse yet, taking him in. I hoped he was true to his word.

We greeted the woman at the entrance as we passed through. She was about our age, but didn't look like a swimmer herself. A little softer and thicker through the middle, but not much.

She smiled and waved us in. "Y'all have a good swim, now."

"Thanks, Lisa," Maggie replied.

I made a mental note of the woman's name for next time, so I could be neighborly, too. We changed quickly and took the one free lane. Even underwater the noise from the pool deck and shallow end was a roar. Inside my head, I whispered to Adrian, *You would love it. All this energy. All this youth.* A deep pang of grief overtook me for a moment. I'd give up my right arm for another swim with Adrian. Then a startling feeling surged through me. I'd give up nearly that to hear my mother's voice chiding me one more time. But I pushed my sorrow away and concentrated on reaching a no-thinking and no-feeling zone. It wasn't long until the rhythm of my kick and strokes hypnotized me and gave me the temporary relief I needed from the mess that was my life.

As we left the pool, I said, "That was a good call."

Maggie turned left where I'd expected her to turn right. "Yep."

"Where are we going?"

"My place."

"Cool." I smoothed back my wet hair then changed my mind. I scrubbed it as hard as I could with my hands to give it body.

Maggie looked at me with high eyebrows, but she didn't say anything.

"I really do love your truck." I rubbed my palm against the creamy leather. It was a milky tan. "Bess, you are quite beautiful."

The truck purred as it jiggled and jounced over the bumps in the road, garnering admiring glances as we passed through town. Bess was not an inconspicuous vehicle.

"She came with the house."

"How could anyone leave her?"

"She was a sight, then. I had her restored. I used to do a little mattress dancing with the guy that fixed her up."

It took me a second to realize what she meant, and then I laughed. With a straight face, I said, "You must be an awfully good dancer."

"Why, yes. Yes, I am." She waggled her eyebrows.

We rode in silence for the rest of the drive to Round Top.

I got a text from Sam: *"Fine."*

I replied: *"????"*

I'd call him tomorrow. When we were a few miles from town, Maggie pulled Bess into the old, colorful wooden house I'd noticed on the drive to Fayetteville. It had a small parking lot in front and a sign over the door: FLOWN THE COOP. The boards were painted in a kaleidoscope of colors, but weathered so the palette was muted.

"This is amazing."

Maggie steered Bess around to an old barn behind the house. "I'm very proud of it all." She parked Bess and shut off the engine. "Come inside with me."

We passed a busy hummingbird feeder by the walkway to the house. An emerald beauty with a ruby-colored throat had staked his claim and was busy fending off all comers. I could hear the buzz of his wings as I passed him and followed Maggie through a back door with a sign on it that read PRIVATE RESIDENCE. We entered into a little kitchen with a butcher-block island in the middle. The turquoise floorboards squeaked under my feet. Cabinets of white-washed reclaimed wood held up the cement countertops with an enormous white porcelain inset farmhouse sink. A gray subway-tile backsplash adorned the walls around the open shelving.

Maggie leaned over and opened the bottom cabinet to the left of the sink. She reached in and pulled out a liter bottle of Texas Single Malt, one-third full of the same amber liquid we'd had the night before.

She held it up by its short neck.

I shuddered. The stuff terrified me.

"Can you believe they make this in Waco?" She set it on the island then grabbed two tin mugs off of the lower shelf above the countertop. She set them down on either side of the whiskey bottle with a clang. "The swim was part one. This is part two."

"Part one and two of what?" I asked her and sidled away from the whiskey bottle.

"Recovery from a hard day." She uncapped the bottle.

She tipped the bottle, filling the cups two-thirds of the way full. She pushed one across the island to me, or rather, along the length of it since I had moved back toward the door, and safely beyond it. The whiskey sloshed a little on its journey.

"Take it." She picked hers up, closed her eyes, and took a sip. She lowered the mug just enough to speak to me. "Burns so good."

"I'm not much of a drinker."

"I saw that last night."

"It doesn't have a mixer."

"Drink it anyway."

The fumes hit me before I had the glass halfway to my face. I let a few milliliters of the liquid pass my lips and swallowed. It burned like fire on the way down. I coughed and sputtered out expensive whiskey.

Maggie laughed. "It takes a few sips to get used to it."

"No, no." I put the glass down.

She narrowed her eyes at me, came around the island, picked up my cup and walked over to me. "Take a seat." She nodded at the stools tucked under the island.

I did as I was told.

"Think of this as an analgesic."

My voice trembled a little. "What do you mean?" Why was I being such a big baby? It was only whiskey. Maggie was still holding the mug out at me, so I clasped my hands around it and nodded. "Thank you."

She took a seat, the feet of the stool squeaking against the wood as she pulled it out. I tried another sip. This time I held the liquid in my mouth a little longer. I got a sensation of butter and molasses and overripe pears. I swished it in my mouth and tasted honey. I swallowed and thought of apples. As I opened my mouth to take another sip, the apple morphed into apple pie with a rich cinnamon and clove aftertaste.

I swallowed. "It's better than I gave it credit for."

Maggie finally relaxed and tipped her tin cup back. "It's all I drink. The best I've ever had, and it's Texan to boot." She raised her cup to me.

I took a few more slugs and enjoyed the warming sensation, from my shoulders out to my fingers and to the tip of my nose. The whiskey enhanced the pleasant silence, and I admired the adorable kitchen, until Maggie set her cup down with a clank.

She refilled it. "So what's going on with you and Rashidi? Or is it you and Blake?"

I sprayed a little bit of Balcones across the island toward the sink as I sputtered. "Nothing. Nothing is going on with me with either of them. They're friends." I covered my face with my cup, drinking.

"It doesn't look like nothing with Rashidi."

"My husband died a year ago. He was, he is, the love of my life—"

"I didn't know—"

"—and my mom just died, too. It's scary loving people. I'm on a break from it." I tried to divert her. "What about you?"

Maggie jumped to her feet, nearly knocking her stool over. She turned and caught it, then pushed it back underneath the island. "My dad died ten years ago."

"I'm sorry. I was actually asking about whether you're in a relationship, though."

She turned around and opened a curtain, revealing a pantry that had a slanted ceiling like it was underneath a staircase. She pulled out a bag of tortilla chips and set them on the island, then grabbed a Tupperware container out of the refrigerator. She peeled the top back and set it beside the chips.

"Nothing fancy." She pulled the sides of the chip bag apart until it released along the top. "Just a little something to line our stomachs." She took her seat again. "I've never been married. I have a long-term non-rela-

tionship based on secrecy and spending as little time together as possible."
She dipped a chip into what looked like hummus.

I did the same. It was hummus. A nice roasted-garlicky one. I popped
one loaded chip then another into my mouth. Through chip and hummus, I
said, "Who is he?" while savoring the delicious melding of olive oil with
lemon juice and chickpeas.

She didn't answer.

"Did you make this?" I asked her. I chased my chips with some more
Balcones.

"Yep. It's a secret."

"So who's the guy?"

"That's the secret."

My lips were starting to feel numb. I bit into a chip. Yes, definitely
numb.

"Besides," she said. "Who said it was a guy?"

She picked up my tin cup, sloshed it around, then filled it from the
whiskey bottle, which was now nearly empty. She slid it back over to me,
not spilling any this time. Just as I was about to laugh at her joke, she leaned
in and kissed me on the lips, soft and long. I was too startled to pull back,
and I didn't want to be rude. Then I felt giggly because I was worrying
about whether or not I was being rude in the middle of the first kiss I'd ever
had from a woman. What would have mortified my mom worse: being rude
to Maggie, or letting her kiss me?

She pulled away from me, watching me with amused, calculating
eyes.

"Oh. Well. Okay."

She laughed so hard she leaned over with her hands on her knees.
When she stood up again, she was still laughing. "You should see your
face."

"Why?" I could feel the heat in my ears, so I was sure my Mexico tan
was red at the edges. I gulped my whiskey.

"Oh, *chiquita*, I'm sorry. You're so adorable. I couldn't resist teasing
you." She squeezed my elbow. "Yes, the relationship—or the non-relation-
ship—is with a guy."

My brain was misfiring, thanks to the whiskey and the kiss. I was just
sober enough to be aware of it and just drunk enough that I didn't care. "So,
you're not a—"

She looked at me and winked. "Lesbian?"

"That."

She smiled. "I'm a free spirit, and I love sexuality in general, but I guess if you had to label me, you'd have to call me straight. Straight, but adventurous." She winked again.

I'd never had a friend like Maggie. I'd never experimented with anyone of the same sex. "I'm not. Adventurous, I mean."

"Sure you are." Her eyes had softened, and now they grew hazy. "You moved out here in a trailer, you're writing Gidget's memoirs, and now you're in her old house trying to fix everything for everybody."

I took a big gulp of the whiskey. "That's a different kind of adventurous."

"True." She raised her cup. "But I like your adventurous side."

"Thanks." My ears felt hot again. "I'll keep your non-boyfriend a secret. We wouldn't want anyone to mistake you for traditional."

She looked very grave. "Thank God."

We bumped cups, and they made a metallic clunk.

The whiskey was working on me fast. "Greyhound has a secret," I said.

"That he does and you should call him."

I thought about it. Whiskey made it hard to think, but I swigged more anyway. I thought about Greyhound and touched my phone in my pocket. "Maybe I should wait until I'm sober." The phone vibrated under my hands and I heard its little text tone, so I pulled it out.

It was a message from Annabelle: *"Where are you? I'm at your house."*

"My house in Houston?"

"No, your house in Nowheresville."

I felt like we were playing "Who's on First?" "The Quacker?"

"No, the old lady's house."

I looked up at Maggie. "My stepdaughter's at Gidget's house."

"The one who just got dumped?"

"Yes. And fired."

"Uh-oh. Time to be a mama."

I nodded. I texted Annabelle: *"I'm at a friend's and need a ride. Can you come get me?"*

She responded: *"LOL, sure."*

"It's kind of far."

"That's OK."

I sent her Maggie's address.

"You're a good mother," Maggie told me.

I set my phone down, faceup in case Annabelle needed me. "Sometimes. Being a stepmom can be tricky. But family is everything."

She scraped up the last of the hummus.

Her comment reminded me of something. "My papa wants to move here."

"Sweet. We can set him up with my mother."

The conversation and whiskey flowed for the next half hour. Maggie's stories could make a sailor blush, but she was interesting and funny. I felt less Tlazol around her. More Itzpa.

The back door rattled as someone knocked. It was Annabelle. She opened the screen door and joined us.

I stood to greet her and swayed, then threw my arms around her. "Here's my beautiful stepdaughter. Belle thizziz Maggie. Maggie, Belle." I released her and swayed again. I covered it up by sitting back down.

Annabelle shook Maggie's hand then turned around and frowned at me. "You're drunk."

"No," I said. "A little tipsy izzall."

"Wasted," Maggie agreed.

Annabelle looked fresh and young and beautiful, with her blonde curls tumbling around her shoulders. But there were dark circles under her eyes and tear tracks on her cheeks. She rolled her eyes at me. "Nice, Michele." To Maggie, she was more polite. "Cool place."

"Thanks. I hear you've had a rough day."

Annabelle leaned over with her elbows on the island and her head in her hands. "It's been awful." Tears welled up.

I did my sober best. "Telluz about it, Belle." I scooched my stool down to her end of the island and put my arm around her.

She put her head on my shoulder for a few seconds then straightened up. "At first, work was cool." She swiped at her eyes.

"Then what happened?" I tucked a curl behind her ear.

"He . . . was . . . um . . . hitting on me. It was gross. He's as old as Papa." Her pale face reddened. No hiding a blush for her.

"Who?" Maggie asked.

"Senator Herrington."

"That sleazeball." She patted Annabelle. "He's hit on me before, too."

I ignored Maggie. "What do you mean, hitting on you, Belle?" My own skin had grown cold and prickly.

"Um, talking about hanging out sometime, or whatever, and um, well, that he liked how my top fit my . . . chest."

Maggie put a hand on her hip. "You shouldn't be working with people like that."

I was white-hot angry, but she needed my empathy, not a display of my temper. "I'm so sorry, honey." I squeezed her again, and then the tears really started falling.

"I told Jay about it, and he was upset about the top I wore." Her cheeks flamed again. "It's just, like, a top, but I guess it does show some cleavage. And it's a little tight. But it's what I wore to class."

I was sobering up fast. I pulled her closer, and she turned her head into my shoulder. "It never hurts to cover up your, um, assets at work, but that doesn't make it your fault. It's not like you asked him to say those things to you or to put you in an uncomfortable position."

"I know." My shoulder muffled her voice.

Anger burned through my buzz. I still felt numb and woozy, but I was more clear than I had been a few minutes earlier. I wanted to hurt Senator Herrington. "I'm sure Jay will get over it, Belle."

She tilted her face up at me. "What if he does? Maybe I should be mad at him."

I used my thumb to rub some mascara off her wet cheek. "Maybe, but just because you're mad doesn't mean you break up. You gotta forgive each other for mistakes sometimes. I'm not saying you have to stay together. If you don't want to be with Jay, then don't be. But if you do, then you can decide whether or not to make this a big deal."

"But I got fired, too. And it's, like, so embarrassing."

She buried her face in my shoulder again. Sobs wracked her tiny body. We were the same height, but she was eighteen and slight and I was forty-one.

"Why'd you get fired, hon?" I stroked her back in little circles interspersed with pats.

Maggie was watching the two of us closely, her face a mirror of our emotions.

"Because Jay told me if what I said was true, then I had to report him, or whatever. So I did, and when I told my supervisor, he took me in to see his boss, and she made me talk to her alone and asked me all kinds of questions, and then said because nobody else saw it happen she couldn't believe me over a senator and that I was a tr-tr-tr-troublemaker." Annabelle's face scrunched up, and her voice was a wail. "Then she told me to never come back." She looked up again, deep into my eyes, and didn't break connection with me even as she choked on another sob. "She told me it was my fault. Like Jay. She said I dressed like a slut."

I put my hands on both of her cheeks. "She shouldn't have said those things. It's not your fault." I stroked her cheekbone with a thumb. "And if you get another job, you should cover more skin." I smiled. "Because it's very pretty skin. And you want to choose who you show all that beauty to."

She smiled and then laughed through her tears.

Maggie broke in. "Do you have the phone number for your boss?"

Annabelle nodded. "She made us all put it in our phones. I almost called her to tell her she's wrong. But I was too scared."

Maggie turned to me. "I think we should call her."

The clock said seven thirty. "Tomorrow. When I'm sober, and she's at work."

Maggie cocked her head at Annabelle. "What's the number?"

Annabelle pulled it up and read it to her, and Maggie punched buttons on her phone. I thought she was just going to save the number, but all of a sudden she was speaking.

"Yes, Julie Sloane. Sorry you're not here right now, too. This is Michele Lopez Hanson, and I'm calling to tell you that I know exactly what the senator did, and he's not going to get away with it." Maggie pressed a button on her phone and shoved it in her pocket.

Annabelle's face lit up, and she crowed. "That was awesome."

I knew there would be damage control for me tomorrow, but in the meantime, I had to agree. It was pretty awesome.

TWENTY-SIX

THE CHIRPS of birds ricocheted in my skull the next morning like gongs. I tried to open my eyes, but they felt swollen and glued shut. I rubbed them, dislodging dried mascara and sleep. I cursed my vanity for putting on water-proof mascara that I wouldn't sweat off the day before. I cursed Rashidi for being the one I'd probably put it on because of. I tried the opening thing again. This time the lids pulled apart with my lashes clinging together with all their might. They gave and light hit my eyes, coming in through the window whose curtains I'd left ajar the night before. I groaned and put my hand up as a shield.

I licked my lips. Hard to believe they could be chapped in 95 percent humidity, but that's what dehydration did to a girl. Not a girl, though. Way, way too old to be a girl. Way too old to drink whiskey from a tin cup and let another woman kiss her. Old, with the breath of a dead buffalo. Foul Tlazol.

I turned away from the light and smacked into a warm body. Again? But the lump beside me had long, curly blonde hair. Annabelle. I smiled, my first of the morning. I took care not to jostle the mattress as I got up.

Annabelle stirred. "Jay?" Then she started snoring.

Little did she know she'd given away the sleepovers with Jay I'd assumed would start when she left for college. I wanted to hug her, keep her the same sweet sprite who'd entered my life six years before in her braces and training bra phase, but I couldn't. She'd gone and grown up on me. Shafts of sunlight streamed across the room, hitting Gidget's *Front Porch Pickin'* in a way that brought out its depth. More than that. I half-closed my eyes, trying to get a fix on a chimera-like image I was seeing. When I locked in on it, I gasped softly. It was a mother and child, painted into the background like a ghostly Madonna. I stepped back, followed the light to her next painting, moved around with my eyes relaxed, and bam, there was another one. *Dios mío.* How had I missed her hidden message? In each painting in the room, the image was the same, hidden in plain sight. Motherhood. It wasn't just me seeing more than what was there. It was real. I studied them closely, looking for other clues, but came up with nothing more than the beautiful simplicity of her statement. I tiptoed into the kitchen, feeling a humming in my chest that was more than the nausea from too much whiskey. The paintings made my soul light and airy. Hopeful.

That lasted until I reached the kitchen. Rashidi had stayed in the Quacker the night before, so there was no coffee made. Damn. I filled a tall cup with water and gulped it. There was no food to speak of, either. I needed heavy, greasy, carby food, and fast. I found a nearly empty sleeve of saltines. They would have to do. I stuffed one in my mouth. It was so dry it stuck to the roof and sides of my mouth. I couldn't even chew it. I had to wait for it to moisten enough that I could lick the adhered white flour, sugar, shortening, and salt and try to swallow it. The dietary lows I had sunk to. I collapsed in a kitchen chair and leaned my head back. I stretched my neck and rolled it, and when I'd finished, I saw a note on the table.

Mom,

Please don't be mad.

It was Sam's handwriting. Sam, as in my nearly seventeen-year-old son, who was supposed to be in Kansas, if I remembered his schedule correctly. I caught sight of a human on the couch. A human with long, bony arms and legs with the lean musculature of a youth athlete, and a dark, floppy head of hair that needed two inches off the front.

I put my hand over my mouth. What was he doing here? I watched him, drinking it in as his back rose and fell with his breath. I walked over to him and laid the back of my fingers against his cheek, my heart molten inside my chest. I decided to let him sleep a little longer. Whatever his story was, it could wait. I made coffee (not as good as Rashidi's) and finished my saltines, sneaking peeks at my son every few seconds. Between the food, the water, the coffee, the girl, and the boy, I felt good enough to slip into my running gear to go sweat the poisons out. I grabbed my Shuffle, my phone, and a water bottle and stepped outside. I was greeted at once by paws on my knees and kisses to my ankles.

"Good morning, Gertrude." I rubbed her hindquarters.

Maggie had forgotten to take Janis and Woody with us to the pool, so they'd spent the night again. I gave them a good ear-scratching, too. The food bowl was still half full, and they had plenty of water.

"Be good, y'all."

I clipped my Shuffle to the neckline of my top and put my earbuds in. With my phone in one hand and the water bottle in the other, I slipped out the gate, pressed play with my thumb, and started to run.

The music gave me a rhythm to pace with. I silently thanked Kevin Fowler for the assist this morning. I'd learned to train through anything building up to the Ironman, but running in the humidity with a hangover was still not fun. Just necessary. I wanted to be present today, to enjoy the kids, and not be weighed down by all the *caca* going on. My feet pounded against the soft dirt driveway. I imagined my foot stomping each of the problems—and problem makers—flat. Take that, Deputy Tank Vallejo and Sheriff Boudreaux, Lester Tillman, Lonestar Pipeline, Nancy Little, Lumpy, Ralph, Greyhound, and even Gidget herself for leaving me this mess. Take that, Rashidi, for showing up and confusing me. Blake, for making Maggie think I was something I wasn't. And everyone else I missed that deserved to be included.

I kept pounding and stomping, out the long driveway and onto the paved road. It helped, as had the arrival of my kids. I was more sanguine, more centered. I even felt a smile creeping up the sides of my mouth after about ten minutes. At half an hour, I turned back. I was eager to be with my family.

Sweat dripped down my neck and torso and even my legs. It worked its way between my lips and into my eyes. Other than the impact of the weather and the hangover, I felt pretty okay. And when Kelly Clarkson's "Stronger" started playing, I picked up the pace. I turned the music louder as my breaths grew faster and harder. I left the pavement, moving onto the forgiving dirt of the driveway again. My lips were moving as I sang all the words.

I was halfway up the drive when in my left peripheral vision a big truck pulled up beside me in the grass and careened to a stop in front of me. My heart rate shot so high the rhythm was like a drumroll in my throat.

I shouted, "Hey!" and put my arm up to keep myself from running into it. It really wasn't all that easy to stop suddenly after an hour of a fast, humid run. My legs wobbled, and I nearly fell. I ripped my earbuds out, and turned to face off with the perpetrator.

My giant neighbor hauled his belly out and to the front of his truck, his face all smiles until he saw mine.

"Are you trying to kill me?" I snapped.

"Didn't you hear me coming?" he asked.

I shook my earbuds. "I believed it was safe to run to loud music on my own property."

"Sorry 'bout that. I just was stopping to say good morning."

I closed my eyes and took a deep breath, my teeth gritted, the air feeling almost cool as it sucked through them. Before I spoke, I focused on his name, determined to get it right, to calm down and discuss my safety in a civil fashion. "Grumpy, listen."

He interrupted. "Lumpy."

I'd tried. Whatever. "Next time, please don't cut in front of me when you want to say good morning."

"Gotcha." He gave me a crisp salute. "Hey, I got a visit from the deputies yesterday."

With the back of my hand I wiped sweat out of my eyes. "About the break-in at my place?" Like I didn't already know.

Lumpy nodded his head several times, nice and slow, and his words—when he spoke—were the same pace. "Yeah, they asked if I'd seen anything out of place. I told them about the picture on your camera, and about"—he paused for a moment, his lips compressing—"a black fella I saw sneaking around here."

My eyes closed again and I tried not to scream. "What do you mean, black fellow? Can you tell me what he looked like?"

His eyebrows drew together. "Black and um . . . well, he had long, braided hair."

I cut in. "You mean dreadlocks?"

"I guess so." He lifted his hands and shrugged, then dropped them.

I crushed my ear buds in my hand. My head bobbed with my words. "What exactly did you see him do?"

Lumpy's pants were losing their fight with gravity. He hitched them up to the shelf of his belly. "Well, I saw him driving in here."

"So, you saw a dreadlocked black man in a car drive to my house?"

"Yep. That's exactly right."

"That doesn't sound like sneaking to me. Lumpy, the man you're describing is one of my best friends." Mentally, I edited it to be "friend of one of my best friends," but he didn't need to know the particulars. "He was here to see me, and he'll be here again. I sincerely hope you haven't caused an innocent man trouble."

"Well, I'm glad he's not trouble for you." He beamed, seeming to miss the fact that he'd just gotten a butt-chewing. "Are you headed back to your house?"

My teeth ground against each other, and I bit back a sarcastic reply about the obvious. "Yes."

"You wouldn't happen to have some coffee for a fella, would ya?"

My head started shaking "no" before the words even came out of my mouth. "No, I wouldn't." Name shame. "Have a good day, Loopy."

"It's—"

I was already walking away, but I lifted a hand in the air. "Lumpy. Got it."

It took a second, but I heard his truck door shut, his engine start, and the sound of him driving away.

My peace had been short-lived and my hold on it too precarious. I used the rest of the walk back to the house to pull my tension meter down to a 6. I was excited to see my son. When I got to the door, I straightened my face a final titch and barged in. I heard noises coming from the back of the house, but I didn't see Sam on the couch.

"Sam? Belle?" I called.

"In here," they said in tandem, giggling.

Their voices came from the second bedroom, and on a light step I made my way toward them. They were sitting cross-legged on the floor with Rashidi.

My eyebrows crept up. "Well, good morning, all."

"Hey, Mom!" Sam leapt to his feet, his limbs unfolding slowly. He took two loping steps and hugged me off the ground.

"Mmph," I said.

"Gross!" He answered and set me back down. "You're sweaty." He looked at his hands. "And buggy."

"And you're a surprise."

Now he found his toes with his eyes. "Yeah, well, we were between camp sessions, and I kinda . . . um . . . missed everybody, and Terrence went home and I didn't get along with the guy that was in charge of my group and—"

"And it wasn't super awesome anymore so you came home."

"Yeah. I came home." He lifted his gaze to me with his face still pointed at the floor. Those big brown eyes, soft and kind underneath his Bambi lashes.

I could forgive him nearly anything. Showing up unannounced? It wasn't the first time.

"I'm not mad at you." I crossed my arms over my chest. "But I do want to know what's going on with you."

"Well . . ." He grinned and stole a glance at Annabelle and Rashidi.

I waved at the floor between them. "When did you get here, Rashidi?"

"Let the boy answer." He flashed his brilliant white smile at me.

"Okay, boy," I said to Sam. "Answer."

"I was thinking that—" He shifted from foot to foot. "That I could get a job here and not go back. I mean, if that's okay with you."

"Did you get fired?" I watched his face closely.

"I didn't get fired before, but I wasn't supposed to leave, either."

"So you'll be fired if you go back?"

He shrugged his shoulders. The boney knobs rose toward his ears and fell comically. He was like an overgrown puppy dog. Not big enough for his long legs and bear paws yet.

I shook my head. "You shouldn't have done it without telling me, Sam. But how about we talk after I've had time to think?"

He smiled then pulled his mouth back down into a serious expression. "Yes, ma'am."

"Don't be celebrating yet. I haven't made up my mind what to do with you." I swatted him on the arm. "Now, the rest of my questions. You." I pointed to Rashidi. "Your story."

"I fetched breakfast. It's in the kitchen." He winked. "And I met Sam and been showin' kids dem how to break a safe."

"It's so cool, Michele," Annabelle squealed.

"I didn't see your car."

"I parked it on the side. Your grass is getting damaged in front." He stood and stuck a toothpick in his mouth.

He was such a nice guy, which made me want to hate him and was probably why I snapped, "Do you have to do that?"

His eyes widened. "What?"

"The toothpick?"

He removed it and stuck it in his pocket without looking at me.

"I'm sorry. I—"

"It's okay."

I tried to fix things, my voice bright. "Do I smell bacon?"

Sam bounced up and down on his toes. "Breakfast tacos. Rashidi brought eight of them, all different kinds with potatoes and bacon and sausage and cheese and hot sauce and—"

"Whoa!" I held up my hands and laughed. "How many have you eaten?"

"Only two."

He was wide-eyed, and I laughed.

I took my Shuffle off my shirt. "I'm going to get some breakfast."

On the countertop, I saw the bag I hadn't noticed earlier. I peeked inside. Black Sharpie identified the different options, and I picked bacon, egg, and potato. Before I'd even unwrapped it, my phone made the sound of voice mail, although I hadn't heard it ring. I glanced at the screen. Greyhound. I made a growling noise.

"Is that yours?" Rashidi asked from the other room.

"Yes. Greyhound. There's a voice mail."

I put it on speaker. Rashidi walked into the kitchen. We both stared at the phone as Greyhound's message played.

"There's a hearing on Ms. Becker's estate today, in about half an hour at the courthouse in Giddings. I wanted you to know about it. You don't have to be there if you don't want to. I've got it covered. It's on the motion I filed for a temporary injunction against the pipeline company and anyone else that the Houston Arts Trust has authorized to do work. And of course the opposing attorney has also filed a motion of her own to stop you from writing the book, as well as one contesting the will." He cleared his throat. "Well, I guess I'll see you later, maybe."

The message ended.

"*Bastardo*," I spat.

Rashidi raised his eyebrows nearly as high as the corners of his mouth. "It's a good day for a battle, don't you think?"

I jutted out my chin. "Damn straight."

TWENTY-SEVEN

With Greyhound's less than timely notice about the hearing, I was pressed for time. I jumped in the shower and threw myself together in the third-least-casual outfit I'd brought from Houston. I didn't notice the big coffee stain on it until I'd pulled up in front of the three-story red-brick courthouse on the square in Giddings.

"*Caca del toro.*"

I stared at the building, starting from the limestone base to the stone arches, polished columns, square clock tower, and distinctive black and gold clock face. It was majestic and deserved a better effort than my dirty above-the-knee light-green shirtdress. I'd never have worn an outfit like this to court when I was practicing law in Houston. But there was nothing I could do about it.

I galloped up the blue granite steps into the building, then ran to the light well in the center of the building, my sandals clopping like horseshoes on the multicolored marble tile. There were signs marking the different rooms and their functions, so I barely hesitated before following the one that pointed to the district court up the stairs. I hauled myself up by the iron balustrade around the well to the second floor. When I reached the entrance to the courtroom, I was out of breath. I stopped for a split second to compose myself, huffing more than I liked. I licked my lips and tasted salt, not wax. I'd forgotten my lipstick. *Oh well.* I threw open one of the massive doors, and it slammed against the wall in the corridor. The sound reverberated both in the hallway and the two-story courtroom. Every head swiveled to see what had interrupted the proceedings, except for the short judge—a watered-down Hispanic, like me. The placard in front of him said The Honorable Judge Raul Gonzales. He looked up at me slowly, glowering from his elevated bench. Over his head four arches towered, decorated in cobalt-blue stenciling. My breath caught in my throat. It was stunning.

"Excuse me." I ducked my head.

I walked to the front row on the left and took a seat. I was the only one on that side of the courtroom except for a few old men I'd passed in the back. If they were anything like the regulars I'd known in Houston, they attended court in lieu of watching Judge Judy. Free entertainment and good local gossip.

In front of me sat Greyhound, pretending he didn't know I'd arrived. The backs of his ears and neck were red, though. *Busted.* He was alone at the plaintiff's table with a big banged-up leather trial case in the chair beside him. It had weathered brass buckles and the remains of what looked like his name embossed in gold.

Judge Gonzales said, "We're ready for the matter of probate in the estate of Anna Becker. Are the attorneys present?"

Greyhound stood. "Eldon Smith for the estate, Your Honor."

A black-pin-stripe-suited woman I hadn't seen before—tall and thin in snakeskin pumps, with long, wavy black hair worn loose down her back—stood. She wore red lipstick and kohl liner and her face was eerily pale.

"Nancy Little for the parties in opposition to Mr. Smith's claims and for the rightful estate, Your Honor." Her voice was deep and gravelly in a small-town drawl that suggested she was faking it to fit in.

She sat and so did Greyhound. Attorney Little took a moment to openly check me out. She dipped her head, but I didn't return the gesture.

The judge licked his index finger and thumbed through the pages in front of him. "We have a number of emergency motions to cover today."

While he was perusing his notes, I surveyed the gallery to the right, behind, and above me. The second-floor balcony ringing the back half of the courtroom was empty. Down below and as expected, I saw Lester Tillman. He was ever the dapper old fop. The old men in the back of the gallery were going to have a field day describing him to their cronies. A woman sat on the same row as him, but it didn't appear they were together. Maybe she was with one of the other defendants. She had dark shoulder-length hair, and looked like she was in her sixties. One row behind them, Jimmy Urban sat hunched over. I kept watching him, but he seemed to find his hands endlessly fascinating. There were several others I didn't recognize, white men in city clothes, except for two guys in the finest Fire Hose and chamois apparel that Duluth Trading had to offer. *Lonestar Pipeline guys*, I thought.

"So, Counselor Smith," the judge intoned.

Greyhound rose, bumping into the table. The water in his glass lapped at the edges.

"You're seeking a temporary injunction that all parties cease and desist any and all pipeline-related work on the property of Anna Becker in Lee County, said property part of the estate subject to probate in this court, and specifically against the Houston Arts Trust, Lonestar Pipeline, Cypress Surveyors, and any contractors they may retain. Is that correct?"

"Yes, Your Honor," Greyhound said.

Greyhound stepped to his right so he was no longer behind the table. I braced myself for something to hit the floor, but he made it without incident. "Your Honor, Ms. Becker executed her Last Will and Testament with me one month ago, a document I prepared for her at her cogent and specific instruction. I duly filed it with the court as prescribed by state law after her death. We are seeking an injunction against the"—he waved vaguely at the right-hand side of the courtroom—"others, most specifically, the Houston Arts Trust and those they have contracted with, comprising, at a minimum, the two parties represented here, Lonestar Pipeline and Cypress Surveyors." He held both hands in front of his hips, palms up. He sounded like a revival preacher, a very old-fashioned one. And he looked like one, too.

"There may be others, Your Honor, but we have not been made privy to that information, if so. Opposing counsel claims to be in possession of a previous will executed by Ms. Becker before her current Last Will and Testament; however, opposing counsel did not file it with the court until she did so in opposition to Ms. Becker's rightful will, already entered into probate. Then, knowing that the issue of disposition of the estate was contested, the opposing parties entered into contractual arrangements with no legal standing to do so, contracts which will result in substantial harm to the property owned by the estate of Ms. Becker in its continued use as a residence and farm. Opposing counsel did not inform me—the attorney for the estate—nor did she inform the executor appointed by Ms. Becker, Mr. Ralph Cardinal. And while we will prove in due course the validity of Ms. Becker's Last Will and Testament filed with the court, we are asking the court to rule that the Houston Arts Trust cannot contract away or in any way diminish the assets of the estate or make substantial and irreparable changes thereto, pending resolution of all probate issues, a ruling which would encompass the work of Lonestar Pipeline, Cypress Surveyors, and anyone they might contract with. We respectfully request that the court rule in favor of our temporary injunction, to protect the estate."

Attorney Little rose like a black swan. "If I may, Your Honor."

The judge nodded. "Be my guest."

"Your Honor, my clients, the Houston Arts Trust and their trustee, Mr. Lester Tillman, are completely within their rights to have not yet filed Ms. Becker's rightful Last Will and Testament with the court because the time period to do so has not expired. In addition, Mr. Tillman acted within his rights in relying upon his valid Power of Attorney on behalf of Ms. Becker in taking steps to increase the value of the estate for its intended purpose as a source of ongoing funds for a nonprofit institution, benefiting the arts in Houston. On the other hand, we have every reason to believe that the document to which Mr. Smith refers, the one he prepared and the one that Ms. Becker signed one month ago, is invalid due to her lack of testamentary capacity."

Her tone elevated my blood pressure, and her faux country accent grated on my nerves. If I could see it, surely Judge Gonzales could too.

"Validity, Ms. Little, will be decided at a later date."

"Of course, Your Honor, but it is germane to the temporary injunction motion, is it not? The injunction, if granted, will cause substantial and irreparable financial harm to my clients. Doesn't it stand, then, that all evidence that supports our position should be considered, to prevent this harm from occurring? We have a witness who will testify as to Ms. Becker's lack of testamentary capacity at the time she entered into this invalid will with Mr. Smith here today. May we call our witness, Your Honor?"

I expected Greyhound to object. When he didn't, I was on my feet before I realized what I was doing. The judge glared at me, and I lowered myself until my butt hovered over my seat. I couldn't help but hiss anyway. "Objection. Objection!" But Greyhound didn't make one, and I felt my insides cave in.

"I'll hear your witness, Attorney Little, if there's no objection from the other party."

The judge was hinting for Greyhound to object. *Come on, Greyhound.*

Greyhound half stood, shaking his head and teetering his chair. He caught it with one hand as he answered. "No, Your Honor."

I wanted to scream. Heavy steps clomped up the aisle. Jimmy Urban made his way from the gallery to the witness box. My brain felt fuzzy. Was he their witness, or was he ours? I put my fist to my mouth, scared to hear what would come out of *his* mouth. The court reporter swore him in.

Attorney Little got right to the point, without asking permission to treat

Jimmy as a hostile witness. "Mr. Urban, you have had occasion to observe Ms. Becker's behavior and mental capacity on an almost daily basis in the last five years. Have you not?"

He nodded.

"You'll have to speak so the court reporter can hear you, Mr. Urban." The judge's voice was clipped and impatient.

Jimmy cleared his throat. "Sorry. Yep. I mean, yes, ma'am."

"How did you come to have this level of interaction with her?"

"Mr. Tillman hired me to keep an eye on her."

I gasped loudly, and Jimmy shot me a dirty look. All his humiliation and anger all those years ago. Darlene told me Jimmy'd found Gidget in Houston, had shown up on her doorstep. So of course Lester had met him, too. Lester knew exactly who harbored a grudge against Gidget. I'd fallen for Jimmy's big-heart-in-a-rough-package routine, and I felt foolish. Anger thrummed hot inside me and burned out my fear of how Jimmy would testify.

Attorney Little craned her neck around to the judge but spoke to Jimmy. "Could you elaborate a little on that, please?"

"Well, uh, I reckon about the time Anna got sick—back in Houston— Mr. Tillman called me up, asking for my help."

"What kind of help?"

"To move her back out to her family place."

"Anything else?"

Jimmy didn't bat an eye. "Report back to him regular on how she was doing." He shrugged. "That's about it."

"And Mr. Tillman hired you to do these things?"

"Yes, ma'am."

"How often did you speak to Mr. Tillman?"

"He'd give me a call once a month."

"And what did you tell him about Ms. Becker?"

I clenched my fists.

"How she was doing."

"In the last year, what exactly did you tell Mr. Tillman about how Ms. Becker was doing?"

"About the same. Not so good."

"And what do you mean by 'not so good' and 'about the same'?"

Greyhound got to his feet, knocking his pen off the counsel table. It rolled across the floor, but no one went after it. "Objection. He's not a doctor."

"He can testify to his own meaning, can't he, Your Honor? He is the only one who can, in fact."

The judge rubbed his chin. "I'll permit it for now."

"Go ahead, Mr. Urban," Attorney Little urged, swooping toward him.

"That she seemed kinda out of it most days. Couldn't remember things, didn't feel good, needed help. Got confused."

He could have been describing me, lately, and I didn't lack testamentary capacity.

"Thank you, Mr. Urban. That's all for now, Your Honor."

"Greyhound?" the judge asked, slipping out of the formality of court-speak for a moment.

Greyhound didn't stand. "So, Jimmy, when you were hired by"—Greyhound's voice sounded like he was sucking a lemon—"Lester, what did he tell you he wanted to hear?"

"Uh . . . how she was doing."

"Let me make myself more clear. What did Lester tell you he wanted Ms. Becker's condition to be?"

Jimmy frowned. "I don't get your meaning."

Greyhound stood, and nothing on the table or chair rattled. "Permission to treat the witness as hostile, Your Honor."

"Granted."

"Did Lester at any point tell you that you were to tell him Gidget had mental issues, like senility, dementia, mental incompetency, or anything like that?"

"Objection, Your Honor." Attorney Little's voice was sharp, pecking. "He's already testified as to what he was to do."

Wrong objection, I thought. Not that I was going to stand up and help her.

"I'll permit it. Go on, Mr. Urban," the judge said.

Jimmy pulled his hand over his mouth, like he was turning a smile upside down. "Well, he told me she was a crazy old bat and I was to let him know if that changed."

A funny warmth started in my belly.

Greyhound looked down at his table, like he was reading notes, but I could see from my seat that his notepad was blank. "Did Lester share with you his thoughts about Gidget's possessions and finances?"

Jimmy snorted. "That she was a slut who'd stolen from his gallery."

Attorney Little exploded while he was speaking. "Objection. Hearsay."

Greyhound turned to her, and I saw his smile in profile. "Mr. Urban is testifying as to statements made to him *by* Lester, in the course and scope of his employment *with* Lester. I believe that's an exception to the hearsay rule."

Suddenly it was clear why Greyhound was rich and famous for his lawyering.

"Overruled," the judge said, his voice dry.

Greyhound smiled. "Thank you, Your Honor."

My tension eased a little bit, but not much.

"Mr. Urban, did you ever have a reason to tell Lester anything about Gidget other than what he wanted to hear? Oh, that was confusing. Let me rephrase that. Did you ever tell Lester that Gidget wasn't a crazy old bat?"

"Uh, no, sir."

Attorney Little spoke without looking up, one hand up with one finger raised. "Objection, Your Honor. Leading."

"He's allowed to lead, Attorney Little, he's questioning your witness."

She made a sound like a horse's laugh. The judge didn't look amused.

Greyhound acted like she didn't exist. "So, Mr. Urban, would it surprise you to hear that I found Ms. Becker to be quite capable and sharp when she met with me about her will?"

"Not really."

Attorney Little started tapping her foot. She was turned away from Jimmy and toward the side of the courtroom.

"Why is that, Mr. Urban?"

"Because she wasn't crazy. She got better and did real good."

Attorney Little studied her fingernails.

Lester shouted, "That lying son of a bitch!"

I smiled.

"Order." Judge Gonzales rapped his gavel.

Greyhound was unruffled. "What do you mean, 'better'?"

"Her memory got better. She wasn't confused. She didn't have those seizures as much anymore. She was the girl I knew, from back in the days when we were courtin'."

The judge smiled for a split second. An image of sixty-four-year-old Gidget flirting with Jimmy as he put flowers in a mason jar on her kitchen table flashed into my mind.

"But you didn't tell Mr. Tillman this?"

"No, sir, I reckon I didn't."

"Why is that?"

"He was paying me. Not much, but some. If I told him she was better, he woulda quit paying me. It's hard to make a living as a chicken farmer, you know?"

The judge actually nodded at this point.

"Yes, Jimmy, I think we do know. Your witness," Greyhound said to Attorney Little as he sat back down.

She stalked to the witness box, her fluid body stiff.

"Mr. Urban," she said in a fakely sweet voice. "So, you're telling us that you've been lying to Mr. Tillman for a long time."

"Yes, ma'am, I'm sorry about that."

"But even though you've been lying to Mr. Tillman for a long time, we're supposed to believe you today?"

Jimmy stewed on her question for a moment. "Yes, ma'am, that's right."

"No further questions, Your Honor."

"Thank you, Mr. Urban. You're excused."

Jimmy lumbered off the stand and all the way out the courtroom door.

Judge Gonzales stuck out his arm and glanced at his watch. "So, what other evidence would you like to present in opposition to the motion that Greyhound—I mean Attorney Smith—has before us today, Attorney Little?"

"I'd like to . . ." She paused for a second and smoothed the waist of her jacket. "There is potential defamation at stake implicit in the terms of Gidget's will."

"I'm afraid I don't understand. *Potential* defamation?"

"Your Honor, Ms. Becker hired a so-called writer to put together a book. In fact, one could say she paid dearly for it as she bequeathed nearly her entire estate to this . . . woman in the will we contend is invalid, then died before the book was written."

My fingernails dug into my palms. I'd socked other girls more than once as a feisty child. As an adult, that was called assault, so I couldn't indulge the urge toward people who deserved it. But that didn't mean I didn't feel it sometimes. Like now.

"We have evidence that we can present in chambers that will show the falsity of what Gidget was having this woman write, her motivation to prevaricate, and the grave harm it will cause."

Greyhound snorted. "If you've got *evidence*, then it sounds like there's a story there to me."

I did a mini fist-pump by my thigh, but Attorney Little went on, not missing a beat.

"To let this continue based upon the input of a mentally impaired woman is reckless to the harm it will cause my clients, Your Honor."

"You haven't proved mental impairment, but I guess I can give you fifteen minutes in chambers."

"And I want to cover this so-called Power of Attorney, Your Honor," Greyhound said.

Judge Gonzales nodded and beckoned the court reporter. "Jane, we'll need you in there as well. Court will resume in my office in five minutes. As to the proceedings here, we are temporarily adjourned." He rapped the bench with his gavel, walked to a side door, and disappeared, looking square from the shoulders down in his unflattering robes.

Greyhound hefted his leather bag and walked past me, on the heels of Little, Tillman, and the woman I'd seen sitting down the row from Tillman. I didn't have time to think about them, because I had something to say to Gidget's attorney.

"What were you doing meeting with Tillman at the Round Top library yesterday, Greyhound?"

He turned around, his voice a low rumble. "Lester wanted to discuss ways to resolve this matter."

"Which he should have done through his counsel."

His face shifted into an angry mask. "I'm comfortable with my decision to meet with him yesterday. And I think it went pretty good in here today."

I almost let up on him, but he knew what he'd done was highly inappropriate. "I guess we'll know that after the hearing in chambers."

"I guess we will." He stormed out.

That went well. I slumped back into my seat. Motion in my side view drew my eyes to the tan and rested face of Ralph at the end of my row.

"I heard there was a hearing. What did I miss?"

TWENTY-EIGHT

Before I could answer Ralph, the bailiff, a black man in his late fifties or early sixties, reentered the courtroom. His voice boomed. "The judge asked me to let y'all know court will reconvene here at one thirty." He was gone as quickly as he'd appeared.

I stood and Ralph hugged me. I returned it, feeling prickly and trying not to show it.

His eyes roamed the room. Proud. Admiring. "Your first time in here?"

"It is."

"That blue stenciling is Wendish." He gazed at the brilliant blue curlicues as he talked reverently. "The Wends wouldn't rest until they'd built the original courthouse and secured Giddings as the county seat. They'd been powerless to protect their religion and culture in Germany. They weren't going to let that happen again here. Course the original burned down and they had to rebuild, but they had more time to make it grand then."

The Wendish roots ran deep here. Gidget's roots. What would it have been like to escape persecution and risk it all for freedom? I hoped I never found out personally. "It's beautiful."

"Can I buy you lunch at Reba's so you can catch me up?"

"Sure."

"My granddaughter is with me, if that's okay."

"My teenagers are in town. I'll call and see if they want to meet us."

He exhaled, his shoulders falling half an inch. "Oh, good. She's already tired of just Grandpa. Meet you there."

In a series of quick texts, I got my kids in motion. I pulled up to Reba's Village Deli & Pizzeria five minutes later, parking in front of a three-foot-high plaster-of-Paris statue of a chef whose face was half pig snout, half whinnying horse. I stepped inside Reba's. It was darkish, even though there were full-length windows along the front of the restaurant and blonde wood on the floors. I had beaten Ralph and his granddaughter there, so I got a table big enough for six. I set my zebra handbag on the tabletop. It looked snazzy against the red-and-white harlequin pattern.

I'd barely sat when I saw Ralph escorting a tall, slender girl about Sam's age to our table. She had long brown hair in a high ponytail, with wisps coming loose around her face. Her nose was lightly freckled and her eyes were green like Adrian's.

I stood for introductions.

Ralph's voice was nervous. "Rachael, this is Michele Lopez Hanson."

"You can call me Michele," I said to her, and stuck out my hand.

She didn't say a word, just took it in a limp, teenage-girl shake with no eye contact. Worry crossed Ralph's face. We took a seat and made small talk. Rachael's silence was awkward at first, but then she got out her phone and started texting, and Ralph relaxed.

The front door burst open, followed by a woman's strident voice, calling for me.

Rashidi's voice answered her, his accent thick. "I tell you she gone. I deliver your message."

I jumped up. "Excuse me, you guys." I trotted around the ugly wooden bar with its faux roof of shake shingles. I found Sam, Belle, and Rashidi at the entrance. Rashidi's face was stern. The subject of his ire was a woman I recognized.

She raised her voice, shrill and frantic. "I need to see her immediately. You have to take me to her."

Rashidi put a hand on her arm. She jerked away, but he held on. "I askin' you to leave, and I askin' nicely. I can ask not nice if you rather."

She gasped and put a hand over her chest with her other arm. "Okay. Let go of me."

"Darlene," I called as Rashidi released her.

She whirled toward my voice. She whispered louder than a shout, "Don't use that name."

Everyone in earshot went silent. Watching us. Listening. I took the last few steps to her at a sedate pace. She looked at me, eyes wide. Terrified?

Confused? She could have a mental disorder. It might explain why she had met me under cloak and dagger before. She could also have a weapon. I'd be careful.

"It's okay." I smiled at her, channeling Papa. When he met with the owners of gravely ill or injured animals, he acknowledged instead of ignored their distress. With the animals, he used a gentle tone and touch. I took her hand and squeezed it, then reached for her elbow with my other hand. "I'm right here."

Her voice trembled. "I have to speak to you alone."

I turned my gaze to Rashidi and the kids. Annabelle and Sam had moved past startled on their way to freaked out. "It's okay, guys. We're good." Sam put his hand on my back and Annabelle scooched under his shoulder. "We go way back. Or at least a few days." I winked at Darlene and she smiled on autopilot. "We're just going to step outside for a brief conversation. I'll be right back. Rashidi, you've met Ralph, right?"

"Yah, mon." His voice was edgy, and his thundercloud eyes told me he didn't like my plan.

"Why don't you take Belle and Sam into the dining area around the corner. Ralph's waiting with his granddaughter, Rachael. She's their age, and I know she's dying to meet them."

Rashidi shook his head at me, and I nodded firmly. Once. Twice. Three times. Until he stopped shaking his head and sighed.

"Le'we go." He put his fingers lightly on Annabelle's shoulder, then clapped Sam on the back.

"This way." I opened the door for Darlene, stealing a quick glance back at Rashidi and the kids. They were all three doing the same toward me. I gave them a thumbs-up. The heat sucked the air out of my lungs. I squinted without the sunglasses I'd left in my handbag at the table.

"My car's over here." Darlene turned and pointed. She led me to a silver Mercedes E-Class. We climbed in and she turned on the engine and full-blast air conditioning. The inside of the car had a cloying scent from a car deodorizer attached to an air conditioner vent. It smelled like an explosion of artificial freesia. Combined with her heavy perfume, it was suffocating. I smelled something more. I flicked my finger on the ash tray and saw the butt end of a joint in a roach clip.

She shoved my hand out of the way as she shut the cover over the marijuana.

I lifted my hands. "I just thought I smelled pot. I'm not a cop, and I'm not judging."

"It's for pain management," she screeched at me.

"Absolutely." I smiled at her. "So, you needed to talk to me so badly that you drove all the way to Giddings to do it. Why didn't you just call?"

"I did. But you didn't call back, and I was given a deadline. I had to get to you before you wrote anything about, well, you know, our conversation, and about Gidget and—" She stopped and stared at her hands.

They were shaking and she clasped them together hard. Her long, skinny fingers were pale and wrinkled. The immaculate manicure of a few days ago was chipped. Several diamond-encrusted gold bands encircled her fingers, with a few rubies, sapphires, and emeralds in the mix.

She claimed she'd called me. Well, maybe she had. The last few days had been insane. Had it been only yesterday I'd left her that voice mail? And had I even checked mine again since then? So much was happening, so fast. I couldn't keep up.

I nodded at her. "Okay. How about you start at the beginning?"

She started to say something, but a sob came out instead. She put her knuckles to her mouth, biting down on them.

"Okay, let me try. I got confirmation that Gidget had a daughter in 1975. Her parents placed her with an adoptive family. So now that I have outside verification of this child's birth—"

"I know nothing." Her voice rose an octave on "nothing" and quavered. "I should never have spoken to you." She wrung her hands again, hard. So hard I wanted to hold them to keep her from hurting herself. "My husband always tells me that I'm a foolish woman. Dramatic. Talk too much. I'm a foolish, foolish woman." The words were clipped off by heavy breaths as she fought for control. She gave a high-pitched laugh. "I made it all up and if you say any different, I'll tell people you're a liar."

I didn't answer her for a moment, just let her breathe and calm down. Her anxiety was suffocating, and I was catching it like it was being forced into my lungs. I picked at a hangnail, then bit at it. Before I could stop myself, I chomped off the edge of the fingernail. Not good. I dropped my hands, then stretched my shoulders, up, back, and in, and crawled a little height into my spine.

"So, Lester got to you." I used a slow cadence and said it as a statement, not a question.

"Lester?" She snorted. "No. He's greedy and an egomaniac and a bad judge of character, but he's no killer. Besides, it's not his secret. All he did was take the dirty money."

Killer? Secrets? Dirty money? The hairs rose on my arms. "I really need to know who scared you."

"You should be scared, too."

"Why? I don't—"

"Powerful people." Tears had pooled at her expensive cleavage, and her false eyelashes drooped. "You have to leave me out of this. And if you're smart, you'll drop it yourself."

Her words had the opposite impact on me. I'd never wanted to pursue Gidget's story more than I did right then. "Drop what?"

"You know. The baby." She chewed the lipstick from her lips, staining her teeth bright red. "I have nothing more to say. You need to get out of my car, forget my name, and never contact me again."

I cocked my head, trying to think of a way to stall her.

"I'm serious," she said. "Please leave my car before someone sees us together."

I chuckled. "Someone in Giddings, Texas?"

Her eyes cut to me, fast, then back away.

"Okay." Before I'd even shut the door behind me, she was backing out. I had to jump to keep her from running over my foot.

I watched her peel out of the parking lot, hands on my hips. The back of my head prickled. I turned, searching for the source of my karmic itch. The woman I'd seen with Lester and Attorney Little was parked in a teal Yukon, watching me. When our eyes met she accelerated and left the other side of the lot in as big a hurry as Darlene had a moment before.

———

Rashidi was monitoring us through a front window as I walked slowly back to Reba's. When I reached for the door handle, he turned and walked back into the restaurant. It had gotten busier in the few minutes since I left it. I pushed my way through staring eyes and halted conversations.

When I reached my table, everyone stopped talking.

"Well," Sam said from his seat beside Rachael, whose cheeks were rosier than earlier. "What did the crazy lady have to say?"

Rashidi couldn't have taken his seat more than a few seconds before. His eyes were dark and his arms crossed.

"She was someone I met in Houston the other day." I licked my lips. "She heard I was writing Gidget's story and is quite anxious for me to write hers, too." I grinned.

My lie seemed to work, mostly. The kids lost interest and started chattering. Ralph made a humph noise and picked up his menu. But Rashidi's eyes bored through me. The only free seat was beside him, so I took it.

"Was that the woman from the coffee shop in Houston?" His voice was so soft I had to lean against him to hear it.

"Yes. I'll tell you about it later. I promise."

The lunch went by in a blur. My mind was still in the Mercedes. In fact, the only thing that really stuck out to me was that Sam had lit up like a firecracker in the presence of Rachael. As we were leaving, he pulled me away from the others.

He put his hand over his mouth to whisper in my ear. "Is it okay if Belle and I go swimming this afternoon with Rachael?"

I put my hand over my own mouth, stood on tiptoe, and whispered into his. "She's pretty cute. Are you sure I can trust you with her?"

"Mom!" He punched me lightly in the arm.

"Have fun. Do you guys need a ride anywhere?"

"No, we don't, but Rashidi will. He rode with us."

When we got outside, the sound of sirens from multiple directions ripped through the air. I hadn't noticed it when we were inside with the hubbub of the lunch crowd, but out on the sidewalk, it was earsplitting. I put on my sunglasses and still had to tent my hand over my eyes in the noonday glare, trying to see down Highway 290 to find the source of the noise.

"Is it a wreck?" Annabelle asked.

A fire truck zoomed past us, its lower-noted emergency signal sounding up and down its scales.

"I can't see it," I said. "But must be, with all this emergency response."

After we went our separate ways, Rashidi rode with me back to the courthouse. On the way, I told him about my odd conversation with Darlene. He was troubled and pensive as I parked.

"Can we talk more 'bout this later?"

I walked quickly beside him. "Absolutely."

People's heads turned when we passed them. I wasn't sure if it was because I'd become notorious, or because he was dreadlocked down to the middle of his back, or because we were a mixed-race couple in a small Texas town. Even though we weren't a couple, I amended.

Ralph hailed us from the door of the courtroom when we were barely to the top of the stairs on the second floor. The three of us walked in together, but it was empty save for the bailiff. He was picking up Styrofoam coffee cups and scraps of paper.

"Are we early?" Ralph called out.

The bailiff straightened. "Nah, the Judge adjourned."

"But I thought court wasn't starting again until one thirty," I said. The clock on the wall said 1:25.

He shrugged. "He said they covered everything they needed to in chambers."

Ralph and I shared a look. Steam built up inside my ears. This felt shady. Secretive and shady, like meetings in library parking lots.

"Seems like crap," Rashidi noted.

"Absolutely," I said. "Which is why we're going to pay a visit to the judge."

"Good idea." Ralph headed for the door. "I know the way."

Rashidi and I walked side by side behind him. When we reached a desk outside an imposing chamber door, Ralph stopped in front of it, clearing his throat to get the attention of a woman with gray pin curls plastered to her head and a strand of pearls hugging the round-necked collar of her white cardigan.

"Is Judge Gonzales in?" Ralph asked her.

She looked up at him and her cheeks pinked. "Ralph."

"Mary Elizabeth." He bowed ever so slightly.

"He left for the day." She whispered, "He's off tomorrow, taking a long weekend, so, you know." Louder, she said, "Can I help you or take a message?"

Ralph looked at me. I shook my head.

"No, thank you."

"Well, you have a nice weekend, Ralph. I hope to see you at church."

"You, too, Mary Elizabeth." Ralph tipped an imaginary hat toward her.

As we turned to go, she added, "Oh, if you guys were going to use 290, you need to find an alternate route."

I hadn't been introduced, but I jumped in anyway. "Why's that?"

"We just got an email." She pointed at her monitor. "A car burned up on 290 in town and they're shutting down the highway in both directions."

"Oh my goodness!" I said. "I hope no one was hurt."

She shrugged. "We don't know anything more yet."

"Thank you," Ralph said.

We walked toward the stairs.

Rashidi said, "That explains all the sirens."

"Do you think we can get anything else done here?" Ralph asked me.

"I don't think so. Not until Monday."

"Well, if anything else happens over the weekend, call."

I nodded, hoping there'd be no need.

Rashidi and I worked our way down the back streets to connect with the road south to Gidget's. I saw the magenta magnificence of Bess in the rearview mirror as we pulled into the driveway. Janis and Woody went nuts when Maggie got out. She'd piled her hair in a messy topknot, and she'd paired blue-jean overalls with a half T-shirt. A honeyed patch of skin showed between the bottom of the shirt and the waist of her overalls. I pulled the Jetta into the open and newly cleared barn to keep it in the shade. The sun was more wicked with every passing day.

"Hey, y'all." Maggie was rubbing the dogs vigorously. They whined and barked happily. "I was just coming to pick up the dogs. How are you two?"

Standing between the enormously sexy Rashidi and his feminine equal, I felt awkward. "Um, fine. What's up with you?"

Rashidi interrupted us. Thank God. "You two coming inside? I have something to show you." Rashidi went into the house without waiting to see our response.

Maggie put her arm through mine. "Game for a surprise?"

"Uh . . ."

She laughed. "Not that kind of surprise." She squeezed my arm. "I had too much single malt last night. Sometimes I push people past their boundaries, I'm told. Sorry."

I wiped pretend sweat from my brow. "Phew!"

"One of these days I'll introduce you to my non-boyfriend, if that will help."

Rashidi poked his head outside. "What're you guys doing? Hurry up."

We hustled into the house after him, and he led us to the second bedroom. He'd made a big mess of metal filings and used-up grinding wheels. The safe still wasn't open.

"So what's the surprise?" I asked.

He brandished the grinder again and turned it on. Using a lot of elbow grease, he applied the spinning wheel to the safe. I tried not to notice that it made the triceps on his arms stand out like he'd been carved from ebony.

Maggie whispered, "You're drooling."

I rolled my eyes at her.

Rashidi turned off the grinder. "Count down from tree."

Maggie and I did it together. "Three, two, one."

Rashidi swung the safe door open.

I shouted, "Hip, hip, hooray!"

Maggie yelled, "Kick ass!" She turned to me. "Picture to blog!"

I snapped a photo of her and Rashidi on either side of the open door. I sent it to the blog, titled "Secrets Revealed."

I knelt in front of the safe and pulled out a high school yearbook. For a split second, I saw Gidget kneeling carefully exactly where I was now. She wore a long white linen gown. It was loose and flowing, open at the neck, and the sleeves hung to her fingertips. All the lights were out and the house was dark. She pushed something inside, then buried her face in her hands and wept.

Maggie sat cross-legged beside me, snapping me back to what was real. "A yearbook? Not what I would have expected."

Next I removed a metal box, unfastening the flip clasp to lift the lid. It was filled with old German coins.

"Anybody know the conversion rate?" I handed the box back to Rashidi and peered back into the safe. "Only one more thing I can see in here." I dragged a cardboard box to the lip of the safe and then wiggled it out. It landed on the floor with a thump.

"Maybe it's full of treasure." Maggie wiggled her fingers. "Jewelry or diamonds."

"Or rocks. They were farmers." Rashidi grinned at her.

"You're both wrong." I tilted the box toward them, spilling some of the contents.

It was stuffed with photographs, news clippings, and other memorabilia. Old black-and-whites, Polaroids, color, posed, spontaneous. Gidget, vibrant and youthful, with other young women and an endless array of notables on the Houston celebrity scene, from musicians to athletes, and many others I didn't recognize. One of a teenage Gidget with Jimmy. Another with Lucy and a preacher, in front of St. Paul. Many with her parents. Gidget in a cap and gown graduating from U of H. A mug shot of Gidget with paperwork from an arrest. The woman in that picture looked decades older, beaten down by life, and so different even from the grandmotherly woman I'd met. A yellowed article about her winning the 1970 Blinn College Grand Prize Art Contest. An invitation to the wedding of Anna Helen Becker to James Arthur Urban. A diner receipt with a cartoon longhorn in ink, and under it a phone number with a 713 area code. Ah, the mystery diner who'd promised Gidget the world, and a phone number to call for the book, and for leads to the daughter. No Gidget with a baby or a pregnant belly. No pictures of babies or children at all since 1975, when she'd given birth. A fragile clipping with an article about her father's heroism, and a picture of him with his car. This and, oh, so much more. It was thrilling, and at the same time disappointing that we didn't learn more.

We catalogued and I lost track of time as we talked over the subjects of the pictures, and Rashidi and I filled Maggie in on the events of the day. Much later, I heard a vehicle engine turn off, then laughter and young voices.

Rashidi nudged me. "Your boy's smitten."

Maggie looked puzzled. "What?" Sam's new friend was one thing I hadn't thought to tell her about.

The teenagers barged in, their voices going off like depth charges.

"Hi, Mom!" Sam shouted.

"Hey," I said. "We're in here. Rashidi got the safe open."

"Cool."

Annabelle and Rachael literally skipped through the doorway, their arms linked together.

"Hi, Mrs. Hanson," Rachael said. Gone was the girl at Reba's who wouldn't speak.

She and Annabelle giggled.

"Hi, Michele," Annabelle said.

"Hi, y'all." I stood up and brushed off the knees of my clothes. "What have you been up to?"

"We went to the pool," Sam said.

"And we drove by where that car blew up," Rachael added.

"Oh my gosh, Michele," Annabelle's hand flew over her mouth. "It looked like the car that woman drove. The one you talked to at lunch."

My stomach clenched. "How could you tell?"

"There was still enough of it, and people said it was a Mercedes. And nobody else in this dump of a town—uh, sorry." Annabelle blushed and looked at Maggie.

Maggie flapped her hand. "Speak your truth, girl."

"If nobody else drives that kind of car, then it had to be her, right?"

My heart started beating faster. "Did anyone say whether the driver had been identified?"

"No. But she was here and she left and then it happened to the kind of car she's the only one who drives. It's pretty obvious."

I couldn't accept it. But was it possible Darlene was dead?

Maggie held up a hand. "Whoa, there. What exactly happened? S-l-o-w-l-y."

Sam took over the explanation. "We were at the pool and people were talking about it being a Mercedes that exploded. You know, like a car bomb went off. Not like a wreck or anything. It just blew up, and it burned up the person inside. The police are questioning people that fit the profile."

I was so horrified it was hard to talk. Hard to think. Darlene. Darlene was scared of someone, and then this happened.

Maggie pursed her mouth. "Fit what profile?"

"You know. Like terrorists." Sam stole a glance at Rachael while she was stealing a glance at him.

"Terrorists in Giddings, Texas?" Maggie's voice sounded skeptical.

"Um, well, I don't know for sure. It's just what people were saying at the pool."

I felt pretty sure this wasn't the terrorist act of a religious zealot. More like the silencing act of someone desperate to keep a secret.

A secret they might believe I knew.

TWENTY-NINE

As if from the bottom of a well—the kind with me under twelve feet of water—I realized Sam was speaking.

"We've got a flat, Mom, and I can't find my jack. Can I borrow yours?"

I mumbled something. He must have taken it as a yes because he disappeared, Annabelle and Rachael with him. I felt hands on me and looked into the concerned eyes of Rashidi and Maggie.

"It can't be a coincidence," I said.

"If it was really her," Maggie responded, squeezing my arm. "And even if it was, it could've been an accident."

"Maybe."

The door burst open and slammed into the inside wall, gouging into the shiplap paneling. I had to replace the kick stop. And put glass back in the broken window.

Sam was buoyant. "Hey, I found a box of old stuff in the back of your car. Do you want it in here?"

I heard the box hit the ground by the door.

"Sure, just drop it anywhere."

"I did," Sam said, missing my sarcasm.

I walked out to it. "Oh man!" I smacked my forehead with the heel of my palm. My brain kept about as much in as a colander. "I'd completely forgot about this stuff. It's all the documents and pictures that Gidget gave me last spring. Thanks, Sam." While she hadn't been very organized,

Gidget had kept a lot of her history. Of course, she lived in a world before digital photography and document scanning and shredding, too.

"No problem. I'm going to go finish my tire. Then can we explore this place? Like walk the perimeter and stuff?"

"If you'll take your mother." I'd been meaning to do it, too.

Sam bounced off like a Labrador retriever puppy. When he opened the door, Gertrude zipped through and side-wound her way to me.

I let the funny dog bathe my ankles. "I'm going to change. For the walk."

Rashidi fanned his dreadlocks. It really was hot in here with the door opening so often. "I hate leaving, but I have to go to a dinner. In College Station."

"Oh?" I hadn't known.

"Yah, they texted me. Command interview performance."

"Oh. Well. I hope it goes great."

He studied me, his face soft. "You'll be okay?"

"You cracked the safe. I've got Sam and Belle. I'm irie."

"And me," Maggie piped in.

I should have been thrilled he was leaving. It should have taken a lot of pressure off me for him to go. Instead, my heart flipped over in my chest. My inner voice chided me. Tlazol. Thank him for this kindness and tell him goodbye. The voice had been right before. It didn't ring as true for me now, but I obeyed.

I stuck my hand out and clasped Rashidi's. I put my other hand over it and shook his, loose-jointed and awkward. "Thank you, Rashidi. I couldn't have done it without you. I hope you're able to learn everything you need and get a great job offer. I mean, if you want it."

His eyes sparked. He pulled me into him and rocked me gently side to side. "Oh yes. I want this job."

I gave in for a second. It felt really nice, but I forced myself to stiffen and pull away. "That's great. Do you need anything before you go?" My voice sounded brittle, falsely bright.

Maggie walked up behind us and made a coughing noise that sounded like "bullshit."

I ignored her.

Rashidi stared at me for a few more seconds then said, "Nah, everything irie with me, too." He stepped toward Maggie. "Miss Maggie, it was a pleasure."

She launched herself into a juicy hug with him. I averted my eyes and told myself I didn't care.

"I hope to see you soon," she said. A knife stabbed into my gut. "You're one of a kind." Stab. Stab. Stab.

"And so are you." Stab. Stab. Stab.

Finally, they released each other. Rashidi saluted me and grabbed his keys from the kitchen table. He walked backwards out the door. His steps were heavy and his eyes sad.

Maggie was shaking her head. "You are one Grade A dumbass, Michele."

I bristled a little. "Thank you." I strode with as much attitude as I could muster toward the bedroom.

Maggie laughed, loud, long, and deep. She sounded wide open, and I felt another stab of jealousy, for her ease. "All right. But somebody else is going to snatch him up."

I wondered if it was going to be her and how her non-boyfriend would feel about it. I shut the door behind me, careful not to slam it and at the same time to make it loud. Angry, yet mature.

"What right does she have?" I muttered as I stripped off my unsuitable-for-court clothes. "She barely knows me." I grabbed a pair of shorts and slipped them on. "She's pushing herself into my life." I reached into my suitcase, rummaging for a T-shirt. "Just like Rashidi. Both of them. Pushy. I do better by myself. I want to be alone. How come they can't see that?" I found a shirt and pulled it over my head.

And that's when the tears started leaking out the corners of my eyes, which made me even madder. I pushed them away with my forearm, but it didn't stop the flow. I sat down on the bed and then gave in, laid back, and sobbed. A few seconds later the door clicked as it opened. Footsteps, soft and slow, approached me. My arms were crossed over my eyes so I couldn't see, but it was clearly the smell of 80 proof, paint thinner, Aqua Net, and sawdust, and that meant Maggie.

The air beside me whooshed, and there was a plop as the mattress bounced down and then back up. I peeked out from under my arms. Maggie had assumed the same position I was in beside me.

"I'm sorry I'm being a bitch. No," I corrected myself. "I've got to pull myself together. My mother—" I started to cry again. "She didn't like it when I—" I cried some more. "It's not right that I lost her so young. We never got a chance to—" I wiped savagely at my eyes and the tears I'd sworn I was done with. "I'm sorry I'm not being nice," I finally choked out. And then in the midst of an enormous sob so heavy that there was no way anyone could've understood me I said, "I miss Adrian so much."

Maggie reached for my right arm and gently guided it down to my side.

She took my hand and held it and we just laid there, side by side, until my crying stopped. "I'm sorry, too."

The front door let in the sound of teenage voices again. The smell of sunshine and the million weeds and grasses I hadn't learned to distinguish yet flowed in on a breath of hot air with them.

"Mom?" Sam called. "Are you ready to go on the walk?"

I muttered, "*Mierda.*"

Maggie laughed.

"Ready," I called. I sat up and the bed bounced.

Maggie sat up, too.

"Sort of." I walked down the hallway toward the kids. "Does everybody have on good shoes, like boots? In case of snakes." I had left mine by the back door. When I got to the door, I slipped my feet into them.

"Do we have any water bottles?" Sam asked.

I laughed. "Do you realize who you're talking to?"

Annabelle went into the kitchen. "She always has water bottles." She rummaged around, found some, and started filling them.

Sam pointed to Rachael's feet. Flip-flops. "Don't you think she'll be okay?"

"I'm used to snakes, Mrs. Hanson. There're rattlers in El Paso."

"Okay," I said. "But I have some boots you can borrow. It's up to you."

She shook her head.

The sun had started to sink on the horizon by the time we left on our walk. Maggie had come so we made five, sans dogs, since Maggie didn't want to get the goldens matted and filthy. There was still plenty of daylight left, but the heat had started to lessen and the shadows were growing longer.

I pointed through the backyard. "So, when I Google Mapped the property, it looked like you could walk to the fence line through the trees back there."

"I want to show Rachael our place and the Quacker."

"Then let's start"—I pointed to my left—"over there at the road. We can find the fence and follow it around and swing out to our place when we come to the junction."

"Sweet," Sam said.

Annabelle had swept her long, curly hair into a ponytail. She fanned her neck with her hand. "It's really hot."

I set off. "Buck up, Buttercup. It'll get cooler in the trees."

"Maybe." Her eyes rolled just a little.

We found the fence quickly and headed along it single file. The pasture was treeless, but there was a line of trees hugging the fence that made it hard to see very far. As we stepped under the protection of the branches, it grew shadier.

Annabelle sighed. "It's not any cooler."

Sam led the way, his long legs eating up big stretches of ground with every stride. The smell grew loamier, damper, almost musty, and even sweet. We came up on a break in the tree line and a small tank and meadow I'd glimpsed from the aerial view on Google Earth. Green-and-purple drag-onflies buzzed over the water. In the clearing, a firework display of Texas-native flowers exploded. Pink Texas stars, black-eyed Susans, yellow-and-brown Mexican hats, delicate daisy-like flowers, tiny yellow-and-orange lantana flowers that reminded me of bouquets, towering lavender horsemint, and thistles with purple pompoms and white cotton fluffs. Bees and yellow butterflies darted every which way. It was heavenly.

"Do you think there're fish in it?" Rachael asked. "I love to fish."

"Me, too," Sam agreed, although I'd rarely known him to fish before. "We can try tomorrow."

Maggie's mouth formed an O, and her eyes twinkled. Not too much farther along, I recognized the stretch of fence we'd crossed the few times we'd walked, and on one occasion, run, between the Quacker and Gidget's place.

"This way." I pointed to the right, but Sam had already ducked under the fence.

"Come on," he said to Rachael, and bounded ahead.

She trotted after him.

"I don't have the keys," I hollered, but they ignored me.

We took a few minutes stomping around the Quacker. I was surprised how much the grass and weeds had grown up in just a couple of days, but they were smashed flat where Rashidi had been parking his car. For a moment, I felt his absence. It added to the loneliness I carried with me all the time from Adrian being gone, which reminded me of Rashidi's find. I went behind the Quacker into the trees where he'd told me he found it. I pressed one hand over the A+M inside the heart carved into the oak, and one over my toasty warm butterfly.

"Your husband?" Maggie's soft voice startled me.

"Yes." I soaked it in for another moment then slipped my arm through the elbow Maggie offered.

We found the kids and headed back toward the fence, pushing through cedar, yaupon, an elm, and some hackberries. Maggie caught her hair in a vine, and it pulled her bump out. She pushed her hair out of her face and stuck the bump in her pocket. She and I were bringing up the rear, because Annabelle had forgotten how hot she was and was keeping up with Sam and Rachael.

"Look what I found!" Sam shouted. He was standing by an old water trough. It was upside down with a rusted-out bottom.

"That's very cool." Maggie knelt by it. "It would make a good planter. I'd sell it for about forty dollars once it was cleaned up."

"If I brought you stuff like this would you buy it?"

"Maybe." She grinned at him. "For the right price."

"Sweet!"

We came to a junction in the fence where we left my property and moved on to Gidget's. The kids continued to call out their finds for Maggie to inspect. There was an old plow, some oil cans, and even a claw-foot tub. Sam made plans to haul it all out to take to Maggie's shop. Better him than me. After about fifteen minutes of walking through thick trees that forced us to stay on the fence line, I spotted the sides of a structure. It felt eerie finding a building where I hadn't realized one existed. I moved forward cautiously.

"A shed!" Sam cried.

"Cool." I remembered the shiny red thing I'd seen on Google Earth. This little building was roughly in the same spot I'd seen it, but it was massive and rusty compared to the patch that had showed through the canopy of trees.

The sides were the same tin as the roof, although they still retained their patina and the roof had rusted. On one side was a wooden door, wired onto the tin in a cutout. It hung askew but mostly closed.

"Can I open it?" Sam asked me.

"Be careful," I said.

"Yeah, yeah," he said. He pulled the door. Immediately an angry buzzing noise flew at us. Sam let go, but the lone wasp was already out. After a few screams and mad dashes around the building, we calmed down. The wasp was gone. Sam opened the door again, more respectfully this time. No buzzing. Rays of light filtered through the trees and in the doorway, catching dust as it escaped in the other direction.

Sam stepped gingerly onto the dirt flooring of the old building.

None of the rest of us moved.

"Tell me if you see spiders the size of your hand or bigger." Maggie called after him.

"What?" Sam shouted.

"Nothing," she said sweetly.

The rest of us laughed.

Then Annabelle shivered. "Are there really spiders that big out here?"

Maggie tapped Annabelle's arm softly with her knuckles. "Not really that big, but there are some big spiders in the forest, mostly harmless, though."

"Mostly." Annabelle shivered.

"I'm more scared of the snakes."

Before Annabelle could get worked up, I said, "But we've got you covered on that," and pointed to her cowboy boots.

"Guys, you've gotta see this." Sam stuck his head back out the doorway. "It's so cool!"

"What's so cool?" I grabbed the edge of the floppy door with my hand.

"It's an old car."

My heart leapt. I bound inside. There were just enough chinks in the joints between the walls and the roof that, added to the light through the door, I could tell it was a very old car. I turned on the flashlight on my phone.

"I know you're excited, but watch where you're putting your feet," Maggie advised, her voice dry.

I shined the light around the ground, illuminating my path. There were winding tracks through the dirt floor, but nothing currently making them. I shined the light on the car. It was dusty, but low, black, sleek, and beautiful with close-fitting helmet wings and a little rumble seat visible under a tarp that was askew. And it was missing a hood ornament.

"Hallelujah." My voice was reverent.

"What is it?" Sam asked.

He was holding Rachael's arm as she made her way cautiously in her flip-flops.

"It's a 1932 SS 1. The antique car that Gidget left in her will to her daughter."

"The daughter you can't find, right?" Annabelle asked.

"Not yet."

Rachael came to stand beside me. "And that's what my grandfather's working on, too?"

"It is. He's going to be so excited." I moved into the best light and activated the flash on my phone's camera. I took several shots then flipped through them and picked the best one. I edited it to make it even lighter. Around me I could hear the conversation of the others, but they had ceased to exist for me. I'd found Gidget's car.

I texted the photo to Ralph. *"Look what we found!"*

And then, riding on a wave of excited accomplishment, I blogged the photo as well. "The Day of the Jaguar."

As I turned my attention back to the inside of the shed and the others, a figure appeared in the doorway and blocked out all the light. Everyone quit talking at once, and a tense silence hung over us. Goose bumps rose all over me. I whirled to face the figure. It was an enormous man, but that was all I could tell because the sun behind him left his face in shadow.

"Eek" came out of my mouth. The Itzpa in me had long given over to the Tlazol, and there was no knife-winged warrior goddess to be found in me.

"Mrs. Hanson." It was a familiar voice. The hulk stepped in the room and light hit his face with its protruding eyes. His thumbs were tucked into the straps of his overalls.

"Jimmy Urban. What are you doing here?"

"Didn't mean to scare you. I come out here sometimes. To think a spell."

"But it's not your place." My voice was shaking and I was being rude, but he'd terrified me.

"The car"—he pointed at it—"reminds me of . . . I check on the car."

I stared at him, or what I could see of him, anyway. Gidget had been his fiancée. I knew how much the car had meant to her and Lucy. Why shouldn't it be important to Jimmy, too? "But you said you didn't know where it was. When I asked you."

"I said it hadn't been around the house. You never asked me if I knew where it was."

Hadn't I? My forehead puckered. Maybe he was right. "But you knew what I meant."

"I knew you'd find it soon enough."

And in the meantime, he'd have a little longer that it was just his. Something to remember a past love by.

"I'll leave you to it." He turned to go.

"Jimmy, wait." I followed him out. "Today, at the courthouse—"

"I'm sorry." He kicked at an old stump low to the ground.

"No—thank you. You helped."

He lifted his big shoulders and they fell. "I don't know 'bout that."

At first I couldn't figure out what he meant. Then I wondered if he knew what had happened in the judge's chambers. "Is there something I don't know?" He took a step away and I snatched his arm. "Tell me. Did something happen in chambers?"

"I can't tell you nothing." He shrugged my hand off. "'Cept that I told nothing but the truth."

I nodded. "Okay, then."

He lumbered away, and I watched him until he disappeared into the trees. When I got back to the shed, the others were coming out.

Maggie wiped her forehead, and dirt from her hand streaked it. "A couple of long-handled tools and some empty old metal containers is about all that's in there besides the car and a back seat full of critters. But the car was a great find."

"Phenomenal."

The kids fell in behind us, and almost immediately we pulled aside to let them pass.

We continued along the fence line and when the younger people were out of earshot, Maggie pounced. "What the heck was that about with Jimmy?"

I chewed the inside of my lip. "He feels closer to her there."

When we got to the edge of the fence closest to Lumpy's place, dusk had fallen and everyone was ready to get home. We broke the tree line and cut left into the field in front of Gidget's house. The laughter of the kids echoed as they widened the gap between them and us. They reached the house and threw the gate open. The golden retrievers came bounding out toward Maggie. Gertrude stayed with the kids, soaking up Rachael's attention. The girl seemed to be enthralled with the funny little dog. Gertrude was quite taken with her as well. We caught up to the kids.

"What are your plans?" I asked Sam and Annabelle.

"Rachael's grandpa said he'd let us build a bonfire and cook hot dogs and s'mores. Can we go over there?"

Annabelle didn't look completely sold on the idea.

"What about you, Belle?"

"I guess, but Jay texted me, and, well, he's on his way here."

"He is?" I tried to dial back my reaction as my eyes widened.

"Yes. He said he wants to talk, or whatever. He knows it wasn't my fault."

World's shortest breakup. "Good," I said. "Have you forgiven him?"

She smirked. "I have, but I haven't told him yet."

Maggie laughed. "Give 'em hell, girl." I wasn't sure that Maggie was the female influence I wanted for Annabelle, but she did have spunk.

"Maybe go with Rachael and Sam and send Jay directions."

"Yeah, I'll do that."

"Cool." I held up my knuckles.

Sam and Annabelle dapped them and turned back toward the house.

"Does anyone care what I'm doing tonight?" I called after them.

They looked at each other, then Sam shook his head. "No, not really, Mom."

Annabelle and I laughed. They disappeared into the house.

"I guess I'll be taking off, too." Maggie brushed her hands off on her overalls. "Unless you want to grab some dinner with me."

My loneliness must have shown on my face. "I don't have any other plans. But what about your non-boyfriend?"

We entered the house just as the kids were blowing out the other direction calling, "Bye, Mom! Bye, Maggie! Bye, Michele!"

We waved to them. As they drove off I said, "Well?"

"You mean you really want me to answer the question about my not-really boyfriend?" She arched an eyebrow high.

"I was kind of hoping you would." I changed out of my boots and grabbed my handbag while she talked.

"He travels," she said. "I see him when he's home." She winked. "If he's lucky."

"Does he live around here?" I slid my feet into flip-flops.

"He's got a ranch in Round Top." She had wandered over to the box from my trunk. It wasn't a big box. She picked it up. "Wanna look through these while we're eating?"

"Sounds good. Why don't you throw Gidget's yearbook in with it?" I put my laptop on the kitchen counter. "Let me just pull up the adoption boards real quick. I want to check for my brother and Gidget's daughter."

She loaded the yearbook and box in her truck while I browsed the site. It yielded nothing, but I felt better for trying. Someday I would get lucky. I switched off all the lights and locked up. When I joined her outside, Maggie was replenishing the dogs' food and water.

I stopped beside her. "Do you mind if I bring Gertrude? She hasn't had much attention."

"No problem. But I'm going to leave these guys here. They're happier lying under the shade trees."

We loaded up, the goldens looking settled and content as they sniffed the evening air. As we drove, we discussed options for food. Maggie suggested we try Giddings Steakhouse for their Thursday night special. We parked, and she ran ahead with the box of documents to secure permission for Gertrude to sit under the table. She was back in ninety seconds, smiling and giving us the okay sign.

The restaurant was a unique and cavernous space. The interior was original eighteen-hundreds brick with visible seams from combining buildings into the current configuration. We picked a table in the back near the salad bar and coaxed Gertrude into semi-hiding.

A leggy teenage girl in blue jeans with a green thigh-length apron showed up, pencil and order pad at the ready.

"We're about out of the special and most of the desserts is running low." She leaned in like she was telling us a big secret. Her brown eyes twinkled. "Most folks eatin' here are a good bit older than the two of you."

"We'll take two of the special then," Maggie said.

"And iced tea," I added. Gertrude licked my ankle and fluffed her locks. Maggie held up a finger. "Me, too."

"Great. Help y'allselves to the salad bar." She disappeared into the back area, her high-tops squeaking on the linoleum as she walked.

We were digging into our salads when the waitress set our iced teas on the table. Mine to the left, Maggie's to the right, which made me smile. She hadn't been trained on formal serving protocols, but she was quick and sincere.

"Sweetener's in the caddy. Sugar's in the jar. Y'all local?"

"I am." Maggie poured sugar in her tea and stirred. I would have to talk to her later about the evils of the white poison, on behalf of Adrian.

I raised my hand. "I'm here for the summer."

"At Gidget Becker's place," Maggie interjected.

She fumbled to put two straws beside our tall plastic tumblers. "Are you the writer?"

"She is."

Busybody, I wanted to say to Maggie. She set down the sugar. Poisoning complete, Maggie peeled her straw and stuck it in the tea.

The girl whispered behind her hand. "There was people here earlier talking about you."

"Really?" I scooted my chair back a little. I felt Gertrude get to her feet. "About me writing Gidget's book?"

She nodded, eyes round. "They said they was gonna put a stop to it."

"Who were they?" I asked.

She screwed her mouth up, thinking, then said, "Some Houston folks. Dressed up sharp. I didn't know 'em."

I said to Maggie, "Probably the attorney for the Houston Arts Trust. She's the enemy."

The young waitress made a disgusted noise. "All I know is they was bad tippers. Mad because they got stuck here on account of the freeway shutdown, I guess, and taking it out on me."

"What are people saying about that? The explosion, I mean," Maggie said.

She put a hand on her chest. "People is wondering if it was some kind of terrorists. I heard there was a Houston lady in there got burned up." She headed away, then stopped. "You know what was weird about them people is they wasn't acting sad about that lady. They was sayin' she had no business here and wasn't gonna be missed nohow." She bobbed her head, emphatic.

"How rude," Maggie said.

"I know." She walked to another table at the front of the restaurant.

We had time after our salads to pull the box between us and get out the stack of documents. I started with the yearbook.

"By the way," I asked Maggie. "What's the special?"

"Hell if I know. It's just better not to order from the menu."

"So you're saying the food here sucks?"

She picked up a piece of paper, and instead of answering me, her lips started moving slowly, forming words I didn't understand.

I bent my head toward the document so that I could read it, too. It was the one in the language that I'd assumed was Wendish. "I think that's Gidget's birth certificate."

Maggie didn't answer. Her lips kept moving and her face folded inward.

The waitress swung her tray from shoulder to hip height and balanced it on a stand a few feet away from our table. Beef tamales with red gravy, rice, and beans. Mexican, at a steakhouse. "Anything else for y'all?"

"Not me. Maggie?"

She shook her head without lifting her eyes from the paper.

As the waitress was leaving, she gave me a look, like *what's up with her?* I shrugged.

I perused the yearbook while Maggie read. The old annual fell open to a page with a scribbled notecard with Julie Herrington monogrammed at the top and a cutout piece of fragile yellow newsprint tucked inside. I looked at the notecard first.

Thank you for helping me come to my senses about Eldon. He'll never leave his wife. I'll just marry Lester—he's a true Southern gentleman—and help him get his gallery, and someday you'll be a famous artist and we'll have fabulous shows for you there. You are the bee's knees.

It was signed *Love, JuJu* in a girlish cursive with flourishes. My vision turned red. Greyhound and Julie? As in Lester's ex-wife, before she married him? Was this the connection clouding Greyhound's judgment? If this note was to Gidget, though, she and Mrs. Lester had been pretty close, too. I'd have to talk to Julie ASAP. Right after I killed Greyhound.

I replaced the picture and unfolded the newsprint. The *Houston Chronicle*. November 2, 1970. "Houston Tycoon Makes Pipelines a Family Affair." A stern-looking man with heavy eyebrows and hair that looked like it was graying—hard to tell in a yellowed black and white—stood behind two twenty-somethings, a man and a woman. I didn't recognize the older guy, but the younger two looked familiar.

"Jesus, Mary, and Joseph," Maggie breathed.

I put my clipping down. "What's up?"

She spoke in a flat voice, eyes still locked on the page, but she handed it to me. "It's my birth certificate."

I stared at it, confused, then at her. "What?"

She smoothed the paper in front of me, pointing. "There. That's my name written in Wendish. Myrtle Margaret. And don't say a word about Myrtle. It's a family name. And there's my birth date. There's not going to be another Myrtle Margaret in the world born on my birthday. But it's not my mother's name on it." She looked up at me, her face pale. "It's Anna Becker."

My voice came out in a too-loud screech. "Anna Becker?" I got control of myself, spoke softer. "Your mother is Anna Becker?"

She shook her head. "It can't be. My mother's name is Charlotte Killian." She put her finger on the scratch-outs over Gidget's name. "Someone tried to cross this out. Maybe they just made a mistake with this one. Maybe Gidget's baby was born on the same day as me."

"This is very strange."

She sat back, rolling her bottom lip in her teeth. "I have a birth certificate. It looks almost just like this. It has my mom's and dad's names and—" She jerked the document back in front of her, holding up a finger as she read the words slowly.

"I can't even believe you can read Wendish."

"Barely. But enough. See." She tapped it hard with her finger. "This part's different. On my birth certificate it says I was born at my parents' house with a midwife. Here it says—" She shook her head, and her face paled. "No, this can't be right. No."

"What do you mean? What can't be right?"

"It says I was born at the Becker farmhouse. At Gidget's place."

THIRTY

Our waitress brought us boxes for our untouched food and expedited our check. Gertrude kept an eye on the to-go boxes for us. And a nose. And occasionally a tongue. We were on the road five minutes later with the birth certificate tucked into the yearbook with the old newspaper article and note to Gidget. It had crossed my mind to post the birth certificate to *Her Last Wish*, but it felt too personal about Maggie to me.

Maggie left a voice mail for her mother. "Mom? It's me. I love you. I need to talk to you. It's kind of an emergency. Please call me."

Maggie floored Bess, and I clung to the armrest. The yearbook slid off the top of the box between us, landing on Gertrude in my lap. She yelped. I moved her gently to the floorboard and opened the yearbook, touching the birth certificate, then the clipping. So much had happened, so long ago in this sleepy town.

It had grown dark outside. Light from above spilled onto the pastures in front of Gidget's house in a magical alchemy of mercury moonscapes and occasional white-gold firefly streaks. The light was bright enough that I caught a glimpse of the news clipping again. Pipeline. I squinted at the article. Buck Herrington. His daughter, JuJu. Her twin brother, Tres, fiancé of Helen Connally, true Texas political royalty, according to the article. The man and his adult kids at the diner, I realized. Was this Gidget's benefactor? Or at least her impetus to leave?

Maggie parked Bess by the side gate. The outside lights were off, either burned out, or maybe I'd forgotten to leave them on. I shut the yearbook and left it on the seat as I scouted ahead for snakes with my iPhone flashlight. Gertrude jumped out of Bess, forgetting about the boxed tamales in an instant. She transformed into the Gertrude that had fetched me from the Quacker before Gidget died. She ran around erratically, barking in a shrill tone. I opened the gate, and she took off like a stubby racehorse toward the house. Whines interlaced her barks. She sprinted back to me, her tail tucked. I pointed the flashlight down at her. She was covered in blood.

"*Dios mío*," I whispered.

Maggie bumped into me in the half-light. "What's wrong?" Her eyes took in Gertrude. "Where are my dogs?"

My chest clenched. Janis and Woody running to greet us, barking and bounding—that's what was missing. Suddenly I couldn't get air into my lungs. I huffed in futile little pants.

Maggie was calling at the top of her lungs. "Janis! Woody!" With nothing to light her way but the moon, she raced around the front yard, then around to the back of the house.

As quickly as it had come on, my emotional paralysis lifted. They were Maggie's dogs. I had to help her. I sprinted to the back door and flipped on the lights, tossing my handbag onto the kitchen table as I did. That's when I heard her scream.

It was high-pitched, operatic almost, drawn-out, and agonizing. "No. No, no, no."

I hurried to her side. Her gorgeous animals, in the prime of their lives, lay side by side, their blood spilling out and pooling black and shiny into one puddle between them.

Maggie dropped to her knees. She put an arm around each furry, bloody neck and hugged them to her, rocking and screaming. Gradually, her cries morphed into rageful sounds. "I will kill the motherfucker that did this. I will kill him. I will kill him."

I had both hands on her back as I crouched over her and her dogs. Their metallic odor was overpowering. I lifted a hand to shield my nose. "Oh, Maggie, I'm so sorry." She didn't seem to notice me.

"Gotta be a sick crazy bastard to hurt a dog. Who hurts a dog?"

My mind raced, and I processed my thoughts aloud. "Could it be about Gidget? Or me?" I stood up. My brain pricked with a delayed thought. My wildlife cam! I'd put the chip back in it. We'd be able to see who did this. I ran to it, knocking into the painted birdhouse, fumbling with the camera case latches. The chip was gone. I walked back to Maggie, processing, processing.

"They were everything to me." Maggie had laid her upper body across the animals, so her voice was muffled.

Tears leaked from my eyes. "Cops first or a vet?"

She shook her head. "A vet won't do any good. Cops not much better." She sat up. Dark splotches covered her face. Even in the moonlight, I knew it was blood.

Gertrude sidled in between Maggie and the two dogs and laid her muzzle against Janis.

A calmness settled over me like a suit of armor. My focus sharpened as Maggie's functionality deteriorated. I heard my voice like I was listening to dialogue in a movie. The general had to take command of the troops. These animals were dead, the chip was missing, but we were alive. Something was wrong, though, and we needed to get it together. "Somebody was here and murdered your dogs. I'm going to call it in and get Gidget's shotgun."

Maggie stood, wiping her eyes with her forearm, smearing blood like war paint across her cheeks. "Do you have a sheet? I want to put them in my truck."

"Oh, Maggie." I put my arms around her and hugged her. She melted, and I propped her weight on me.

The blood from the dogs was sticky, and now it was all over me, too. Keeping one arm around Maggie, I half-carried, half-dragged her into the house. When I turned on the lights, I didn't scream, even though it was a shock. The place was trashed. Papers and photos were strewn everywhere. Cabinets stood open with broken dishes and glasses on the kitchen floor. Artwork was tossed around the house, and the walls were bare.

I steered Maggie toward Gidget's room, for the shotgun and the sheet. In the master bedroom, clothes had been thrown all over the floor. Someone had shoved the mattress and box springs off the bed frame. The shiplap was broken in places, ripped down, hammered, or drilled, or maybe all of the above. Whoever had been here had worked fast. And probably had been watching us, waiting for us to leave. We'd only been gone—I looked at my watch—forty-five minutes. An hour, at most.

"Holy shit!" Maggie breathed, rousing enough that I let go of her. She picked up a picture.

I waded over Gidget's possessions and picked a sheet off the floor, thinking aloud as I did. "This has to be about Gidget. But why now? And what are they looking for that they couldn't have found when she was alive or in the last two weeks?"

I dug between the mattress and box frame. Eureka, the shotgun was still where I'd shoved it the other night, with the shells. I loaded the gun and stuffed shells in my pockets. On the other side of the room, a window was broken outward. Shotgun in hand, I inspected the window. Shards of glass still hung in the frame in jagged teeth, but there was enough space that a person could have exited this way, painfully. I leaned out. Glass littered the ground along with the wooden crosspieces from the window. From close range, I saw bright red blood running down one of the shards. A tiny scrap of denim hung from the point of the glass.

"Look at this." My voice sounded normal in my own ears, even though I should have been scared out of my mind.

"I'll kill the son of a bitch!" Her wild eyes flitted in every direction, looking out through the window.

I took the picture from her hand, intending to put it on the bedside table. "We have to get out of here."

I glanced down at it. I'd seen it before. Lester, Gidget, and a plain, brown-haired woman. I did a double take. I'd seen her before. *Mierda*. I'd seen her more than once. She'd been at the gallery in Houston. She'd been in the courtroom today. She'd been in a picture with Lester I'd pulled up online. She was Lester's imminently forgettable ex-wife, Julie. Julie Herrington. Julie *Herrington*. *JuJu* Herrington. Daughter of Buck. Pipeline heiress. Pipeline . . . Lonestar Pipeline. *Oh God*. I'd been so stupid not to see it sooner. A return address handwritten on an envelope lying on the table the day Gidget died. From the office of Julie Herrington Sloane, campaign manager for Boyd Herrington. Was Boyd *Tres*? So much made sense in a heartbeat, but so much still didn't. Most importantly, I didn't know who had been here or what they wanted. Or whether they'd left.

"I'll call the cops." Maggie pulled her phone from a pocket of her overalls.

The front door creaked opened, chasing all thoughts of JuJu and Tres out of my head.

"Sam? Annabelle?" I called.

Maggie moved to the bedroom door, her finger poised above the screen of her phone, her eyes moving toward the front of the house. I heard a pop noise and then a thud in the back wall of Gidget's room. Maggie dropped her phone and yelped. Everything moved in slow motion for me. I grabbed her by the arm and dragged her to the window, kicking the last of the glass out. I tossed the shotgun through, a little past the blanket of glass below. With one arm, I pulled Maggie after me and dove, releasing her in midair and landing with one hand on the gun and the other right on a big sharp chunk of glass. My knees were next, and they caught glass, too. It stung.

Hijo de puta. Maggie landed on top of me, and her weight dug the glass deeper into my palm.

No time to think about the pain. Time to get the hell out of here. "Get up! Run!"

I leapt to my feet, grabbing the shotgun. Maggie struggled up, too. I looked through the yard, back at the house, and into the trees. The cars. But I had tossed my handbag onto the kitchen table when I'd turned on the outside light. I had no Jetta keys. And no phone, either. Mine was in my bag, and I'd just watched Maggie's fall to the bedroom floor.

"Are your keys in the truck?" I whispered, moving toward the back gate.

"No. I dropped them. When we found Janis and Woody."

Caca. Big piles of caca. But my calmness stayed with me, and I didn't panic. "This way." I pulled her toward the darkness of the forest, flicking off the safety and pumping a shell into the chamber as I ran down the trail I'd first seen a week before and never taken. I cursed my priorities, reset the safety, and tucked the shotgun tightly under my armpit, one hand holding it for dear life, the other one dragging Maggie.

"Black mask," she panted. "Man," she panted again.

I didn't want to give him sound to follow. "Shh."

Maggie crashed through undergrowth I was taking pains to avoid. My sandals weren't good running shoes and were even worse protection from snakes. Maggie was wearing her boots. She was loud, but still I envied her. I steered us down the widest opening between the thick trees on either side. Maggie slowed, then stopped. She was completely winded, and I couldn't budge her.

"Do you think he followed us?" she said between heaving breaths.

I didn't answer. When Maggie stood, I jerked her forward again. Suddenly we all but smashed into the shed we'd discovered that afternoon.

"I can't go any farther," Maggie gasped.

"Get in here." I pushed the shed door open with my sandal, analyzing like a supercomputer as we went inside. The SS 1 was the only possible hiding place inside. We could hole up with the gun ready for anyone who came through the door. I opened the passenger door. A raccoon chittered at me, an angry sound. Her body rose up and exposed the nest of babies she was protecting and the overpowering odor of urine and feces. I shut the door.

The "Jaguar" had a rumble seat, though. I'd seen it in the pictures. There was a tarp covering the back end of the car. I pushed it to the side, uncovering the rumble seat. The latches were rusty and resistant, but adrenaline spurted through me, and they gave way to me. Holding on to the tarp and going by instinct and common sense, I pushed the rumble seat back and into position. Dust billowed into my nose, and I coughed. No critters jumped out, though.

"In here."

Maggie climbed in first. I handed her the shotgun, then I got in and pulled the tarp over us. Pitch blackness descended.

"I don't want to think about what might be on this floorboard." I shuddered.

Maggie stuck her boot downward and kicked. "Nothing crawling around." She pushed to rearrange herself and her boot slipped. "There's something down there, though."

I heard noises in the woods. "Shh."

I rearranged the shotgun pointed up and away from us and flicked off the safety. Our breathing slowed, but I was sure anyone within a hundred yards could hear my thundering heartbeat. Quiet footsteps growing louder approached. They entered the shed. We held our breath. They circled the car, and someone opened the driver's side door, pissing off mama raccoon again.

"Shit!" The voice was androgynous, but muffled.

I put my finger over the shotgun trigger. The tarp whipped back, and a spotlight shone in our eyes.

"Well, hello, ladies." He raised a handgun with a fat silencer at the end of the barrel.

I pulled the trigger.

THIRTY-ONE

THE THUNDEROUS BOOM of the shotgun exploded against my eardrums as it slammed against my shoulder. The spotlight ping-ponged like a laser around the shed, then fixed on the ceiling. In the echoing silence, Maggie let loose a soprano scream that melded with a tenor oomph and groan outside the car, followed by the thud of a body hitting the ground. Dazed, my ears ringing, I realized I'd dropped the shotgun. I grabbed for it and slammed the butt of the stock to my shoulder, pumping it and jumping to my feet in the rumble seat, yelling like a banshee over the opera around me.

Maggie quieted, and the groans stopped. The shot had peppered holes through the walls and ceiling, and faint moonlight streamed in—a constellation of sorts. I peered over the edge of the rumble seat. A figure in black writhed, hands clutched to the gut. Short dark hair stuck out of its mask in the back.

"I've got the gun pointed at you," I said. "Don't move."

The man spat out, "Fuck you." The groaning resumed.

"No, thank you." I kept my eyes on him. "Maggie, do you have anything we can tie him up with?"

I heard pats as she searched her body.

"I don't," she said. "Sorry."

"We've got to get out of here and go call the cops." I thought of my phone back in my handbag.

Maggie slipped as she stood. "Dammit." She reached into the floorboard and came up with something sheathed in plastic. She shook it.

While Maggie was otherwise occupied, I hopped out and grabbed the man's Glock, stuffing it in the back of my waistband. Then I snagged his light from the shed floor. I couldn't stand the thought of leaving our accoster to follow us. Using my left hand for the flashlight, I went to the door. Baling wire snagged the sleeve of my shirt. I was so happy about it I didn't even mind the rip. There were three lengths of it holding the door up. I mined the lower two, leaving the door hanging from one strand at the top. I took my makeshift restraints back inside. The man in black swiped at me when I crouched beside him, but his aim was off and his arm fell to the earthen floor without touching me. His breathing was ragged and shallow.

"Save your strength." I wrapped wire snuggly around his ankles. Moonlight through the roof glinted off little blond tufts of hobbit hair on his fingers as I closed the wire like a twist tie around his wrists. "Stay put."

Maggie had freed herself and the plastic package from the rumble seat. She was standing beside me, watching.

"Let's go," I said.

We ran along the path back to the house, the only sounds our footsteps and our heavy breathing. Maggie dragged behind me, barely able to keep up. When we reached the backyard, the back gate was open. We burst into the house through the door by the kitchen, passing Janis and Woody again. I averted my eyes. Maggie's breath intake was sharp, and then she moaned. I laid the shotgun on the kitchen table. After a moment, Maggie joined me inside and set her package beside the gun.

"I'll get my phone," she croaked, and took off toward the bedroom.

I looked back at the table. Where was the handbag I'd left there?

Maggie squeaked, then I heard a cracking noise, a thump on the floor, and running footsteps coming toward me. *Maggie*, I thought, and then thought ended and instinct took over. I snatched the shotgun from the table and bolted out the door. I hurdled the side gate and crouched behind Bess. I breathed in and out once to steady myself. *There'd been more than one of them.* I half stood. The shotgun was pumped, and it had two shells left in it. I put the barrel over the edge of the truck bed. A short person was sidestepping through the door frame in shadows. It looked like the hunchback of Notre Dame. *Not now*, I told my imagination, but as the figure drew closer, I realized it wasn't my mind playing tricks on me. It was thick and dark but with something smaller and light colored moving jerkily beside it.

"Stop right there," I yelled. I didn't want to shoot. I hadn't wanted to the first time tonight. But I would if I had to. The choice between me and a bad guy wasn't a choice at all.

The voice that answered exploded in my brain. "Michele!" Annabelle screamed.

I didn't understand. Annabelle's voice came from the figures on the back porch, but how? The how didn't matter, and the mama tiger in me roared. "Let go of her!" But my command was toothless, and I knew it. I couldn't shoot now. Even if I was a good enough shot, a shotgun was too imprecise and there was no way I could avoid hitting my daughter. In frustration, I aimed away from them and pulled the trigger anyway, hoping to scare whoever was holding Annabelle into releasing her.

It didn't work. A woman's voice, tight with an edge of desperation, called out to me. "I'm leaving with her. Put your gun down and come out with your hands up where I can see them."

I fumbled with the shells in my pocket, loading another to replace the one I'd wasted. "We shot your partner and called 911. It's over. Let her go before anyone else gets hurt, and you make this worse for yourself."

She cackled. "Your friend didn't make it to her phone. Nice try."

Annabelle started to sob. "I'm sorry, Michele."

The woman jerked her, hard, and Annabelle's cries intensified.

I had no choice. I tossed the shotgun into the open.

"Good start. Now come on out, hands high."

I was on my way, I was going to comply, but I never got the chance. A rifle shot cracked, and the woman crumpled. Annabelle screamed more shrilly than even Maggie had. Out of the darkness, Lumpy appeared, rifle in one hand. He grabbed something from the grass at the woman's feet and stuffed it in his belt, then snatched Annabelle up. He ran past the lifeless dogs, kicking open the gate, with my precious daughter in his arms. He set her on her feet, and I wrapped her in my arms, squeezing the stuffing out of her.

"Thank you, thank you, thank you, Lumpy," I called to my ex-Texas Ranger neighbor. I was going to be a little nicer to him from now on.

But he didn't seem to hear me. He was back in the yard, bent over the woman in the grass. She screeched as he pulled her arms behind her, not bothering to be gentle. Annabelle sobbed against my shoulder.

"Shh. It's going to be all right," I told her, rocking her side to side, one hand cupping her silken head, the other rubbing in circles on her back. The sound of a car pulling up the driveway chilled me. "Lumpy, someone's coming," I shouted.

"Probably the sheriff. I called 'em on my way," he grunted, wrestling with his prisoner.

Sirens wailed, growing closer fast. The car materialized in the moonlight. But it wasn't the sheriff.

THIRTY-TWO

It was Rashidi John who jumped from his car and ran toward us.

"It's okay. He's a friend," I shouted at Lumpy.

Annabelle babbled what she knew of our story to Rashidi, and he hovered over us, apologizing over and over for leaving. He said his sense of unease had grown through the afternoon and into his interview dinner, until he couldn't stand it. He'd made excuses halfway through and driven like a bat out of hell the whole way back.

The sheriff himself and my two favorite deputies pulled up less than a minute after Rashidi.

Lumpy waved to the lawmen. "Over here." The sheriff and Tank headed straight to him without acknowledging us. Junior peeled off our way, though.

"Maggie," I told him. "She's in the house. Hurt." I hoped she was only hurt. "And I shot a man who tried to kill us. I tied him up. He's in a shed on the back of our property." I described the exact location.

"Alive?" Junior asked.

"When we left him, alive and ornery."

He nodded. "There's an ambulance on the way. I'll call another." He moved off quickly toward the house, where he conferred with his partner and the sheriff then disappeared inside.

"Stay with Annabelle?" I asked Rashidi.

He nodded, and I slipped away, closer to the house, into earshot.

Lumpy was telling his story to the sheriff. "I been keeping a closer eye on things. This house is the last'un out on this road, and I'd seen Ms. Hanson and Maggie drive into town, then a car went by and didn't come back. I got suspicious and drove down the road. 'Bout that time, I saw Ms. Hanson and Maggie return. Then I found a passenger van, no one in it, on the side of the road. I went home, stewed on it, remembered I'd seen one like it before when it shouldn't'a been here, and reckoned I'd better check things out here, quiet-like. I walked over, called you on the way. Saw this here woman holding Ms. Hanson's daughter, and Ms. Hanson out yonder." He gestured toward where Rashidi and Annabelle were huddled next to Bess. "She made Ms. Hanson throw down her gun, so I shot her in the shoulder."

Tank snapped a set of metal handcuffs around the woman's wrists. She howled in pain, but I didn't feel sorry for her. More bright lights spun their way up the drive. An ambulance this time. Tank pulled the mask off the woman's head. Behind me, I heard an enraged Annabelle shout.

"That's the woman who fired me from Senator Herrington's campaign. Mrs. Sloane. What's she doing here?" Annabelle had run to my side as she yelled, Rashidi keeping pace with her.

Tank had dragged her to a sitting position, and I got a better look at her. Dark shoulder-length hair mussed by the ski mask, late middle age. My handbag on her shoulder. I recognized her, too, and my fists balled. Lester's ex-wife. Julie Herrington Sloane, the Lonestar Pipeline heiress. Why on earth would she break into Gidget's house and hold a gun on Annabelle? And if she did those things, what else had she done? I started toward her, a snarl on my lips, but it died as Maggie wobbled out the door with Junior trailing behind her.

She weaved the last few steps to me, her hand to her head. "I think I'm going to throw up."

"You've probably got a concussion," Junior said. "I told you not to get up. Come back to the house."

Maggie sunk to her knees, then on her haunches. Luckily, her dogs were out of her line of sight. A phone rang, and she groaned, holding up her hand. Her ringing phone was clutched in it. It stopped ringing. Maggie stared at her screen, squinting. "I can't read it. The letters are squiggly."

Annabelle grabbed it and read aloud. "Mom."

"Shit. I wanted to talk to her."

The phone sang out its voice-mail tone. Junior walked up to Maggie with an ice pack. She pressed it to the back of her head. Then he met the new paramedics at the gate. They took off into the woods carrying spot-lights and a stretcher.

"You want me to play it?" Annabelle asked.

"Sure."

But before she could, another car pulled up out front.

"It's Jay!" Annabelle thrust the phone at me. "I was meeting him here." Which was the answer to the question I hadn't asked, and the reason for her very bad luck in running into Julie Sloane, I guessed.

"I'm sorry about tonight," I said.

She shot me a brilliant smile as she trotted toward Jay, who was climbing out of his car. "It was scary, but you're a badass, Michele, and it was kind of cool." She disappeared into the darkness between the cars, and I heard the sound of Jay's voice. I smiled, just a little.

Maggie slumped over with her head in the grass, the ice pack crowning her head. "She doesn't know the half of it."

The paramedics rolled a stretcher toward Julie Sloane. The tall woman who had helped Gidget was one of them. She was focused on her patient and didn't glance my way. Just as I was about to play Maggie's mother's message, her phone rang again.

"It's your mother," I told her.

Her voice was muffled by the grass. "Put it on speaker." I sat cross-legged beside her and did. "Hi, Mom," Maggie mumbled.

"What's wrong, darling?" a woman's voice asked. It was a caring voice, a sweet voice with a little quaver to it. "You don't sound like yourself."

"I got hit in the head, and I'm a little woozy." Maggie straightened up to a kneeling position and readjusted her ice.

"Oh no!"

"And somebody killed my dogs."

"Oh, honey, I'm so sorry."

"And I just saw a copy of my birth certificate, but your name wasn't on it."

The line went silent. I drew in a deep breath and held it.

After a few seconds, her mother cleared her throat. "What do you mean, dear?"

"I'm at Anna Becker's house, Mom, with my friend Michele Lopez Hanson, who's writing a book about Ms. Becker. I've been helping her. I found a picture of you and dad with Anna's parents. Were you friends?"

"We were, but what does this have to do with the birth certificate?"

"It was in Wendish. It looks just like the one that I've had all these years

—with my name and birthday—except for two things. The name of the mother was Anna Becker and the place of birth was here at the Beckers' farm."

"Oh . . ."

"Mother?" Maggie said. "Do you know anything about this?"

The silence this time was even longer. When her mother answered, her voice was small, and the quaver more pronounced. "We all promised we wouldn't ever tell. I didn't even know such a document existed."

"What do you mean, you promised you'd never tell?" Maggie's eyes had opened and she had dropped the ice. Her voice was stern.

"We promised the Beckers." Her mother sniffled. "Oh, Maggie, we've always loved you as if you were our very own. We tried for years and weren't able to have children. The Beckers knew. When Anna showed up at her parents' pregnant and in labor, they called us."

Maggie cut in, her voice sharp, her face pained. "So you're saying Anna Becker is my mother?"

There was a sob on the other end of the phone. "I am your mother. I have been your mother since the moment you arrived in this world, but Anna gave birth to you."

I reached for Maggie's hand. It was cold from the ice. I squeezed it hard. Tears had welled up in her eyes. To my surprise, I felt them in my own.

The tears didn't show in her hard voice, though. "So who's my father?"

I sucked in a deep breath and held it. Another ambulance pulled up in the Grand Central Station parking lot that was the strip of grass beside Gidget's house.

"Anna wouldn't tell her parents. I'm so sorry, darling. I really am."

I exhaled, feeling a flicker of disappointment. It was enormous to learn that Maggie was Anna's daughter. But the part of me that was writing Gidget's book as well as the part of me that was Maggie's friend wanted desperately to know the identity of her father. Tank motioned for me to join him on the back porch, so I squeezed Maggie's hand again and released it, leaving her talking to her mother. I glared at Julie Sloane as I walked past her. What in the world was taking them so long to get her off the property?

He took me in the house to the kitchen table. "I need a full account of the events of tonight from you."

"I already told Junior, but sure."

Sheriff Boudreaux stuck his head in the door. "We need you," he said to his deputy.

Tank shot to his feet and pointed at me. "I'll talk to you later."

He hustled after the sheriff. I sat at the table, gathering my thoughts and just breathing. The package Maggie had brought from the car was still on the table. I stared at it now. It was a square, more than two feet on each side, wrapped in butcher paper and layer after layer of plastic sheeting.

I looked down at myself. Bloody hands and knees. Dirt streaks. Ripped clothes. I was a sight. From my seat in the kitchen, I could see Maggie had taken the phone off of speaker. She squatted, phone to ear. Rashidi and Lumpy were talking like old friends, and I saw Lumpy clap Rashidi on the back. Annabelle was in Jay's car. No one needed me right that second. I looked back at the package. I wanted to know what was in it. I got a knife from a drawer and carefully sliced open the layers of plastic on one edge. Then I did the same thing on the other edges. I pulled the plastic and paper away, revealing a waxed-canvas portfolio. I unzipped it. I reached in and found a hard-edged object wrapped in tissue paper. I felt like I was pulling apart Russian nesting dolls as I unfolded the corners of the paper. Finally I came to the baby doll in the center: a painting of a man and a woman. But not just any painting. An extraordinary painting, as the wrapping job had hinted, in a style I'd recognize anywhere. I put my hand to my throat. Could it be? I peeled the tissue back from the bottom right-hand corner. My head felt light, my mouth was dry. Andy Warhol. I ran my fingers gently over the canvas and felt the ridges and whorls left by the brush of the artist himself.

I picked it up and ran outside. "Maggie," I called. She kept talking to her mother. "Maggie!" I shouted, my voice sharper.

She put her hand over the phone. "What is it?"

"You've got to see this."

Maggie stood and winced, her hand cupping the ice to the back of her head. A male paramedic wheeled a stretcher toward her. She waved it away.

He said, "You need to get that checked, ma'am. You probably have a concussion."

She said, "I promise I will, but not right now."

The paramedic shook his head as he pushed the stretcher back to the ambulance.

Maggie put the phone receiver against her chest. "What is it?"

"Look," I said. "It was in the package you found in the car."

The paramedics working on Julie finally started wheeling her toward the ambulance.

Maggie stared for a few seconds and said, "Is that an Andy Warhol?"

Julie Sloane gasped.

"It's so much more than that. Do you know who the people in it are?"

"They look familiar, but I'm not sure." She looked at me, her eyes confused and concussed.

"It's Gidget, with Boyd Herrington." I beamed. "Your parents."

As she rolled past us, Julie hissed. "It's just a painting, not a paternity test. You have no proof."

THIRTY-THREE

THE NEXT DAY, Maggie parked Bess in front of Senator Boyd Herrington's ranch house. I'd made an appointment, and we'd driven past a gauntlet of media at the entrance to his property. We got out, and she shot me a nervous smile then wiped her hands on her thighs, hitching her skirt up a little bit when she did. I took her arm as we walked up the flagstone path to the blue front door.

The restored old ranch house was white with a wraparound porch and a multitude of roof lines on its second story. It was a second home to the senator and his wife, whose primary residence was in Austin. They'd taken great pains to restore the wooden structure to its former glory, while enlarging it tastefully and with architectural integrity.

Maggie stood in front of the door and started whispering something to herself.

I jerked on her arm. "What are you saying?"

"Trying to get my courage up."

"Want me to do it?"

"Yes!" But she laughed, and I knew she was kidding. "My head hurts. I don't want to do this."

"Yes, you do." I rang the doorbell.

The senator opened the door. "Ms. Hanson. Maggie. It's nice to see you. Won't you come in?"

Maggie shook her head. "I'm not sure that's a good idea."

"Oh?" One of his eyebrows rose higher than the other, like a set of mismatched parentheses.

"We came to give you some information," I said, trying to prompt Maggie.

She turned to me, her eyes wide with unshed tears.

"And what might that be?" he asked, looking back and forth between us.

I took pity on her. "Maggie's your daughter."

His eyebrows reversed course, down with a furrowed brow. "Come again."

"Yours and Anna Becker's. Your sister and your father bribed Anna not to tell you. That's the information Julie was trying to cover up when she tried to kill us, the information the whole world is about to find out."

"Slow down. My father, my sister, oh my God." He put a hand to his forehead. "Wait, Anna had a baby?"

Maggie waggled her fingers at him. "Me."

He looked between her and me. "I knew we bought Anna a share in Lester's gallery, but I thought it was just—"

"A break-up present," I said.

His face flushed. "That sounds pretty terrible doesn't it?"

I nodded. "'Fraid so."

He stepped outside and closed the door behind him. "My wife's in bed with a migraine. As you can imagine, this has been a very tough time for our family, with Julie and all." He shook his head. "I never told my wife about Anna. I want to tell her myself, not have her overhear it. So, start from the beginning."

I drew in a deep breath. "Julie invited Greyhound to visit her at the hospital this morning. Did you know they had an affair before she married Lester?"

He looked puzzled. "I didn't."

"After Gidget died, Julie went to see him. Greyhound. She blackmailed him into helping her. Which he did. He entered into an agreement in chambers to squash the book about Gidget for her."

"Oh no," he said.

I kept going. "So today she called for Greyhound and asked him to defend her in all of this. He said no, but he said she poured the whole story out anyway. Afterwards, he came straight to me. I'm sure he only told me all of this to keep me from reporting him to the bar association—or worse—but he said a reporter had called him. He didn't talk to them, but the media is going to figure it all out. About Julie. You and Anna."

Sitting in Gidget's living room across from Greyhound earlier, I'd clasped my hands in my lap to keep from throttling him, at least until he'd told the story. I'd already figured a lot of it out, but he was able to confirm details and pull the rest of it together for me. It was going to make one hell of a book, at least, and I'm sure that would have made Gidget very happy.

The senator nodded. "We've got to get out in front of it with our story, whatever it's going to be. Go on."

The sprinklers came on in the flower beds in front of the porch. The senator motioned us to the other side.

I walked in front of him, talking over my shoulder. "Greyhound said you and Julie were with your father when you all first met Anna at a diner in Brenham. That your father wooed her to Houston, where she worked for him. That he paid her generously so she could study art and art history at U of H."

He nodded. "That was a long time ago. But yes, that's right."

"Julie was jealous of Anna. Anna was gorgeous. Julie was only rich. They partied together—Julie providing Anna's entrée to the Houston social scene—until the day Anna confided she was pregnant, and that the baby was yours."

The senator leaned against the porch railing. "Why didn't she just tell me?" His eyes were bleak.

I didn't have an answer to that, so I launched back into my tale, nearly to the climactic events. "Julie went straight to your father, and they came up with a solution that wouldn't end your engagement to the perfect woman for the political future Daddy Buck envisioned for you. In their eyes, at least, everyone would get what they wanted. Lester would get money for his struggling art gallery, Anna would get her dream career in the art world, and Buck would get to set you up to make a run for the Presidency. All Anna had to do was say yes, agree not to tell you or anyone, and abort the baby."

He propelled himself off the railing, landing in an almost pugilistic stance. "They made her promise to get rid of my baby?"

"That's what Julie told Greyhound. And they thought Anna'd done it, until she met me and I agreed to write her biography. She mailed you a letter to let you know you have a daughter. Julie intercepted the letter." I paused, remembering my conversation with Greyhound. That had been the end of his tale. He'd begged me to forgive him. It took everything I had to defy good manners and ignore his apology, but I did it. I think my mother would have approved. I shook the memory off and continued. "I don't have proof she killed Gidget, but I believe she did, to keep her quiet."

The senator's fists balled. "If she did, it wasn't for me. It was for her, and for my father. I mean, Julie's my sister, and I love her, but I can't believe what they did to me. What they did to Anna. And to you, Maggie." He turned to my friend and put a hand on her arm briefly. "It's unforgivable."

Maggie's cheeks colored.

I told the senator the rest of what I knew. About Gidget's correspondence with Warhol, and his painting of the senator and Anna. About Darlene, what she'd told me and what she hadn't. How she died. About all of it. He asked a few more questions, but mostly he just listened, his face pale and grave. Maggie watched him taking it in, while pretending not to.

When I was done, he said, "Forty years of my life has been replaced in an instant with a new version." He crossed his arms over his chest like he was cold. When he spoke, his voice was careful. "I'm horrified about what Julie's done. But that's about her. Part of what you came to tell me is good news. Maggie, I wish I'd known you were my daughter from the beginning."

She looked lost and young. Uncertain.

The senator smiled. A small one, but a smile. "Welcome to the family. They'll all love you, once they get used to the idea."

My jaw nearly dropped. From Julie's extreme decisions and actions, I would have expected that the senator would have treated the news that he had a daughter like the end of the world. Except that Julie was protecting herself and her father from their bad choices. None of this had ever been about whether Boyd Herrington would have welcomed a child with Anna.

Maggie's lower lip quivered, and she almost got emotional. Then she rallied. With sparks in her eyes, she took a shot at him. "Now that I know you're my father, all I can say is thank God I never slept with you. Not that you didn't try."

"Whoo, yeah, thank God for that." He laughed, but it was a nervous sound. "Listen." He reached out and put an arm around her. "I may not be a great husband, but I'm not a completely amoral human being."

I had planned to let this be Maggie's moment, but I blurted it out anyway: "I heard you hit on my daughter."

"What?"

I put my hands on my hips. "I heard you made a pass at my not-yet-nineteen-year-old stepdaughter, Belle Hanson."

He opened his mouth, closed it, then said, "Ms. Hanson, I'm really sorry. I think that was all just a misunder—"

I didn't want to hear it. "Julie fired her when she reported it."

His eyebrows did the mismatched parentheses again. "I hate to hear that. I'll make it right. I promise."

"How?"

"Well, I've suspended my campaign, so I can't offer her a job—"

"I wouldn't let her come back to work with you."

"—so how about a scholarship instead?"

I nodded. "It also would be nice if you quit hitting on women young enough to be your granddaughters."

He sighed. "Does it help any to know that my therapist says the same thing?"

The view out my front window was pretty wonderful. Sam's 4Runner—Adrian's old car—was coming up the drive. Gertrude must have thought so, too, because she stood with her feet in the window frame, barking and wagging her tail. Jimmy had put glass back in the window for us, and it had nose prints all over it already, but I didn't mind. Smudges were small stuff. Right now I was much more concerned about whether law enforcement would be able to prove that Julie killed Gidget and Darlene. I was praying that Reggie, the guy I'd shot, would rat her out.

I put the paint roller down. Between a few intense makeup workouts and my traitorous body, I hurt. A lot. I folded forward, grabbed my elbows, and swung side to side. I'd just have to do the best I could with what I had. I stood back up. Sunny yellow paint droplets covered Gertrude and me from head to toe. I had gotten permission for a few updates to the place from my new landlord, Maggie. I had declined Gidget's bequest now that she had an heir. Maggie would get everything, which made me very happy.

I had a feeling my book on Gidget's life would do just fine—the story was sexy and had celebrities and politicians in it, after all, and my blog following was growing exponentially every day—and I was working on it around the clock now. Except for redecorating breaks.

My phone chimed with a text. I found a dry spot on my shorts and wiped my hands. It was from Rashidi. I hadn't talked to him since he'd gone back to College Station that crazy night when Julie Sloane had almost killed Maggie, Annabelle, and me.

"Congratulate me on my new job."

Dark spots danced in front of my eyes. Rashidi living an hour away terrified me. Was I ready for a relationship? With him or anyone? I wanted

Adrian back, not someone new. But Adrian wasn't coming back. With my only paint-free finger, I touched the warm butterfly hanging from my neck, then texted him a thumbs-up and typed "*Tell me more,*" then added "*Congratulations.*"

I opened the door to Sam, who was carrying my groceries on each hip.

"Whoa!" he said. "It's bright in here."

"You mean, hey, Mom, it looks good and you've been working so hard!" I pointed to the kitchen counter tops. "Put them in there, and thank you."

He laughed. "It does look good. It's just mostly on you, not the walls." Gertrude escorted him to the kitchen.

Sam set the groceries down and started putting them away. Doing more than he was asked to do?

I smirked and picked up a paintbrush. Time for a little cutting in. "So, do you want to talk to me about something?"

"Huh?" He dropped a soup can, and it rolled across the floor with Gertrude giving chase.

I stifled a laugh. Kids never realize how transparent they are. "So, what is it, son?"

Sam galloped after the can and took it back to the pantry. He planted himself in front of me, swung his floppy bangs off his face, and put his hands in his pockets, shifting from foot to foot. "About . . . you know . . ."

"Your job?" I squatted and painted carefully above floorboards.

"Yeah, about my job."

"Have they fired you? You've been gone over a week. Nearly two weeks, in fact." I dipped my paintbrush.

"Um, yeah. I just wanted you to know it's official, but that I have another job offer."

"You do, huh?" I stood and looked him in the eye.

"Yeah, uh, the pool here needs a lifeguard."

I crouched and painted a little more, but it dripped. I lapped the extra paint up with my brush and redistributed it. "So, what are you saying?"

Out of the corner of my eye, I saw him pull his hands out of his pockets then jam them back in. "Well, I was wondering if you could talk to Dad and maybe I could live with you and work here for the rest of the summer."

I put the paintbrush in the tray with the roller. "I don't think Dad's going to have a problem with you living with me."

"I know. I just mean so he won't be mad at me about the baseball camp job."

Maggie poked her head in the back door. "Anybody home?"

"Hey, Maggie," I said.

"I've got something I want to show you guys. Can you come outside?"

"Uh, sure, but, Mom, about what I said?"

"I think that'll probably be all right." I breezed past him. Inside, my heart was doing cartwheels.

We stepped out into the midday sunshine and followed Maggie to Bess. "I was doing some picking at an estate sale near here. The owners had died." She grinned and gestured in the open back door to two curly-haired baby goats on a red-and-blue plaid blanket.

Sam's eyes popped wide. "Are those goats?"

"Listen to you, city boy. Of course they're goats." I dove in the back seat, filling my arms with tiny, soft bodies. "This is what you picked?" I held the black one out to Sam, and he took it awkwardly, then grinned.

"Not really. The mama goat gave birth in front of me, then just keeled over and died. There was nothing to do but pop them in the truck and run for supplies."

I looked in the floorboard. Baby bottles with thick rubber nipples. A bag of something called Doe's Match. "Don't they have an owner?"

"I'm not sure. There was no one around. If I'd left them, they would've died. I've been calling everyone I can think of, but they just tell me to keep them." She laughed, shaking her head. "What am I going to do with two baby goats?"

Sam was carrying the black one around whispering to it. Gertrude ran in circles around his feet. "They're so cool. I can help you if you want. You should name them. Biggio and Bagwell. You know, the Killer Bs from the Houston Astros."

"Baseball players? I don't think so." She leaned her head to the side and stroked the head of the one in his arms. "Omaha and Nebraska. The town I was gigging when I first heard one of my songs on the radio."

A horn honked. It was Papa. He'd moved into the Quacker and was commuting a day or two each week to help his old partner out with the practice until the new vet arrived to take his place.

"You'll only be here for another six weeks or so to help out, Sam." I pressed a finger against the curls on the red goat. They bounced back like they were spring-loaded.

"About that. I was thinking, Giddings may go to State this year, and Bellaire, well, they basically suck, and the baseball coach here said they need a pitcher."

Papa joined us, and we exchanged hugs and greetings. He and Maggie chatted goats while I turned my attention back to my son. "You want to move here for the rest of high school?"

"I like it here, Mom. I kinda think we've found our place, don't you?"

I thought about the book I was writing, of how I would start with the Wends who exiled themselves in the name of freedom of religion only to watch their culture and values all but slip away in a few generations, and move on to Anna/Gidget, whose pursuit of freedom from her religion led her back to it. I thought about the woman herself, this farm, and the daughter she left behind, and marveled that she had basically, without even knowing it, bequeathed me an entire life. I may not have found my brother yet, which hurt, a lot, but I had found a sister in Maggie. And I had a brother, so I wouldn't give up until I found him.

I lifted my face to the sun and breathed in deeply. The scent of goat formula, baby animal, and sweaty boy eased my disappointment and made room for the happiness of now.

For the first time in many, many months, I felt as if my husband slipped his arms around me. The sensation was so real I could feel his chin on my shoulder.

I let myself smile. "Yes. I think we've found our place."

NEXT UP: Michele and Rashidi are back in *Searching for Dime Box*, the 3rd Michele book in the addictive *What Doesn't Kill You* series.

A drug-dealing defendant. A stricken infant. A deadly new strain of murder.

Indulge in the thrills with Michele in **Searching for Dime Box on Amazon** (free in Kindle Unlimited) at https://www.amazon.-com/gp/product/B07CZ3WC8R.

But wait...did you miss Michele's 1st mystery, *Going for Kona?* Then your best deal is a **half-price three novel box set**, *The Complete Michele Lopez Hanson Trilogy* (free in Kindle Unlimited), here: https://www.amazon.com/gp/product/B07FCSDHV3

Or **get the complete WDKY series** here: https://www.amazon.-com/gp/product/B07QQVNSPN.

***

And don't forget to snag the **free** *What Doesn't Kill You* **ebook starter library** by joining Pamela's mailing list at https://www.subscribepage.com/PFHSuperstars.

To my one and only: no Rashidi for me!

OTHER BOOKS BY THE AUTHOR

Fiction from SkipJack Publishing

The *What Doesn't Kill You* Series
Act One (Prequel, Ensemble Novella)
Saving Grace (Katie #1)
Leaving Annalise (Katie #2)
Finding Harmony (Katie #3)
Heaven to Betsy (Emily #1)
Earth to Emily (Emily #2)
Hell to Pay (Emily #3)
Going for Kona (Michele #1)
Fighting for Anna (Michele #2)
Searching for Dime Box (Michele #3)
Buckle Bunny (Maggie Prequel Novella)
Shock Jock (Maggie Prequel Short Story)
Live Wire (Maggie #1)
Sick Puppy (Maggie #2)
Dead Pile (Maggie #3)
The Essential Guide to the What Doesn't Kill You Series

The *Ava Butler Trilogy*: A Sexy Spin-off From *What Doesn't Kill You*
Bombshell (Ava #1)
Stunner (Ava #2)
Knockout (Ava #3)

The *Patrick Flint Trilogy*: A Spin-off From *What Doesn't Kill You*
Switchback (Patrick Flint #1)
Snake Oil (Patrick Flint #2)

Sawbones (Patrick Flint #3)

Scapegoat (Patrick Flint #4)

Snaggle Tooth (Patrick Flint #5)

Stag Party (Patrick Flint #6): 2021

The What Doesn't Kill You Box Sets Series (50% off individual title retail)

The Complete Katie Connell Trilogy

The Complete Emily Bernal Trilogy

The Complete Michele Lopez Hanson Trilogy

The Complete Maggie Killian Trilogy

The Complete Ava Butler Trilogy

The Complete Patrick Flint Trilogy #1 (coming in late 2020)

Nonfiction from SkipJack Publishing

The Clark Kent Chronicles

Hot Flashes and Half Ironmans

How to Screw Up Your Kids

How to Screw Up Your Marriage

Puppalicious and Beyond

What Kind of Loser Indie Publishes,

and How Can I Be One, Too?

Audio, e-book, and paperback versions of most titles available.

ACKNOWLEDGMENTS

When my husband, Eric, and I moved to Nowheresville, the tiny community welcomed us with open arms. Thanks to Stephanie for plot inspiration and a super white linen gown which belonged to the "real" Gidget. I wore it while drafting *Fighting for Anna* to summon the muse. Hugs and appreciation also go to Tiffany, the owner of the real Flown the Coop—where she repurposes, reuses, rethinks, and upcycles junk aka industrial, vintage, retro, and primitive antiques pieces—which you totally need to visit in Burton, Texas. She and her husband Jeff also lovingly drive a vintage magenta Ford pickup identical to Maggie's. They call it . . . wait for it . . . Maggie. It's a coincidence, but a good one.

Thanks to my husband, Eric, for brainstorming *Fighting for Anna* with me despite his busy work, travel, and triathlon schedule. He always manages to fit me in first, and never leaves me hanging when it comes to the writing. I am a lucky woman, in so many ways. Eric gets an extra helping of thanks for plotting, critiquing, editing, listening, holding, encouraging, supporting, browbeating, and playing miscellaneous other roles, some of which aren't appropriate for publication.

Thanks to our five offspring. I love you guys more than anything, and each time I write a parent/child (birth, adopted, foster, or step), I channel you.

To each and every blessed one of you who have read, reviewed, rated, and emailed/Facebooked/Tweeted/commented about the *What Doesn't Kill You* books (so far, this includes Katie, Emily, and Michele, but watch for Ava, Laura, and Maggie, in the next few years), I appreciate you more than I can say. It is the readers who move mountains for me, and for other authors, and I humbly ask for the honor of your honest reviews and recommendations.

Editing credits go to Rhonda Erb and Sara Kocek. The beta and advance readers and critique partners who enthusiastically devote their time—gratis—to help us rid my books of flaws blow me away. The special love this time goes to Marcy, Melissa, Ridgely, Candi, Lindsay, Linda, Pat, Ginger, Nell, Vidya, Michelle, Dina, and Susie. Thanks to Bobbye for putting up with heavy breathing and animal noises while transcribing the original recorded draft.

Kisses to princess of the universe, Heidi Dorey, for fantastic cover art. Thanks for evolving with us as we evolve with the world of publishing.

New thanks this time, as our publishing world is changing at SkipJack, to Rhonda, Bobbye, and Candi, our first employees, and real jewels. I can't wait for the world to discover Bobbye's and Candi's books, because they are both wonderful writers as well. SkipJack Publishing now includes fantastic books by a cherry-picked bushel basket of mystery/thriller/suspense writers. If you write in this genre, visit http://SkipJackPublishing.com for submission guidelines. To check out our other authors and snag a bargain at the same time, download *Murder, They Wrote: Four SkipJack Mysteries*.

ABOUT THE AUTHOR

Pamela Fagan Hutchins is a *USA Today* best seller. She writes award-winning romantic mysteries from deep in the heart of Nowheresville, Texas and way up in the frozen north of Snowheresville, Wyoming. She is passionate about long hikes with her hunky husband and pack of rescue dogs and riding her gigantic horses.

If you'd like Pamela to speak to your book club, women's club, class, or writers group, by Skype or in person, shoot her an email. She's very likely to say yes.

You can connect with Pamela via her website
(http://pamelafaganhutchins.com)
or email (pamela@pamelafaganhutchins.com).

PRAISE FOR PAMELA FAGAN HUTCHINS

2018 USA Today Best Seller
2017 Silver Falchion Award, Best Mystery
2016 USA Best Book Award, Cross-Genre Fiction
2015 USA Best Book Award, Cross-Genre Fiction
2014 Amazon Breakthrough Novel Award Quarter-finalist, Romance

What Doesn't Kill You: Katie Romantic Mysteries

"An exciting tale . . . twisting investigative and legal subplots . . . a character seeking redemption . . . an exhilarating mystery with a touch of voodoo."
— *Midwest Book Review Bookwatch*
"A lively romantic mystery." — *Kirkus Reviews*
"A riveting drama . . . exciting read, highly recommended." — *Small Press Bookwatch*
"Katie is the first character I have absolutely fallen in love with since Stephanie Plum!" — *Stephanie Swindell, Bookstore Owner*
"Engaging storyline . . . taut suspense." — *MBR Bookwatch*

What Doesn't Kill You: Emily Romantic Mysteries

"Fair warning: clear your calendar before you pick it up because you won't be able to put it down." — *Ken Oder, author of* Old Wounds to the Heart
"Full of heart, humor, vivid characters, and suspense. Hutchins has done it again!" — *Gay Yellen, author of* The Body Business
"Hutchins is a master of tension." — *R.L. Nolen, author of* Deadly Thyme
"Intriguing mystery . . . captivating romance." — *Patricia Flaherty Pagan, author of* Trail Ways Pilgrims
"Everything about it shines: the plot, the characters and the writing. Readers are in for a real treat with this story." — *Marcy McKay, author of* Pennies from Burger Heaven

What Doesn't Kill You: Michele Romantic Mysteries

"Immediately hooked." — *Terry Sykes-Bradshaw, author of* Sibling Revelry
"Spellbinding." — *Jo Bryan, Dry Creek Book Club*

"Fast-paced mystery." — *Deb Krenzer, Book Reviewer*
"Can't put it down." — *Cathy Bader, Reader*

What Doesn't Kill You: Ava Romantic Mysteries

"Just when I think I couldn't love another Pamela Fagan Hutchins novel more, along comes Ava." — *Marcy McKay, author of* Stars Among the Dead
"Ava personifies bombshell in every sense of word. — *Tara Scheyer, Grammy-nominated musician, Long-Distance Sisters Book Club*
"Entertaining, complex, and thought-provoking." — *Ginger Copeland, power reader*

What Doesn't Kill You: Maggie Romantic Mysteries

"Murder has never been so much fun!" — *Christie Craig,* New York Times Best Seller
"Maggie's gonna break your heart—one way or another." — *Tara Scheyer, Grammy-nominated musician, Long-Distance Sisters Book Club*
"Pamela Fagan Hutchins nails that Wyoming scenery and captures the atmosphere of the people there." — *Ken Oder, author of* Old Wounds to the Heart
"You're guaranteed to love the ride!" — *Kay Kendall, Silver Falchion Best Mystery Winner*

OTHER BOOKS FROM SKIPJACK PUBLISHING

Murder, They Wrote: Four SkipJack Mysteries,
by Pamela Fagan Hutchins,
Ken Oder, R.L. Nolen, and Marcy Mason

The Closing, by Ken Oder
Old Wounds to the Heart, by Ken Oder
The Judas Murders, by Ken Oder
The Princess of Sugar Valley, by Ken Oder

Pennies from Burger Heaven, by Marcy McKay
Stars Among the Dead, by Marcy McKay
The Moon Rises at Dawn, by Marcy McKay
Bones and Lies Between Us, by Marcy McKay

Deadly Thyme, by R. L. Nolen
The Dry, by Rebecca Nolen

Tides of Possibility, edited by K.J. Russell
Tides of Impossibility, edited by K.J. Russell and C. Stuart Hardwick

My Dream of Freedom: From Holocaust to My Beloved America,
by Helen Colin

FOREWORD

Fighting for Anna is a work of fiction. Period. Any resemblance to actual persons, places, things, or events is just a lucky coincidence.

CPSIA information can be obtained
at www.ICGtesting.com
Printed in the USA
LVHW011609060722
722867LV00014B/74